spring,

summer,

autumn,

us

# spring,

# summer,

# autumn,

# us

FIONA COLLINS

LAKE UNION
PUBLISHING

Text copyright © 2023 by Fiona Collins

Published by Lake Union Publishing, Seattle

www.apub.com

Amazon, the Amazon logo, and Lake Union Publishing are trademarks of Amazon.com, Inc., or its affiliates.

ISBN-13: 9781662507236
ISBN-10: 1662507232

Cover design by Emma Rogers

Printed in the United States of America

spring,

summer,

autumn,

us

# Prologue

Rachel was dreaming. Not bedtime dreaming, but wide-awake, sitting-on-the-landing dreaming. She shifted on the carpet and stretched her nightie over raised knees, turning them into pink blancmange domes like her mum used to make on hazy summer afternoons. The radiator on the landing was still on and Rachel leaned against it, liking the almost-burn on her bare right arm.

Mum and Dad were down in the hall, shouting. Torpedoing words at each other like the coloured plastic sticks in KerPlunk – a jabbing, spiky mesh of scaffolding they could not reach each other through, even if they wanted to, and they did not want to. They only wanted to shout.

'What you've done can never be *undone*, Gary!' shouted Mum.

Rachel absently tapped the wrapped chocolate biscuit on the carpet beside her, making sure it was still there. She often stole a snack when dinners were forgotten to be made.

'You keep driving me *back* to her, Frances!' shouted Dad.

Rachel half-slid the biscuit under her right foot. She was only semi-hearing her parents' words, as she was somewhere else in her head – a different house to this, a house that was calm and quiet always, not just in patches of days when everything seemed all right again. When her dad stayed and didn't go.

'You just make everything so bloody difficult! You make this house *miserable*, Frances!' shouted Dad.

'Don't go to her tonight, Gary! I'm *begging* you!' shouted back Mum.

Rachel heard these words, despite trying to dream them out. She knew her father would disappear tonight. He would take his brown shoes from the understairs cupboard and slip out of the front door.

She closed her eyes. In later life she would think of herself on this landing, a just-turned-teenage girl, a dreamer, who could never have imagined that the life she lived in this house, with her mum and dad, and their ups and downs and back and forths, would end in tragedy in just a few short days.

Rachel opened her eyes and stretched her nightie further over her knees until the middle of the blancmanges were translucent, then she picked up the chocolate biscuit from the carpet and carefully peeled back the silver paper from one corner.

# SPRING

4 May 1986

# Chapter One

Rachel stepped off the back porch and into the bluster and cloud-shy sunshine of an English garden in early May, followed by Tatiana, known as Teddy to all who loved her, who shoved her hands in the fraying back pockets of her denim boiler suit and scanned the sky.

'It won't come here, Rachel, will it?' Teddy frowned, as low clouds like draught excluders shunted sideways on the horizon and the cottage garden's scatter of pansies and lilacs and irises shivered in their beds.

'What won't come here?'

Rachel was staring at the washing line, thrashing about with merry jeopardy in the freshening wind. Her work aprons. The darks and lights of Jonny's socks, flapping like the ungainly wings of crows and doves.

'That poisonous air,' said Teddy. 'From Russia.'

'From Chernobyl? No, I don't think so, Teddy,' said Rachel. It had been headline news for eight days, the explosion. That terrible accident. 'It's such a long way from Oxford,' she added, smoothing the skirt of her dress. 'Try not to worry.'

They started walking down the steep slope of the garden to the small wooden gate at the bottom. *Teddy is a worrier*, Rachel thought. Jonny's eight-year-old daughter worried about school and nits and dogs and fitting in.

'What's it called again?' Teddy asked. 'The stuff I'll throw when you and Daddy get married?'

They were on the lane below. A petal-rain of blossom, from the huge magnolia tree in their closest neighbours' front garden, fluttered down on them, Rachel catching some in her palm, Teddy plucking at the air and putting a few of the flowers in her back pocket.

'Confetti,' Rachel replied.

'How many days away is it?'

'Well, it's going to be quite a long engagement,' said Rachel. 'We need to save up. It'll be more like *months*, actually.'

'But one day soon you'll be my *step*mum.'

'Yes, one day soon I'll be your stepmum.'

Teddy's face broke into one of her rare grins and she skipped a little, through the ruffling pink blossom carpet at their feet. They were off to the Wetheringtons' annual Spring Luncheon at the 1930s villa towards the end of Hedge Hill Lane, one of the big houses sprawled behind hedges and iron gates and overlooked by Rachel and Jonny's tiny black-and-white cottage on the hill. Rachel could just about make out Rupert and Rosemary, two of the lane's genial middle-class, middle-England neighbours, heading into the Wetheringtons' front porch.

'What time will Daddy be coming to the party?' asked Teddy.

'In about an hour, I expect.'

'Is Nanna Florence coming?'

'No, darling. She wouldn't have been invited. Besides, she finds this kind of thing insufferable.'

'What does that mean?'

'It means she's busy, darling.'

Rachel and Jonny were invited to most of the 'dos' in Hedge Hill Lane despite being, at twenty-five and twenty-seven, at least two decades younger than the rest of their neighbours and, potentially more alarmingly, having been *living in sin* for the last five years. This was on top of Jonny being *divorced*, and a *father*, of course, but he was charming, and the nearest the village had to a celebrity, and the neighbours were kind. Rachel and Jonny often found themselves walking down this pretty lane to attend parties and lunches and suppers and barbecues – the *youngsters*, as they were called, or as Jonny referred to them, the *successors*.

An overhead canopy of trees, dense dapples of dark and light green, shimmied as the wind stippled coolly through their leaves. Rachel tried to put her arm around her stepdaughter but Teddy was like water, impossible to grasp. *We could never be mistaken for mother and daughter*, Rachel thought. Teddy was tall, gangly and almost Scandinavian blonde, with bright blue eyes the colour of Smurfs. Rachel was tiny, with straight-with-a-kink dark brown hair and green eyes. And everyone in Fincham St George, Oxfordshire, where Rachel had lived her whole life, knew Teddy's mother was Nancy Littlen-Green.

'Will Faith be there?' asked Teddy, having hopped herself to a safe distance.

'Not this time,' replied Rachel. At the Wetheringtons' last Spring Luncheon, her boss, Faith, had brought a *glittering* sort of party atmosphere – plus a bottle of tequila – not many were ready for. 'I think she's going on a date.'

'And what about Adrienne?'

'No, she doesn't know the Wetheringtons. Besides, she's in Torremolinos. Spain.'

Rachel had two jobs. She was waitress and occasional baker at Fincham's, St George's only cafe, Monday to Wednesday, where her boss was her best friend Adrienne or 'Wren', as she called her. And she was assistant at the village's art gallery, Picture This, Thursday to Saturday, where her boss was Faith.

'Wren is nice,' commented Teddy, as she flicked a windswept chunk of vanilla-blonde hair out of her face. 'But not as nice as you.'

'Thank you,' said Rachel. *Nice* was her thing. Nice was what she tried to be, every day.

'Except when you don't let me have Hubba Bubba.'

'Bubble gum is highly dangerous,' said Rachel wryly, 'so, no.'

They were at the Wetheringtons' gate now.

'Welcome, welcome!' Martin Wetherington was at the door, wearing a striped apron and a wide grin. 'Come on in, the sausage rolls are just cooling.'

Rachel smiled. Martin's legendary sausage rolls were part of the blueprint to the afternoon, which also included gin and tonics stronger than paraffin, enough food to have everyone rolling home and, sometime after 5 p.m., Christie putting her Barry White tape on and the women dancing on the sitting-room carpet, sherry glasses at dangerous angles. The men would light cigars and the cheese and biscuits would come out, until it got so late they really had to think about making a move, 'busy day tomorrow' . . . There would be hugs, and jokes and banter. It was fun, it was predictable; it was life in pretty Fincham St George and picturesque Hedge Hill Lane.

'Thank you, Martin,' Rachel said, on the doorstep. 'In you go, Teddy.'

They crossed the threshold and were swallowed up in the welcomes and the friendly fussing. Rachel had a drink thrust into her hand by Martin. Teddy got leaped on by a kindly lady with a taloned elbow clutch and a 'Haven't you *grown?*' And they were swept into the sitting room where Fincham St George's finest were gathered in their Sunday best. Every spring.

The same faces, the same 'spread', the same golf jumpers and court shoes and burgundy leather loafers, and hearty whisky laughs and lipsticked smiles and handshakes. Despite her age, Rachel felt strangely at home among all these well-to-do neighbours. She knew Jonny did, too. As the *successors*, Jonny imagined the two of them moving seamlessly along life's conveyor belt behind the Wetheringtons; that one day they would stop at the right point and it would be their turn to open up their big house (because Jonny's plan was to have one, on Hedge Hill Lane. His plan was to have *everything*) and invite the neighbours in. To do a 'spread' and provide ridiculously strong drinks and watch as an impromptu and jubilant conga caterpillar-ed out on to the lane and up as far as the post box.

And it was Rachel's plan, too, to get the things she'd always wanted, which were – as she mentally counted them off in her head, *often* – home, family and security, and to erase the worst bits of her past and repeat the best. She was on the path to that, with Jonny Trent, local author and the love of her life, and she had no intention of getting off.

'Lisa from your class is here,' said Rachel to Teddy, in the crowded sitting room. 'Do you want to go and talk to her?'

'Not really,' said Teddy. 'Can I have a Coke?' She took off her cardigan and gave it to Rachel.

'OK. Why don't you go into the kitchen and help yourself?'

'Stay here, then.' Teddy looked a little nervous.

'I'll be here,' said Rachel.

Teddy edged into the crowd. Rachel shrugged off her own cardigan, looked around her at those she would follow on Jonny's conveyor belt, and prepared to join in the fun.

# Chapter Two

The conga – a straggly affair, exuberant arms and legs sticking out like cocktail sticks from a cheese and pineapple hedgehog – burst from the Wetheringtons' front door at about half past four, but instead of grabbing Margery Westgate's floral waist as it sashayed past her in the hall, Rachel stepped back into the heaving sitting room and checked her small gold watch.

Jonny had given it to her for her twenty-first birthday. It was from Elizabeth Duke at Argos, and even as Jonny gave it to her, he was apologising and promising that one day he'd buy her a watch from Cartier. But Rachel loved it. She *liked* Elizabeth Duke. Her engagement ring was from there, the one Jonny had given her on New Year's Eve, in the backyard of the pub – down on one knee on both the ice and a crystallised packet of pork scratchings. She loved how the cubic zirconia 'diamond' caught the light. She loved that it represented Jonny's promise to her, that he would marry her and make her happy forever.

*Half past four*, she thought, and he had still not arrived. Teddy had disappeared, too. She was upstairs somewhere with Emily Wetherington, reluctantly playing 'Sindys'.

'Rachel! How simply darling to see you!'

Bustling across the patterned carpet in full sail was Mrs Bottomley, local postmistress. A vision in swathes of pleated purple polyester, she had a large drink in her hand.

'Twice round the gasworks,' Jonny always said about her, with a little wink and a warm smile, and Rachel would laugh, despite herself, as she tried not to be unkind to anyone, but Jonny always made her laugh. Made her laugh like a drain.

'You must meet Gabe,' Mrs Bottomley trumpeted, and in her purple polyester wake was a man Rachel had not seen before. He had dark hair and blue eyes. A cornflower-blue jumper over a buttoned-up white shirt. A sheepish smile that suggested he had been dragged around for a while now, by the good ship Bottomley. 'Gabe McAllister.'

'Hello,' he said.

Oh, he had an American accent, thought Rachel, and he was young, too, her age. He was tall. His jeans were very dark blue, almost black. He was wearing lace-up brown shoes.

He held out his hand for her to shake.

'Hello,' replied Rachel, and she took his hand, briefly aware of her thumb against the soft, warm pulp of skin between his thumb and his forefinger.

'You have a very nice face,' he said.

'Oh!' she replied, a little startled. 'Do I?' Did he not see a lot of nice faces? Was it unusual? Rachel thought most faces were nice and if not nice, interesting. She'd never yet met a face she hadn't appreciated, in one way or another. 'Well, so do you.'

Mrs Bottomley roared with laughter. Rachel blushed. He *did* have a nice face.

'Yours is like sunshine,' Gabe said, smiling at her.

He said it quite innocently, like a child, or someone making a simple observation – looking out of a window and reporting it was raining.

'A face like sunshine,' she echoed, blushing even more. 'Well, there we are.' She could still feel the warmth of the side of his palm

11

against her thumb, although they had both returned their hands to their sides.

Mrs Bottomley roared again. 'Oh, you Americans!' she trumpeted. 'What a hoot! Rachel Smith lives at the cottage at the top of the hill,' she expounded. 'You've left your washing out, by the way, dear. And Gabe here is Julia's nephew. You know, Julia March.'

'From the Mill House?' asked Rachel, determined to ignore Mrs Bottomley's barb about her laundry.

'Yes,' said Gabe, the American. 'I'm staying with her for a few days.'

'Oh, I see. It's lovely there, isn't it? And how are you finding Fincham St George?' Rachel asked politely. *I like his accent,* she thought. She didn't know much about Americans. Apart from what she knew of reclusive Julia March, who had been here so long, apparently, no one thought of her as American any more, Rachel had only ever encountered them in films and TV. *Yanks,* she'd seen on telly last week. Richard Gere. But Richard Gere never said things like, 'Your face is like sunshine.'

'I'm finding it very . . . English,' he said.

She laughed. 'You've never been here before?'

'No.'

'And do you like it?' she pressed. Mrs Bottomley had been distracted by a passing plate of spring rolls and had turned away from them.

'Sure,' he said. 'I've met some pretty nice people so far.' Gabe smiled at her. Rachel noticed he had quite long eyelashes. 'People say "sorry" a lot,' he added. 'And other people seem to be permanently afraid.'

'Afraid?'

'"I'm *afraid* I can't find my spectacles."' He spoke in a terrible British accent. 'I'm *afraid* I don't know the time, *sorry* . . . I do worry for you folk,' he said, with an easy laugh.

12

'Please don't worry about us,' she said, with a grin. 'Politeness may be an affliction but it's a rather pleasing one, wouldn't you say? And don't all you Americans go around wishing everyone "Have a nice day!" all the time?'

'We do,' he said, 'and for that I'm *afraid* I'm very *sorry*. Are you having one?' he asked.

'One what?' *He's handsome*, she thought – objectively, for she had Jonny. Handsome and immediately funny, though not as funny as Jonny, of course.

'A nice day.'

'Yes, I am,' she said. 'Lovely, thank you.'

'Nothing to be afraid of then,' he said and he held her gaze, just for a second or two longer than it ought to be held, she felt, and he was smiling at her, and if she didn't have Jonny she might have thought being smiled at by him was a little like sunshine, too.

Mrs Bottomley turned back to them, holding three huge spring rolls hammocked in a serviette.

'Well, I'll leave you young things to chat,' she trumpeted. 'I need a little top-up,' she added, and she steered her bulk away and headed off to the drinks table. Rachel tinkered with her own glass, a prohibitively strong G&T. She suddenly felt incredibly shy and a little woozy. Maybe it was the three and a half hours of sipped drinks through solid chit-chat; maybe it was the room's maelstrom of mingling colognes, most of which she had clinging to her neck from hugs and kisses. She placed her left hand to her collarbone and her fingers felt hot. Where *was* Jonny?

'So, do you know many people here?' asked Gabe.

'Mostly everyone,' replied Rachel. 'How about you? Apart from Aunt Julia, of course. Is she here?' she asked doubtfully. If she were here, Rachel would have noticed. As well as being seldom spotted, Aunt Julia was tall and angular and resembled a smart hat stand.

'No, I think she was quite horrified when she got the invitation. She's at home wrestling with the *Sunday Times* crossword and a lamb shank, and sent me in her place. It's been an eye-opener,' he added, 'the gin, the Barry White, the conga . . .' He leaned towards her a little, conspiratorially. '. . . These are the people who'll recapture their youth, later tonight, by having sex to "Bolero" . . .'

Rachel burst out laughing. She covered her mouth with her hand, blushing furiously. 'There's *always* a conga,' she said, recovering herself.

Gabe leaned back. 'I also know someone called Sally Henderson-Something, and you, now. Plus, the formidable Mrs Bottomley, of course . . . Man, you'd never get a surname like that in America,' he smiled.

'I wouldn't know,' said Rachel. 'Whereabouts in America are you from?'

'North Dakota. A miniscule town called Jud. I'm pretty sure you wouldn't have heard of it.'

'No,' Rachel concurred. 'I don't think I've heard of *anywhere* in North Dakota. What's it like?'

'Quiet. Conservative. In the middle of nowhere. Escapable. It's OK,' he added, with a shrug. 'Jud's called "The City of Murals",' he continued. 'Folks in Jud like flowers and chickens painted on the sides of their buildings, what folk there is, of course – the population currently eighty-four.'

'Wow, well, the murals sound really interesting, and that's not very many people at all.'

'It's better that way.'

'Why?' She was being nosy again. She tried to maintain a tidy existence, to not create ripples, but now and again a nosy question – a *why?* or a *how come?* or a *what?* – meant she coloured outside the lines, as her dad would have put it; maybe because there was a time, as a kid, when she never got any answers.

'Less people talking,' he said. 'Less people judging.' Someone had just turned up the stereo, so it was hard to catch his last words – Barry White was rumbling another intro as court shoes were slipped off. As she leaned in to check if she'd heard him correctly, Rachel noticed Gabe, the American, had eyes the colour a child would paint the sky.

'Gabe flew into England from Chernobyl last weekend,' announced Mrs Bottomley. She was back in orbit, juggling a plate of cheese and crackers in one hand and a full glass in the other. 'Did he tell you? He took off three hours before the explosion.'

'*Chernobyl?* Really? What were you doing there?' Rachel was taken aback. At the same time, she thought how easily this place, this word – *Chernobyl* – tripped from everyone's lips, as easily as saying 'How awful' or 'What a terrible tragedy'. 'And what extraordinarily lucky timing,' she added, almost shivering at the horror of it.

'Yes, incredibly lucky,' said Gabe. 'And I feel so incredibly guilty, too, you know. That I got out . . .' He sighed. 'But, yes, it's true, I was in Gomel, Belarus, around a hundred miles from the accident. I left a couple hours before it happened. A few of us did, from the same scheme; back to Europe, Morocco, Canada . . . We travelled to the airport together. None of us knew anything about it until we landed . . .'

'I'm so sorry,' said Rachel. 'What were you doing there?' she repeated. She suddenly felt woefully parochial. She'd only ever been to Greece. This man had been to Russia. To *Chernobyl*. 'You said something about a scheme . . .'

'Gabe was on an outreach project,' interjected Mrs Bottomley, waggling her fingers against her glass. '*Art*. Some kind of exchange, wasn't it, Gabe?'

'Yes. I was there for three months. I was one of a handful of resident artists from various countries, at a facility there. Belarusian artists went on exchange to our countries. One of their guys went to New York, I think . . . Lord knows if he'll ever be able to go back . . .' He shook his head, his eyes looked faraway. Distant. The deeper blue of an approaching dusk at the end of a long summer's day. 'And I'd made a couple of local friends there in Gomel. Drinking buddies, you know. I've got no idea what's happened to them. I can't get through by phone. No one can. Phoning Belarus can be difficult at the best of times . . .' He looked anxious, disquieted, his humour and his ready laugh vanished.

'I'm so sorry,' Rachel said again. His words had sounded so incongruous against the background of this middle-class party. Behind him, a man in a beard laughed uproariously. 'What a horrible end to your trip.'

'Thank you,' he said. 'It was such an interesting place. It was . . . stark, you know. Different. The people were amazing though.'

Rachel realised he was nothing like the impression of American people she had gathered from films and TV. This man was tinged by sadness. Introspective. And he seemed *older*, older than he should be. Perhaps it was because he had travelled to places like Gomel.

'What a worry,' she said. 'All those people. Your friends. I hope they're all right.' They weren't, though, were they? Everyone knew that much already. 'So, you're an artist . . .' she said. It felt weak to change the subject, but she didn't like the sadness in his eyes.

'Yes. For my sins. An impoverished *creative*. Thank goodness for those bursaries from the North Dakotan Artist Fund keeping me in bread and water.' He smiled wryly, and she thought him a little ridiculous for a second, but those blue eyes, on closer inspection, were amused, and she suddenly got the feeling she had seen him before somewhere. That he was known to her, this appeared-in-their-midst American blown to England and safety, from close to Chernobyl.

16

'And now he's An American in Oxford,' Mrs Bottomley added excitedly, her bright cherry nails scraping at the edge of her cut-glass tumbler. 'Sounds almost romantic, doesn't it? Now, if you'll excuse me again, my pets,' she added, turning on a robust heel, 'I have an appointment with some coronation chicken.'

She blustered off, her mast fully up and the wind in her sails.

'So, what do you do, Rachel?' asked Gabe.

Rachel was surprised. She was never asked this. No one asked what women did, even if it was the 1980s and there was one in charge of the country. Even if lots of women were now working, often in what had been men-only jobs. In Fincham St George, plenty of women worked: Maureen Peters, who did a few hours up at the council offices; the women at the library; Linda and the other ladies who worked in the tiny branch of Midland Bank; Mrs Bottomley at the post office – all in the little crescent of quaint Tudor buildings facing the green. And Rachel, of course. But they would never be asked by anyone, let alone a stranger from North Dakota, what they *did*.

'Well, I work in a cafe and in an art gallery. The cafe on Rose Glen Street and the gallery, the far side of the green, by the war memorial, if you know it. Picture This?'

'Yes, I've walked past there,' Gabe said. 'I haven't had a chance to go in as yet.'

Rachel looked at his blue eyes, and the way his hair curled around his ears a little, and realised that she had, indeed, seen him before.

'Oh,' she said again, and she laughed. 'It was you with the bike.'

'The bike?'

'Yes.'

She felt rather delighted. 'I was at Brando's last week, sitting by the window. You came past pushing an enormous bike with a basket on the front.'

17

Brando's was the one and only restaurant in the village, an Italian. She'd been having lunch with Wren. She'd been stuffing her face with carbonara and giggling at a story about Wren's husband when a man had walked by, pushing a bike with a large wicker basket attached to the handlebars. Rachel had her fork to her mouth and remarked to Wren on the handsome man passing the window and Wren, catching the rear of him, said he had a 'nice bum'.

'Were you eating spaghetti?' he asked.

'Yes, I was.'

'It looked like you were having a really nice time. That was Aunt Julia's bike,' he pointed out. 'Just so you know. I don't think it had seen the light of day since 1965.'

Rachel giggled. 'So, no time for painting since you've been here?'

'I've squeezed in a little.' He looked boyish now.

'What do you paint?'

'I paint trees.'

'Interesting. Well, how lovely. What is it about trees?' Jonny would say she was being *really* nosy right about now. He'd be poking her in the ribs, his eyes glinting. She wondered again what time he'd be showing up.

'Trees are everything,' he said. 'Oh God, I sound pompous, don't I!'

'Well, no . . .' She smiled at him.

'I do, I'm sorry. But what I mean is, to me at least, they reflect permanence, certainty, but at the same time they're always changing, dying and being reborn, as the seasons change.' He looked impassioned, earnest. He *was* a little pompous. 'Do you know the Oscar Wilde story? About the old oak tree?'

'The one about the giant with the tree in his front garden?' She nodded. It was one of the stories her father used to read to her as a child. It was sad and beautiful. The children who played in the

18

giant's garden, which turned to winter when he shooed them away but grew abundant again when he allowed them back in. It was allegorical, her father had said, when he'd had time to sit with her in the evenings. Before the arguing. Before *her*. 'It's a lovely story.'

'I adored that story growing up,' he said. 'There was something about it that just got me. I still live with my parents, unfortunately, but there's a house in Jud I think about buying one day, because of that story. It's on a corner plot with a great oak in the front garden.' He looked like a small boy when he said this. Earnest and happy. 'I'd like to sit and watch that tree from my front window, as spring turns to summer and autumn turns to winter. I'd like to imagine children playing under it as I paint.'

Rachel felt a familiar hope sweep her at his almost poetic words, as she imagined children playing under an imaginary oak tree, both in a corner plot of a house in Jud, population eighty-four, and here, one day, in a garden in Fincham St George.

'You live with your parents?' she asked, and she was aware she was bursting his poetic bubble slightly.

'Yes, well, it's me and my grumpy dad, mostly. My mom's in and out of . . . institutions.'

'Oh, I'm sorry.' She was dying to ask more but reined herself in. It was not as though she could bear to talk about her own parents, *Frances and Gary*, and the hollow ache in her they had left behind.

'Anyway, *you* know about art,' he said. 'You work in a gallery.'

'True,' she replied, 'but I only—'

'Would either of you care for a vol-au-vent?'

Dray Briggs, forty-something local solicitor and casual social groper, was at Rachel's elbow. He was hanging on to a stainless-steel dish toppled with a pyramid of vol-au-vents.

'Thank you,' Rachel said, taking a vol-au-vent with a napkin. Gabe took one too and looked at it curiously. Did they not have vol-au-vents in America? Rachel wondered. She imagined another kind of American enquiring in a loud voice if this was 'Some type of a funky *pastry*?'

'Are you monopolising our Quiet American?' Dray enquired affably.

'Oh, well, trying not to,' Rachel said. *Was* he quiet? she wondered, getting the Graham Greene reference. He was quite outspoken, confident – almost – but there was a lot going on behind the exterior, certainly. She had the oddest feeling it was a pity she was never going to find out *what*, exactly.

'Let some of us others have a go,' smirked Dray, his lips crusted black from red wine and pursed convex above his huge wine goblet.

'I'm not a fairground ride,' quipped Gabe, with a wide grin.

'No. Quite the spectacle, though, *Americans*. We don't see any round here. There's probably not been any since the war, and those were the days, or so I've heard.'

He slapped Gabe heartily on the back. Rachel flashed Gabe a sympathetic smile.

'Well, I'm going to go and circulate, anyway,' she said. 'He's all yours, Dray. Bye for now,' she said to Gabe, 'lovely to meet you,' and she moved away from them, taking her vol-au-vent with her. She would have been interested in talking to him a bit longer, she thought, as the throng of blouses and jumpers swallowed her up. She liked most of the Fincham St George neighbours, and enjoyed the community here, but all topics had been exhausted: house prices, lawn feed, the dreadful state of modern music ('I mean, what kind of a name is *Pet Shop Boys*, anyway?'), the babysitting circle, Margaret Thatcher . . .

*A face like sunshine*, she thought, amused, as she passed the buffet table and resisted the urge to look back through the colourful Sunday Best tableau to where Gabe was still talking to Dray Briggs and refusing further vol-au-vents. It was funny he should say that. She had strived to be sunny all her life, if sunny meant smiling, amenable and polite. She had been brought up to be a light in the world, that's what her father once said; she should be a little light to illuminate the world when it was so dark in so many of its corners. Funnier still that some of its darkest corners had been created by her father himself.

'Rachel!'

Here was Jonny – at last – stepping in like a thunderclap through the conservatory doors.

'Here!' she called. He was wearing one of his jaunty little neckties (they made him look like a *real* author, he said). He had a cheeky look on his face, like he always did – expectant, too, of the reaction he would get coming in, and he always got the same. Delighted smiles. Hearty handshakes. Hands moistened by Yardley hand cream placed up on his shoulders by women panting at him like excited Labradors. He was a young and handsome and *brilliant* local celebrity in Fincham St George, after all.

'Hi, darling,' she said, as Jonny neared her, his hair all gelled and perky in its customary artfully messy quiff, and he hugged her fiercely, like he hadn't seen her for days. Sometimes it seemed to Rachel his hugs were like hanging on to a life raft as it went over the edge of a waterfall. But she loved those hugs, and she would often giggle in his ear while wrapped in one of them and whisper 'Silly' to him and he would say, 'I love you, Smith,' and she would reply, 'No, I love *you*, Trent,' and she would go over that waterfall with him, both of them clinging on to each other and giggling like fools. She would go anywhere with him. And he knew where he was going. He had *always* known.

'Where's Teddy?' he asked.

'Upstairs, playing.'

'That's nice.' He held her tighter. She could smell that aftershave she loved.

'Silly,' she whispered in his ear, when he still refused to let her go.

'I love you, Smith.'

'No, I love *you*, Trent.'

'I can't wait to marry you.'

'Me neither.'

His breath, in her ear, was hot and sweet. 'This will be us soon,' he whispered. 'Holding parties like this. Popping champagne and serving canapés. When I'm famous. Do you doubt it?'

He often asked her this – if she doubted their future, if she doubted *him* – and her answer was always the same.

'No, I don't doubt it,' she said. She never had, since she had first spotted him under the concrete bridge in Fincham St George with his little notebook. He was going to be properly famous, one day. One of the most famous authors in the country.

Finally, laughing and full of love, Jonny released her.

'Time to party,' he said. 'Lead me to the devilled eggs.'

# Chapter Three

It was Jonny who had the job everyone asked about. Jonny who had spent the last eighteen hours in the study at the back of the cottage on the hill. He had a rickety desk with a folded-up beer mat propping up one leg, a second-hand office chair and a flask of coffee. He had still been in his dressing gown, hunched over his typewriter with his quiff collapsed, when she and Teddy had left for the Wetheringtons'.

'Nearly there,' he'd said, from his typewriter. 'Nearly there. I'll be along shortly, I promise.'

Jonny wrote spy thrillers set in Russia, big fat ones, published by a small publishing house in Maida Vale, London. 'Posh office in a Grade II listed building,' Jonny would say in awe. He would also say this was only the beginning.

'I'm on the brink, Rachel,' he would declare, hope shining in his eyes. 'The *brink*.' Sales were low, though. There had been . . . disappointments, but Jonny kept saying it would hopefully be only a matter of time until he was a huge success and Rachel could give up the two jobs that supported them – and he was so grateful that she did – and they could buy a house on Hedge Hill Lane and make babies, lots of them.

'Did the muse grab you for a bit longer?' Rachel asked, at the Wetheringtons' buffet table, where Jonny was helping himself to the last cheese and pineapple stick from the tin foil hedgehog. 'You said you were nearly done when Teddy and I left.'

'I was, sorry, but I got carried away. Then Nancy called and I had to pop to the woods and sort Teddy's bed for her. The bottom bunk had collapsed.'

Nancy lived in a farm cottage in the woods. Jonny used to live there too, when he and Nancy were married. They had been teenage village sweethearts, caught up in the romance of both being charming and good-looking and certain everything would work out, when it hadn't.

'Nancy really shouldn't keep calling you to fix stuff in her house.'

'I know,' said Jonny, shaking his head and rubbing Rachel's arm affectionately. 'But who else would she ask?'

Jonny and Nancy had been married for a year when Jonny had realised Nancy wasn't his forever love, after all. That she wasn't easy to live with, that she was untidy, unfocused, and cared neither for well-stocked cupboards nor colluding in a set plan for the future. That the pair of them being charming and good-looking – with willowy limbs and extremely long blonde hair, in Nancy's case – and *so* excited about being *so* in love, so *early*, wasn't enough, not for a lifetime. Jonny had broken Nancy's heart, that's what everyone in the village said, but they'd been so *young*; wasn't it inevitable one of them would change their mind?

'I suppose so,' said Rachel. She found it hard sometimes, that Jonny had been married before and had a child. She didn't like the thought of him promising his whole life to someone else, however impermanent that marriage had been. But she knew *her* cupboards were always well-stocked – an occasionally haphazard childhood food supply had guaranteed that. And colluding in a set future with Jonny, for her, was both easy and everything.

24

'It was for Teddy,' shrugged Jonny. 'I couldn't say no.' Teddy was Jonny's whole world. She was three months old when he and Nancy had split up; custody was shared between them and Jonny adored her. He was the kind of dad who carried his daughter on his shoulders around the village. The kind who wrote Teddy her very own bedtime stories and performed them in silly, hilarious voices. 'Anyway, guess who I bumped into, on the way out of the woods? By the pheasant keeper's hut? Old Mrs Forrester. I gave her a lift to the Co-op, she was mumbling all the way about her sciatica. I had to drown her out with Level 42!'

Rachel laughed. 'Well, I'm glad you're out of that dressing gown, anyway,' she said, nuzzling into him and smelling the after-shave on his neck. 'You're all spruced up.'

'Can't let the side down,' he replied. 'What would the neighbours say? So, how's it been?' he asked, popping a cube of cheese in his mouth. 'Friendly chat? Shoes off? Dancing?'

'Yes to all three. And you missed the conga. So, the writing went well?' she asked.

'Really well, really well,' he nodded, his eyes glazing over happily as though he had re-entered his snowy Russian fictional landscape. He was always in his books to some degree. And when he finished one, he was in the next, plotting, planning. His eye on the prize. To be one of them. The famous, bestselling authors.

'Good,' she said. 'That's really great. I'm glad.' She slipped her hand into his, palm to palm, like they were two schoolchildren in a playground.

Jonny swept his eyes hungrily along what was left of Christie's spread: flopped-open sandwich triangles and soggy slices of quiche.

'Not a devilled egg in sight,' he lamented. 'You've eaten though? Done the rounds? Has there been any gossip?'

There was *always* gossip in Fincham St George. 'No,' she said. There was nothing she wanted to retell. Nothing interesting except there was an American in town, she thought. But that didn't matter now, as Jonny was here. And once her wonderful fiancé was around, *nothing* else mattered.

'I've brought along a copy of *Nikita's War*,' said Jonny, prising a thick paperback from his back pocket. 'A signed copy for Martin Wetherington's sister-in-law,' he said, slapping it lightly against his palm. 'She works for the Arts section of the *Observer*, apparently,' he grinned, 'and Martin said he would pass it on. So, you never know. Could get a mention. Fame at last?' he queried, with a wink.

Rachel smiled hopefully at him. Fame was what Jonny craved, writing his designated means, but Rachel knew he would be a rock star if he could. Or an actor. They went to Live Aid last year and Jonny had stared, transfixed, at the likes of Freddie Mercury and David Bowie, up on stage, like they were in a club he deserved to be a member of. But what if he *wasn't* on the 'brink'? Rachel sometimes worried. What if they were always going to be exactly where they were now?

'Do you know where my other shoes are?' he asked abstractedly, looking down at the trainers on his feet. 'My party ones. I couldn't find them.'

'They're where you left them,' she said. 'By the front door.'

'OK, let's do the rounds!' he declared, slapping the cover of his book again. 'A couple of hours of convivial chat and let's see if I can get a few verbal sales, and none of this "I'll get a copy from the library" nonsense,' he added charmingly, taking her by the hand and leading her into the centre of the room. 'I need *sales* from these beautiful people, baby.'

It was half past six. Rachel was taking what her father used to call 'a breather' at the kitchen doorstep, filling her lungs with that fresh

May breeze and letting it free the clinging perfumes and aftershaves from her neck. She glanced up to their cottage on the hill, but all was motionless there, apart from the flapping washing – still out. Jonny, with much apology, had disappeared again, this time to fetch three copies of *Nikita's War* for raffling off at the next Lions Club AGM, and he still hadn't returned. He was probably sat back at that desk, thought Rachel, succumbing again to the muse and raking his hand through his James Dean quiff. She'd leave the Wetheringtons' soon, if he didn't reappear. Skit quickly around the whole place kissing the friendly, fragrant people goodbye, then escape.

Teddy wasn't here either. At six o'clock, Nancy Littlen-Green had turned up at the Wetheringtons' front door wondering if her daughter wanted to come over for tea, and Teddy had rushed up to Rachel asking if she could, as her mother had 'Findus Crispy Pancakes and please, Rachel, I'm so bored! I've just had to talk to one of my *own teachers*!' It wasn't Nancy's weekend, of course, but Rachel had let her go.

'Mum says she'll drop me back at eight,' Teddy had said, and Rachel had seen her off at the Wetheringtons' doorstep, where Nancy had given one of her usual off-ish smiles from under her fringe, appraising Rachel for just a fraction too long with her cool and beautiful eyes.

From her vantage point on the kitchen doorstep, Rachel could just make out her Great Aunt Florence's house, further down the valley. Smoke from the little wood burner was coming out of the chimney, Charles and Diana tea towels were still fluttering on the line. Rachel smiled at the sight of them. Florence would be pottering around her kitchen, making herself some supper. Flicking through the *Radio Times* for tonight's programmes. Moving through the cosy terraced cottage that enveloped her in the memories of her long, happy marriage and her amazing life. Rachel was due to see her on Wednesday, for another welcome visit to her second childhood home.

She'd better go back in. Rachel stepped over the uPVC threshold, witnessing lunch-do stragglers – through the square serving hatch to the dining room – bopping to Elton John and Kiki Dee.

Rachel walked over to the sink, unrolled two pieces of kitchen roll from the side, wetted the wad under the cold tap and applied it to her neck. Cool and soothing, it wiped away all those people, for now. As she stood at the sink and pressed it to her skin, she noticed a tin of corned beef on the worktop. The wooden bread bin was open, a sliced white squatting inside. Christie wouldn't mind, would she? If she rustled up a corned beef sandwich for Jonny, for when he came back? She popped the wet kitchen roll in the pedal bin, took the little key from the side of the tin, slotted it into the metal band near the base and started to wind. A ribbon of metal slowly curled around the key, creating a thin horizontal slice.

'Ow!'

Damn, she had cut herself. A bulb of blood appeared on the tip of her index finger and started dripping on to the counter. She dashed to the sink and ran it under the cold tap. Blood mixed with water and cascaded into the plughole. She watched it, strangely fascinated.

'Taking some time out?' said a voice.

She grabbed a tea towel from the side, wrapped it around her finger and turned to face the American, Gabe.

'Oh Lord, are you in the wars?' said Gabe. 'You OK?'

Blood was already seeping through the tea towel.

'Yeah, I'm fine. Absolutely fine. Corned beef tin. Those blasted keys, you know how it is.' She *was* a little light-headed. 'My Grandpop Jim always called them "damned abominations".'

'We are similarly afflicted across the Atlantic,' said Gabe. 'Here, let me.'

28

He took her arm and unfurled the tea towel from her finger, then held her hand at the knuckles and examined the cut.

'Needs pressure,' he said, as though he knew what he was doing, and he grabbed a loop of kitchen roll and made a pad of it, which he pressed firmly against the cut. 'There,' he said, and they stood facing each other for a few moments. 'I think we've stopped the bleeding,' he announced, a little regally, and he released his pressure, removed the blood-smutted wad of kitchen roll and chucked it in the bin. The red on white reminded Rachel of her dad and how he would stick a torn-off coin of toilet paper on his shaving cuts until the blood had dried. It always made Rachel think of a crimson version of the 'black spot' that Pew, the blind pirate, would place into the palms of those about to die, in *Treasure Island* – something else her dad had read at bedtime.

Gabe touched the base of the offending finger with this thumb. 'OK, yep, you're good,' he said. 'No need for a trip to the emergency room. Let's see if our hostess has any Band-Aids.'

He started opening Christie's cupboard doors.

'Here we are,' said Gabe. He had unearthed a tube of Savlon, a roll of fabric plaster and some gauze. He dabbed Savlon on the tiny slice in her finger, unwound a stretchy ribbon of plaster, wrapped it around her finger – pressing the end firm – then helter-skeltered the gauze, securing it finally with a knot.

'Are you sure you're an artist and not a doctor?' Rachel laughed.

He laughed too. 'Let's just say I was in a lot of scrapes, as a kid. All done,' he added. 'I think you'll live to fight another day.'

'Thank you,' she said, but it came out in a bit of a whisper, so she said it again, a bit louder. They stepped back from each other and Rachel searched her brain for something to say. 'Do *you* like corned beef?' she asked, like a bandaged fool.

'I don't eat meat,' said Gabe.

'Oh. Don't you?'

'You expect me to be chowing down on a big ol' burger or something all the time because I'm American?' he asked. His grin was wide and teasing. His eyes were not.

'No, of course not! Well, maybe . . .' She shrugged.

'I'm a vegetarian. My dad used to be a truck driver before he became a logger. Used to haul around carcasses. You could say I saw too much,' he said dramatically.

'Oh, right. I'm sorry. I've never met a vegetarian before.'

'We're a rare breed, if you'll excuse the pun, and *very* rare in my small town. I'm a curiosity. Viewed with suspicion when I walk into the local diner. My dad doesn't like it much either, me being a vegetarian. But then he doesn't like much at all. I see you're engaged, Rachel,' he added. He was looking at her left hand.

'Yes,' she said, wondering why she felt a little strange when he'd said her name. 'I'm engaged to Jonny. He's here . . . well, he was, and his daughter, too. Tatiana – Teddy. She's gone home with her mum and Jonny's gone home to get some books. He *writes* books. He's an author.'

'What kind of books?'

'Spy novels set in Russian winters, usually. The colder and snowier the better. He's never been to Russia, though,' she volunteered, acknowledging Gabe's timely escape from Belarus. 'But he does a lot of research. He looks up the weather in guidebooks, or *National Geographic* magazines.' This sounded lame. She felt she was being disloyal, treacherous, even, placing one of Blind Pew's black spots in the palm of Jonny's hand . . . 'He also reads loads of similar books, to get the milieu just right. He knows lots about his Russian settings. *Tons*,' she added. 'Maybe you could talk to him, when he comes back. Tell him about the winter in Belarus.'

'It was pretty brutal,' admitted Gabe. 'Snow, sleet, hailstones as big as golf balls. The temperature dropping to minus sixteen sometimes, at night. Although that also happens in North Dakota.

We get harsh winters. Lots of snow. Wind chills of minus fifty, sometimes.' He grasped his upper arms, as though warming himself. 'What's your favourite season?'

She and Gabe had both manoeuvred themselves to lean against opposite worktops. Rachel considered his question. 'I like all of them,' she said. 'There's always something to like. Something lovely to look forward to in each.'

'Yes, I can imagine you're the sort of person who feels like that,' said Gabe, and she wondered what he meant and why he was looking at her so intently. 'There's not always *something* to like, though,' he continued. 'There are floods, fires, gales, landslides. Despair. Misery. It's all year round, you know.' He aimed that last sentence at her like a challenge. His face had a sudden brooding shadow to it.

'That's rather . . . dark,' she noted. She thought what a peculiar mixture of a person he was – light, funny, serious, dark, a little risqué, a little sad, all in one.

'Sorry, I can be,' he said. He smiled, but his eyes were fixed on hers. 'Can't you?'

'Be dark?' she asked. She suddenly felt like she was in an odd and earnest little play, set in a suburban kitchen. 'No. But I haven't just left Chernobyl,' she added, 'so I think you're excused.'

'I guess you're just a happy person.'

'You make that sound like a negative,' she bristled. 'I don't think it is. I try the best I can, yes, to be *happy*. To make a good, secure life for myself . . .'

'To know where you're going?'

'Yes.'

'To fit in?'

Where was *he* going? she wondered. 'Do you travel a lot?' she asked. 'Or was the artists' exchange your first?'

'I travel a lot,' admitted Gabe. 'Last summer I did an artists' exchange to South America. The year before I hitch-hiked to Canada. I'm an occasional backpacker,' he said. 'I like to get away when I can. I like to do my art and to party – when the mood takes me.' He grinned shyly. 'How long have you known the Wetheringtons? Christie and Martin?' he asked, resuming his questioning.

'All my life, I suppose. They've always lived in the village.'

'You seem young for this crowd.'

'I suppose so.'

'Don't you want to be in a different circle?'

'What kind of circle? These people are our neighbours. They're lovely.'

'Is that what you really think?' he asked. 'That you find everything and everyone in the world *lovely*?'

'No, of course not,' she said hotly. *What* is *this?* she thought. She was not sure how this conversation had become what it had, but she fought the urge to defend herself to this man, to say she had decided to find everything lovely a long time ago, to *be* lovely, if she could. To align herself away from the darkness and the danger of the world. But why should she defend herself to this stranger? Why did he care what she felt about things? Rachel hoped Jonny was back now, with his paperbacks and his best Paper Mate pen. She wanted to leave Christie and Martin's kitchen and return to his side, to be held fast by him, just how she liked it.

'Sorry,' Gabe said. 'You just seem so unbelievably nice.'

'There's nothing wrong with being *nice*,' she protested.

'A niceness that appears to be unconditional, even.'

'Unconditional? Nothing's unconditional,' she replied. What did *he* know? What did he fancy himself as, some kind of sage? she thought crossly. And what did he want her to *say*? That with Jonny she loved and was loved, under a condition – that neither of them

32

would cheat or stray. That they would support each other, laugh together, write their own blueprint and discard those from the past that had caused so much damage. That Jonny would be her safety. Her security. Her comfort. Hadn't he promised her all those things?

'I'm sorry,' he said, 'I just envy those who live in lovely little bubbles.' Now he was mocking her. She knew what this Gabe was all about. He was one of those men who liked to get into intense, psychological conversations with a woman – any woman – and flatter them with a patchy analysis. It was irritating sparring she didn't want to get involved in, however good-looking or intriguing or *American* he was.

'So what if I do?' she challenged.

The air rippled between them. His amused eyes were narrowed. Again, she felt like a female character in a strange play, in a headscarf.

'It's interesting,' he said. '*You're* interesting.'

She laughed. Rachel had spent the best part of seven years being the least interesting half of her and Jonny, and she was perfectly OK with that. Perhaps Gabe was bored. Perhaps, as a fish out of water, an American in Oxford, he thought it fun to stir things up with complete strangers. Whatever, this was pointless. This was just a random and unnecessary chat, soon forgotten, between two people who would never see each other again.

'Does it really matter?' she asked, and the question hung in the air, in the cream-and-white space of the Wetheringtons' kitchen.

'No, I suppose it doesn't. You're good to talk to, that's all. Forgive me,' he said. He folded up the tea towel and placed it on the worktop. Wrapped the corned beef tin in yet more kitchen roll and discarded it carefully in the bin. 'Unless you think anyone still wants this?' he said, with an impish smile, as the lid closed.

Rachel shook her head. 'It's a dangerous weapon,' she said, 'the bin's the only place for it.'

'Everything OK?'

Christie Wetherington appeared in the doorway and came swishing in holding a large jug, the contents of which she emptied with a great whoosh down the sink. 'I'm just replenishing the Buck's Fizz,' she said, 'it's gone a bit flat. Oh, are you OK? Have you hurt yourself?' she asked Rachel.

'Just a cut on a . . . beer can, silly me,' Rachel said. She didn't want to admit the corned beef. She could see Gabe grinning at her, behind Christie, and was that an attempt at a *wink*? The man was four seasons in one day.

'Oh, I'm so sorry. It looks like you've been well bandaged up, though,' Christie said, checking out Gabe's handiwork. 'You must be Julia's nephew,' she added, turning to Gabe. 'I've been hearing all about you. You flew in from Chernobyl, I hear.'

'Yes,' said Gabe, and Christie started asking him questions about it.

'Thank you,' Rachel mouthed to him, as she left the kitchen. He raised his eyebrows and gave her another, proper wink. She blushed a little, despite herself, and stepped into the hall, where she bumped straight into Jonny.

'Darling! There you are! Where've you been? You're missing everything. Jeremy from The Mallards is up on the table being Cher.'

Rachel laughed with relief at seeing Jonny's cheeky and cheerful face, the stack of books in his arms. *Sod quiet Americans with their darkness and their psychoanalysis of strangers*, she thought. Here's *Jonny*. Her life, her love, her future.

'I cut my finger,' she said, waggling her bandaged finger at him. 'I was trying to make you a corned beef sandwich.'

'Oh, you're sweet. I hope it wasn't a serious injury.'

'Not at all. Teddy's gone to tea at Nancy's,' she added. 'I thought that was OK. Nancy will drop her back at eight.'

'Fine with me. Poor kid must have been bored out of her mind. Has she got her cardigan in case it gets chilly later?'

'Yes, she has her cardigan.'

Jonny held out his arms and Rachel fell into his laughing embrace and the evening ended as it always did, with shoes-off dancing and toes in flesh-coloured pop socks and pastry flakes on the carpet in the sitting room. Cigarettes smouldering in ashtrays and half-finished whisky tumblers on the mantelpiece. Ruddy faces above lambswool jumpers and M&S blouses pulled free from too-full waistbands.

Another spring had rolled around in Fincham St George and Rachel was happy to be one of them, here at this *do*. In a happy circle away from shame and devastation; a place of safety and comfort. Soon to be married. Soon to be complete. As she let Jonny twirl her around to Jackie Wilson and his 'Sweetest Feeling', she was vaguely aware of the quiet American leaving the room and heading for the front door.

# Chapter Four

'I've just remembered it's my mum's birthday on Friday.'

Jonny was at the open door of the study, the mug of coffee Rachel had just presented him with in one hand; she was halfway up the stairs with a slice of cake and a book on Van Gogh, having finished her shift at the cafe at three.

'So it is,' said Rachel. She wrote it on the calendar every year, transferring it with all the other family birthdays from the one before, but she'd forgotten to turn over the page yet this month.

'I'm so sorry, and I know you've just finished your shift, but I don't suppose you'd be able to go into the village and sort a card, please?' he asked, pulling a pained and conciliatory face. 'I'm in a tricky bit with Nikita.'

'Of course,' said Rachel. 'I need to pop to the bank, actually. I could go and do that, too. Padded with a nice poem inside?'

'Yes, please. You're a darling. Ms Ivanov's being a right pain this afternoon.'

Rachel smiled. Nikita Ivanov was the main character in all Jonny's books, a Russian girl-spy (inspired by the Elton John song), currently infiltrating a European spy ring at the Kremlin, apparently. And Rachel was happy to head into the village and get a card for Jonny's mum. He had a nice, normal family. Sweet, over-fussing mum; bumbling, joking dad. *Margaret and Malcolm.* They lived on the outskirts of the village.

'Oh, I also have this cheque.' Jonny momentarily disappeared then came back with a cheque in his hand, plus a paying-in slip. 'Just some small royalties. Nothing earth-shattering. Thanks, Rach.'

'No problem.'

Rachel parked in the little car park behind the library. Half the sky was charcoal and ominous; the other, a deep blue. As she walked quickly to the bank, she spotted Sally Henderson-Bright peering into the latticed casement window of the florist's.

Sally was lit by uncertain sunlight in a bright red raincoat, her blonde hair a neon. Rachel's heart sank. There was no way she could escape walking past, and once you started talking to Sally, it was hard to get away; a conversation with Fincham St George's stalwart Power Lady was like putting your head in one of those woodwork clamps at school and having the winch turned.

'Rachel, *hi*! How are you?'

'Good, thanks, Sally. You?'

Sally was striding assuredly towards her late thirties in Gloria Vanderbilt jeans and silky tucked-in shirts. She had bouncy hair, a handsome salt-and-pepper husband, a story-book daughter, a huge house, a yellow sports car, a cleaner *and* a gardener . . . and every year she and her handsome husband held a Winter Ball at their house which was the talk of the village.

'*Great!* Well, can't complain, anyway!' Sally had a throaty laugh that demanded attention. 'Did you park by the church? It's so *busy* today! How *are* things? How's Jonny? Is he a millionaire yet?' She put her hand on her hip.

'No, not yet.' Rachel wished she hadn't stopped. She was already imagining herself in the bank, at the card shop, coming home again. Anywhere but stuck outside the florist's, talking to Sally.

'Oh, I'm sure he'll join the club soon. Only a matter of time and all that.' There was that throaty laugh again. 'Hey, did you hear about the Steinems? *Apparently*, Jill has run off with Damian Cross from the estate agent's.'

'Yes, I heard,' Rachel said vaguely. She found talk of such things upsetting.

'We do have to keep our other halves on a tight leash, don't we?' Sally husked. 'Well, *you* don't need to worry – you're young. Once you get to my age, it's a different story.'

Rachel doubted there was cause for concern with the Henderson-Brights. They both exuded a wealthy sexual confidence and were often spotted necking in David's parked sports car, outside the pub.

'Well, I must go,' said Rachel. 'I'm going to the bank.'

'OK, yes, off you go. I'm going to buy David an enormous bunch of lilies. An apology for being an absolute *cow* last night.' She pulled a delighted grimace. 'Followed by make-up sex. See you.'

'Bye, Sally.'

Always so *up front*, Rachel thought. Rachel had only tried to be all-out sexy on rare occasions, like the time she and Jonny went to a Vicars and Tarts party in the next village and she had been more of a wholesome *apple pie,* really, despite her short dress and her mussed-up hair. Jonny had liked it though.

Rachel headed to the bank, two cheques slipped inside her leather cheque-book holder. Jonny's royalty cheque, and a dividend that had arrived in the post this morning from her father's solicitors. Some small figure from an investment he'd once made.

As she stepped through the propped-open door of the Midland Bank, it started to rain and she brought some drops in with her on to the rubber mat and the scratchy carpet. The women behind the counters were waiting with convivial smiles and twiddly biros on chains, which wrote all splodgy, and charity money boxes where you put 2p in a slot and it excitingly rolled its way to the bottom. Her mum's oldest, best friend, Linda Spencer, had been stationed here since time began, or the late 60s at least, and here she was this afternoon, in a red jumper and a huge gemstone necklace like a multicoloured Stonehenge on a string.

'Well, hello,' said Linda, as Rachel approached. 'How are *you*? How's Jonny? You're looking well, love. Have you set a date yet?'

'No, not yet, Linda.'

Linda shook her head sympathetically. 'Not getting cold feet, either of you?'

'No, we just want to save up.'

'Right. Well, that's good. Young love, eh? It's a joy to see. We need to have more of it in the village.' Rachel knew that if Linda wasn't behind that counter, she'd be giving her a hug. Linda's hugs were the best. 'So, is Jonny writing another book?'

'Jonny's always writing another book,' replied Rachel. She was staring at Linda's necklace and remembering how Linda used to arrive at their family doorstep with Kendal mint cake and a leather bookmark from Penrith Castle, every single summer, after her annual holiday. How Dad used to let her in and call for Mum, who was usually in the garden, and Mum would arrive in the hall pulling off muddy gloves and running a futile hand through bird's-nest hair to greet her, but looking happy. That was before, of course, before 'that woman', Stephanie Kerridge. Mum never looked happy after. But Mum and Linda would sit in the garden and Linda would tell Mum all sorts of things she shouldn't be telling her, because Linda had a tongue as loose as a barn door, that's what Mum always said.

'Well, that's exciting!' Linda said. 'I'm always talking about him.'

'I'm sure you are.' Rachel smiled.

'And how's your little job? Still at the cafe, isn't it?'

'And the art gallery,' prompted Rachel. She slid the cheques and two paying-in slips under the glass. Linda reached out her stubby hand – bright red nail varnish, thick stack of gold engagement, wedding and eternity rings – and picked them up.

'Ah, from *Dad*,' she said, looking at the first one, and Rachel felt tears prickle behind her eyes. She remembered Saturday morning trips to this very bank, a small hand in a large one, her father holding her up to the counter, so the tips of her leather shoes butted against the smooth front and she pretended to fill out paying-in slips; pretended to be a grown-up. They would come here, then meet Mum outside the bakery next door and Dad would wear his brown shoes, the ones with the long black laces he had to knot twice, and she would wear her Rupert Bear trousers and her pink jumper.

'Yes,' Rachel said as Linda looked like she might be about to say more, but instead she smiled sympathetically and enthusiastically stamped the back of the first cheque and the waiting stub in the paying-in book. Stamp. Stamp. Smile. Smile. Rachel was swamped by emotion; for the longing for her errant father was so deep and wide she thought she might go down with it, like a sinking ship.

'Much missed,' said Linda eventually, as she handed Rachel back her paying-in book. 'And your mum. Much missed. Such a terrible shame.'

'Thank you,' whispered Rachel. She waited while Linda stamped Jonny's cheque and paying-in slip, then shoved her cheque-book holder back in her bag and fled, dragging that tidal wave of emotion with her even as she breathed in the air outside. She could imagine her father standing next to her, stamping his feet and slapping his pockets searching for his cigarettes; she could see her mum bustling out of the bakery with a brown paper bag stuffed full of hot sausage rolls, for them all to eat in the car.

She dashed to the car park behind the library. Got in the car, switched on the radio. 'Don't Stand So Close to Me' by The Police was playing and she turned it up, sang the last fading few lines of the chorus out loud for comfort, to absorb and banish the memories of her parents, although they were good ones – the sausage rolls and the big, warm hand, and coming in from the garden, smiling – but good memories always led to bad and the worst one of all.

Even sitting in the car, the rain now steady and nonchalant on the windscreen, reminded her of them. Of crumbs brushed from laps. Of rustly brown paper bags. She could feel the tears coming and wondered whether to let them or not. Whether to give in to her feelings. She couldn't remember if she'd feel better or worse afterwards.

The DJ mumbled something and the next song came on. Well, that was settled then – James Taylor's 'Fire and Rain' started up, its opening bars melancholy and familiar. An inevitable tune for a good old sob. She didn't cry for her parents when she was at home. Jonny always cajoled her out of it, said that it was better for her if she didn't. Said she'd feel better if she hugged him instead and thought of happy things, like their brilliant future. Twelve years it had been. Since the accident. It felt like yesterday. It always felt just like yesterday.

Raindrops striped and merged into one another and she turned her key in the ignition and put the wipers on. One of the windscreen wipers squeaked and the other had a wet leaf stuck under it, which it carried with it, up and down, up and down. She cried, and James Taylor sang about seeing someone's face again. Then she saw him. The American from the lunch party. *Gabe.* He was walking through the car park and she saw him glance towards her car and glance again and, oh no, he'd seen her. Rachel put her head down, but there was a tapping at the window, and his face was there, behind the misted-up glass. Wiping the tears away with her hand

and ladling on a bright smile, she turned off both the radio and the windscreen wipers and wound down the window.

'Hi,' he said, and then his expression changed. 'Oh God, are you OK? Have you been crying?' He immediately pulled a navy hanky from the pocket of his dark blue denim jacket, currently absorbing raindrops like flicked paint from a paintbrush, and held it out to her. She didn't take it, but instead waved her hand back at him.

'No, I'm fine, honestly. I'm absolutely fine, thank you. I'm just being a bit silly.'

'Take it,' he said, still holding out the hanky, and she remembered how he had irritated her in Christie Wetherington's kitchen, trying to assess her personality, holding it under some sort of a spotlight, but it was difficult to recapture that irritation now; it slid from her like one of the plump raindrops streaking down the windscreen. Large spots of rain landed on his hair and instead she remembered how he had bandaged her finger and tied the gauze.

'Thank you,' she said. Their fingers lightly touched. The hanky was soft and very well-worn. Rachel wondered if Aunt Julia had put it in Gabe's pocket. She dabbed under her eyes with it, feeling self-conscious.

'Anything I can help with?' he asked, his hair darkening in the rain, his face damp. Raindrops on his lips.

'No, no, not at all,' she said. 'Sorry. So, what are you up to?' she added, in an attempt at sounding chirpy, but she sniffed at the same time so that didn't really work.

'Just running some errands for Aunt Julia. Without the bike this time,' he said, with a grin. 'Drug store, you know.'

'*Drug store?*' She put the balled-up hanky on her lap. 'Oh, you mean the chemist's.'

'Yes, the *chemist's*,' repeated Gabe, rubbing at the back of his increasingly wet head. 'Are you sure you're OK?'

'Yes, I'm fine. It's just . . . memories,' she said. 'Just silly memories.'

'Family?' asked Gabe quietly. The rain was heavier now. He looked like he needed windscreen wipers for his face.

She nodded. 'My mum and dad,' she said. She couldn't help it. Something about his face made her say it.

'I understand,' he said drily. 'I have a mom and dad, too.'

She nodded. 'Why does your mum go into institutions?' she asked, then she realised this was a very abrupt and nosy question indeed, and too heavy for two virtual strangers – one sitting in the driver's seat of a car and the other standing outside, being heavily rained on.

'Long story,' he said wryly, and she felt it was a story he might tell in a bar somewhere – an American bar, like in a movie, where a neon sign on a darkened street leads to a snug, dark space and a man might tell a woman the story of his life. But they were not in America. They were in a rainy car park in a village in England.

'Mine is very *short*,' she said, with a short laugh to go with the short story she would not tell him either.

He looked at her, his eyes serious. She was suddenly aware of the dried tears on her cheeks.

'Can I get in?' he asked.

'Erm, OK?' she replied, and before she knew it, he was in through the passenger door and on the seat, flicking wet hair out of his eyes and smiling at her.

'Shoot,' he said. He looked like a mischievous child.

'*Shoot?*'

'If you want to talk. Shoot, go ahead.'

'I don't want to talk,' she said, winding up the window. 'I was just crying in peace.' But she had the weirdest sensation she could tell him anything and it was disconcerting, this sensation, because it appeared to upend everything she had known or felt up until this moment.

They both looked at the windscreen. Rachel stared at the fattest descending raindrop. After a while, Gabe spoke. 'My dad had an accident when I was twenty-one,' he said. 'It was on my last night of college. I was at a bar, celebrating, when I got a call from his boss. They'd been trying to get hold of me for hours, my name got called out by the barman when I was downing a shot of tequila. Dad was a logger, felling trees up near the state border. A mitre saw slipped and . . . well, I won't go into gruesome detail, but he has big mobility problems. Left leg.'

'I'm sorry,' said Rachel.

'Thank you,' said Gabe. 'And my mom, well, she suffers with her nerves, that's what they call it, although it's a lot worse than that. She often has to go away to an institution in Fargo. To be looked after, settled, so she can bear to come back. My dad makes her life . . . difficult. Mine too.' He sighed. 'He takes it out on us, his hatred of life. He lashes out. I escape, when I can – I'm not sure I'd be in Jud at all if it wasn't for Mom – but then I feel guilty about it. I feel guilty now, that I'm away. We used to be happy, the three of us. But it's not like that any more.'

He paused. He swept back his hair from his face again. 'I don't tell many people this,' he grinned, but his eyes were sad.

'I'm sorry,' she said again, 'it sounds like an incredibly tough situation.' She remembered how she had once been part of a 'three of us' too.

There was a pause. Gabe was looking at her expectantly. She thought, in his sadness and his openness and his silent encouragement, how handsome he was. Maybe it was the way his hair curled at the nape of his neck and above his ears. Maybe it was the colour of his eyes.

'Am I supposed to speak now?' she asked, trying to turn herself the right way up, to be light and breezy and unaffected by his handsome face.

'If you'd like to.'

'Is this how they do therapy in America?' she asked. 'In the front of cars, with the therapist talking about themselves first?'

He laughed. 'No, I don't think so. I just thought it might help. I don't like to see anyone cry.'

She fell silent again. She turned from him. 'I was in the bank,' she said. 'It reminded me of my dad. We used to do errands on a Saturday morning. My mum too. We'd get sausage rolls from the bakery next door.' He nodded. She continued. 'They died when I was thirteen. In a car crash.'

'I'm so sorry,' he said.

'Thank you.'

Everyone in the village knew how Rachel's parents had died, and that the night it happened Rachel had been sleeping over at Nanna Florence's and Grandpop Jim's cottage as Frances and Gary were in one of their brief patches of 'trying' (a word Rachel heard bandied around the house occasionally) and were going out for a 'little dinner' at a local Indian restaurant. The proposed dinner had followed a few days of an unspoken peace treaty – from arguing about *her*, from Dad slipping out, and from Rachel creeping on to the landing in her nightie to hear them flinging arrows at each other – and had meant her parents had been almost happy, or so Rachel liked to think, the night they died, driving out in the car for dinner together, the affair with Stephanie Kerridge temporarily on hold, until a misjudged turn and the tragic surprise of a huge cement bag squatting in the road . . .

Rachel sighed. 'It was a very hard time,' she continued, amazed she was spilling out this stuff to him. 'I was full of teenage hormones, all the angst and emotion of puberty. I wasn't equipped for

45

such a loss. I couldn't deal with it; I couldn't talk about it. I was a closed-off kid anyway and this just shut me down completely,' she shrugged. 'People in the village kept asking me how I was feeling all the time. "How are you?" "How are you feeling now?" as if three, six or nine months after the accident would make any difference. As if two years would, or three. I just wanted to shout in people's faces. I just wanted them to go away. I wanted *everything* to go away. Sorry,' she said. 'Sometimes it all just comes back to me. Sometimes I have to cry about it. Especially when a sad song comes on the radio. It was James Taylor,' she added.

'"Fire and Rain"?'

'How did you guess?'

'That always gets people,' he said. 'James Taylor has a lot to answer for.' She smiled then, and he grinned back at her. He had the beginnings of creases at the corner of his eyes. 'What happened to you?' he asked. 'After?'

'I went to live with my great aunt and uncle,' she said. 'They were my only family. I didn't know my grandparents – my dad's parents both died before I was born. My mum's, not long after. A *lot* of death in the family.' She grimaced.

'I'm sorry.'

'That I went to live with them? Don't be. We had a lovely time.' He spared her an eyebrow raise at 'lovely'. 'They were wonderful, actually. Well, my great auntie still is. She lives here in the village. My grandpop – I call them Nanna and Grandpop – died four years ago.'

'I'm so sorry, again. But I'm glad you had them. And were you closed off with them?'

'Well, they didn't encourage dwelling on things,' she said. 'They encouraged happiness and laughter, so that was good, in its own way. I see my nanna all the time. She's pretty amazing.' She smiled as she thought of Florence.

'Tough break, though, kiddo,' he said. 'I know what you mean about being a closed-off kid. I was one of those too. It's not easy.'

'No.' She couldn't believe she'd just told him all this. This story that reached from the past right into the present. She hadn't spoken about it for a long time. And he had called her 'kiddo', so American, and strangely affectionate.

'And you're an only child?' he asked.

'Yes.'

'Tough,' he agreed. 'No one to share anything with.' And they both fell silent.

'Well then,' she said eventually, hooking an unruly piece of her hair behind one ear. 'Am I supposed to feel better now I've told you why I was crying?'

'Do you?' he asked, his kind eyes anchored on hers.

'Yes,' she said, looking away from them, bashful, 'actually. Thank you.' She thanked him for his kind eyes and his friendly smile and his own confession. She prayed no one would see the pair of them sitting in the front seat of her car, in this car park. And she wondered why Jonny thought it was better to focus on the future, but Gabe had encouraged her to talk of the past.

'OK,' he said, and just as quickly as he'd got into the car, he was out of it again and back round at her window. She wound it open.

'Keep the handkerchief,' he said. 'I have plenty more.'

'Oh, thanks.'

It was absolutely chucking it down now. Gabe's hair was fast becoming drenched again and the shoulders of his denim jacket were deepening into a darker blue.

'Well, great to see you, Rachel.'

'You too.' *What an odd encounter*, she thought. Intense and odd. Like in Christie Wetherington's kitchen but in a different way, and now he was out of the car she felt she'd only imagined him

47

being in it. That she'd only imagined the quickening of her heart when he'd looked at her.

He turned away. Then he turned back again.

'You're not working at the gallery today?'

'No. Thursdays to Saturdays.'

'Oh, right. Listen, can I drop in sometime? See the art?'

She hesitated. 'Well, of course you can.' She hesitated again. 'Hey, did you bring any of your paintings with you to England?' she added. 'The ones you did in Belarus?'

'Yes, a few,' he said. 'I left the rest at the art facility there.'

She nodded. The word 'Belarus' and the thought of what was currently happening there hung like a shroud in the air. 'You should bring them with you, if you come into the gallery. I'm sure Faith would love to see them.'

'Faith?'

'My boss.'

'Right. And you? Would *you* like to see them?' His smile was teasing. His face sopping wet.

'Yes, I would.' Her heart quickened again.

'OK. I'll come in. In the next couple of days.'

'Great,' she said. 'You're getting soaked,' she added. 'It's stair rods.'

'*Stair rods?* I thought it was cats and dogs.' He laughed, rubbing the back of his head, then he shook it comically and dislodged a small shower that landed inside the car. 'OK, stair rods it is. Go figure,' he shrugged, his grin wide. 'OK, well, bye then, Rachel.'

'Bye, Gabe.'

Rachel wound up the window. She watched him walk away in the rain, flipping up the collar of his denim jacket and dipping his head down into it. She turned the key in the ignition, put the windscreen wipers on and pulled out of the car park, then remembered she'd completely forgotten to buy Margaret's birthday card. She'd forgotten herself, too, in this encounter, she realised, as she

48

shunted the car irritably into reverse. She had momentarily become someone else entirely.

◆ ◆ ◆

When Rachel finally got home, after parking again and popping to Martin's the newsagent's, it had stopped raining and Jonny was sitting out on the tiny patio at the back of the cottage, his feet up on a chair in weak spring sunshine, reading a Stephen King novel.

'Hi, baby,' he said. 'I missed you. How was town?'

'Quiet.'

'You were a long time.'

'Not really.'

'See anyone?'

'Only Linda, at the bank. Mum's old friend.' She didn't tell him she had bumped into Gabe, the American staying in the village. Or that he had sat in her car while she told him about her parents. Or that she had invited him to bring his paintings into the gallery. Rachel couldn't explain it to Jonny, and she couldn't exactly explain it to herself. How everything had happened so easily, like raindrops slipping down glass, and had ended in an invitation she now wasn't sure about.

'I've made us dinner,' Jonny said. 'Shepherd's pie. It'll be ready about seven.'

'Oh, great! Cheesy topping?'

'Cheesy topping. Come here and give me a cuddle.'

Jonny patted his lap, and she went over to him and climbed on, slotting her face into that familiar space between his shoulder and the crook of his neck. He stroked her leg, played with the hem of her cotton skirt, looking thoughtful. Happy. 'I think this next book's going to be the one, Rach,' he said.

'Really?' He'd said this before. He'd said this twice already. But each time something – and nothing possibly his fault, it was the market, the climate, the zeitgeist, not enough luck in the air – had fallen short. 'Well, that's great, Jonny. That's really great.'

'And you'll be with me, every step of the way, won't you? Every step, good or bad?'

'Of course I will.' It didn't matter that she'd told someone else her story. It didn't matter that she'd been weak today and cried in the car, or that her heart had foolishly quickened at the sight of another man's – a passing stranger's – handsome face. Her story was her life with Jonny. When she was with him, Rachel didn't need to cry any tears. And she didn't need anyone else. She never had.

Jonny enveloped her in a tight, tight hug.

'I love you, Smith.'

'I love you too, Trent.'

'It's always been us, hasn't it, you and me, in this together? And that's how it will stay? Forever?' He snuggled in tighter. Clung on to her, like a child, and she loved how he needed her.

'Forever, Jonny.'

It had been forever almost from the moment she had first laid eyes on him.

# Chapter Five

As an only child, Rachel spent a lot of her childhood wandering around the village on her own, before Wren arrived in 1976. Rachel would aimlessly amble down fragrant country lanes picking up interesting-looking flowers. She would wander into building sites and make secret solo dens out of breeze blocks, where she would bring her paint-by-numbers, or her Enid Blyton *Mystery* books and enjoy them in solitude. She would wander down to the stream under the concrete bridge that went over Church Street and sit and listen to people walking overhead, like the troll from the Billy Goats Gruff. Except this troll would be ten years old and wearing check shorts, an embroidered gypsy top and red Start-Rites.

One September morning, in her second to last year at primary school – before Stephanie Kerridge and all the shouting – she was wandering down the dried-mud bank to the stream when she saw there was a boy already there, under the bridge. He was sitting crossed-legged and scribbling things in a notebook with a yellow-and-black striped school pencil, in *her* place, her space to hide. Yes, she knew bigger boys and girls came down here in the evening and smoked cigarettes and laughed about things nobody but them would understand, but in the afternoons, after school, this place was hers.

He didn't look up, not even for a second. She stood and stared at him, then she silently crept backwards up the crisp-mud bank and on to the street.

The following Monday, the boy started at her primary school, in the year above, sauntering into assembly halfway through the second chorus of 'Lord of the Dance', grinning his head off, loosening the tie that would be in his pocket for his entire time at that school, and wearing a gold-plated, dazzlingly unbreakable *confidence*.

'All right?' he said, to no one in particular, although *everyone* was looking at him, and he took his cross-legged place at the end of his class line, the line up from Rachel, and sang the final chorus of 'Lord of the Dance' with such gusto that all eyes remained on him. His were devilish blue, under thick eyebrows, and framed by soot-black lashes. He had a mouth that was always inclined to smile. Slightly uneven teeth. He was an Artful Dodger of a boy, who played that very character in the Christmas production the following winter and received a standing ovation.

Jonny Trent hit the school like a hurricane. He was interesting. He used to live at Magdalen College, Oxford, the story went round. His parents had worked there, as a gardener and a cook. Jonny's dad now worked at Fincham Cricket Club and his mum was a dinner lady at a school in another village. Jonny was cheeky, but just the right side of insolent. He was also *great* at English, excelling at it in a magnificently unselfconscious way. It was not usually *cool* to write long, very funny poems about fireworks night or sweet, inventive ones about the burgeoning of spring flowers, and have them displayed in the school's corridors. But Jonny was cool. He was also up for fighting, when fighting was required – he had a rash, reckless side that brushed easily with trouble, but also led to ready confession.

When Jonny's year moved up to secondary school, Jonny didn't go with them. He passed his eleven-plus and got into the local grammar school. But Rachel still saw him about. Hanging around street corners of the village, slouching near the war memorial. Sometimes under that concrete bridge, where she now knew there was a stack of dog-eared 'dirty magazines' (which she had once thought meant *Good Housekeeping* had got muddy).

She also read his words, later. Young Jonny Trent got a gig writing for the local newspaper: perky and obliquely scathing reviews of local am-dram productions or summer fetes, that seemed positive unless the partly interested reader read between the lines, and Rachel was always more than partly interested and could read everything that was intended. But although she absorbed his written words, every one of them, he never once spoke to her, if she saw him around the village. She was never a receiver of one of his 'All right?'s. When he was one of a group of teenage boys down by the bridge, crouching over those magazines, he would just turn and look at her, his eyes glinting under thick eyebrows, and she would scuttle away, skittering on the loose stones.

It wasn't until *much* later that they used to go down there together, the world walking above them but as far away as it could possibly seem. When he would scribble in another notebook and she would be the first to read what he had written. When the footsteps of those above them faded into nothing, for they had each other and that was all that mattered. When it was *only* she who he asked if she was all right, and the answer was, when she was with him, 'Yes' . . .

◆ ◆ ◆

'You were miles away.'
   'Sorry.'

Faith, Rachel's boss, was lingering at a painting of a golden-haired child sitting in a wicker egg chair in an English garden.

'I love this,' Faith said, with a happy sigh. She held the painting at arm's length and tilted her head to one side. 'Look at the light.'

'Yes, it's great,' said Rachel. She had been standing at the large Georgian front window of Picture This, Fincham St George's art gallery, with a giant mug of coffee and thinking about Jonny. About the hurricane of him. His megawatt smile and the unshakeable belief he had in himself. How he loved her. This morning he had grabbed her from behind, in the kitchen, as she'd been standing at the sink, washing up, and had spun her round to tell her so. To tell her he adored her, that she was perfect for him. She'd been smiling at that memory as she looked out from the window at the picturesque village green with its 'Fincham St George' wooden sign, adorned with a hanging basket of bursting hydrangeas and freesias, and the wooden bench on the pavement where her Grandpop Jim always used to sit, to watch the world go by.

It was still outside. Weak sunshine peeped through stretched clouds. It was a warm-in-the-sun, chilly-in-the-shade afternoon. When she finished here, later, she was walking to Florence's house for their customary Thursday visit.

Rachel smiled at Faith, trying to get her face to match her words. She really didn't like that painting. If truth be told, and she never told the truth to Faith as firstly, it wasn't her place and secondly, she liked her boss – Faith was a lovely woman with a warmth that negated her terrible taste in art – it was pedestrian and parochial and dated, and that new word, *cheesy*.

'Shall I put it over there next to the pink Pierrot?' asked Faith. 'What do you think?'

'Yes, why not?'

Faith walked to the back wall of the gallery and held the painting up next to a large picture of a pink clown with a downturned mouth and an enormous ruffly collar. Faith liked portraits of Pierrot clowns with tears descending from kohled eyes or wistfully holding roses. She liked shiny Athena-type posters – close-ups of giant glossy lips, or monochrome portraits of bare-chested hunky men holding babies. She liked sub-Warhol prints of ice lollies. And she *loved* angelic curly-haired children on wicker furniture. It was just a shame nobody else in the village seemed to.

'There,' said Faith. She had hooked the painting on the wall now and stepped back to admire it. 'I so love this artist,' she added. 'I wonder what she'll bring in next.'

*More of the same, unfortunately,* thought Rachel. 'Who knows?' she said cheerfully.

Faith laughed randomly, a warm, expansive laugh that drew people to the gallery to have a *look*, at least. 'Shall we have a coffee?' she asked. 'Just one sugar for me, as I'm slimming.'

Faith kept a Slimcea loaf – the one in the white packet with the illustration of a tape measure round it – in the small fridge at the back of the shop, where Rachel stored her snacks of apples and Ski yoghurts. Faith was permanently 'slimming' the smooth Sindy-doll figure she dressed in tight-fitting polo necks cinched at the waist with thin leather belts, dog-tooth pencil skirts and high heels with huge bows at the back. Her hair was tiger-striped, flicky and enormous; her lips lined in brown pencil. Since she had hired Rachel, via a card in the local job centre, Rachel had been rather in awe of her.

They stood and drank their coffee. It was slow this afternoon; it was always slow in the gallery. They had seen a few stragglers and the local bag lady, coming in for shelter, plus a couple of passing ramblers on their way to the cafe. Rachel wasn't really needed, position-wise, but she knew Faith liked having an assistant – someone to say, 'Faith will be with you shortly' or 'Faith will know, she's just popped out the back' or someone to run to the chemist's for Faith, for emergency 10-denier stockings. But Rachel liked Faith, and she loved working in the gallery.

'I'm going to get my hair done at two,' Faith said. 'Would you mind locking up for me this afternoon, please?'

'Yes, of course.' Faith was a former hairdresser herself; she had been working at Upper Cuts on Trebor Street when the gallery had come up for sale. Fancying it, she'd begged her then husband to buy it for her but admitted to Rachel she knew 'sod all' about art, an admission corroborated by poor sales and low footfall, yet bankrolled by maintenance payments from her ex-husband, keeping Picture This open.

'Sally Henderson-Bright might come in,' continued Faith. 'Well, today or tomorrow. I know it's super early for the Winter Ball, but she wants to look at some of Forrest Chaplain's work. You know, the Catskill Mountains landscapes.'

Rachel nodded. At their Winter Ball, Sally and David Henderson-Bright displayed a piece of art, always with a wintry theme, at the top of the grand staircase in their entrance hall, to which over three hundred guests in black tie paid homage while they nibbled on Marks and Sparks canapés and sank fine wines. The Winter Ball often hosted a live band, playing in the Henderson-Bright's enormous sitting room, and, occasionally, ostentatious fireworks in the back garden. This would be their sixth year; last year, Jonny had brought along five of his books, placed them on various windowsills, mantelpieces and occasional tables, but had been saddened to find one abandoned on the floor of the downstairs cloakroom.

'I just wish I knew what Sally had in mind for this year,' said Faith. 'There's *this* one of Forrest's . . . ?' Faith click-clacked to the back of the gallery and gestured with a burgundy talon to a bound and wrapped canvas at the back of the shop. 'Could you be a sweetie and unwrap it for me? I can't manage it with these nails.'

It was a lavish oil painting. A snowy scene, with a pond, creepy-looking background woods and a huge moon in a black sky, reflected in the water. The only thing it had going for it, in Rachel's opinion, was that it was gigantic and would cover a good part of the Henderson-Brights' designated wall.

'It should be fine,' Rachel said.

'But will *Sally* like it?'

'Hopefully, yes. It's very . . . striking.'

Rachel liked art that made her feel something, art she could look at for ages and still find more layers of meaning in. Art that gave her *joy*. She pored over art books at home. She sometimes went on a coach to London, to one of the big galleries. She had never been a good artist herself – she was too imprecise, too sloppy; she coloured too far over the lines – but she had a good appreciation of it. When she was ten years old, her dad had taken her to the Tate Gallery to see a Turner exhibition – he'd been given some free tickets through his job as a building contractor – and she had been transfixed. Consumed. It started an obsession for art books from the library (taken out one Saturday and returned the next) and meant she'd applied for this job immediately when she'd seen that card in the job centre.

'Great. Well, if Sally comes in, show her this one. Thanks, Rachel. OK, got to fly!' Faith cried. 'See you in the morning!'

She grabbed her designer handbag and was out of the door, a blur of warm Opium perfume and big-cat hair.

'Bye, Faith,' said Rachel and she closed the door. She *loved* having the gallery to herself. She wandered round, revelling in the space. The late afternoon sun cast a pale square of light in the middle of the polished floor, and Rachel stood in that square and rejoiced that it was spring, the skies lightening and the days lengthening, just a little, every single day. That her soul would lighten, too, and stretch up to greet the ripening sun.

'Warm your bones,' her dad always said, and she always did just that, in the spring and summer months. In early childhood, she would play dolls in a sunny back garden while her mum weeded and her dad sat in a deckchair, reading the paper. In her early teens, she would sprawl on a pink candlewick bedspread and bask in the sun, Radio 1 turned up to drown out the arguing from the open windows of the house. Since she and Jonny had moved to the cottage, she would lie on the sloping lawn with a book and the silence, knowing Jonny was typing in his study indoors – her world all nice and peaceful, with no confrontation, for what was there to confront, in the life the two of them shared?

Rachel walked to the back of the gallery, where her boss kept a tape recorder. She rifled through the stack of cassettes in the drawer of the desk – Whitney Houston, Madonna, Phil Collins, The Cure – and pulled out The Cure, a compilation album. A few years ago, she and Wren had found themselves unexpectedly and hilariously on *Top of the Pops* and they'd danced on a podium to 'The Love Cats', twirling ecstatically in each other's arms.

As Rachel took the tape out of the case, a brown ribbon of tape bulged from it. She wound it back in, then snapped the tape into the tape recorder and forwarded – four attempts, five – to the right place on the tape and the track she wanted. 'In Between Days'.

The music burst into the space: clanging, jangling, filling it, every corner. Rachel walked to the sunshine square on the floor, and she started to dance. First, swaying her arms, on the spot, as the short burst of drums heralded the galloping guitars; then, when they really kicked in – layer upon joyous layer of them – she started spinning and spinning, hopping on both feet and waving her arms in the air. And when Robert Smith started to sing, she joined in, letting her clear, out-of-tune voice rise to the small skylight at the top of the gallery.

The music was like a carousel with her on board, the wind in her hair and the sun in her eyes as she lifted her face to the skylight and turned and turned.

*See, Dad*, she thought, as she sang and twirled, and hopped and spun, holding out her arms like the wings of a bird of prey. *I am warming my bones!* She missed him, her father, and in that moment, she could almost forgive him.

When the carousel came to a stop and the last bars of the song faded to nothing, she gave herself an ironic little bow and laughed at her own ridiculousness, in the sunny square in the middle of the gallery.

'Bravo.'

There was someone standing behind her. Amused eyes. Hands half raised as though deciding whether or not to applaud ironically. A bashful smile at his interruption.

'Hello,' she said. *This is the third time he's caught me at something*, she thought. The not-so-quiet American. In the Wetheringtons' kitchen, in the car and now here. Catching her spinning like a fairground windmill to The Cure.

'Hello,' he replied, and she knew, quite suddenly and irrevocably, that this man was dangerous to her. That he had come to interrupt and upset her carefully planned life, walking into the room of her existence to shine a light into one of its dark and empty corners when she'd thought her corners were far from dark and empty. Wasn't she currently standing in a shape of sunlight and warming her bones? Wasn't she *happy*, on this spring day?

She knew it, as she looked at him. She looked at his face and she knew this man could make her question everything she'd ever wished for.

# Chapter Six

'The door was unlocked. Sorry.'

'That's OK. We haven't closed yet.'

'Nice dancing.'

'Would you actually call it that?' She laughed as she walked to the back of the room, ejected the cassette from the player and put it back in its case. She whispered to her heart to quieten.

'Some people might.'

'They might be idiots.'

'And you can't beat The Cure,' he added.

He was wearing jeans again, a white T-shirt. A navy kind of tennis shoe. His hair looked just combed but those curls were there, at the nape of his neck, escapees.

'You have it in America?' She didn't want to step back towards him, although she knew it would be odd to stay here at the safety of the table. She didn't want to see what shade of blue his eyes were today, or the curve at the corner of his lips.

'Music? Yes, we have music.' His smile was playful. She was in danger.

'No, The Cure.' Why had she said 'it'? Rachel still didn't move. She was worried he would see his effect on her, that he would know. How his face and his body, in this space, unnerved her. *He's going soon*, she told herself. *This is transient, fleeting, it means absolutely nothing. He's just a different kind of man, that's all. Different to Jonny. That's all this is.*

'Yes, The Cure have reached North Dakota. I'm a big fan. And I like badly applied red lipstick on a man.'

'Me too,' she said, trying not to let that handsome, mischievous smile absorb into her skin, take hold of her completely. 'And hair spiked up with soap.'

Gabe laughed. He started walking around the room, his hands clasped behind his back. Rachel steadied hers on the edge of the table. 'It's a very modern gallery,' he commented, looking at the painting of a giant pair of jewelled sticky lips pouting into the receiver of a red telephone.

'You mean awful?'

'Well, contemporary, let's say – very of the decade. No chances have been taken. I hope you don't mind me saying that.'

'It's not my gallery,' she shrugged. 'And Faith's out having her hair done, so it's fine.'

Gabe smiled and continued to move around the walls of the gallery. She wanted to stop watching him, but she watched each step. Every tilt of his head. He stopped in front of a bland painting of a poppy field just right for the top of a tin of biscuits. 'This is nice.'

'Stop taking the mickey.'

He laughed, and she was surprised how quickly she had found this *ease* with him. When had the line become crossed? she wondered. In the car park, when she was explaining her tears and he was telling her about his mom and dad? When they were in the Wetheringtons' kitchen and he had accused her of living unconditionally and she had called him *dark*? Or the first time she'd ever laid eyes on him?

'It is,' he insisted, but his grin told her otherwise. 'I like the light. Are they all local artists?'

'Yes. Faith likes to support the local community.' He was too close to her. She slipped from the table to the window and pretended to watch a car driving past the green. 'So, where are your paintings?' she asked, eventually turning back to him. She wanted to move things along. Hasten the afternoon. Get him out of here, so she could bring her heart back in line and return to her life.

'Hang on,' he said. He stepped out of the door and appeared a few seconds later with a long cardboard tube. Popping off the cap, he gently let a rolled-up column of parchments drop on to the floor.

'How many are there?' she asked, walking over.

'Six.'

She was already unwrapping the first painting from its thin cotton shroud. She was eager and impatient, as ever, to see new work by new artists; hoping for a jewel among all the slurry, not that it was ever her choice.

'Oh, it's pen and ink!' she cried, once the first artwork was unrolled.

'Biro,' said Gabe with a self-deprecating grin. 'Good old blue Bic biro. I've been experimenting.'

'Wow,' said Rachel, and her eyes roamed over the work she had unfurled. It was the most startling drawing of an oak tree – barren, all leaves shed – its branches stretching to the edges of the paper and trailing off with no end. The tree was made up from thousands, perhaps millions of intricate tiny pen strokes, enmeshed with each other: a road map for the eyes and, between the branches, nestling in hollows among the twigs and the leaves, were symbols and tiny figures – hearts both plump and spindly, elongated; two clasped hands; a tightly furled rosebud; a two-pronged fork; a couple, entwined, their arms wrapped around each other's bodies like curled feathers; a sleeping infant, a comma in the cupped palm of two intersecting oak leaves. And the face of an old man, with a thick beard and rheumy eyes staring from a notch in the bark.

'This is amazing,' she said, 'truly wonderful.' And Rachel looked up at Gabe and into his smile and his enjoyment of her praise for his drawing, and she felt something pass between them, as if one of those endless indigo branches of the stark oak tree had reached from him into her – something imperceptible and intangible. She felt almost like he had touched her.

'How long did it take you?' she finally managed to ask.

'About two months. Maybe slightly less.'

Rachel looked through the others, spending time with each one. The others were in pale strokes of watercolour and each painting was of the same tree but in different seasons: bare and under its winter shroud; sprouting with spring buds; full and leafy in summer; wilting and in the process of decay in the autumn. There was an air of hope to spring, and a descent of drear and darkness about the winter oak. They were beautiful. *Faith would hate them*, she thought. She would frown prettily and say 'No, not modern enough, too depressing . . .' and move happily on to a painting of a woman in a long cream dress looking out across a wheatfield.

'They're all wonderful,' she said.

'Thank you,' said Gabe.

Rachel was now sitting cross-legged, the paintings across her lap. Gabe was on his haunches with his hands in his back pockets. A slice of light – a miniature window in the deep blue of his right iris – was threatening to transfix her.

'Where is this tree?' she asked, gesturing to the intricate biro drawing. 'I mean, I know it's in Belarus, but whereabouts?'

'It's near a hospital in Gomel. I used to sit on a bench every morning with my back to the building and draw it. I walked there with my friend Daniil when he went to visit his grandmother. I found the grounds very peaceful. I really liked this particular bench and this tree.' He smiled, then a shadow crossed his face. 'I dread to think what's going on in that hospital now.'

She nodded, shuddering a little. She also thought of her grand-pop's bench, opposite the gallery. 'I'm intrigued by the symbols between the branches,' she said. 'Tell me about them. The babies, for instance?'

'I'm young. They both scare and fascinate me,' he said. His eyes were cool and steady fires.

'I would like them,' she said quietly, looking into those eyes. 'One day. And the old man?'

They were sitting so close to each other. His face was amazing. Rachel was dazzled, actually, and felt the extremity of that reaction to him, while praying he didn't notice it in her. That he didn't sense she might be falling, somehow, when falling was not allowed.

'My grandfather. He died when I was a child. He was in hospital for a long time and I was never allowed to go see him. My dad didn't think it was right, for me to see him in pain like that. To witness that decay and death. But of course, then, I had to imagine it all, and in my imagination, I believe it was worse.'

'I'm sorry,' said Rachel. 'You never got to say goodbye?'

'No. So while I was sitting on that bench outside the hospital in Gomel, I added him to this piece. And I knew Daniil was some-where in the building behind me visiting his grandmother in her final days and it was kinda comforting.'

Rachel nodded. She thought of Florence, her great aunt, who she was seeing tonight. The woman who had brought her up, when her parents died; the woman who, along with Rachel's loving and steady great uncle, had shown her the model of what real love and real marriage was; who'd had an amazing past and a husband who'd supported her all the way. Rachel wasn't ambitious, like her great aunt had been, but she wanted what they'd had in their marriage. Those years of love and stability.

'And the fork?' she asked.

'Hmm. Well.' Gabe looked a little embarrassed. 'It represents mistakes, the wrong path. I've taken a few and I think I probably have a few more to come.'

'What wrong paths did you take?' Oh, she was being incredibly nosy again; what on earth would Jonny say? What would Jonny say about *any* of this? She was ashamed to even think of him as she sat on the floor of the gallery with this American stranger.

Gabe hesitated. 'Oh, just relationships,' he muttered boyishly. 'Too many of them, too many of them not working out. A couple of failed engagements.'

'Oh, right,' she said. 'Well, you're still young.' *She* was young, and she had found her forever love, although she was Jonny's second, of course. 'You just haven't found what you're looking for.'

'Nope. Not even close.'

His face closed down. Four seasons in one day again, she decided. Changeable. Serious one minute, flippant the next. Open, then closed. Dark, then light.

They both fell silent. Gabe rocked off his haunches and sat down on the floor, his legs stretched out in front of him. The right toe of his tennis shoe almost touched the right toe of her sandal.

'You said you were impoverished,' she said, remembering their first conversation, at the Wetheringtons'. 'You don't sell as much art as you'd like?'

'No,' he said. 'I'd like to sell a whole lot more, but nobody knows who I am. It's a bit of a struggle, getting known. I hope I don't leave it as late as Van Gogh.'

She didn't know if he was joking or not. Comparing himself to Van Gogh was a bit . . . much. She also thought of Jonny, struggling to make sales too, and always so vocal and so determined about it. 'But you survive?'

'With the help of the Arts Fund, yes. I live a pretty simple life.'

She wanted to laugh. He sounded so earnest, so Dickensian. He had travelled, she also remembered, and not just for exchanges, so he couldn't be *that* poor. And she wondered if his failed relationships were down to his wanderlust and his partying in other continents, escaping from home.

'Tell me,' she said, stretching both legs out in front of her too. 'As I'm always interested in these kinds of details. How do you work? What's your daily routine?'

'Well,' he said, 'I wake about eight. I walk to the local diner – the Jud Bar & Grill – where I eat Hal's excellent scrambled eggs – he's the diner's grouchy owner. I drink coffee and read the newspaper. I come back and start working. I work all day without a break, then I have dinner and watch a little TV with my folks, then I go to bed. And the same in Belarus, except I swap the morning diner for a sparse little cafe and the *Minsk Times*. As I say,' he smiled, 'a simple life.'

'What did you eat in Belarus?' she asked. It was the easiest thing in the world to talk to him, she realised. To picture him in his 'simple' life. She was charmed by it, but at the same time she was resisting the inclination to laugh at him a little.

'Whatever was on offer,' he shrugged. 'Borscht, potato pancakes . . . sometimes I'd go to Daniil's house and he would make me pierogi – potato dumplings. In return I'd bring candy bars I brought with me from the States.'

'You have a sweet tooth?'

'I guess so,' he grinned.

She loved the *candy* and the *borscht*. The little touches. 'I like chocolate too,' she said. 'Candy bars. I'm particularly partial to a Curly Wurly.'

'A curly *what*?'

'It's a British thing.' Now she *did* laugh.

The sun reappeared. The square of sunlight from the skylight window boxed in their knees with its warmth. They basked in it for a while.

'What's your role here?' Gabe asked, looking highly curious, his gaze steady as sunlight danced on their legs.

'I'm Faith's assistant.'

'Sounds almost allegorical.'

'Doesn't it?' She smiled at this.

'What would you do with it, if this was your gallery?'

'It's not my gallery.'

'But if it was?'

'Well . . . I'd support local artists too, like Faith does, but . . .'

'But what . . . ?'

'I'd only choose good ones.'

He laughed. 'What else would you do?'

'I'd change everything.' Rachel had never dared to articulate this before, let alone say it out loud to anyone. But she felt she could tell him, as they sat on the floor together, their legs close and in a square of sunlight. 'I would paint over the yellow walls with fresh, clean white. I'd banish the bowl of potpourri on the desk and replace it with pale pink peonies; in fact, I'd replace that dark oak desk altogether with something in painted white wood. I'd strip and repolish the floors. I'd have a yearly event – a summer party, which I'd hold in the gallery, but which would spill out into the tiny courtyard garden to the rear . . . well, that space you walked through when you came in through the back – I'd *turn* it into a courtyard garden . . . I'd serve Pimm's and have a small exhibition from a yet-to-be-discovered local artist . . .' She stopped.

'You've thought about this.'

'Yes. I guess I have. But it doesn't matter, as it's never going to happen.'

She felt she had whispered her private dreams to him down a late-night telephone. Her face hot, Rachel stood up and brushed imaginary dust from her trousers.

'Anyway,' she said. 'Thanks for bringing your work in. I love them, I really do.'

'I'm glad,' he said. He stood up, too. His T-shirt rose a little and she caught a glimpse of his taut stomach. 'Sometimes I think my direction is a bit stark, which is why they're not selling,' he added, with a sheepish smile.

'They'll sell when people *discover* them,' she said. 'When people know who you are. What will you do with these when you get back to North Dakota?'

'Same as I always do, try to get them exhibited somewhere. Keep on keeping on.'

'I'm sure it's only a matter of time,' she said.

He nodded, then started roaming the gallery again, examining the paintings. The sun had gone in. The square of sunlight on the polished floor had disappeared. He disappeared too, to the other side of the pillar where there was a terrible picture of a combine harvester immortalised in mock sepia.

'This one's interesting,' he said, and she could hear the smile in his voice.

'I know,' she replied, from her side of the pillar. 'The artist is Faith's sister, Marina. She has a certain . . . style.' Marina was the worst artist over the age of nine Rachel had ever seen, with a curious attraction to Victorian farmyard machinery.

'First one you'd ditch?'

'Absolutely.' There was a beat. 'I think my role in life is to be an assistant,' Rachel blurted out, from the safety of the pillar. 'A supporting player in someone else's life. Which is OK, I mean, I know other people have the talent – in some cases, not Marina's, obviously – so it's fine, really. I just . . . assist and support, a lot . . .

I sometimes feel like a piece of blank paper. Or an undecorated cake. Or a branch without leaves . . . What stupid analogies. They don't even make sense. I—'

'Who else are you an assistant to?' Gabe asked, and he stepped out from behind the pillar, and she had the strangest feeling she wanted to walk right up to him and lay her head on his chest.

'Adrienne, at the cafe,' she said. 'Although she's my best friend. And Jonny, maybe. A little bit. Sorry, I don't know where all this has come from . . .' She wished she hadn't said his name. Hadn't she already betrayed Jonny enough this afternoon, with this man?

'And does Jonny support and assist *you*?'

'Of course he does!'

'Behind every great man is a great woman and other bullshit . . .' Gabe made a snorting sound and Rachel looked at him, astonished. 'Men *shove* women behind them. And it should work the other way too, although sometimes a great woman can be great all by herself. A woman could be *greater* if she could only step out from behind the man's back.'

'How very forward thinking,' she commented dryly. 'Anyone would think a woman could become the leader of a country . . .' Gabe laughed, but Rachel wasn't laughing. 'You don't know anything about Jonny and me,' she said hotly. 'You've never even seen us together. And now you sound pompous,' she added.

Gabe looked at her curiously. 'As long as you have your own adventures,' he said.

'Adventures? I don't need *adventures*.' She was really riled now. What was any of this to do with *him*? Just because he liked to gallivant round the world, breaking hearts by the sound of it . . .

'If you don't have adventures, what memories will you have?'

'Family, a good life,' she objected.

'An easy life?'

'You don't know me,' she repeated. She wasn't sure how the conversation had ended up here. 'And if I knew *you* better, I'd say you were running me down.'

'I'm not running you down,' he said gently. 'I'm trying to build you up.'

'Why? I don't need *building up*. I'm fine as I am.'

'The eternal assistant,' he smiled.

'That's quite rude. Especially for one person to say to another when they're basically strangers.'

'*Are* we strangers?' asked Gabe. 'It doesn't feel like that,' he added softly. 'I'm sorry. Forgive me. I'm really not trying to run you down.'

'I know.' She'd started it, after all, hadn't she? She'd said that thing about being an assistant. She'd mentioned Jonny when she hadn't meant to. She was happy with all her choices. She knew where she was going.

'I really am sorry,' he said.

She was exhausted. They had spoken about so much, in so few words, this afternoon; their words tumbling out like wooden blocks to land scattered on the floor, about art and life and roles and dreams, but they were not blocks that could be built upon. He and Rachel were two people who would never see each other again.

'OK,' she said. 'Anyway, I need to lock up now. I don't mean to kick you out or anything . . .'

'It's OK,' he grinned. 'I need to get back to Aunt Julia and her lamb shank. It's been in the oven since Sunday.' She looked at him in surprise. 'Just kidding. Thank you for looking at my pieces.'

'Thank you for bringing them in.'

They both moved to the back of the gallery, where Gabe's paintings had scrolled in on themselves. Rachel held the tube while Gabe rolled them up and dropped them in. 'When are you leaving?' she asked him.

'Are you trying to get rid of me?'

'Yes, I think I probably am.'

They laughed, the tension of their last exchange released. But she did need him to go now, to leave Fincham St George and Oxford, so he couldn't unsettle her any more.

'I'm leaving on Sunday,' he said, popping the cap on the tube. 'Before that, it seems I have the pleasure of attending something called the "Blitz over Fincham St George".'

'The PTA thing?' she said lightly, but her heart was immediately heavy, saturated; she would be seeing him again. 'Well, yes, they have a themed party every year,' she continued, as airily as she could muster. 'Last year it was a medieval theme. This time, Second World War. Sometimes they get a little messy.'

'Messy?'

'Drunken.'

'Oh, gotcha. Drunk Brits at a costume party, that's a spectacle I would really like to see.'

'You'll love it,' she said, trying to sound frothy. 'A real eye-opener.'

He put the tube under his arm, like a general, and walked to the door. 'So, are you going?' he said, his hand on the handle.

'Yes.'

'What's your costume?'

'Either land girl or WREN – women's Royal Navy. Haven't decided yet.'

'Fantastic. I'm thinking of going as Winston Churchill. I'll borrow Aunt Julia's big wool coat and one of Uncle Trevor's old bowler hats.'

'I can't wait to see *that*,' smiled Rachel. 'Sounds like another spectacle not to be missed.'

He grinned back at her. 'Right, kiddo,' he said, in the open doorway. 'I'll guess I'll see you on Saturday night.'

'I guess you will.'

Rachel shut the door behind him. She didn't watch him walk away, the tube of paintings under his arm. She didn't imagine him letting himself into Julia March's cottage and surprising her with a hug and a joke. She didn't dwell on his words or her own this afternoon, or how he had caught her dancing. She didn't think forward to Saturday night and seeing him again. Instead, she exhaled long and slow, locked up the gallery and set off down the lane to visit Florence.

# Chapter Seven

Florence Toms' backdrop was a sea of Charles and Di memorabilia: mugs, cups, saucers, plates, tankards and egg cups on the shelf above her head. Her soundtrack was both the eternal blare of the television and the loud tick of Grandpop Jim's retirement carriage clock on the mantelpiece opposite her.

The Shloer was poured, the Dairy Milk had been snapped into rows and shared out between them, on tea plates that rested on the arms of their squishy floral armchairs.

'Well, then,' said Florence, like she always did, as Rachel sat down. 'What's news with you?'

'No news, Nanna.' Rachel realised she had sat on a *Woman's Weekly* and pulled it out from under her.

'I'll have that,' said Florence, holding out a hand for it. She tucked the magazine down the side of her seat cushion, then sat back, alert in soft navy slacks and a bright pink T-shirt, and fixed her blue eyes on her great-niece. 'Nothing?' she enquired. 'Can't you make something up?'

It was always the same exchange. 'No, Nanna.'

'Shame. Cafe OK? Gallery OK?'

'Yes, Nanna.' She didn't want to think about the gallery and the afternoon she'd just spent there.

'When are you going to branch out?'

'I don't want to branch out.'

They had long been in an ongoing tennis match. Florence served; Rachel batted back. They each snapped off a square of chocolate and put it in their mouths. *Murder, She Wrote* was just starting. Angela Lansbury was typing her way through the opening credits.

'Very *unfortunate*, this Jessica Fletcher woman,' sighed Florence happily. 'I mean, how many murders can one person reasonably stumble across?'

'Hundreds,' Rachel laughed.

'Only in America,' Florence said. She snapped down the wooden handle on her recliner and launched herself back forty-five degrees, her fluffy-slippered feet and robust ankles ricocheting upwards on the footrest. 'You wouldn't get any of that nonsense in England. Murders every ten minutes.'

Rachel laughed. Florence Toms was sixty-five years young. She was no-nonsense, unsentimental, with a determinedly active social life: the WI, the Fincham Ladies, the Fincham St George Throwers' Darts League. She had a full and purposeful calendar. She was *busy*.

'How's Jonny? How's little Teddy? Do you want a top-up of Shloer, or are you all right?' Florence asked, turning to reach into her little cocktail cabinet, mounted on the woodchipped wall beside her.

'No, Nanna, I'm all right, thank you. And Teddy's great and Jonny's very well, thanks.'

Flo turned back. 'Have you set a date yet?'

'No, not yet.'

'You'd better get on with it.' She broke a chunk of chocolate from its row. 'What are you hanging about for?'

'We're saving up,' said Rachel.

'In my day we didn't worry about things like saving up,' Florence said. 'If you wanted to get married you just went and did it. None of this fannying around. Having big parties. Huge meringue dresses. Well, Diana had a huge meringue, of course, but Diana is Diana, Lord bless her.' Florence raised her chin in deference to the egg cups and tankards above her head. 'In my day, you went to the church, returned to your Auntie Jean's front room for a bit of cake and just got on with it.'

'I know, Nanna,' said Rachel; she had heard this all before. 'That's because there was a war on.'

To the right of Grandpop Jim's ticking carriage clock, on the mantelpiece, were photographs in silver frames. Nanna and Grandpop on their wedding day in September 1943, framed in the pretty arch of St Edwin's church. Nanna and Grandpop on their weekend honeymoon in Skegness, in the penny arcades; Nanna beaming in an austere coat and victory rolls, Grandpop laughingly bringing down the handle of a slot machine. Nanna, standing proud and exuberant in front of a Spitfire in flying suit, boots and goggles . . .

Florence didn't like to talk about it all that much, but she'd been rather a big deal in the Second World War – an Attagirl, one of a select band of women who ferried planes from factories and maintenance units to air bases for the ATA (Air Transport Auxiliary). Without radios. Or instruments. Just a compass, maps and a watch. They were quite the daredevil heroines of the war. Florence had been reluctantly featured in magazines, periodically, for as long as Rachel could remember. She had even been persuaded into an interview, once, on BBC Radio Oxford. In true Florence fashion, all her war tales were told with great self-deprecation and humour, and if too much praise and amazement greeted them, especially from her great-niece, they were brushed away, her spectacular war effort dismissed as nothing.

'You smell nice today, Nanna,' said Rachel, reaching for her etched cocktail glass of Shloer, but still looking at the photos. After the war, Florence stayed in the industry. There was a photograph of her at RAF Benson, standing with three other women in uniform outside the control tower, on a blustery autumn day. Rachel was sorry Flo's career in the Air Force had had to end when her parents died, in 1973, when her big-hearted great aunt and uncle stepped up to be her guardians, but the photos were there, and Rachel loved looking at them. The proof of Nanna's former life.

Rachel wanted to change the subject from her wedding date. The truth was she and Jonny could afford to get married now – just – but he wanted to wait until they could do it in style: the village party, the meringue for her; top hat and tails for him. 'Did you buy a new bottle of Charlie?'

'Yes,' said Florence, staring at Jessica Fletcher, who was investigating a murder in a theatre where one of her nieces was putting on a play. 'You can have any that's left.'

'Left?' Jessica Fletcher was nosing around backstage, looking for clues. Rachel snapped off another square of chocolate.

'Yes,' said Florence matter-of-factly. 'I'm probably not going to be around much longer.'

'Why, where are you going?' Rachel was bemused.

'Heaven, with any luck. To be with your grandpop. Bless him. He's waited a long time for me. It's been nearly five years now, since he went.'

'You won't be going yet,' said Rachel, letting the square of Dairy Milk melt on her tongue. 'You're only in your sixties.'

'No, I haven't got long left,' said Florence brightly. 'I can feel it coming. Probably my ticker.'

'You only had your *ticker* checked a month or so ago,' said Rachel. 'It's perfectly fine, isn't it?'

'No, I don't think it is. What will be will be, though, and if the end's coming then I'm ready for it. I must warn the ladies at the Lions Club, though . . . I'm not sure anyone else can minute as well as I do . . .'

'Don't be silly, Nanna!'

Flo hoicked herself up higher in her chair. 'I'm being the opposite of silly,' she said sternly. 'It's silly to pretend death isn't waiting for us all, in the end. It's sensible you know what must be faced. And I want to be with him now, I've had enough of waiting. I'm ready to go.'

'Oh, Nanna.'

'You make sure you make the most of it,' said Florence. 'Life. All of it. Shall we have an ice-cream sandwich?'

'Yes, please.'

Florence shot herself from her recliner and strode into the small kitchen just off the sitting room – which always smelled faintly of gas and caraway seeds – and Rachel leaped up to help her. They sandwiched slabs of raspberry ripple ice cream between two wafers and, back in their armchairs, worked on them in tandem as the loud clock on the mantel ticked and ticked and Jessica Fletcher caught the baddie.

'I hear there's someone new in town,' said Florence finally, when mouths had been mopped and sticky hands washed.

'Someone new?'

'An American. Julia's March's nephew.'

'Oh, yes, that's right.' A little heat rose to her face.

'That feisty old firebrand,' smiled Flo. 'Not that anyone ever sees her. You seen her lately?'

'No,' Rachel replied, with as much unconcern as she could conjure up.

'I heard about her very exciting visitor on my *very* reliable grapevine. The postman.' Flo grinned and so did Rachel. 'Have you met him?' she asked. 'The American?'

'Yes,' said Rachel, desperately indifferent. 'I met him at the Wetheringtons' do.' *Among other places.*

'Is he handsome?' enquired Florence. Her normally sharp blue eyes were slightly wistful, her body poised for information.

'Not *all* Americans are handsome, Nan.'

'I've heard he is.'

'Well, then you don't need to ask me.'

'I heard he's an artist,' Flo continued. 'That he flew in from that pollution place in Russia. I hope you were careful around him.'

Rachel almost laughed. *No, I haven't been careful around him at all*, she thought. 'He flew before it happened, Nanna. From Chernobyl. He got out in time. So, he's perfectly safe.' Oh God, she had to see him again. On Saturday night. She was thrilled, frightened, excited, panicked, everything . . . at the prospect. The memory of him in the gallery this afternoon filled her head. His wonderful artwork, the infuriating way he had challenged her, his gentle reflections of Belarus.

'I knew an American once.'

'Did you?'

Florence had a faraway look on her face. She was staring absent-mindedly in the direction of the mantelpiece. Her wartime photos, those black-and-white images of her wedding day, her honeymoon, the photo of her in front of the Spitfire, a pair of flying goggles on her head, the clouds in her eyes and war all around her.

'Well,' Flo said absently, 'there were lots of them, in the war. Lots of Yanks who came to Fincham St George. I knew one in particular.' Her eyes stayed on the mantelpiece.

'Did you?' asked Rachel, her interest piqued. 'You never told me this. A *special* American?'

'Quite special,' nodded Florence. 'But I never wanted to be disloyal to your grandpop, that's why I've never told you the story of him. But an American in the village . . .' She sighed and Rachel felt she was no longer here, in this room, but somewhere else entirely. 'It's made me remember, not that I ever really forgot. Although, actually, I suppose there was never very much to tell,' said Flo, turning her face towards Rachel again. 'As I chose your grandpop.'

'Chose him?' echoed Rachel. 'You chose him over another man? An American? Nanna! You need to tell me this story!'

Rachel knew the wartime tale of Florence and Jim well. That they grew up five doors from each other. Jim Toms didn't go off fighting in the war because he was a vital worker in a reserved occupation, on the railways. Every day he shovelled coal into a firebox and serviced ammunition and troop trains, coming home in the evenings covered in soot and carrying an empty tin from the sandwiches Flo had made him. He lived with his elderly father – his mother having died of TB when he was a child – and ever since he and Flo had started courting, when she was sixteen, she and her older sister (Rachel's grandmother, who would marry her childhood sweetheart and give birth to Rachel's mother, Frances, at the beginning of the war) cooked for both Jim and Albert. At six o'clock each evening, Flo and her sister would walk five doors down the street, carrying plates under check tea cloths.

Florence and Jim married in the autumn of 1943 and stayed married for thirty-eight years. That was the story. Rachel had heard it many times and it was a story she loved. It was a story she was trying to retell herself. A lasting marriage. A love that endured across the decades. Stability. Safety. Nanna had never said anything about an American.

'Well,' said Flo, and Rachel realised she was literally on the edge of her floral seat, waiting for Florence's words, while Nanna sat back in hers and took a deep breath. 'Do you know, there was so much excitement when those Yanks first came into the village. With their nylons and their chewing gum. Their suntans and their accents. Women went quite silly over them – Mrs Jones from number seven, in particular, went completely doolally. She was cleaning her front windows when they first came up the street, in their big trucks, and she nearly fell out, silly woman. I didn't. *I* had your grandpop.'

Rachel nodded. 'Go on,' she said.

'Well, one spring, during the war, Jim went away for three nights – taking a consignment of medical supplies to the war hospital at Cambridge, on the train – and I met an American at the Clarendon Hotel.' She hooted with laughter suddenly, the memory lighting up her eyes. 'Remember I told you I worked for the Ministry of Food, before I joined the ATA? That I did the dull old coupons and the boring old leaflets? Well, I was having a bath in the Clarendon.'

Flo had told Rachel that she and the other girls at the Ministry of Food were sometimes allowed to take a bath in one of the unused bathrooms on the upper floors of the commandeered Clarendon Hotel, and how blissful it was.

Flo smiled. 'It wasn't his fault, and he was ever so sorry about it, but a man came in, as I was sitting on the edge of the bath in a towel. An American. And I shrieked, as you would, and he dashed out, muttering apologies, and after I got dressed and came out, he was waiting for me outside. To apologise again, you know. And I was all suitably frosty and said it was perfectly OK or something like that. He said he didn't make a habit of it and I said you never knew, with the Yanks.' Flo's eyes were dancing with merriment. 'He was ever so handsome. I said I hadn't seen him around before, and he said he kept himself to himself. That he didn't want to be like all the others, you know, running through the local girls like water, leaving johnnies in the churchyard. Oh, don't be shocked, Rachel. The young local lads used to put them on the end of sticks and wave them at people!'

'Blimey,' said Rachel.

'He didn't actually say that, about the johnnies. He was far too gentlemanly. Anyway, I went to a dance that night, with my friend Cynthia – there was a servicemen's club on the ground floor of the Clarendon and we danced . . . and well, we saw each other afterwards . . . for four days, actually . . . he was about to be posted to North Africa . . .'

'. . . And you fell in love,' Rachel interjected, as a half-joke, but Flo's face was serious.

'Yes, we did,' she said. 'We fell in love.'

'Oh, Nanna.'

'He was so different to Jim,' she said, eyes watering a little. 'My safe, sensible Jim. Four days me and the American spent together. Four days when we took trips in his jeep to Bicester and Banbury and Broughton Castle and we talked and talked. About everything. About nothing. About big things and small. About our lives. Our hopes and dreams. About his role in the war, over here. The things he'd done . . . And then I had to make a choice.' She looked at Rachel, then closed her eyes. 'I had to decide whether to continue on the path of life I was on or take another.'

'With him.'

'Yes, with him. He said he would wait out the war for me. That when it was over, he'd come back and get me.' Flo sighed. She opened her eyes. 'And I thought of nothing else for two days. Scott – that was his name, my American – was leaving by train, on the Friday morning, the same morning Jim was coming back from his trip to Cambridge. I was in the cafe at Fincham station – I'd got the bus there – I could see Scott waiting, on the platform the other side of the track. And Jim's ammunition train was due in any minute. I remember that day like it was yesterday. It was raining – full on "stair rods", as your grandpop used to say.'

Rachel smiled, remembering Grandpop with love, and also marvelling at how people could keep secrets locked away inside themselves for so long. 'What happened?' she asked, as though she didn't know the answer.

'I sat in the cafe and I thought that my view from my kitchen window might change, that I could swap one life for another – in New England, because that's where he was from – but would it be any better than the one I had? Would this *risk* – because it was a huge one – and all the uncertainty of it, and all the hurt it would cause, be worth it? I loved Jim and I loved this man too, and perhaps it was a better love or a more grand, passionate, once-in-a-lifetime love, but I had promised myself to Jim – and his father, in effect. I had already chosen the path my life would take. Scott was . . . well, he was still just the idea of a man. And I was a sensible girl. Practical. The grass isn't always greener, just because it looks it from a distance, you see,' said Florence, leaning forward in her chair. 'Grass is grass, whichever window you look at it through; it's just *different* grass. I made my decision. I waited for Jim's train to come in and I walked out of the cafe and went to meet him. I couldn't see Scott any more, over on the other platform,' she said sadly, 'and when Jim and I left the station, I expect he had boarded his train and gone.'

'And do you regret your decision?' asked Rachel, almost in a whisper.

'No,' said Florence emphatically. 'I had a wonderful life with your grandpop, just wonderful.'

'And you didn't ever wonder – all those years – how it might have been if you'd chosen Scott?'

'Of course I did and I still do, sometimes. But I made the right decision. I truly did, Rachel.'

Rachel remembered how proud her grandpop was of her nanna. Always. As a teenager, who cooked for him and his father. Her time at the Ministry of Food, her dutiful war effort at the Clarendon, issuing the coupons and distributing the leaflets. Her transfer, later in the war, to the ATA, and White Waltham in Berkshire, where she first worked as an administrator and then applied, 'on a bit of a whim', as she always said, to an 'ab initio' training programme to become a female ferry pilot – without prior experience – to deliver all kinds of aircraft, from factories and maintenance units to squadrons, all over Britain. To become one of the feted Attagirls.

'I never thought I'd be accepted,' Flo always said, after being coaxed into telling her wartime stories, 'but maybe they saw I had a bit of spunk, or a bit of fire,' she would shrug. 'Who knows?'

'Of course they did!' Jim would always say proudly. 'They saw it *all* in you, my girl!'

Grandpop was proud of her all his life, Rachel remembered; he said he felt so lucky to be with this amazing woman, that he barely deserved her – a quiet, boring thing like him – and Flo had always snapped good-naturedly and said, 'You are a good man, Jim Toms, and don't you ever forget it! I've been very lucky to be with you. To have your encouragement and your support. I'm the lucky one!'

'Do you think Scott was your true love, though?' asked Rachel. 'Your truest love?'

'What does that even mean?' asked Flo. 'You must live your true life, that's what you must do. And that's the end of it. I owe my life to your grandpop. Make sure Jonny gives you the same,' said Flo. 'Make sure he lets you fly. Now, do you want some more Shloer? I'll do us a top-up.'

'Yes, please.' Rachel didn't want to fly though. She wanted to stay grounded, stable. She knew how life was when a person in a marriage flapped their wings too hard. Made waves with their own selfishness. Caused dangerous ripples. Jim had given Flo space to spread her wings in safety; Rachel didn't need to. She liked her wings tucked underneath her, her space confined to her and Jonny, closeted and safe. He was her truest love, wasn't he?

'I'm glad you stayed with Grandpop,' said Rachel. She smiled and Flo smiled back. Flo leaned forward and wrapped her cool fingers around Rachel's as tears sprung to both their eyes. 'And I'm glad you had your wonderful life together,' Rachel added. 'Thank you for giving up your career in the Air Force to look after me. To bring me up. It was amazing what you did.'

'Pfft,' said Flo. 'I'd had my adventures. You were simply my next one.'

They held hands, sparkly eyed, for a few seconds until Flo muttered with a chuckle that they were 'sentimental fools!' and took her hand away with an affectionate pat. They watched an old movie. They polished off the bottle of Shloer. Florence was quiet at times, low on pithy comments and like she wasn't really watching the film. Rachel wondered if she was thinking of her American.

When the movie ended, Flo shunted forward and sprung herself upright, bending round to the concertinaed cupboard doors of her cocktail cabinet, where she kept the Martini and the packs of cards.

'Ah,' she said, when she had found what she was looking for. It was a tin. Not a Charles and Di one, but a burgundy tin, flattish, hexagonal, with gold edging. It looked quite grand.

'I want you to have this,' she said, handing it to Rachel, 'and I'm giving it to you now, before I go, so it definitely goes to you. I don't want there to be some dreadful house clearance, after I've gone, with things getting lost.'

Rachel put it on her lap. It was cold, and light. 'You're being ridiculous,' she said, 'there's not going to be a house clearance for at least another twenty years!'

Florence ignored her. 'There's a key for it. Here you are.' Flo placed a small silver key in the palm of Rachel's hand. 'You can open it when I'm gone. It's just a few photos, but quite precious ones. Please take good care of it.'

'I will,' Rachel said. 'Thank you. I'll take care of it, I promise. Are there any—'

There was a jaunty rap at the window and a holler of 'Hello, girls!' A face, full of merriment and sticky-up hair. It was Jonny, holding up a bulging Co-op carrier bag. Rachel jumped up to let him in the back door, and he came in and theatrically emptied all the things Florence liked – Mr Kipling Bakewell Tarts and Tunnock's tea cakes and a box of Liquorice Allsorts – on the largest of Flo's nesting tables.

'Oh, thank you, Jonny, very kind,' said Florence. 'I've got something for you as well.' She walked into the tiny kitchen and came back with a knotted clear bag full of rhubarb, from the garden, and a bag of monkey nuts. 'To snack on, while you're writing,' she said, 'although I'm aware Rachel usually has a million things in her cupboards. And I know you like my rhubarb.'

'Thanks, Miss Florentine,' said Jonny. It was what he called her. 'I'll make a beautiful crumble.' He put the sundries in the empty carrier bag. 'Are you ready to go?' he asked Rachel.

'Yes,' she said, standing up. 'I've had a really lovely afternoon,' she added, giving her great aunt a hug. Flo smelled of Charlie and lavender talcum powder and love.

'Me too, pet. You take care of yourself.'

'I will do. You too, Nanna.'

Flo waved from the kitchen window, as she always did, once they were on the lane, her face shrouded by one half of the net curtains. She waved until they had gone round the corner and were on Church Road.

'What have you got there, Rach?' asked Jonny, glancing towards the tin in Rachel's hand as they walked in the cooling sun of early evening, and he jauntily swung the carrier bag with Flo's other gifts in it. Their cottage was just visible, at the top of the hill.

'Oh, just an old tin of photos,' said Rachel, the key safe in the coin pocket of her jeans.

'Pop it in the bag,' said Jonny, opening the mouth of the carrier bag to her, and she carefully placed the tin on top of the rhubarb. 'I missed you,' he said.

'You, too.'

Rachel was extremely pleased to see him, after Nanna's surprising story and all this talk of handsome Americans and doing the right thing, and *risk*. She didn't want to think about handsome Americans now, nor did she want to take any risks. Rachel wanted to stay safe with Jonny. To keep her view the same. To forget the strange afternoon in the gallery and all the words she and Gabe had said to each other, and all the things she had felt. To pretend she wouldn't be seeing him on Saturday night dressed as Winston Churchill.

She took Jonny's hand. 'I love you, Trent,' she said.

Jonny laughed. 'I love you too, Smith.'

Rachel knew where she was going. She could see it from here. She was on her way home, and home was Jonny.

# Chapter Eight

'Oh, look out!' Jonny said genially, as they turned into Coopers Row.

A car was pulling up alongside the kerb. The driver's window was painstakingly being wound down.

'All right, mate?' The car was a mustard-coloured Ford Capri, a 70s relic with a souped-up exhaust and racer stripes. The driver was Lee, Jonny's new sidekick.

'Yes, mate,' Jonny cheerfully replied. Lee was eighteen, a local plasterer. Jonny had met him at a rally at the library.

'Get in,' said Lee, fag at the wheel. 'I'll take you both to the pub. It's Sausage Night.'

'Oh, not for me,' said Rachel, 'I've got things to do. But you two go,' she said, noting Jonny's hopeful, puppy-dog expression.

Lee bared his teeth at her in what she hoped was a smile. He had a smirk that could morph into a sneer and vice versa; you never quite knew where you were with him, but she suspected it was never a good place. She didn't really like Lee. When Fincham St George's promising young author had led a march through the village last month, culminating in a megaphone speech from the back of a trailer outside the library, against its potential closure, she wouldn't have expected someone like Lee to be in the crowd. His applause for Jonny's words were the loudest. He had looked out of place in his workman's clothes, splattered with putty-coloured dashes and spots. Still, people always surprised you, she'd thought as she watched him clap with loud, rigid hands and wolf-whistle at Jonny's closing hail, and yes, Lee had surprised her all right. He had surprised both of them.

A 'clarion call', Jonny had jokingly described his efforts at the library that afternoon. He wondered, with a laugh, if he would make the local papers, but sadly his call was barely reported – meriting a single mention in the free brochure the village store gave away. When he got home that night, far later than planned, and as yet blissfully unaware of the damp fizzle his crusade had made on the world, a young man had slunk in through the back door with him. The young plasterer's applause and whistles at the rally had been rewarded with a trip to the pub, apparently.

'This is Lee,' Jonny had hiccupped happily, about nine o'clock, as the youth, still in his work clothes, staggered over the threshold and steadied himself on the kitchen wall. 'Lee loves my books. He's my new friend. I thought I'd invite him in for a nightcap, if that's all right, Rach?'

'Of course,' Rachel had smiled. 'Come on in, Lee.'

'Thanks for having me,' said Lee. He was half grinning, half sneering, his eyes unfocused.

'Pleased to meet you,' replied Rachel. She poured out fingerfuls of whisky for them, which soon became fists. She sat up with them for an hour, nursing her own small glass. Jonny kept sweetly kissing her and calling her his 'love'.

'Lee's an aspiring playwright,' he told Rachel. 'What was it you said, Lee? That you want to emulate the lyrical characterisation of Steinbeck and the tragic realism of Tennessee Williams?' He winked at Rachel. 'I said I'd give him a helping hand, for what it's worth.'

Lee smirk-sneered, then nodded. 'That's right,' he said gruffly, his eyes all over the place, 'I'm looking for a mentor.'

'And I now have a protégé,' Jonny had said proudly. 'How hilarious! Cheers to that!'

'Come back tomorrow, lad!' he'd yelled out, joyously, later – sometime around 3 a.m., after Rachel had eventually excused herself at midnight. She'd heard plonking steps down the front path from her bed. 'Come whenever you like!'

The front door had slammed, and Jonny had crept upstairs, giggling as he hopped across the room trying to take his trousers off and shushing himself. The next day, the *lad* did indeed come back, and the next after that. Johnny had a protégé and he was very generous with the time he spent on him. Jonny would discuss his characters, new and existing. He let Lee read chapters of his work in progress. He gave Lee advice on writing plays, not that he knew the exact discipline, but writing was writing, right? Rachel only tolerated Lee. Jonny obviously saw something in him, but there was something about Lee that suggested he knew where the bodies were buried.

'I'd quite like the sausages,' Jonny said now. Rachel knew Jonny had another 'Nikita' plot thorn he wanted Lee to help him untangle. 'If you're sure that's OK with you, Rachel?'

'Get in anyway,' Lee said to her. 'We'll drop you home first.'

'Erm.' She hesitated. 'Well, just drop me at the war memorial and I'll walk the rest. If that's OK?'

'OK.'

She got into the back seat of Lee's Capri. It had sticky tan plastic seats, ripped in places, exposing white lint. It smelled of cigarettes and spearmint. She placed the Co-op carrier bag in the footwell at the other end of the seat, as hers was stacked with what looked like the dirty magazines once enjoyed under the concrete bridge. She gingerly sat back. The radio was blaring.

Lee drove like a maniac. Rachel was at the war memorial, slightly breathless, in mere terrifying seconds.

'See you, Rach,' Lee breezed over-familiarly, as she clambered out of the car and shut the wayward door.

'Thanks, Lee,' she said, shaking slightly.

'I love you!' called Jonny from the passenger seat. 'I love you forever! See you later.'

'I love you too!' she called.

Lee roared off, the radio cranked up higher. Bon Jovi. 'Livin' on a Prayer'.

'Bloody idiot,' she muttered under her breath. Speed kills, everyone knew that. She set off smartly down the road, as birds tweeted in the bushes and the sun began its descent behind the ripped, shredded clouds of early May.

It was only after she had let herself into the cottage that she realised the carrier bag, and Nanna's tin, were still in Lee's car.

# Chapter Nine

The day Rachel had fallen in love with Jonny, when she was nineteen and he was twenty, had been the day in summer when horses from the brewery traditionally paraded through the village, before being taken to a nearby field and given troughs of the finest local beer to drink. Rachel had ended up standing next to Jonny outside the newsagent's. He was hard to miss. The handsome young man expertly holding the baby.

*Jonny Trent*, she had thought. *Well, I never*. He was writing for the paper still; she had read the odd funny and acerbic article by him. She'd heard he'd got married at nineteen and had had a baby. It was big news in the village and *huge* news when it came out that he and his wife had got divorced.

Rachel knew he would not have remembered her from primary school. He didn't look at her, anyway; he was smiling at the big bonny baby in his secure arms; pointing things out to her; glancing down at his shoes as one of his laces was undone. Rachel was in her work outfit from the local Wimpy, her awful cap shoved in her pocket; she wished she was already in her new dress, the one she was going to wear tonight to the disco at the village hall.

'Hold her a minute,' he'd said, out of nowhere, suddenly placing the baby into Rachel's astonished arms. 'I need to tie my shoe-lace up.'

Rachel held the baby fearfully, not sure how to do it. The baby grinned and made a grab for Rachel's cheek, clutching a painful wodge of it in a chubby fist, her other hand brandishing a soggy flapjack.

'Hey, thanks. Sorry, she's assaulted you, I see. You've got an oat on your cheek.'

Jonny gently plucked off a piece of flapjack and popped it in his mouth, then he held out his arms and Rachel passed back the baby. His face lighting up, he snuggled her on to his hip and sniffed delightedly at her hair.

'What's her name?' Rachel had asked. Although she already knew what it was. Everyone in the village did.

'Tatiana. It's Russian.'

'It's lovely.'

'Thanks.' He finally bestowed that cheeky grin on her, the one she'd coveted at school. 'She's fourteen months old. We call her Teddy.'

'She's beautiful.'

'Thanks. You work at the Wimpy?' he asked her, looking at her awful red outfit.

'Yeah,' she said, ashamed. 'The one by Fincham station. The pay's pretty good,' she justified. 'I read your articles,' she added. 'In the local paper. You're an excellent writer.'

'Nobody ever reads my articles,' he said, staring at her curiously.

'*I* do,' she said, blushing, and the look in his eyes told her he liked that.

'Are you going to that disco tonight?' Jonny asked. 'The one at the village hall?'

She nodded.

'Me too. Well, I wasn't going to, but I think I will now. I'll ask Nancy if she can have Teddy.'

'OK.'

'What time do you think you'll be there?'

'When it starts? About eight o'clock?'

'Great. I'll see you tonight, then.'

He grinned at her and moved off into the crowd, his baby on his hip. Rachel wasn't quite sure what had just happened. But when she arrived with Wren at the village hall that night, Jonny was slouching at the bar with a smile on his face, apparently just for her, and she ended the night snogging Jonny Trent against the memo board outside the ladies' toilets.

After all the snogging, Jonny invited Rachel back to his, a clean but horribly cramped garage conversion he was renting, with a metal door down the side that stuck in the winter and a roof with tarry edges you could climb out on to in the summer and poke your fingers into. They creaked up the threadbare stairs past Tatiana's bedroom – which Rachel saw in the morning Jonny had painstakingly painted in candy stripes – and into Jonny's, where she could only make out the shape of the bed and the shape of Jonny, his arms held out to her, in the veil of the puttering street light outside his window.

A year later, she moved in. Florence and Jim helped her bring her stuff and made tearful jokes about 'getting rid of her'. Jonny cooked dinner and plucked some flowers from the garden to put in a vase. That weekend, up on the flat roof with the grey shingle that needed three layers of beach towels to lie on, they had picked at bits of tar from the edges and told each other the stories of their childhoods. Jonny told Rachel about living at Magdalen College and how he hated growing up there, how ancient walls fenced him in, and stupid gowns made him feel very small. How he would hide, sometimes, in one of the students' rooms that was never locked during the day, sitting at a leather desk, peeking at half-written essays and staring out of leaded windows on to the cold courtyards below.

'I was called "the rat" by laughing Henrys and Henriettas, when spotted scuttling in the shadows,' he said, flicking a piece of tar between thumb and forefinger, and he told Rachel his time at Magdalen had triggered an 'I'll show them!' attitude in him, which had led to him writing blockbusting spy novels with a kick-ass heroine.

'And what about Nancy?' she asked, a while later. 'What was the story there?'

'We married too young,' he said. 'We were so sure of ourselves. That it was brilliant, that it would last just because we wanted it to. But Nancy wasn't right for me, in the end – I couldn't live with her. Not like you,' he beamed, joy flashing in his eyes. 'I'm going to love living with you.'

Rachel had felt ridiculously happy. 'Everyone talked about it when you split up,' she said.

'"Marry in haste, repent at leisure",' Jonny grimaced, 'I bet that's what they said. And that's what *did* happen. I was really sorry about it, but I've always been impetuous, I suppose, and I have Teddy . . .' he added, with a smile. 'So that's really something. And how about you?' he asked her gently. 'Do you want to tell me your story?'

He had listened carefully, for he knew the story, like everyone else in the village, of the evening her parents had set off for a local restaurant and had never come home again, and he took her hand when she spoke of the aching terrible *loss* of it all – then he had looked at her and said, 'Rach, you never need to talk about that again. It's you and me now. You'll be safe with me.'

She looked back at him and she knew it was true. That this man she was up on the roof with, on three layers of cheap beach towels, was destined to be her safety, her comfort and her forever. That whether they were living out the melting tar days of August or the warm bed days of December, the chill rains of March or the toasted days of October, in every season, he was *home*.

◆　◆　◆

Jonny wasn't at home. The cottage was quiet. It was 1 a.m. and Rachel was attempting to read in bed, but thoughts about the afternoon in the gallery were creeping, unbidden, into her mind. Dancing to The Cure. Gabe. His paintings. Thoughts she'd betrayed Jonny, temporarily stepping from the safety of his promises and into a dangerous square of light. She'd had feelings she wasn't supposed to feel. She had shared things she shouldn't share. She had let in the idea of another man, when her very best idea had been Jonny.

Where *was* he? she wondered, as she tried to read the same page again. Had Sausage Night ended in one of the landlord's famous occasional lock-ins?

This afternoon with Gabe had been nothing, she decided. Just a silly nothing. As was their time in the car park and their conversation in the Wetheringtons' kitchen. She would avoid him, at the Blitz do. Florence was right; stay with what you knew, stay where you were safe. The grass was not greener because you looked at it through a different window. The *idea* of a different man was just an idea. And, most of all, Gabe would be gone in a few days and her life, interrupted by him, just for a moment, would resume.

Rachel closed her book and waited for Jonny. She wanted to feel the familiar warmth of him. She needed him to fold his safe arms around her and hold her close. She expected him to smell faintly of sausages when he snuggled up to her and told her 'I love you'.

She listened for Lee's horrible car coming up the lane, too fast, bringing Jonny home to her, or Jonny's footsteps up the lane, but her eyes closed and she fell asleep before he was back. The lane with its hushed spring blooms lay quiet and the moon hung in the blank night sky, outside her bedroom window, indifferent to her best-laid plans.

# Chapter Ten

'I hope no one else has come in the same costume,' Jonny murmured conspiratorially to Rachel, as they walked up the steps to the double doors of the red-brick Victorian village hall at the end of Rose Glen Street. 'Blitz over Fincham St George' was being manned by two PTA ladies dressed in pneumatic Second World War nurses' uniforms, taking tickets and stamping people on the wrists with the smudging purple lozenge of 'FOFS' – Friends of Fincham School.

Rachel was hanging on to the back of Jonny's jacket. She had come as a land girl. A pair of Jonny's double pleat chinos – legs rolled up – and a pale blue shirt – sleeves rolled up – were accompanied by an old headscarf of her mother's and, last minute, she'd decided to eschew clumpy lace-up boots for her favourite gold 70s disco heeled sandals. They made her a little unsteady but, if anyone asked, she'd say she was a land girl who was going straight out in the evening – in 1978.

Jonny had come as a Biggles fighter pilot. He'd been to the big fancy-dress shop in Oxford and hired jodhpurs, a leather flying jacket with a sheepskin trim, Air Force cap and goggles and a wired cream scarf permanently whipped up at a forty-five-degree angle as though caught in a tailwind. He looked funny and fantastic, but Rachel was still a little cross with Jonny. About Florence's tin. When he had finally rocked up at two o'clock in the morning after the Sausage Night lock-in, signalled by the apologetic crashing of bins and the shamefaced smashing of a treasured ornament in the hall, there had been no sign of it.

'I'm so sorry, Rachel, no idea,' Jonny had shrugged painfully the next morning, stinking of garlic and vaguely of a heady perfume she'd recognised as that of the hug-prone landlady.

'Is it still in Lee's car?'

'Yeah, maybe. Sorry, Rach.'

It wasn't. She got Jonny to phone Lee and Lee had gone to check.

'Maybe you took it into the pub and left it there?' she suggested. Rachel walked to the pub and looked for it, but it wasn't there. It would turn up, she had thought. It was probably in Lee's car after all; he would bowl in with it next time he inflicted himself on them.

'Tickets, please,' said one of the buxom nurses. Jonny flicked his wind-stiff scarf comically at them as they walked into the hall, making them laugh. Rachel took baby steps behind him in her heels. She forgave him, her lovely funny Biggles, and the tin was sure to come to light.

The village hall as they knew it – Rachel, most recently, from Teddy's years at nursery; Jonny from casual book signings he had sheepishly organised for himself – was almost unrecognisable. Above them was a frantic criss-crossing of red, white and blue streamers. At table level were Union Jack tablecloths, paper cups and plates. On the walls were suspended gas masks with streamers threaded through them. A trestle table to the left bowed under wine boxes and cans of Party Seven beer. The stage at the back of the hall was already clustered with two-thirds of a local Glenn Miller tribute band. And huddled at the bar was a small squadron of soldiers, sailors, nurses, land girls and three Royal Air Force Biggles pilots.

'Oh no,' Jonny said. 'Do you think I look the best?' he asked hopefully.

'The handsomest Biggles ever,' confirmed Rachel, giving her fiancé a reconciliatory kiss.

'Wine?' he asked her.

'White, please. But just half a glass.'

'Oh, come on,' said Jonny. Jonny didn't do things by halves. He was always in for the whole hog, with a huge smile on his face. 'Let your hair down.'

'I can't. It's in a headscarf.'

Jonny laughed and squeezed her tightly to him, before heading to the bar.

Rachel leaned against the wall and quickly scanned the room. She waved to a couple of WRENs she knew. Said 'Hi' to a passing Eisenhower. Waited for Jonny, who was laughing at the bar with the other pilots. She wished Wren was here, but Wren said she would rather sit in a vat of cold sewage than go to a fancy-dress PTA do at the village hall. There was no sign of Gabe and Rachel hoped he wouldn't come after all. That he'd flown home early. Or he'd caught a cold, or Aunt Julia had, and he had to look after her. She felt embarrassed about the times they'd talked, how intense they'd been. How out-of-herself she'd felt. If he did turn up, she'd be pleasant and brief and friendly, comment on his costume and wish him both well and goodbye.

She felt a hand on the side of her bottom.

'Looking good, young lady.' It was Dray Briggs, local groper, dressed in chinos, white shirt and the pointy cap of a US Navy SEAL. He looked like Virgil from *Thunderbirds*.

'Oh, hi, Dray,' she said unenthusiastically.

'You can come and work my land any day of the week,' he said, looking her up and down. 'Pretty shoes,' he added, looking at Rachel's feet.

98

'Thank you,' she said. She didn't know what she was thanking him for. She felt she wanted to say the opposite of 'Thank you' but she didn't know what that was.

'Here, have my bubbly,' he said, handing her his glass.

'No, thank you.' There, that was the opposite of thank you. As simple as that.

'Hope we can have a dance later,' he said, looking directly at her chest.

'Maybe,' she would have said, normally. She'd have said 'Maybe', and hoped he would go away and not bother her again. Tonight, she said, 'No, thank you' – again – and waited for his surprise.

'Gone all stuck up, have we?' he frowned. 'That's not like you.'

'Hello, Dray,' said Jonny, approaching with a pint of beer in one hand and a large glass of white wine in the other. 'What's going on here?' He gave the wine to Rachel and flashed Dray a warning look.

'I was only asking Rachel if she wanted to take a little turn on the dance floor with me later,' he pouted. 'What's wrong with a little dance? Why do women always have to get so hysterical?' Rachel felt a chill in her heart, below the pocket of her land girl shirt. Hysterical. That's what her father always called her mother. And she hated the way Dray said it now, with that special sneer reserved for women.

'Leave it out,' said Jonny. 'That's a bit much, mate.'

'*Lighten up, shweetheart*,' postured Dray to Jonny, in a bad American accent. 'Rachel,' he added pointedly, and he gave her a wink and strode off, his buttocks fighting each other in his GI Joe chinos.

'Old pervert,' winced Jonny. 'Just keep away from him.' He put his arm round her and pulled her to him, his ridiculous scarf squishing against the side of her face. 'I love you,' he said. 'You look gorgeous. No one else is allowed to get near you. Oh,' he then added, flicking his eyes to a group of people behind them, 'there's Robert Tandy. Do you mind if I go and have a quick word with him? Sorry. I'll be right back.'

'Of course not,' she fibbed. 'I'll wait here for you.' She felt safer with Jonny by her side. She didn't want to leave *his*, the whole night. She idled by the wall, sipping her wine and resisting the temptation to survey the room, but she heard Nancy Littlen-Green's laugh over by the fire exit and risked a glance to see she was also a land girl, one with a red bra on show under a front-tied white shirt and a tight pair of rolled-up jeans. She looked beautiful, actually; didn't she always? Like a very cool member of Bananarama. Jonny was in the circle of people behind her, talking to Robert.

'Hi! Rachel!'

Faith was stage right, striding across the floor in a very glamorous Andrews Sisters' outfit, complete with jaunty hat and tiger-y victory rolls.

'You look great,' Rachel said. 'Fantastic, actually.'

'And you look cute,' Faith laughed. 'What do you think of my hat?'

'Very nice.'

'I daren't take it off! I'd have the most horrific helmet hair. And do you know, this outfit was one that originally belonged to . . .'

Faith's happy voice trailed out of Rachel's consciousness as a man in a white Navy officer's uniform entered the periphery of her vision. He was walking in via the fire exit. He was accompanied by Mrs Bottomley – dressed as a hospital matron and wielding an enormous see-through barrel full of raffle tickets, which later on Mrs Pickering from the greengrocer's would spin and announce with a shrill voice, 'Pink ticket, number 344, that's pink ticket, number 344 . . .' until some excited person ran to the front to collect a tin of butter beans.

Rachel focused on that barrel, on silly thoughts of the raffle, as she didn't want to focus on Gabe. Why hadn't he come as Winston Churchill? A bald one, with full prosthetics and a limp? She couldn't take her eyes off him, in his white jacket, and his cap. In profile, he looked like a movie star. He passed her, about five people away. Five heads and shoulders and moustaches away. Gabe clocked her. He raised his eyebrows good-naturedly and grinned; she grinned back, feeling like her stomach was its own turning barrel – a kaleidoscope of excitement she hadn't felt since . . . well, since Jonny had kissed her, not far from here, in front of the memo board.

*I'm in trouble*, Rachel thought to herself, and the words climbed into her brain and took up squatters' rights there. *I'm in trouble. I shouldn't be, but I am. I don't need to be, but I* am. She wouldn't talk to him, she decided. She would be with Jonny and she would end this night walking through the safe quiet streets with her fiancé . . .

'And then, just as I put the stockings on, I got an enormous rip in them, and had to start all over again . . .' Faith was still talking. Gabe's immaculate white back headed to the bar. 'Anyway, I'll see you later, Rachel,' said Faith. 'I need to go and freshen up before my dance card is marked. Cheerio for now.'

She wriggled off towards the back of the hall. Rachel gripped her wine glass. She couldn't see Gabe now. Hopefully he'd be very popular tonight, in that uniform, and she wouldn't encounter him. She wouldn't be in *trouble*. It had just been a fleeting attraction. It had nothing to do with her life.

The band started to play: Glenn Miller's 'In the Mood'. People started moving, grabbing each other's hands, jiggling and twisting. No one knew how to jive properly and why should they? Rachel stood and watched them and bet Nanna knew how to jive. And Grandpop. They probably did it all through the war. She wondered if Florence jived with her American, Scott, at the dance on the ground floor of the Clarendon Hotel. She wondered what they had whispered to each other. Whether it was as they'd danced that they'd fallen in love.

*Where* is *that tin?* Rachel thought. When she had washed Jonny's jeans after Sausage Night, she'd found the shell of a monkey nut in one of the back pockets, but Jonny had still been none the wiser. The whole thing would have to remain a mystery and she wouldn't tell Florence, yet, that the tin had been mislaid.

An arm slid around Rachel's waist.

'There you are,' a voice said.

*Dray.* She looked wildly around for Jonny but couldn't see him anywhere. Gabe was peeling away from the bar, stacked pint glasses wedged between his hands, then he disappeared.

'I don't like taking no for an answer.' Dray held out his meaty hand, already glistening with sweat, and yanked on hers, launching them both into an unexpected and unwanted jive. She wanted to protest but he was holding her fast, and she thought it easier to go with it for a couple of seconds, then get rid of him. It was horrible. Dray bobbed and stepped and kicked his feet out; he spun her out like a reluctant top, then reeled her back in. He jived up behind her, holding her round the waist, then he was next to her, his arm a bridge across her shoulders, yelling 'Good, good!' She looked frantically across the crowded hall for Jonny but there was no sign of him.

The band segued into 'Chattanooga Choo Choo'. Dray showed no glimmer of relinquishing her. She was being swung around like a soap on a rope.

'You're so pretty,' he said, all yellow teeth and darkened armpits. 'So, so pretty.' Refusing to let go, he threw her out then pulled her in again, shunted up behind her like a trailer to a lorry. Inched his right hand a little too close to her right breast. Pressed a grotesquely hardening groin against her chinos. Her heels were skidding on the increasingly slippery floor.

'May I cut in?'

She looked up from the stifling straitjacket of Dray's waist cinch and Gabe was standing there. Movie star American officer's uniform. Curt smile. A welcome hand, held out like a lifebuoy.

'Yes!' she cried with huge relief and gratitude as she looked up into the bluest of American blue eyes. 'Yes, you may.'

# Chapter Eleven

'You can't just *cut in*,' huffed Dray.

'You can where I'm from,' said Gabe.

Dray removed himself from Rachel's waist. He stepped beside her, swiped at his flopped comb-over with a chastened hand, then stuck his tongue out childishly.

'Boo,' he said to Gabe, 'you can have her. She wasn't much cop anyway,' and he shuffled off into the crowd, hitching up his trousers.

'"Not much cop?"' Gabe queried, still holding out his hand. Rachel took it gratefully.

'It means I wasn't very good.'

'Ah,' said Gabe. 'Well, neither am I.' Gabe's hand was cool and dry in comparison to Dray's paw. 'I hope you didn't mind me cutting in,' he added. 'You didn't look like you were particularly enjoying yourself.'

'No, I wasn't.'

'Shall we?' he said, and Rachel nodded.

Gabe was clearly not a jiver, to Rachel's joy. He didn't spin her or grab her, or throw her out and reel her in. He just kind of swayed from side to side, a little self-consciously, to the jazzy Glenn Miller vibe, and allowed her to do the same. She was free, rescued. But at the same time, she was almost as thrown as she had been by her previous partner. Gabe's eyes were dancing with merriment. His skin looked warm. His lips were tilted into an easy grin. Hers couldn't help but reciprocate. She worried about Jonny. Would he see her? Being manhandled by Dray Briggs was one thing; dancing with this quiet and handsome American was entirely another.

'Everything all right?' Gabe asked her.

'Yes, and with you?' she responded politely.

'I'm just swell,' he said, and she didn't know if he was teasing her.

'What do think of our little village party?' she asked him, trying not to look at his lips, eyes, eyebrows, cheeks, face.

'Not enough drunk Brits yet,' he replied, and she laughed.

'Give it time.'

The crowd of people dancing just behind them shifted and expanded and, with a cry of 'Rachel!' from a woman Rachel knew from the library, soon the two of them were engulfed in the same circle, dancing to Glenn Miller. Gabe was laughing now, as they did their ineffectual sway, like two old-timers at a wedding. She liked that laugh rather too much.

'Man down!' shouted August Collier, the local estate agent. Rachel turned and saw the retired dentist on his back like an overturned beetle. Gabe helped to grab his pleading jazz hands and heave him up.

'Quite the spectacle,' Gabe whispered to Rachel, once the man was relaunched into frenetic dancing.

'Quite,' she agreed. They found themselves on an appendage, suddenly: an outcrop.

'Shall we take a break?' he asked her.

She nodded. They moved slowly over to the side of the hall and stood near a table strewn with streamers and discarded glasses. The village hall doors had been shut to seal off noise and the room was really heating up. Someone had brought along a smoke machine, making things worse.

Gabe took off his cap and ruffled at his hair, then removed his jacket, which he threw over the back of the nearest chair. He waved his hand through the encroaching smoke.

'This is terrible.'

'I know.'

'We'll need those gas masks in a minute.' Gabe gesticulated to one, on the wall.

'I'm afraid we might.' She realized her hand had found its way on to the back of the chair and the shoulder of Gabe's jacket. The jacket felt both crisp and warm. She retracted her hand, put it down by her side.

'I like your headscarf,' said Gabe.

'Thanks.' She patted at it self-consciously, averting her eyes from his.

'You look pretty.'

'Thank you.' She looked back at him, her heart racing suddenly. She had the terrible feeling she would like to hear Gabe call her 'pretty' for the rest of her life. 'I like your costume,' she said. 'It's really smart.'

'Winston wasn't viable,' he replied. 'The coat had mothballs and Aunt Julia's cat had been sitting on the hat. I hired this from a fancy-dress shop in Banbury, last minute.'

'It suits you.' A tiny piece of her wondered if he had changed costume because of *her*, so he could be a smart naval officer instead of a comical Winston Churchill.

'Thank you, ma'am.' She didn't even want to examine how she felt when he called her 'ma'am' in that delicious accent, but she imagined it was how some of the sillier women had when the Yanks came to town, or perhaps how Florence had felt, with *Scott*. 'My grandfather was a naval officer. In the war,' continued Gabe. 'Served in the South Pacific. Man, those guys. So young, most of them . . . My grandad was only in his late teens. Were your great aunt and uncle in the war?'

'Yes,' she said. 'Nanna worked at the Ministry of Food, and then the ATA, sometime later, and my great uncle was on the railways, reserved occupation.'

'The ATA?' asked Gabe. 'What did your great aunt do at the ATA?'

'Flew planes,' shrugged Rachel, smiling.

'She was a *pilot*?'

'Yes, eventually. Ferrying planes between factories and bases.' Rachel thought again of Florence's photo, in front of that Spitfire, both the sun and the clouds in her eyes.

'That's pretty amazing.'

'I know.'

'I bet Aunt Julia would have done something similar. Something *gung-ho*, if she'd been old enough.'

'Really?' enquired Rachel. 'When did she come to England?' she asked.

'Nineteen fifty-one,' said Gabe. 'She came over here when she was twenty-two, on an academic sabbatical. Married Trevor March, professor of maths – God rest his soul – within a year, and never went back. My father's never forgiven her.'

'Why not?'

Gabe frowned. 'He felt she had betrayed the family, by going. Left him behind. Denied her roots, all that garbage. He was jealous, probably, of her sense of adventure, the ease at which she shrugged off the small-town mentality. The whole academia thing . . . Books and travel, that's her thing.'

'Travel?' Rachel was surprised again. 'I thought she was a recluse?'

Gabe shrugged. 'She doesn't leave the Mill House much, but when she does, she packs a suitcase and goes *far*. Anyway, she wanted to visit Dad when he had the accident, but he told her "no". They're officially estranged.'

'I'm sorry.'

'It's OK,' said Gabe. 'It's easy to become estranged from my father. He's really not the approving or forgiving kind.'

Rachel looked at Gabe's face as the partying throng – a meshing thump and twirl of side-partings and victory rolls – romped behind them.

'What does he disapprove of in you?' she asked.

Gabe laughed bitterly and ran a hand through the back of his hair. 'Where do I start? My career, or lack of it, as he sees it. "Who ever made a living from art, boy?" . . . My "sensitive" nature – that was a good one, growing up. My tendency to roam, my failed relationships, though he never gave me the blueprint of a decent one.'

'Even before the accident?' Somewhere, in the smoky distance, she heard Jonny laugh. It floated into the air like a balloon on a long string, far from her. She couldn't tear her eyes from Gabe.

Gabe sighed. 'There was never any love between my parents. Not real love. Yes, there was tolerance, and subservience and fortitude and effort – from my mother, before and after Dad's accident, until she literally got *sick* of trying – but not real love.'

Rachel nodded. 'Go on,' she said.

'My mom was a really good artist, one of the murals in Jud is hers, a pair of pheasants. She painted it on the side of a saddlery store when she was a teenager. My dad promised her a studio, when they got married, but that never materialised. Whenever art was mentioned, he was scathing. Scathing is kind of his thing.' Gabe gave Rachel a rueful smile. 'She had a coffee-table book, on nineteenth-century paintings. Her favourite artists are Suzanne Valadon and Toulouse-Lautrec. My dad hated that book, said it was artsy smartsy and a load of crap. While she was at the grocery store one time, he chucked it out with the garbage, but when I was sixteen I ordered another copy from a bookstore in Fargo and she hid it in her sweater drawer.' He smiled, boyishly, at the memory. 'I think it's still there. My mother loved a particular series of paintings by Lautrec,' he added. 'The paintings are titled "The bed", "*Le lit*". They're of women. Prostitutes, from a Paris brothel.'

'I like those, too,' said Rachel. She remembered the series of paintings well; two women, heads on pillows kissing, or lying in bed, sleeping or embracing.

Gabe looked pleased. 'My mom always said *that* was love, real love, even though it was two women – you can imagine what my dad would think of that! She told me, "Look for that, it's what you're aiming for, that love." They never had it, my mom and dad. And the not having it sent my mom crazy, eventually.' He sighed. 'And I guess that's what I'm looking for.'

'Real love,' said Rachel softly.

'Yes. I know it's out there. It has to be, so I can honour Mom somehow. Until then . . .'

'You'll be a lost and wandering soul,' said Rachel, with a gentle smile. She was teasing him, just a little.

'Yep,' agreed Gabe, his smile matching hers. 'I know exactly what I'm looking for. I just haven't found it yet.' His eyes didn't leave her. There were flecks of mirrorball in them. Light and dark. They made her feel punch-drunk. 'And you?' he asked. 'Have you found it?'

'Yes. I believe I have.' She heard Jonny's laugh again, hearty. Soon she would walk away from this man and she would go to him. She had to.

'You're certain of it?'

'Yes,' she said. But she felt precarious, here with Gabe at the edge of the hall.

'Then I envy your certainty,' he said. 'Your contentment.'

'Not always,' she replied, thinking of her own parents, and the terrible blueprint of their up-and-down marriage; the dark days and the awful moments. How she *missed* them, felt their loss like a big, hard rock inside her, its sharp edges threatening to puncture her skin. But she had *certainty*, didn't she? She planned to love Jonny for a lifetime. Real love had come her way one summer's day when there he was, holding his baby. At the same time, she overwhelmingly felt she wanted to put her arms around Gabe and hold him close to her. Feel the warmth of him, through his white shirt. Raise her face to his.

'I think falling in love should be as easy as saying "Hello",' he said, his eyes steady and serious, and she was jolted sideways, then, in a comical swipe, by an out-of-control dancing Army couple, victory rolls and khaki.

'Pardon me,' said Gabe, steadying the woman.

'No problem, handsome,' the woman replied, as they spun away again.

'Are you OK?' Gabe asked Rachel.

She nodded. 'Yes, fine.' She saw Jonny, out of the corner of her eye, appearing from the entrance to the kitchen. 'I need to go,' she said to Gabe. 'Sorry. Thank you . . . for the dance and the chat.'

'OK,' he said. 'Maybe I'll see you again before the end of the evening?' He looked a little hurt.

'Maybe,' she said.

'I'll be seeing you?' he pressed, but she had already left him. She was walking towards Jonny, who spotted her and headed in her direction, his flying jacket off and his silly scarf discarded.

'Got to love Glenn Miller . . .' mused Jonny, grabbing her and pulling her into him. 'You know what, I'll be in the mood, later. You look fantastic, Rachel.'

'Thank you,' she said, 'so will I.' She was so relieved to be back in her intended life. Whatever she had felt with Gabe – a moment in time, an aberration – had to dissipate into the chokingly smoky air.

'Shall we go and get a drink?'

'Yes, please.'

They headed to the bar as her heart tried to gather itself in her chest, lock doors around it and pretend what had happened was inconsequential – that her life could glide on, on its set runners, without this catastrophe throwing her to the ground. That tonight she would walk home, with safe, lovely Jonny, in the cool streets, and nothing could ever change.

# Chapter Twelve

It was 11.45 p.m. Rachel was standing in the porch of the back door of the village hall, looking out into the car park and breathing in the night air. It was still unbearably hot in the hall, where people were jiving like joyous maniacs, staggering to and from the increasingly depleted bar and hanging off each other like cheap coats. Newly and surprisingly formed couples (there would be a few red faces in the Co-op in the morning) were snogging on the dance floor, the curtailments of the wartime spirit sparking an urgent lust. There were fifteen minutes until the lights were switched on and all the carnage of the night was exposed under the glare of parish council strip lights.

Rachel found the mundane sights of the car park a calm oasis. Mr Griffith's old Morris Minor, badly parked at a hurried angle, like he'd swerved in, chased by robbers. A cat squatting with disdain on top of a yellow salt bin. A crumpled shoe discarded without its mate at the base of a tree in a concrete surround. Above her, the exit sign winked and spluttered, the 'I' missing. Behind her, an overly yellow hallway sat bright and sterile. Radiators. Stainless-steel hooks. A stack of green paper towels on a windowsill. Village life. She loved it, all its quirks and its craziness and its people. She loved its companionship and its safety.

The cat jumped off the salt box and went over to sniff at the shoe. An owl hooted from a hidden branch somewhere. And a man emerged from the small copse of trees to the right of the car park, hitched a crisp white jacket further over his shoulder and walked towards her.

'Hello,' Gabe said, like it was the beginning of the night and not the end.

'Hello.' The top button of his shirt was undone. Rachel noticed an escaped curl of hair around his right ear.

'You getting some air too?' he asked. 'I was just checking out an old oak, over there.' He gestured in the direction of the copse.

She laughed. 'Busman's holiday,' she said, and Gabe looked mildly confused. 'But yes, I'm having a bit of a breather. It's all a bit much in there now.'

'Sure is,' he smiled. 'Been having a nice time?'

'It's been lovely. You?' They had returned to being ultra-polite. Strangers.

'I've had fun, yes. But now I'm beat. I've got an early start in the morning. Plane to catch and all that. Say, do you know if I can cut across the back of the car park here, to get to Sidmouth Street?' He said Sid-*mouth* and not *Sidm'th*.

'Yes,' she replied. 'Go through the gap in the wall over there – see? – and head past the King George pub, on your left.'

'Gotcha. Thank you.'

He looked at her, his eyes clear and studied.

'So, I guess this is goodbye, Rachel,' he said.

'I guess it is.'

She had preferred the 'I'll be seeing you' of the dance floor. She had spent the past two hours laughing and dancing with Jonny. She'd desperately tried to forget Gabe was still in the room. Talking to other people. Giving them his warmth and his smiles.

'It's been lovely meeting you, Gabe.'

'Likewise.' He held out his hand to her and the touch of it was a promise of something that couldn't be promised. An evocation of a life that could never be lived. He would travel and party and escape his life in North Dakota, meeting strangers and challenging them with his *four seasons* curiosity; she would be here in Fincham St George, quietly living hers.

'Goodbye, then.'

'Goodbye.'

She was certain he felt the same thing. This promise. This non-promise. A feeling that threatened to overwhelm her but was already leaving her. He finally let go of her hand and turned away, and she turned away too, to step back into the bright, sterile hall.

'Can I just say something?'

She looked back and Gabe smiled, a slow sweet smile that made her want to crumple to the cracked quarry tiles.

'I know you're engaged,' he said. 'I know you have a life planned with your fiancé. I know I'll never see you again, but I just wanted to say that I think you're beautiful. You may be the most beautiful woman I've ever seen.' He half shrugged, smiled a downturned smile, looked with blue eyes into hers, for too long. 'I believe if things were different, so many things, that I might love you. If you're ever free, come find me, won't you?' And he turned and strode off into the car park, his jacket over one shoulder, out through the gap in the brick wall to head past the King George pub and on to Sidmouth Street.

'Goodbye,' Rachel whispered, astonished, as Gabe walked out of her life and this May night held its breath for just a moment, and so did she, then the owl hooted again, somewhere within the branches of the old oak tree, and she gathered her life once more to her – a coat discarded in the first warmth of spring sunshine but retrieved after a late frost catches an English morning by surprise – and stepped back into the village hall.

# SUMMER

## 20 July 1997

# Chapter Thirteen

Sunlight streamed in through the dining-room window. Rachel scrutinised the last knife. Everything on the table – mats, charger plates, wine goblets, flowers, candles and linen napkins fluting from silver napkin holders – sparkled in the sun, as behind it, on the marble mantelpiece, a ticking clock marked the morning. Rachel went to the large bay window and opened the left-hand elevation. She leaned far out and breathed in the seductive summer scent of honeysuckle and cut grass. The front garden was beautiful in summer: dog roses and delphiniums and snapdragons competed from deep flower beds either side of the bright green lawn to be the prettiest and most fragrant of the season.

'Hi, Mrs Trent!'

Mrs Bottomley's grandson, Freddie, waved at her from behind the front hedge, a pair of secateurs in his hand. He came every Wednesday to garden for them and today, after he'd done the hedges, he was going to put some miniature hurricane lamps along the path, to welcome tonight's guests.

'How's the table looking?' Jonny called from the kitchen. He had decided to 'help' her today; he'd unearthed a navy-and-white striped apron his mother had given him three Christmases ago and had spent most of the morning enthusiastically stirring things that didn't need to be stirred.

'Wonderful!' she called back. The kid next door was playing his Oasis album again and 'Champagne Supernova' drifted over the fence. The TV was on behind her, at the end of the large open-plan living-room-diner they'd knocked through when they'd moved in. Sky News was reporting from the South of France where Princess Diana was on a yacht with a rumoured new love interest who was something to do with Harrods. Rachel closed the window until it was only a couple of inches ajar.

'Shall I add the dill now?' Jonny called.

'Not yet!' she called back.

'There's a fly in here. I need to swat it. Where are the washing-up gloves?'

'Where they always are? In the cupboard under the sink!'

'Right-o!'

Tonight, they were hosting a celebratory dinner, marking two hundred thousand copies sold of Jonny's latest book, *Nikita in Moscow*. On the guest list was Jonny's agent, his publicist Zoe, Teddy and the ubiquitous Lee, who hovered round this house like a fly that could never be successfully swatted, no matter how many times you swiped at it with the washing-up gloves.

They had been here almost eight years now, at Crofters on Hedge Hill Lane. The house had come up on sealed auction in the autumn of 1989 and Jonny and Rachel had been in the fortunate position to make a very generous offer, having always admired the house's Georgian façade and neat gardens, and further falling for its high ceilings, huge kitchen and the room in the attic for Teddy to hide away in, when she wasn't staying elsewhere in the village.

'A step up we'll never fall from, Rach,' Jonny had said, as he'd carried Rachel over the threshold, the afternoon they'd moved in, and placed her gently on the sumptuous pink hall carpet – now replaced – that the estate agent had pronged back to perfection behind them, on their first viewing, with a tiny rake. It was *that* sort of house. The sort of big, beautiful house perfect for hosting the old Hedge Hill Lane crowd, with parties, summer barbecues and get-togethers, in reception rooms big enough for dancing in and a pine-tree-lined rear garden they could linger in for hours, over Pimm's, and to a backdrop of Jonny's ready laughter. The sort of house couples in their early thirties thought themselves extremely lucky to get.

Things could only get better, Tony Blair and his Labour crew had promised at the beginning of May this year, and things already *had*, for Jonny and Rachel. Since 12 March 1989, in fact.

'What time are you popping to Vivaldi's?' Jonny called out. Rachel came away from the window and walked into the kitchen, where her husband was leaning against the worktop with a glass of red. Flushed and grinning, his new haircut was all perky (less quiff, more well-tended spike), his slightly expanding belly proud under the stretched stripes of the apron. He still looked rather like the cheeky schoolboy he once was, at thirty-eight years young.

'Any minute.'

'What are you wearing tonight?'

'My red dress. The one you gave me.'

'Oh, sexy! You'll look amazing. I thought I might drag the old tux out. Scrub up a bit. Do you know where my dress shoes are?'

'No, sorry.' She opened the fridge and checked they had milk.

'OK, I'll find them. What time are we expecting Teddy?'

'I'm not sure. About five, hopefully. I hope her and Lee aren't going to be a problem tonight. You know what they're like.'

Jonny made a noise, a *humph* mixed with a humoured snort.

'We could always *un*-invite Lee,' she said.

Jonny frowned. 'Come here,' he said, putting his glass of wine on the worktop.

'What?' she asked, but she knew he would take her in his arms and tell her he loved her.

'I love you,' he said, enveloping her and kissing her on the cheek with lips that were all red wine and garlic.

'I love you too.'

'Off you go, then,' he said. 'I'll finish off here. A well-stirred sauce is a beautiful thing.' He began to sing tunelessly to himself, as he busied himself with wooden spoon and pan.

It was a glorious afternoon, bright and still, with a bristling yellow sun in a wide-eyed sky, as Rachel walked down the lane, heading for the village. The trees and shrubs around her were bursting with greenery and saturated with light; the flowers in the hedgerows winked at her from their hiding places. She was wearing a navy cotton shift dress and her beloved Birkenstocks. Tonight she would change into that dress Jonny had bought her from Selfridges, on his last trip to London, a vampy ruby-red satin dress with spaghetti straps. It was not quite *her*, and she wondered, at thirty-six, if she could get away with it, but Jonny said it was a total 'wow'.

She continued into the village and down the main street. Oh no, there was Nancy Littlen-Green, walking ahead of her, opposite the park. Rachel slowed her pace. She and Jonny tried largely to avoid her. In the early days Jonny used to hide behind Rachel, rather comically, if they saw Nancy out and about in the village, saying he didn't have the energy to talk to her, that she always gave him a cool look that communicated he should feel guilty. These days, Rachel didn't want to catch up with Teddy's mother, make clenched-teeth talk about the weather and pretend not to notice how Nancy was still beautiful, but now wore shabby-looking fleeces with wolves on the back, and odd T-bar shoes – or to judge them *both* for not bringing up what was really important: Teddy's state of mind.

'Hey, Rachel!'

Ugh, it was Lee, coming out of the Co-op on the other side of the road with a slack-jawed face and a swinging carrier bag. Rachel smiled an approximation of a smile and did half a wave.

'Looking forward to tonight!' he called over to her, but as it was Lee, it was more like a heckle.

'Me too!' Rachel's half-smile faltered and died, and she carried on walking, muttering all sorts of unladylike things under her breath, while he turned and went the other way.

*Lee Hope.* He was a blight on their lives, that man. Bad enough he had inveigled his way into Jonny's but now he was in Teddy's too and Rachel hated it.

She quickened her pace. She remembered – with absolute clarity and rage – the morning she had found Lee in Teddy's bed. Rachel had walked into the attic room with a cup of tea and a restorative bacon sandwich for her stepdaughter, after what had been a *monumental* party for Jonny's thirty-eighth birthday early this year, and was horrified to see a puny leg sticking out from under Teddy's butterfly duvet cover and a horribly familiar pair of scruffy black trainers on the floor.

'What the bloody hell?'

As she stood in the doorway, Rachel had been overwhelmed by a feeling of utter inevitability. A feeling that all roads, as far as poor Teddy was concerned, had led to this repugnant destination. She loved Teddy fiercely, but she was . . . troubled. The sweet, often serious little girl Rachel had once held hands with on the lane had long since departed and in her place was a young woman who was hard to reach and even harder to help.

It started in her teenage years, which had not been good to Tatiana Trent. They were when she had needed her mother the most, but Nancy had become more and more 'hands off' in recent years, distracted by a stream of impermanent men and a meandering 'career', setting up short-lived candle businesses, second-hand furniture enterprises and pyramid schemes involving aloe vera hand cream and hair vitamins. She was never really around for the teenage Teddy, and Rachel, always there to step up and love her

121

stepdaughter to the best of her ability, soon started to feel power-less. At thirteen, Teddy became withdrawn and sullen, alternatively sneering at Jonny and Rachel or barking illogical demands at them. At fourteen, she started hanging around with unsuitable friends – 'feral types', as Jonny decreed them – who smoked under the concrete bridge and stomped around glaring at people. At fifteen, Teddy started to go to house parties in the village, every Saturday night. She began smoking weed; Rachel found 'roll-up' butts in her school bag but wasn't allowed to tell her off. It was Jonny's job or Nancy's, she was constantly told, but useless Nancy wasn't going to do anything, and Jonny had spoiled Teddy enough in the preced-ing years that it was far too late for him to lay down the law now.

He *had* spoiled her. Always a fun playful dad, now Jonny's career had taken off he replaced little outings and time spent deal-ing with homework and friendships and boys with buying Teddy *things* – clothes and jewellery and make-up. And saying 'yes' to her. To pretty much everything. The teen years spiralled downwards. At sixteen and seventeen, Teddy was snappy and belligerent, going out with the wrong sort of boy and barely attending sixth form. At eighteen, she dropped out of college, just before she was sup-posed to take her A levels. She worked here and there around the village – behind the bar, in the pub, at the chicken factory, down at the farm shop on Rectory Road, counting out potatoes . . . She became a drifter who never settled to anything. Listless. Depressed? A frustrated and very concerned Rachel thought she might be. They took her to the doctor and Doctor Harris had looked at all three of them coldly and said there was nothing wrong with her.

And then Teddy got involved with Lee.

'I could call the police!' Rachel had cried from the doorway of the attic room, but she knew there were no grounds to. Teddy was nineteen; Lee was, what, twenty-nine? No laws were being broken. Except the laws of decency and morality. Rachel had seen them talking together, by the fireplace, at the end of Jonny's party, had overheard Lee bending Teddy's ear about his interminable plays (the most recent had been put on at the Yarnwell Playhouse, to a lukewarm reception). She'd clocked Lee's charming, gratifying smile, something he turned on when he was after something, and Teddy's face lit up by it. But she'd never expected this.

'What for?' Lee had asked, sitting up in Teddy's bed and revealing his puny chest. She felt sickened. Sickened that this creepy, sycophantic cling-on of Jonny's had weaselled his way upstairs with her stepdaughter.

'Well, I'll be telling Jonny,' she threatened.

'What will he care?' drawled Lee, his voice croaky. 'His best girl and his best mate together. Won't he be pleased?'

'I very much doubt it.'

Teddy lifted her head out of the duvet then, hair everywhere, panda eyes bleary. She didn't even have the decency to look ashamed.

'I thought you'd have your standards set much higher than this, Teddy,' Rachel said.

'I *like* Lee.' Teddy yawned, pushing the hair out of her eyes. And Rachel had despaired, and stormed upstairs to Jonny to blurt out the horrible truth and at first, to his credit, he had looked taken aback. He'd sat down on their bed and stared out of the window, at the blank January sky.

'Right,' he'd said finally. 'Right.' Then he'd said they were both adults and what was the problem, really, when you thought about it, and Rachel had raged at him, had protested about the ten-year age gap, and it being under their roof, and didn't he want to just go up there and kick that utter toerag out on to the *street*, and Jonny had said better *here*, in this house, than somewhere else, and they were old enough to know what they were doing, surely, and Lee was all right, he was his friend, after all . . .

Friend? Rachel had thought, looking at her husband as he sat on their bed and told her it was acceptable, that man in bed with their Teddy. Why? Why did he go to the pub with this insidious man, have him round for supper and drinks, invest in his God-awful plays like Lee was the next bloody Harold Pinter? Of course, she knew why. It was the adoration, the hero worship; the ego-thrill Jonny got from being someone's benefactor. Jonny had beckoned her to the bed, then put his arms around her and held her close. And his breath had sounded a little ragged, but he said it was fine, it would all be fine. It would be a one-night thing, no big deal, and forgotten in a week or two.

'Don't you worry?' Rachel had said, into his chest. 'Don't you really just *worry* about her?' He didn't feel the same compulsion she did, she thought, to keep everyone around them safe, secure and protected, especially Teddy.

'Of course I do.' Jonny had stared out of the window again, over her shoulder. 'Of course I do.'

It hadn't been a one-night thing and it hadn't been forgotten in a couple of weeks. Nothing Lee or Teddy did was ever *forgotten*. Everything they did was escalated or overdramatised – the pair of them brought the kind of disaster into her house that Rachel had tried to avoid since the drama of her childhood – a drama she had recently discovered, quite accidentally, held a devastating additional scene that had been well-meaningly but purposefully kept from her.

Lee and Teddy (how Rachel hated saying or even thinking of those names together as a *pair*) were still together, although it was a very on-and-off sort of together. There were times Teddy stayed over at Lee's small bungalow at the edge of the village for three days and came home blissfully happy. Other times, there were slammed car doors and shouts in the lane and Teddy would lock herself away in the attic room indefinitely.

*Tonight could be explosive or it could end with them in each other's pockets*, Rachel thought, as she continued to walk up the road towards Vivaldi's. Her need to protect Teddy was strong, to keep her from harm – as she'd found out had been done for *her*, by those who loved her – but if no one else was in collusion with that, what power did she have? Jonny still said it might fizzle out; Jonny said Lee wasn't that bad. She passed Grandpop Jim's bench and reached into her bag for her keys. She would put the Lee and Teddy situation out of her mind for now. She was going to her happy place.

Vivaldi's front window shone in the sun, making it almost impossible to see the huge seascape painting behind it, displayed on a giant easel. Come rain or shine, whatever the season, the black-and-white sign above Vivaldi's filled Rachel with joy. A local sign-writer came and painted it for her seven years ago, on a scorching day like today. She had brought him pints of orange squash and stood and watched as he painted new life into her world, with those white words on polished glass.

It was hers, this gallery. Two years after Jonny's dramatic change in fortune, and the day after his third *Sunday Times* bestseller, Faith had told Rachel she was selling up – that she had met a man at step aerobics and was moving away with him. She had told Rachel she was so sorry she would lose her job, but maybe she could up her hours at the cafe, 'not that you need the money, these days, what with Jonny and everything', before hugging her tightly. Rachel had said yes, she could maybe increase her hours at the cafe, then she had walked very slowly home from the gallery that afternoon, and that evening went to Jonny with a proposition.

'You'd like me to buy the gallery for you?' he'd said, over his typewriter, his new Pierre Cardin glasses teetering on the end of his nose.

'No, I'd like you to lend me the money so *I* can buy it and then I'm going to pay you back.'

'OK,' he'd replied. 'Let me see what I can do.' Three days later he'd written her a cheque. Six weeks later she'd signed the lease on the gallery. Three years later she paid him back, every penny.

Rachel unlocked the door and walked in, placing her keys on the desk and looking round her, with that almost astonished air she knew she always had, that she had done it.

Vivaldi's was hers.

# Chapter Fourteen

As soon as she'd signed the lease on the gallery, Rachel left her job at the cafe with lots of well-wishes from customers and a huge hug from Wren and set to work transforming Picture This.

First she took down all the paintings on the buttercup-yellow walls and kindly returned them to their artists, then she spent three days redecorating (up and down a ladder in dungarees and an old Katharine Hamnett T-shirt, listening to Radio 2), painting the walls in stark white, before a man in a green bandana came in to strip and sand the floors and stain them dark oak. She put the pine desk outside on the road with a label on it saying 'free' to whoever wanted it, replacing it with a vintage white console table with cabriole legs that she always placed a pretty vase of flowers on. And she themed each of the four sides of the gallery to the four seasons, in rotation: spring, summer – as the current season, on double-sided easels in the window – autumn and winter, and she kept the central pillar bare, as she'd always thought it looked cluttered.

She stood in the gallery now, remembering the transformation, and she also remembered she'd told someone, once, of her plans. Today she had come to fetch the art magazine she'd wanted to show Zoe, Jonny's publicist, at dinner tonight.

She walked to the console table and opened the drawer. When she pulled out the magazine, a photograph fluttered out with it, a beloved one of Florence, laughing behind an enormous cake Rachel had baked her for her sixtieth birthday. Rachel kept a few photos of Florence in the drawer, along with brochures, postcards advertising the gallery and neat pairs of wrapped digestive biscuits; she liked to glance through the photos sometimes, at quiet moments, although they could easily lead to tears.

Florence had died two mornings after the Blitz party. A neighbour had knocked on the door to ask her if she wanted anything from the shops, expecting to be invited in for cake and a chat, but had seen her through the net-curtained window, slumped forward in her armchair. On the telly, apparently – for Florence's neighbour, Pat, who had immediately let herself in through the unlocked door, was known for the enthusiastic recounting of small details – was *Murder, She Wrote*, the one where Jessica investigates a murder in a small family circus. What had made Rachel cry even more, also recounted by Pat, was that there was a half-drunk glass of Shloer on the little table in front of Flo and, on the doily armrest, a row of Dairy Milk squares.

The funeral had been packed, absolutely packed; people spilling outside the church and down the lane. Rachel had helped carry Nanna's coffin and read the eulogy she had taken great care in writing, making sure to reflect Nanna's great spirit, kindness and humour. Afterwards, they had a little do in the pub, with ten bottles of Shloer pride of place on the bar next to an Airfix model of a Spitfire. A woman from the RAF, no less, turned up to pay her respects. She brought a copy of Flo's old flying certificate, from 1943; it had been passed round the pub with careful fingers and grateful smiles.

Rachel missed Florence tremendously. She thanked Flo for protecting her; she understood her reasons for keeping secret what Rachel had discovered about the death of her parents a few months ago, and why that protection could never have lasted forever. Rachel loved looking at all the old photos. She sometimes wondered about that missing tin, which may have contained more. But she didn't have time to indulge in tears. She slipped the photo back into the drawer, between two floral postcards, and was startled by a sudden rap at the gallery window, looking up to see Sally Henderson-Bright standing there, all red lipstick and huge sepia sunglasses.

'Cooee! Thought I saw you!' Sally called, through the glass. 'You're not opening on a Sunday, are you?'

'No, I had to come in and pick up something,' Rachel called back.

'Oh, right. Let me in, would you?'

'The door's unlocked.'

'So . . . how are things?' asked Sally Henderson-Bright, striding into the gallery and plonking her enormous designer handbag on the console table, a threat to the vase of peonies.

Sally always asked Rachel this, usually with a slight head tilt. Sally knew all about Teddy. Everyone in the village did. Sally had a 'Dominique' who had been a model teenager and was now a model university student down at Exeter, getting an 'A' for every essay. She didn't have a 'Teddy' who was scrubbing potatoes down at the farm shop and sleeping with the local ne'er-do-well. Rachel felt passionately defensive of Teddy when Sally brought up her wonderful *Dominique*. She would tell her Teddy was going through a phase and was at heart a lovely girl who would come good soon.

'Good, thanks, great. And how are things with you?'

'Fabulous, thanks.' Sally was flouncing around the gallery, her white cotton sundress billowing behind her. 'Any *news*?' she asked, with a second head tilt, for Sally knew other things too.

It was always asked with a head tilt. The real question. It was gossamer-thin code for 'Are you pregnant yet?' and Rachel always wanted to reply with anything but the 'no' she had to give, and turn away from the string of platitudes that would follow it, an unravelling rope tossed down a very deep well.

Things like: Oh, I'm sure it's only a matter of time. You'll have a great time practising. It will happen, probably when you least expect it. Go on holiday or something; I know someone who tried for years and as soon as she stopped trying and went on holiday, poof, just like that, she got pregnant! At least you're having loads of sex, must be such *fun*. Such a shame, you know, my cousin got pregnant on the very first try. Have you stopped trying? You'd make such a lovely *mum*, well, you've always had Teddy, of course, but it's not the same as having your own flesh and blood, is it? Don't leave it too late, will you, you're not getting any younger, and if you want to make time for a second one . . . ah, well, I hated being pregnant, perhaps the universe is trying to tell you something! Being a mother is hard, it's not the be all and end all, anyway you've probably still got plenty of time . . .

Rachel had made the mistake of going for an impromptu coffee and bun with Sally at the height of her and Jonny's fertility woes, when they'd been trying for a baby for a miserable four years. Well, Jonny wasn't miserable; the thwarted baby-making didn't seem to make him suffer like it did Rachel – that monthly alternation of hope and despair. It didn't help that Wren had had two children in that time, so easily. Rachel had cried as she'd wrapped newborn gifts for Wren's babies – soft bears from Mothercare in layers of tissue paper and cute wrapping paper – but had smiled and cooed over Wren's precious bundles when she saw them, had held them and tried to stop her heart from breaking . . . And she didn't want it to, she tried so hard for it not to happen, but a sad and hollow distance had gradually created itself between them since the babies, which Rachel was so sorry for. They still saw each other, but not very often, and it wasn't the same. The truth was, Rachel often couldn't bear it – the reminder of what she couldn't have.

Rachel had broken down on Sally in Debenhams in Oxford, where they'd bumped into each other in the lingerie department and Sally had been kind and sympathetic as Rachel had cried and said 'sorry' for crying and snivelled into a tiny paper napkin the size of a doll's hanky. There'd been a few too many 'Poor you's from Sally – a woman who'd had three children, two of whom had been conceived over the age of forty without medical intervention – but Sally had let Rachel pour out all her woes, like milk from the miniature stainless-steel jug that cooled their coffee.

When she got home, Rachel had been truly sorry, though, as it seemed she'd now signed a devil's pact with Sally. Each time she saw her, she would get that inflection of sympathy, that head tilt and those coded questions; a silent 'Poor you' weaved through her words like a ribbon through the cuff of a baby's bootie.

'No news,' said Rachel, wondering if Sally was going to take her sunglasses off. 'How's Dominique?' It was utter self-flagellation to ask this, of course.

'Oh, Dominique's tremendous,' trilled Sally. 'Lots of sunbathing in the back garden, simultaneously pre-empting next term's reading list. She wants to be ahead of the pack, you know?'

'Great.' Rachel didn't know. The only thing Teddy was reading was *Just Seventeen* magazine and the local rag, looking for her next low-paying job.

'How's Teddy?'

'Oh, you know,' Rachel mumbled, 'on her way to great things very soon . . .'

'Such a shame,' tilted Sally. 'Still, at least you know you're not to blame. Not in her case. You're only the stepmother, after all.'

'Right.' Yes, that was her. Only the stepmother. The stepmother who adored her stepdaughter but could not help her. The stepmother who cared but could not console. Always the stepmother, never the *mother* . . . Rachel had the sudden urge to scream, very loudly, in Sally's face. 'So, what are you up to?' she asked instead. 'This afternoon.'

'Just a few errands,' pouted Sally. She walked over to the winter wall of the gallery, her expensive sandals smacking on the floor. 'Winter's looking good,' she commented, 'nice to see another piece by Missy Wainwright. I might be interested in one of hers for the ball this year. Still, there's plenty of time yet.'

'Yes, there's plenty of time,' nodded Rachel. It was always hard to imagine winter on a day like today, even with one whole wall of brilliant pastel snowstorms and bare, frozen landscapes to take her there. Missy Wainwright did highly sellable, atmospheric oil paintings of birds in the snow, in beautiful muted colours and exacting brush strokes. She hoped Sally would choose one of her works, maybe the one of the goldfinch on the greenhouse roof? She could spend a long time looking at that painting.

'Anyway, I must dash. Just thought I'd pop in for a *chatette*, as I saw you through the window. See you soon, OK?' Sally touched Rachel's arm with shiny nails, flashed a brightly sympathetic smile; scooped up her bag and slung it on her shoulder. 'I hope this month is *the* month, Rachel,' she postured.

Rachel knew it probably wouldn't be, as she and Jonny had decided to take a break from the Olympic lovemaking and the obsessive temperature checking (on her part). To just relax a bit, see if that famous 'stopped trying miracle' might arrive. Well, Jonny was relaxed, at least. Rachel was just sad.

'Actually, I have got some news,' Rachel called, as the hem of Sally's billowing dress and a final waft of CK One disappeared through the door of the gallery.

'Oh?' Sally popped her head back round. The sunglasses were finally lowered.

'I'm going to Morocco tomorrow. Marrakesh. On my own. To meet an artist.'

Rachel liked how Sally's face looked, her mouth an 'o' and her thin eyebrows arched in surprise. 'Oh, wow! Well, fabulous, how *exciting*!'

'Yes, I mean Vivaldi's has been very successful, with its local artists, but I came across this chap in a London arts' magazine, the tiniest article on him, actually, and I really think there's something there . . . something people here might like . . . So, yes, I am very excited. This artist could be really great for the future of the gallery.' She was babbling, beaming – but she didn't care.

'Well, good for you.' Sally's eyes had glazed over. Rachel knew Mrs Henderson-Bright wasn't really into art at all, despite the Winter Ball. She had no real passion for it, just a surface liking for pretty pictures and having something on her wall others might admire at a party. Luckily, these days, Rachel was able to persuade her towards the good stuff.

Sally tapped her red nails on the door frame. 'Right, bye then!' she said – and she was gone.

Rachel sighed with relief then picked up *Art Matters*, the magazine. She flicked to page thirty-two and the one-page profile of Khalid Ziani, the Moroccan artist.

Khalid was originally from Tarfaya, a desert region of sweeping dunes and Berber settlements, and had moved to Marrakesh ten years ago. He did rich, opulent paintings of the dust and heat of the streets of the old town, or medina; hyper-saturated and impressionistic pieces in shades of russet and terracotta and amber, overlaid with fine black lines depicting notions of people and animals. His work was incredibly commercial and perfect for her summer wall and she was booked on the 9 a.m. flight to Marrakesh in the morning.

Rachel smiled to herself with excitement and happiness. She would be staying at Hotel Felicity, just outside the city, and was planning to meet Khalid at an exhibition in a tiny gallery in the heart of the medina – as arranged by a crackly telephone conversation – then hoping to persuade him to exhibit some of his work in Vivaldi's.

She reread the article, popped the magazine in her bag and locked up. She stepped from the gallery into the bright sunlight of the afternoon and made her way back home through the pretty streets of the village, the wild summer flowers showing their little faces. As she neared Crofters, she could hear music. Jonny was listening to the radio again: '2 Become 1' was issuing through the trees and she could spy him, dancing like a charming elf on the lawn of the front garden, a slight builder's bum below the ties of his apron and a glass of red wine held up like a football trophy. She couldn't help but laugh as she reached their front gate. This was solid gold Jonny.

'Join me!' he shouted, as Rachel opened the gate, so she set her handbag down on the path, which was now lined on either side by hurricane lamps, and walked over to him for a comedy waltz, there in the front garden, to the Spice Girls.

'My wife!' he declared, as she twirled in his arms, and he lowered her to the ground in a ballroom dip.

'My husband!' echoed Rachel, with a giggle. 'And what a glorious sight you are!'

'Do you still love me?' he asked, a sparkle in his eyes and red wine on his lips.

'Until the end of time,' she replied.

# Chapter Fifteen

Teddy was in the kitchen. The contents of the fridge were being gloomily surveyed by a gangly figure in a red vest top and a low-rise denim skirt, dirty heels hanging off the back of worn flip-flops.

'Teddy! Hi, how are you?' Rachel held out her arms for a hug and Teddy slouched into them.

'Fine,' said Teddy, her mouth muffled into Rachel's shoulder. 'Thank God Dad's turned that terrible music off.' Jonny was in the study now, having abandoned his apron on the bottom of the banisters. He'd warned Rachel that Teddy had arrived, and that she wasn't in the best of moods.

'You don't like the Spice Girls?' Rachel asked, releasing her stepdaughter – who smelled of cigarettes and Thierry Mugler's Angel – back to the fridge.

'Do I *look* like I like the Spice Girls?'

'I guess not.'

Teddy looked more like a Marilyn Manson fan. She had black circles under her eyes, straggly hair, dry chapped lips and sooty make-up that looked three days old. She also seemed terribly thin and not all that well. Rachel felt worried for her, a worry that never went away.

'Were you drinking last night?' she asked.

'Don't start.' Teddy pulled listlessly at a packet of ham then flicked it back on to the shelf.

'Well, I'm just asking, love. You look hungover.'

A shrug. 'Might be.'

'What about smoking? Weed?'

'Maybe.'

'You need to look after yourself better.'

'I'm nineteen.'

'Nineteen-year-olds still need vitamins and a decent night's sleep.' Rachel tried to take Teddy in her arms again, but Teddy resisted.

'Nah. Lee still coming tonight?'

'As far as we know,' Rachel replied. 'Why don't *you* know, love?'

'I've not seen him for a couple of days. I've been at Tina's.'

'Oh. You had a row with him.' A statement not a question. There were far too many rows with Lee.

'Yeah.' Teddy slammed the fridge shut with her elbow.

'What was it about?'

Sudden tears filled Teddy's eyes. She leaned heavily against a cupboard. 'He can just be an absolute *bastard*, you know?'

'I know.' Tears threatened Rachel's eyes too. 'So why are you with him, sweetie? You don't have to be. You can do anything you like. Your dad and I will be here to help pick up the pieces.'

'No, I can't do anything I like.' Rachel wondered if she and Teddy were *both* thinking of the dead-end local jobs. The dropped A levels. The substandard GCSEs. The sadness of Teddy's life nobody seemed able to save her from.

'I mean, in a relationship. You don't have to be beholden to him. Women don't have to put up with stuff like they used to.'

Teddy did an enormous snort. 'Like you don't?' she scoffed.

'What do you mean?'

'You're *beholden* to my dad. You're always cleaning and washing up and stuff and putting up with things.'

Rachel laughed. 'That's not the same, that's just domestic stuff. When you love someone, you'll want to do all that for them. Dad does things for me.' She remembered, though, she had once told a man visiting from America she was an assistant, and that she had revealed that information like a wound.

'God, *I* won't. I'm not ever getting married . . . into slavery.'

'Slavery! I wouldn't put it quite like that! Marriage is lovely!'

Rachel and Jonny had married on a June morning in 1991, at St Edwin's. There had been a meringue and top hat and tails. They had celebrated with a sumptuous wedding breakfast in a marquee in the back garden of Crofters, and dancing into the night. Their marriage was to be nothing like her parents'. It was to be joyous and long-lasting. She shuddered when she thought of how her parents' marriage had ended, and the 'why' of it she now knew.

'And, well, you might change your mind,' Rachel added. *As long as it's not with Lee.*

'I won't,' said Teddy. 'I believe you can sustain a successful relationship without the stranglehold of marriage.'

Rachel laughed again. 'When it's love, you might think differently,' she said, but she thought again of her parents, and yes, their marriage had been a stranglehold on them both, and the fresh, terrible knowledge Rachel had on their demise was a stranglehold on her too.

'Oh, I love Lee. It's all-consuming,' Teddy added dramatically.

'Yet he's still a bastard . . .'

'You wouldn't understand,' said Teddy, with a superior sigh. 'There's no constraint to our relationship, no predictability, no monotony.' She sounded so earnest, so sure of herself, Rachel wanted to laugh, and then cry. 'There's a freedom in our unpredictable union.' Her stepdaughter sounded like a character in one of Lee's plays. His most notorious to date, *Love Comes A Stealthy Night*, featured a woman in a see-through nightie who spent a twenty-minute monologue lamenting the passing of a man who had once beaten her black and blue. 'And, knowing *me*, I guess I'm always going to be the sort of person who goes for bad boys.'

'Seriously, Teddy,' Rachel said, taking her gently by the shoulders. 'He's not good for you, love. Please don't waste too much of your time on him, *with* him.'

'We love each other,' Teddy repeated simply.

'Sometimes love isn't enough,' said Rachel. 'Sometimes you have to think about your life, the whole of it. Where it's going. Where it's going to end up.' She wanted to implore Teddy to leave Lee, to tell him she was better than him, that she deserved better, to walk off into the sunset. But there was currently no sunset for Teddy, no horizon beyond the confines of Fincham St George. And as long as Teddy stayed in the village, Rachel couldn't see her being free of Lee Hope.

'Do *you*?' asked Teddy. 'Do you know where your life's going?'

'Well, of course I do.' Teddy's face was beginning to set in that stubborn look she had, the look that could turn to quick anger. Rachel didn't have time now to explain everything to her, that if your goal was home and family and security, you would do anything to keep it, you'd be that occasional assistant, you'd turn away from chance encounters that might undermine everything you'd ever worked for. You wouldn't rock the boat too hard in case it capsized – she knew that now, more than ever. 'Anyway,' Rachel continued, purposely lightening her voice, 'I hope Lee is kind to you tonight and the evening ends on a happy note.'

The doorbell rang.

'You should get that,' Teddy said chippily, walking out of the kitchen. 'I'm going for a shower.'

Jonny's agent, London literary legend Michael Sallis, was standing in the porch. He was a slight man, shaped like a runner bean, with a penchant for a striped blazer whatever the weather.

'You're early, Michael!'

'I know, I know, forever at the mercy of the British railway timetable . . . I'm *so* sorry,' he said, stepping over the threshold and shrugging off his blazer to hand to her.

'It's fine, honestly. How lovely to see you! How are you?'

'Strange to be out of London, dear girl,' he said, wiping his forehead with a handkerchief. 'I feel quite discombobulated.'

Rachel had met Michael several times over the years. Mostly when she had been what Jonny called 'dragged up to London', as though it had been a terrible inconvenience for her to stay at the Marriott and have lunch at The Ivy.

Rachel loved London. She loved the cool, pale buildings and the light between them. The busyness, the people. And dragging Jonny back to Oxford would be more apt; he always got over-excited and drank too much on these occasions, looking around him in The Ivy like an excited child. She practically had to wrestle him back on to the train afterwards, where he would clasp her hands and kiss her at intervals and say how lucky they both were, how very, *very* lucky.

'A glass of cold Chablis, Michael?' Rachel suggested.

'Perfect.'

'Michael!' declared Jonny, appearing from the study. 'Marvellous to see you!'

'You, too, dear boy.' They shook hands. Transformed it into a hug and a backslap. 'How's the work in progress coming along?' Michael asked.

'Oh, swimmingly, swimmingly,' said Jonny. 'You know how it is.'

'Well, indeed I don't,' said Michael, following him into the sitting room, 'but as long as you're putting pen to paper, or fingers to computer keyboard, that's the main thing . . .'

They disappeared into the sitting room, where Rachel knew Jonny would sit in the big leather armchair and Michael would be directed to the chesterfield sofa, and they would hitch up the knees of trousers and await their drinks.

'Here she is,' said Michael, as Rachel appeared with two glasses of white wine. 'Just what the doctor ordered. Oh, and speaking of which – you might like to hear this, too, Rachel,' he added, patting the sofa cushion next to him. 'The publicist has had a call from the *Observer* – they want to talk to you about the accident, Jonny.'

'Again?' Rachel sat down next to Michael.

'Again,' he continued. 'People are still fascinated by it, you know. As long as you keep churning out those fantastic books, I think they always will be.'

Jonny nodded. 'OK,' he smiled. 'Just point me in their direction.'

Jonny was great with the press. He enjoyed talking to them – print, radio, television if he was lucky. He told hilarious and slightly embroidered anecdotes about mishaps and things that had happened to him at parties. He told not so hilarious stories – detailed, honest stories – about bigger things: his early childhood at Magdalen, his struggles to find success. And the accident was the biggest story of all.

'Tuesday?' said Michael. 'The publicist will call you to set things up.'

'Excellent.' Jonny took a glug of his wine.

Rachel stood up. 'I need to get on,' she said. She had the starter to finish, then she needed to go and get changed, make herself dinner party presentable. As she excused herself to the kitchen, Jonny and Michael started to talk about the timeframe of the interview. How it would no doubt be preceded by a photo shoot at Maida Vale and followed by a lunch with the reporter.

The accident had changed everything. It was funny, really. Jonny used to say, 'I would be so good at being famous.'

And then he was. Because of the accident.

Jonny became famous and then he became a famous author.

# Chapter Sixteen

Jonny had been at a book event in the ballroom of the Fordham Hotel in London, in the spring of 1989, when there had been a gas explosion in its adjacent kitchen and eight people had been killed, including the famous author Bertie Hinch-Wells, creator of the multimillion-selling Alistair Atkins detective novels.

Jonny was the sole survivor of the accident. He had been found wandering, dazed and confused, on Wardour Street, with an ashen face, dusty hair and a series of strangled sobs. He'd only been in that ballroom that morning because his small publisher was friendly with someone at Bertie's big publisher and a favour had been served up, allowing Jonny to 'piggy-back' for the day. Both he and Bertie had recently published new books: Bertie's expected to fly to the top of the fiction charts; Jonny's likely to sink without a trace.

'Please help,' Jonny, the piggy-backer, had said, as he'd collapsed on the pavement at some poor woman's feet, but not before a photographer from the *Telegraph*, on his way to the scene, had captured his face: blackened, despairing and destined for the front page.

An hour later, the police had called Rachel and she'd rushed up to London. There had been a clutter of camera people in Jonny's hospital room, a starchy bed from which he wept for the kitchen staff and the members of the publishing team who'd died. He wept for Bertie Hinch-Wells, said he'd tried to save him, but it had been impossible. Sobbed about a heavy beam he could not wrench from him, before he'd staggered to a fire exit and on to the street.

Rachel had held his hand as he'd told his story and thanked God he was alive. Hadn't there been too many accidents in her life, too many loved ones ripped from her? So much loss. She was so thankful, she couldn't think beyond his hospital room, or pay heed to the future waiting for them outside. She had no idea what a strange, fortuitous turn of fate the explosion was going to bring about in Jonny's life.

Michael Sallis, top London literary agent, phoned Jonny three days after he got home from hospital. Michael Sallis – who'd been Bertie's agent, missing from the event because he was at his villa in the South of France – had devoured all three of Jonny's books. Michael Sallis – having seen, along with the rest of the nation, Jonny Trent's dazed, heartbroken face in all the papers, next to a photo of the portly Bertie Hinch-Wells, and under a headline about how this accidental hero had tried to save the much-loved author – wanted to become his agent.

Jonny was no longer on the brink; he had been propelled over the edge and lifted high . . . higher than a soaring eagle or a jumbo jet or a bloody NASA spaceship. The metaphors came thick and fast that afternoon from Jonny, after Michael's phone call. He and Rachel finally concluded their celebrations with a slice of Battenberg and a glass of Asti Spumante, out in the sloped garden of their tiny cottage, and Jonny's final metaphor of the afternoon was that he was the *Very Hungry Caterpillar* who had finally become the butterfly. Then they had both grown sad, as this good fortune had come from tragedy, from eight lives lost, but, as Jonny had put it, 'it was just one of those awful, awful things, but if the best could be made of it, for someone, then wasn't that OK?'

Today, Jonny was number one in the *Sunday Times* bestseller list. He asked if maybe she could take a photo of his book on the shelves at WH Smith when she flew to Morocco tomorrow.

'If you have to go, that is,' he added, uncharacteristically grumpily. He had grunted and harrumphed this morning, and said she'd better bring him back a Toblerone and not to talk to anyone on the flight – hadn't Nikita met her warring lover, Andre Androvski, on a flight to Islamabad?

She would miss Jonny, of course she would, on this trip to Morocco, but she was excited. *It's going to be great for Vivaldi's,* she thought, as she stood at the kitchen sink, *and great for me.* There was a bird in the garden, a chaffinch, hopping along the back hedge. Absent-mindedly, she admired the way its neat wings tucked into themselves.

There was a commotion at the back door and Rachel could make out Lee's rangy shape behind the frosted glass. He shuffled in without a word, but with three bulging Tesco bags of things they didn't need: huge round French cheeses, bottles of own-brand red wine (Jonny now used a posh mail order company for his vintage red), a massive bunch of dusty black grapes in a brown paper bag and a very ugly beige candle in a glass Kilner jar – all which he pulled from the bags and plonked on the kitchen worktop with a lacklustre flourish.

'You shouldn't have,' Rachel said truthfully.

'Just my little contribution,' Lee smile-scowled, twisting the huge gold signet ring on the little finger of his left hand back into position. The ring was a sign of Lee's newly acquired wealth. Somehow, he had ended up buying the building company he'd worked for as a plasterer, and he now did people's extensions. He also had a spindly beard, which Rachel imagined he tugged on, his eyes narrowed, as he priced up a job. The beard was great for the whole playwright gig, too, she reckoned, adding that touch of gravitas.

Lee had turned up the evening after the accident, in 1989, when Jonny was home from hospital, and the pair of them had got straight on to the whisky, nursing giant tumblers of it until 3 a.m. and talking in loud then gradually muted voices. Rachel had gone up to bed at ten and she found Lee on the sofa in the morning, the end of his spindly beard flapped on to one of her chenille cushions. Not long after, plans emerged for Lee's first play – a pastiche of *Of Mice and Men*, set in Chipping Norton.

'Where shall I put everything?' Lee asked now, over the round French cheeses.

*Back in the shops?* thought Rachel to herself. She put the cheese and the grapes in the fridge, the wine and the ugly candle in the utility room.

'Aren't you going to put that out?' he asked.

'Maybe later,' she said.

Lee hopped up on to one of their high stools, leaving his pipe-cleaner legs, in board shorts, dangling.

'Jonny tells me you're leaving him.'

'For Marrakesh?' Rachel said, wiping down the counter where the cheese had been. 'Yes, I'm flying there tomorrow,' she said happily. 'Going to see about an artist.'

'Nice,' he said disinterestedly. 'Is it going to be hot?'

'About eighty, I think – thirty-two degrees.'

'Nice.'

Jonny wandered into the kitchen, followed by Michael.

'We've come for a replenishment,' Jonny said. 'Evening, my friend. This is Lee,' he explained to Michael. 'My playwright buddy I was telling you about.'

Rachel silently rolled her eyes.

144

'Pleased to meet you,' said Lee, limply shaking Michael's hand. 'You really OK with letting your missus fly off to foreign lands?' he asked Jonny, once the introductions were over.

'Of course,' Jonny said with an indulgent smile, resting his hand on Rachel's shoulder. 'The lady appears to be going places.'

'What about all them Arabs? Those predatory men . . . ?'

'They won't go after Rachel!' laughed Jonny.

'Charming!' Rachel said, whacking him teasingly with her dishcloth.

'They want blondes,' qualified Jonny. He gestured for Michael to sit down on another stool. 'Anyway, my Rach is far too serious and sensible to go off with a Moroccan, aren't you?'

'That's hardly a flattering description of me, but no, of course I wouldn't.'

'You'd never leave me, would you, Rachel?' He pretended to pout, pulling her closer to him.

She laughed and patted his hand on her waist. 'You know I wouldn't.' She'd seen what leaving did to the people left behind. She'd felt the numbing pain of her dad slipping off to Stephanie's house; she'd soaked up her mother's misery and bitterness. And when they'd both left her, in a way she'd absorbed the full truth of it, like blood into bone, after that unexpected revelation, she'd vowed her own life would be knitted together so tightly it could never be unravelled.

Jonny tickled her in the ribs. Yelping, she tried to wriggle away. 'I'm happy for her,' he said. 'I'm happy with everything she does. Proud, too.' He planted a tender kiss on her forehead. 'You know I love you,' he said.

She let herself melt into that kiss, that touch. 'Yes, I know you do.'

'*Hello*, Lee.'

Teddy was in the doorway, her face pinched and drained; heavily made-up eyes and a plum-coloured lipstick on her tiny rosebud lips. She was wearing a long black slip dress and a black velvet choker.

'Hello, lover,' said Lee, making Rachel cringe. He went over and embraced Teddy, grabbing at her bottom through the silk of her dress. 'How are ya?'

'Good, thanks,' said Teddy breathlessly. She slipped her hand into his and Lee turned on his charming smile for her to bask in. Rachel excused herself to go upstairs and get changed. When she came down, a rumbling diesel taxi was pulling up outside and a woman heavily accessorised with towering platform sandals and an enormous gilt-chained handbag fell out of the back and staggered up the front path, laughing her raven-haired head off.

'Call off the cavalry!' Zoe giggled, 'I'm here!' and in a drench of Trésor and a tumble of tanned limbs, she was bundled into the house and immediately handed a glass of champagne.

'Lovely to see you,' Jonny beamed.

'Likewise,' she slurped. 'Congratulations.'

'The gang's all here!' declared Jonny, 'except my editor, of course, but she's out of town and missing all the fun,' and he led them to the dining table. Rachel had sat Lee and Teddy apart, but Teddy switched the place cards as soon as they got to the table and Lee slipped into the chair next to her with a wolfish grin. Rachel glanced at Jonny, but he was settling Zoe and patting Michael convivially on the back. Once the candles were lit and their glasses were full, Jonny raised a toast.

'To me, I guess!' he grinned.

'To Jonny!' echoed the crowd and Rachel slipped from her seat to the kitchen. He deserved it, this night, she thought, as she opened the fridge and took out the pre-plated smoked salmon. He deserved every second. He was a huge success and rightly so, with his wonderful books that had finally caught everyone's attention as they always should have done. And she knew exactly how it would flow, this celebration. Jonny would get happily drunk, turn the music up then lead everyone into the back garden for an under-the-stars disco. Michael would start the evening telling delicious literary snippets about Virginia Woolf and George Orwell, then get very silly and attempt the Macarena. Zoe would chain-smoke Marlboro Lights all night, get black lips from red wine and hitch her AllSaints dress into her knickers for the garden disco. And Rachel could tell just by looking at them that Lee and Teddy's toxic on-off relationship would be back on by the end of the evening. That they would slope off down the lane to Lee's bungalow around midnight, a gangly arm slipped round a slight shoulder and the tips of their gesticulating cigarettes fireflies in the night.

And Rachel would toast her husband's success and dance under the stars too. She'd take Jonny's shoes off for him at the end of the night, as he lay on the bed with all his clothes on, and place them on the floor. She'd slip into the cool sheets beside him. But through it all, the anticipation of her trip to Morocco would be like a jewel held in the palm of her hand.

Rachel loaded a gilt tray with the *amuse-bouches* and walked into the dining room to loud cheers and Jonny wolf-whistling.

'Oh, stop it,' she protested. 'You're acting as though I'm bringing in the Crown Jewels, or something!'

'As good as,' said Jonny, slipping his arm round her waist as she balanced the tray on the edge of the table and started offloading the plates. 'As good as.'

And Rachel thought of that jewel of anticipation and knew that, during the course of Jonny's night, she would polish it until it shone.

# Chapter Seventeen

'. . . and the outside air temperature on landing will be a balmy forty-two degrees.'

Some of the passengers, including Rachel sitting in the window seat of 34A, 'Ooh'd loudly. One man, a few rows in front of her, a shiny bald head crowning merrily above his seat, happily exclaimed 'Bloody hell!' and high-fived the grinning woman next to him. They would be the same people who clapped when the plane landed, but Rachel would too.

Forty-two degrees . . . July so far in Oxfordshire had been quite glorious, but this was something else. Unaccustomed. Exotic. Rachel planned to bathe in Marrakesh's heat, luxuriate in it; soak up every North African ray of sun and every new experience this business trip offered her.

She settled back in her seat for the landing. A baby, propped over its father's shoulder on the seat in front, stretched its pudgy hand into the gap between the seats. Rachel resisted the urge to touch it, to squeeze that soft, doughy and delicious flesh. In a few minutes, when they landed, elderly people on their way to the exit would coo 'Oh, wasn't she good?', while Rachel's heart would be at risk of expanding, then contracting to a shrivelled raisin. From all the wanting. The longing. But she wouldn't let it. A baby in a dinosaur Babygro would not derail her today. She closed her eyes and let the plane take her down to Marrakesh.

Twenty-five minutes later, the baby was bobbing up the aisle, Rachel moving slowly behind. She had clapped on landing. She felt pure joy as she emerged into the bright sunshine at the top of the metal stairs and breathed in the dry heat of the air, pulling her sunglasses from her handbag.

The taxi into the centre of Marrakesh had air conditioning but Rachel opened the window so she could continue to feel that North African air. The taxi sped and sputtered through streets of beige and dusky pink: pink, low-rise commercial buildings; beige, chalky pavements. There were helmet-free people on puttering mopeds, children and baskets and bags and livestock almost toppling off them. Meandering men, in djellabas and scuffing sandals, staring at her with detached curiosity. Sparse areas of scrubby wasteland. Crusty, half-finished constructions, skeletal with scaffolding. And the dusk, coming now, and slowly turning everything khaki.

'Lady!' a woman called to her, holding up a handful of coloured beaded necklaces and proffering them with a gap-toothed grin, as the taxi slowed at a junction. '*Madame!*' And Rachel waved a 'no, thank you' at her as the taxi beetled away.

She was welcomed at the Felicity Hotel by a fruity cocktail and a uniformed bellboy, who heaved her case on to a gilt trolley and trundled it away while she checked in. She was given a key and directed to the lifts at the far side of the lobby. There were a few people lounging in the lobby, which opened, through double doors, to a tiled courtyard and, beyond, the pool area.

Three storeys up, at the end of a hushed corridor, her room was all mahogany and cloisonné lamps, with a view over a small yard, where tea towels hung motionless on a line and she could make out two sleeping cats curled into each other in a yin-yang circle, under an olive tree.

The bellboy knocked at the door, with her cases.

'Thank you so much. What time is dinner?' she asked him.

'Seven until ten,' he said. 'Majorelle Room.'

She thanked him again and tipped him five dirham. Heaved her suitcase on to the bed and started to unpack. There were two gifts at the bottom of her case, one wrapped clumsily in stripy paper, the Sellotape ill-applied and curling; the other in a waxy paper bag, folded over at the top and secured with a pink paper-clip. They were birthday presents from Jonny and Teddy, plus a thin stack of pastel-coloured cards wrapped inside a beach dress. It didn't matter to Rachel that she was away for her thirty-seventh birthday. Birthdays had not been a big deal to her since her parents died. She placed the gifts and the cards on top of the safe in one of the wardrobes.

Her case unpacked, she reached for the telephone. Jonny would be in his study, frowning over Nikita and her latest antics, before cobbling himself some burnt scrambled eggs and exasperatedly taking off to the pub for something decent. As she picked up the receiver and dialled their number, she could already hear herself laughing at his tales of expedited domestic ineptitude and answering his queries about where things were.

He answered on the second ring.

It was quiet in the Majorelle Room. The lighting was low, sourced from hanging lanterns of red and gold; the buffet helmed by chefs in white hats smiling behind gleaming stainless-steel counters. Many different languages floated in the air around her: Arabic, Moroccan, English, German . . . Rachel ordered a tagine and enjoyed the mild spice of it, the chunks of butternut squash, the spindly shards of okra. She nursed a tumbler of warm red wine. In her eyeline was a businessman in a cheap suit, dining alone with a box file in front of him. Every time she looked up, he was staring at her, until she didn't dare look up at all. When she finished eating, she found he was standing there, right by her table, his lapels and his too-long sleeves almost static with polyester.

'I hope you enjoyed your dinner,' he said, in a French accent.

'Yes, very much, thank you.'

'How do you like our city of Marrakesh?'

'Well, I haven't seen it yet,' she said. 'I've only just arrived.'

'Are you here on business?'

'Yes, I am.'

He was staring at her chest. She wanted him to go away.

'Can I join you?' He began to pull out a chair.

'No, thank you,' she said, standing up. 'I'm about to go back to my room.' Oh God, why had she said *that*?

'Maybe tomorrow night? I'm here for three nights. I come from Casablanca. I would really love some company.'

'No, thank you,' she repeated. 'I don't want company at all. Now, if you'll excuse me . . .'

She had never said 'Now, if you'll excuse me' in her life. As she walked away from the table, she felt his eyes boring a hole in her back. She didn't want to wish this, this early on in the trip, but she wished Jonny was here. It was 1997 and nothing had changed. Things didn't always get better, for women.

Up in her room, she looked down into the yard, where in dim lamplight she saw one of the cats stretched out on its back, turning over and over on the soil beneath the olive tree. The tea towels had gone. She stayed at the open window for a while, breathing in the warm night air, which was still twenty-eight degrees, even at 10 p.m., then came to the bed to read through some notes she had made for her meeting with Khalid Ziani tomorrow.

Ten thirty a.m., they had agreed, on that crackly phone call. She couldn't wait to meet him. Satisfied she knew each of his exhibited paintings by title and by detail, that she could explain how his work would fit so beautifully into Vivaldi's, she turned on the television and half-watched an Arabic soap opera until midnight, when the humming air con and the slamming of a distant door became her only acoustics.

Her adventure was only just beginning.

# Chapter Eighteen

*Who knew 10 a.m. in Marrakesh could already be so fearsomely hot?* thought Rachel, as her taxi driver dropped her off at the Bab Agnaou gate to the medina. As she got out of the car, she was immediately hit by a mingling cauldron of smells: spices and horse manure, hot cement and minty ancient stone, un-fragrant drains.

Life was in full, mid-morning bustling flow. There were men everywhere: in robes and sandals, strolling, talking in groups, shouting to each other from across the street. Women – far fewer of them – in hijabs and paving-slab-sweeping coloured kaftans (*djellaba* – long-sleeved – and *gandoura* – short-sleeved), clutching flimsy cloth shopping bags. She'd studied both traditional Moroccan dress and the dress code for Westerners, in the library, choosing her own outfit for today carefully: loose-fitting linen harem trousers, a vest top and a huge sweeping chiffon scarf, wrapped over her front and arms.

Traffic swarmed and horns blared, and taxis stopped and started, and a horse and cart scuttered into view and out again and, beyond her, just through the crumbling gate, was the medina and the maze of alleys in the belly of the city.

Rachel walked through the gate. She was in a tiny lane, uneven cement tiles underfoot, cross-hatched wooden or metal canopies above, patching over the sky at intervals. To either side, mysterious wooden doors were carved into ochre or slate blue or pale terracotta walls, with intriguing and ornate knockers; some of the doors were tiny, like from *Alice in Wonderland*. An ambling donkey was being led at a distant turn in the alley, the chime of a bicycle bell echoed ahead and then a moped appeared, careering up behind to overtake her, beeping furiously; one rider's foot on a pedal, the other in flip-flops, trailing on the ground as it slalomed past. Another moped approached, its rider two feet wider than his charge, wobbling pre-cariously. These moped drivers had impassive faces and shouted words in French or Arabic it was easy to guess the meaning of.

'*Allez!*' '*Aibtaead!*' – 'Move!' 'Out of the way!'

As she walked further, stalls and shops appeared, with a cor-nucopia of wares. Tiny square shops set into the walls, stuffed with leather handbags or rolled-up Berber carpets or watches or kaf-tans – layers and layers of them, hanging from rails. Ceramics and piles of spices and jewellery. Copper kettles and urns tied up like bunches of balloons, high in shop doorways. Tradesmen working in open-fronted workshops, cobbling shoes and shaping metalware.

She felt like she was in a painting. A woman in harem trousers and a wrapped scarf, caught in the maze of streets in Marrakesh. A woman who knew exactly where she was going, although she didn't, actually. She knew the gallery was on Rue Céline. She had a map. But there were so many twists and turns, and so much to distract, she knew she had probably gone wrong already.

Rachel stopped, hopping out of the way of another moped. She squeezed into an ornate doorway, cooking smells beyond it of lamb and mint, and studied the map again, as a donkey laden with ornate rugs and cushions trundled past.

'Lady, lady! You lost? Where you going?'

A young Moroccan man in a bright blue tracksuit, idle on a straddled pushbike – his elbows propped on the handlebars – was calling to her from the other side of the alley.

154

'The Céline Gallery,' she called back. 'Rue Céline?'

He cruised over to her, riding high off the saddle, a flip-flopped foot stretched languorously down to the lower pedal.

'I can show you.' He held out his palm. 'I show you for dirham.'

'Oh, you want money?' She rummaged in her bag, pulled out a ten-dirham note and placed it in his hand. He bounced up on the saddle of the bike and took off on it, flicking his head over his shoulder.

'This way,' he said, with a grin. 'Follow me.'

He cycled slowly, his bum above the saddle, swaying a huge 'Nike' at her. He turned left, then right, then left again, taking her deeper into the maze of alleys. Bikes buzzed and chimed past; locals and tourists trailed through and around them; a donkey weighed down with more of those bronze goblets clanked as it swayed past. Rachel stepped in and out of shapes of sunlight, on the cobblestones and stetches of uneven concrete, as the swaying 'Nike' led the way and the makeshift canopies overhead created a jigsaw of shade and light.

When she felt she'd been following it for ever, finally the Nike bottom came to rest in front of a small wooden doorway in an expanse of crumbly ochre wall.

'Here,' her guide said.

'Here?' There were no windows, no shop front, just this wooden door with hammered panels and a small brass ring knocker.

'Yes. You want me to wait? I wait for ten dirham extra?'

'No, it's OK,' she said. He nodded, alighted his bike and sailed off, loudly whistling 'Wonderwall', for her obvious benefit. She approached the door – had she been conned? Was this really it? Yes, this was Rue Céline; there was a small sign further along the wall. She rapped hesitantly at the door and waited. Nothing. She tried again with the brass knocker. Still nothing. Then she turned the ring and the door swung lazily open on to a tiny chalk-white vestibule. She stepped down into it, immediately feeling the damp coolness of the place, inhaling the fragrance of mint and stone. There was an arch to the right, which she walked through.

A small square room with rough peach walls and a white pitted floor was filled with the art of Khalid Ziani. Rachel feasted on the colours, moving from one painting to the next, soaking up the hyper-oranges and golds, the ruby reds and aquamarine blues, the tart earthy browns and saturated yellows. The richness and vibrancy of Marrakesh in a kaleidoscope of glory. Then, the intricate line sketches, overlaying the blushes and strokes of colour; flicks and tendrils and suggestions of people and buildings. Each painting drew her in and refused to let her go until her eyes had roamed over every inch. She was right to come, she knew. There was something really special about these paintings and she wanted them for Vivaldi's.

It was just after ten thirty, the allotted meeting time. She would wait. Or she could try that little door at the back of the gallery? Behind it was an elderly gentleman, eating a pastry at a wooden table, the sleeves of his djellaba swishing golden crumbs on to the uneven floor.

'*Bonjour,*' she said.

'*Bonjour, madame.*'

And that was the limit of her French. 'Do you speak English?'

'Yes, a little.'

'I'm looking for the artist. Khalid Ziani,' she said. 'I was supposed to be meeting him here. At this time.' Oh God, she was doing that awful thing of speaking with the inflection, and almost the accent, of the person she was talking to. Her dad used to do that all the time, on holidays to Greece, those holidays that used to be fun but were punctuated, later, by him wandering off, cigarette in hand, and making furtive phone calls from payphones with plastic surrounds.

'Khalid? Sometimes he come, sometimes not come. You can wait. Or come back. He not tell me,' he added.

'He was *supposed* to come,' she said. 'We arranged it?'

The man looked blankly at her. 'You may wait,' he said, inconclusively. He returned to his pastry.

'I'll wait,' she echoed.

She moved back into the gallery and stood in front of a painting of market morning in the Jemaa El'Fnaa – Marrakesh's main square, in the centre of the medina – and marvelled at Khalid's depiction of the bustling people, the fruit stalls, the market sellers; the elongated shapes, the almost neon of the colours. She should go there. Perhaps she should start to plan all sorts of excursions, in case she didn't manage to meet Khalid after all.

'Oh well, at least you had a nice holiday,' Jonny would say if her mission were thwarted. He would be sorry, but he would say there were other artists and other opportunities. Mostly he would just be happy that she was back at home, with him.

A small group of people entered the gallery. French tourists, she imagined, from their stylish Marrakesh sightseeing clothes and the lyrical sound of their voices. Rachel smiled at them shyly as they moved from painting to painting, uttering exclamations. She stepped towards a small painting, only six inches square, and placed quite near to the ground. She crouched down on one knee.

'Wow,' she said to herself. The painting was of the Jemaa El'Fnaa at night: ghostlike figures in djellabas blurring across a dark blue background as lights of gold and butterscotch streaked behind them. It was beautiful. She stayed in her crouched position and simply stared at it, for a long time. Absorbed and transported to a place not far from here that she was yet to explore. She must go there at night, Rachel thought. She must do that while she was here.

'It's fantastic, isn't it?'

A man was standing behind her. From her crouch, she could make out sandy-coloured suede shoes. The hem of khaki linen trousers.

'Yes,' she said. She could feel her heels against the cotton of her harem pants.

'An all-round improvement on a Pierrot with a balloon, wouldn't you say?'

The voice was American. Rachel's heart hitched like it did when she almost tripped on the carpeted bottom stair at home, or when she remembered something she'd forgotten.

'It *is* you, isn't it?' the voice said, and – holding her breath – Rachel turned around.

# Chapter Nineteen

Gabe – astonishingly, inexplicably, he was there – was wearing a black T-shirt above khaki trousers and suede lace-up shoes. His hair was shorter, with a little grey – just a hint – at the sides. His blue eyes had a sunburst of fine lines from each corner.

'Hello,' he said.

'Hello,' she replied, her voice hesitant, disbelieving.

'I thought it was you,' he said. He was smiling at her, like he had before. Ten, eleven years ago? *Eleven* years ago. Suddenly she wasn't here, in Morocco, but back in another gallery – hers, before it *became* hers – where a man had sat back on his haunches and she had sat cross-legged on the floor, very close to him, and her heart had felt the same as it did now. Not safe within her.

'And it's you,' she replied. The quiet American who liked The Cure and once pushed a bike with a basket past the window of a restaurant. Who'd bandaged up a cut finger and tried not to notice she'd been crying in the front seat of her car. Who'd told her she was beautiful, on the back step of an English village hall.

She stood up, smoothing down the front of her scarf and her hair away from her face.

'It's good to see you,' he said gently.

'And you.' She drank him in, curiously, like Alice drank from that tiny bottle. His face, his hair, his eyes. How he looked different and yet not at all so.

'What are you doing in Marrakesh?' His eyes were fixed on hers and hers on his.

'I'm here to look for this artist,' she said, gesturing rather foolishly with her hands around the gallery. 'Khalid Ziani. To talk to him on behalf of the gallery. How about you?'

'Khalid is a friend of mine,' said Gabe. 'We met in Belarus.'

'Oh!'

'The exchange programme, if you remember?'

'Yes, I think I do.'

'I came for the exhibition,' Gabe added. He smiled at her and she felt like a butterfly was tentatively opening up its wings inside her and spreading them to all her corners. 'I come to Marrakesh when I can. So,' he said, 'I guess Faith sent you here?'

'You remember her name,' Rachel replied.

'I remember everything.'

She realised her hands were clasped behind her back, like a young girl standing up in assembly, about to do a reading. She was sure her cheeks were almost as red as a schoolgirl's.

'Faith doesn't own the gallery any more,' she said, as the memory of his eyes, his lips, his face and his words blended with the sight of him now. 'I do.'

'Really?'

'Yes, I bought it. It's mine.'

'Amazing. And did you do all the things you said you'd do?'

'Yep,' she grinned. She remembered listing all her fantasy plans to him. *I've made them all come true*, she thought – including the tiny courtyard garden, at the rear of the gallery, for parties.

'Did you get rid of the Pierrots?'

'Every single one.'

He laughed. How wonderful and disconcerting it was to hear that laugh again. 'Well, that's fantastic, Rachel!' he said, and when he said her name, she felt like she had stepped off a cliff into nothing at all. 'Congratulations! How did you discover Khalid?'

'In a magazine. I've come to find out if I can exhibit him in Vivaldi's – that's the name of the gallery now.'

'*The Four Seasons*? Of course,' Gabe nodded. 'Very you. I like that.'

Rachel blushed a little more. He had remembered her love of all the seasons, she mused. She had thought about their conversations many times. She remembered he'd been intense and curious and challenging and infuriating. Rachel wondered what had changed about him, in all these years, and what had stayed the same.

'This is so weird,' she said.

'Yes,' he said, 'and nice.' He smiled at her again, his eyes kind and so pleased to see her, it seemed, that the years that had passed since they last saw each other both expanded to a lifetime and contracted to a moment.

'So, were you expecting Khalid to be here?' she asked, when the moment had pulsed between them for far too long. She tried to make her question sound normal, unaffected, like it was nothing much to bump into him here, like this. 'I had arranged to meet him at this time but he's not here, and the man out the back doesn't seem to know anything.'

'Ah, that's Loco,' commented Gabe. 'And I arranged to meet Khalid here today too, but he's not that good with arrangements. If he's not here, then he's in his studio,' he added, and he looked at her and smiled again. 'Want me to take you?'

'Take me?' Her hands were now on the cool wall behind her, steadying her.

'Yes. If you'd like to see him. It isn't far from here.'

'He won't mind me pitching up?'

'He stood *you* up,' said Gabe. 'Shall we?'

She nodded, light-headed, and then she was back out in the criss-crossed shade of the alley, but not quite into reality, as Gabe was still with her. There were more men sitting in the doorways of their shops, on little stools. More running children in Adidas vest tops, shorts and sandals. More mopeds. A large man swayed past with a small child balanced on his lap, a row of signet rings almost welded to the handlebars. All these people and things were hazy moving images with her in the middle. Gabe was here. In Marrakesh.

'This way,' he said, and they walked to the end of the alley, past market stalls and crusty ochre walls, studded with more doors of varying size and mystery – the ground beneath their feet uneven.

'So, you came to Marrakesh especially to see Khalid?' she asked him eventually. She felt shy. The surprise of him had completely turned the already extraordinary day on its head and she was looking down on it, dazed.

'Yes,' Gabe said, and she noticed the grey at the sides of his hair a little more, in the sunlight. It suited him. 'I was due a trip – it's been a coupla years, actually – and I thought why not? Just get on a plane. Come to Marrakesh. See my old buddy.' He grabbed her arm and pulled her out of the way of another carousing moped, coming up behind them. 'This way,' he said, and they turned left, into an alley that looked just like the one before, in this maze. A man from a watch shop tried to call them over but Gabe took his hand from her arm and waved him a 'no, thank you'. 'You? You didn't come with Jonny?'

'No. I'm here by myself.' She saw Gabe glancing at her left hand, her rings glinting in chequered sunlight. It was the arm he had touched; she could still feel the tips of his fingers.

'I've been hearing about him. I hear things are going very well for him and his Nikita.'

162

'Yes, very well.'

'I'm sorry he got caught up in that explosion a few years ago.'

'You knew about that? Thank you. Yes, it was awful.' She remembered the one Gabe had escaped. They passed a tiny kiosk selling water and packets of sweets. Lay's crisps.

'Would you like some water?' Gabe asked. 'It's pretty hot. Shall we stop?'

'Yes, please,' she replied gratefully.

Gabe bought two small bottles of chilled water, condensation dripping down their sides, and they stood and sipped from them. Two strangers who had just bumped into each other after a decade, like they were no more than a photograph to each other, with a line or two of scant details scrolled on the back.

How strange it was, yet not strange at all. Rachel wondered what he thought of her now. He had chanced upon her lost in a painting. Did he notice the little lines around her eyes? The slight softening of her features? Did he look at her and remember what he'd said to her in the car park of the village hall? The words she'd been so surprised by but had never forgotten.

'Shall we walk again?' he asked.

'Yes.'

'How many times have you been to Marrakesh?' she asked him. She had been staring at mysterious doorways in mysterious walls, trying to make herself wonder who or what was behind. Trying not to look at his face. *His* new lines, that unfairly made him look more handsome.

'Maybe five, in total,' he said. 'I love it here. I love the craziness. The colours. The noise. The smells.'

They both laughed. They were passing another old and not particularly fragrant donkey.

'Each time to see Khalid?'

'Yes. And you?'

'First time,' said Rachel. The bottle of water was slippery in her hand. 'And I love it so far, though I really haven't seen anything yet.'

'There's lots to see,' he said. 'And to sample. Have you tried the mint tea?' he asked.

'Yes, I had some at dinner last night.' She remembered the creepy businessman and hoped she wouldn't see him again. The sterile oasis of her hotel was far removed from this real Marrakesh: the hot dusty maze of streets, the slices of sun between buildings, the hubbub and chatter in both French and Arabic. The peril of bumping into someone from long ago, for wasn't there peril and consequence and danger everywhere?

'How's your art?' she asked. 'The trees?'

'The trees are good,' smiled Gabe.

'Did you buy that house? The one on the corner with the oak tree in the front garden?'

'I did buy that house!' laughed Gabe, looking at her curiously. 'It's a lovely spot. Have you seen Aunt Julia at all?' he asked. 'Well, I write to her, of course, and she came out to see me, in Jud, a coupla years back. I know she's rarely spotted in the village, but does she look well?'

'There was a rare sighting at the greengrocer's recently,' said Rachel. 'She was arguing about the price of cabbages and looking very well indeed.'

Gabe threw his head back and laughed. 'Same old Aunt Julia,' he said. 'Glad to hear it.'

'How is Jud?' she asked, marvelling at that laugh and how she could have ever let herself forget the sound of it.

'Population eighty-six,' he smiled.

'Growing,' she nodded.

'Exponentially,' he grinned. 'So, what else has been going on in your life?' he asked, as he steered her past a sleeping man in a doorway, a sapphire-coloured duvet over his prone body.

164

Her face crimsoned. Was he asking her about children?

'Well, I've moved house,' Rachel said, a little too breezily. '*We* have. Jonny and me. We moved down to the lane where that lunch party was, you know, that day?'

'How could I forget? The overbearing Mrs Bottomley,' he smiled. Gabe was looking at her closely again. *He knows I don't have children*, she thought. He knew it from her face. How she walked. How she carried herself. She was marked with it. He knew it and she knew now he wouldn't ask.

'And how is your stepdaughter? Tatiana, is it?'

*You remember.* 'Challenging,' smiled Rachel sadly. 'And a real worry. Teddy's nineteen, floundering, really . . . I'm not sure I'd have time to tell you about her, really, before we get there.' And she didn't want to get upset about her. Not here, not now. 'How far are we from the studio?'

'About four more streets away. Nearly there.'

They walked in silence for a while, navigating people and transport and animals and the uneven stone path. A mother carrying a child in a sling, big eyes staring at her as he sailed past. *Always a stepmother, never a mother*, she thought. Her window of hope was shortening, gradually being shut. The baby on the plane *had* affected her. The white Babygro, the snuggle of a soft cheek. She feared she would never walk up the aisle of a plane with a baby on her shoulder.

'Are you OK?'

'Yes.' Rachel suddenly wanted to blurt it all out to him as they walked. The hurt, the pain, how the swinging pendulum of hope and disappointment was brutal and cruel. Instead, she looked away from his face and to the clutter and clatter of another alleyway.

'Here we are,' Gabe said finally.

They were at a doorway more than Gabe's height, with double doors in studded iron set into a rough and smooth peach wall.

There was a single doll's house window, high up on the wall, and a miscellany of barrels and old bicycles.

'We're here?' she asked.

'Yes,' said Gabe, smiling at her, and she put away her losses and her disappointment and let excitement in – at being here, and being here with him. 'Let's find out if Khalid is.'

# Chapter Twenty

Gabe gestured for Rachel to go in first and she stepped on to a patterned tiled floor of reds, greens, yellows, cobalts and coppers. It was cool in the narrow hallway, under a domed ceiling – and at the end of the hallway was an arched narrow doorway.

'Yes, through there,' said Gabe. 'Go ahead.'

'Oh!' she exclaimed. She was in a wide, low-ceilinged room, drenched in colour – on the walls, floor and ceiling. It was daubed with overlapping and jubilant swipes and ticks and swashes of paint – flashes of metallics – silvers, golds and bronzes – among the matts: blues, red and oranges. It was a womb of colour. It was crazy and joyful. She turned, taking it all in. And 'Oh!' she exclaimed again, as in one corner, almost camouflaged – as he himself was a rainbow splash of swooshes and paintbrush marks, on a great, engulfing smock – was a man on a low stool frowning at a canvas, a paintbrush clamped between his teeth like a matador with a rose.

She and Gabe stood silently watching as the man decided on a last stroke to complete a small dog, burrowing under a cloth bag. Finally, under his giant purple headphones, the man seemed to sense them, and when his eyes rested on Gabe, he leaped up, grinning.

'Gabriel, *mon amie! Bien venue, bien venue!* It's so good to see you, my friend. *Ahla oushela!*' He came rushing over, clasped Gabe by the shoulders, then went in for a hug.

'My old friend!' exclaimed Gabe warmly, from inside the hug. 'It's great to see you too, Khalid.'

Khalid held Gabe at the shoulders, slapped him gently round the cheeks, then hugged him warmly again, rocking them both from side to side. Rachel wondered if she should give a little cough, to signal her presence.

'Ah,' said Gabe, motioning at Rachel for her to step forward. 'This is Rachel. She was supposed to meet you at the gallery this morning but you're an unreliable rogue, so I brought her here.'

'Rachel? *Rachel!* From the gallery in Oxford! Oh, *tiens!* I'm so sorry!'

'It's OK,' Rachel said. 'Please don't worry about it. It's really nice to meet you.'

'That was today? I lose track of the day, like an old fool. *Attends.*' He clapped his hands together. 'Let me make mint tea for the both of you.'

He wafted in his billowing smock over to the back of the room where, on a mosaic-topped table, there was a polished urn and four upturned glass cups on a silver tray. Khalid expertly poured the tea from a great height into three of the glasses, steam rising to the studio's low ceiling.

'Come, sit, Gabe,' Khalid said, motioning to the seating there. 'And come, Rachel. Sit here, next to me. We can talk.'

They sat on low Moroccan pouffes. Rachel sipped at her mint tea, which was blisteringly hot; Gabe and Khalid blew on theirs to cool it. *They both look so happy to see each other*, Rachel thought. So tremendously thrilled. And *she*? she wondered. Was she truly happy to see Gabe again? Rachel didn't know. She wasn't certain, suddenly, that this wasn't the worst thing to have happened.

'So, how is everything?' Khalid asked Gabe. 'North Dakota? The trees? The art?'

'North Dakota is good. The art is good,' said Gabe. 'I recently showed at Fargo again and it went pretty well.'

'Great, great. I'm glad, my friend. I love your trees. And Sarah, how is she?'

'Sarah's good,' said Gabe and Rachel's heart froze a little, though it had no right to.

'Another one bites the dust,' said Khalid and he laughed, seemingly at his excellent use of idiomatic English.

'Sarah will be OK,' Gabe said, looking thoughtful before blowing on his tea again. 'She knows I was definitely not capable of making her happy.' He shook his head.

'So, still you search,' said Khalid.

'Hope over experience,' grimaced Gabe, and Rachel looked down at her lap.

*Sarah is an ex*, she thought. She remembered what Gabe said he had been looking for – real love, far from what his parents had experienced. That he'd described himself as a lost and wandering soul. She wondered what Sarah looked like.

'But you're OK?' urged Khalid. 'You're OK, my friend?'

'I'm good,' Gabe replied. As Rachel looked up, his smile returned and Khalid grabbed his upper arm and shook it affectionately.

'So, Rachel,' said Khalid, turning to her again, 'you've been to the Rue Céline and seen the exhibition?'

'Yes, I have,' she said, 'and it's truly wonderful.'

'Thank you.' He crossed his legs, under his expansive smock, and she could see he was wearing lime-green trainers. How strange she should find herself here. With these two men. A man she was seeking and a man she thought she would never see again, who was already making her feel and wonder things she couldn't quantify. Somehow, all roads had led her here, to this room, on this late morning in Marrakesh.

'I love all of your paintings, Khalid,' she said. 'I love your studio. I love the pieces you're working on now.' Her eyes cast around the studio, drinking in the dozens of canvases, the paintings, propped against the daubed walls. 'Can we talk shop?' she pressed. 'It's why I came to see you, after all. You don't mind, do you, Gabe?'

'Go for it,' said Gabe, sitting back on his stool, an amused look on his face. 'Strike while the iron is hot.'

She focused fully on the artist. 'I would love to exhibit five or maybe six of your paintings, Khalid, in my gallery, some new work, if you agree, of course . . .' she said, impassioned, 'as many pieces as you would like to give me . . .'

'In England?' Khalid stroked his chin.

'Oxford, yes.'

'Is it near the university? Your gallery?' he asked.

'No, not near the university, it's in a village.' She suddenly felt terribly parochial. 'A really pretty one, actually. I've brought my brochure,' she added, swiftly reaching into her bag, 'and we hope one day soon to have a website, you know, on the internet.'

'The world wide web? Yes, that is an opportunity for us all,' Khalid nodded, taking the brochure from her with paint-splattered fingers. 'The future is exciting, *non*?'

'I hope so.'

He flicked through the pages. 'And you have themed to the seasons?' he asked, looking at the photos of her current featured art.

'Yes.' She leaned forward on her pouffe, trying to gauge his reaction.

'And you're thinking of summer wall, for me?'

'Summer wall, yes,' she replied.

'Come,' he said, standing up and letting his smock billow, 'let me show you what I've been working on.'

He directed her over to the wall where three canvases stood overlapping one another. They were all paintings of souks and stalls within the medina, the colours even more vibrant, the overlaid lines stronger and more defined. Rachel had a feeling he had turned the lights up high in the studio when he painted these, that he had painted with both purpose and fire.

'Is this the sort of thing you want for your exhibition?' he asked.

'Oh, absolutely! I adore them!'

'And three more . . .' He spread his palms wide to indicate hypothetical works either not yet completed or stored elsewhere.

'Three more would be wonderful.'

Khalid nodded. 'And Gabe – has he exhibited in your gallery?' Gabe had stood up now too, and was wandering the studio, perusing the paintings. 'Is that how you know each other?'

'No, I met Gabe in England when he was visiting his aunt, who lives in the village. But he showed me his art.' Rachel remembered dancing to The Cure, circling round and round, and how Gabe had disturbed her. She wondered how the tree in his front garden in North Dakota looked in summer, when it was full of leaves. She wondered if the tree in front of the hospital in Belarus would ever grow leaves again.

'He is very good, *non*?'

'Yes, he is.'

She sent a shy smile over to Gabe and he shot one back at her, those sunbursts of thirty-something wrinkles at the corner of his eyes. He watched her closely as she turned her smile back in Khalid's direction.

'So, can we talk?' Rachel asked. 'Can we talk some more about you exhibiting with me? Maybe tomorrow, or . . .'

'You must come to my party tonight,' said Khalid. 'The opening. Will you come?'

'An opening party? I don't know,' she said. 'I . . .' Rachel couldn't help but look hesitantly over to Gabe again, who was standing in front of another night-time scene of the Jemaa El'Fnaa.

'You should come,' Gabe said.

'Come!' insisted Khalid.

'OK, well, yes, I suppose I could. Thank you . . .' she replied.

'And we will talk more there? Tonight?'

'You are a persistent lady,' smiled Khalid. 'Yes. We will talk. Gabe, you will bring her?'

'You don't need to bring me,' she said to Gabe.

'I've been to the gallery many times,' he answered. 'I know how easy it is to get lost, particularly at night.'

'Actually, I *did* get lost,' she conceded. 'I had to pay some bloke on a pushbike ten dirham to show me how to get there.'

'That's settled then,' Gabe said. 'So, I'll come and meet you at your hotel?'

'Oh, I didn't necessarily mean . . .'

'It makes sense. I'll pick you up in a taxi and we'll go together. We can't have you getting ripped off again,' he grinned. 'The going rate for directions is usually five.'

Rachel smiled. 'OK, well, if you're sure.' But she wasn't sure she wanted him to come and meet her at the hotel. Her wedding ring, tight on her finger, began to pulse and she twisted it, trying to ease its pressure.

'I'm sure.' And Gabe's face was so warm and kind and so familiar to her, she almost fled from the studio.

'Let us have more tea,' said Khalid. He and Gabe started talking amusingly about Gabe's last visit to Marrakesh and how they had hired a car and gone up to the Atlas Mountains together. They included her in their conversation, making sure her tea was topped up and declaring, 'You see, Rachel?' and, 'Rachel, now *you* would understand this . . .' There was lots of backslapping and plenty of ready laughter.

Rachel watched the pair of them curiously, fascinated by their easy friendship and banter. Their delight in catching up with each other.

'And then the front axle fell off!' exclaimed Gabe and Khalid fell about laughing, slapping his thigh through his paint-splattered smock. 'Sorry,' said Gabe, to her, tears of merriment in his eyes. 'Sorry. We must be boring you senseless.'

'No, it's fine,' she said. 'I'm enjoying myself, really.' He was not so serious now, she thought. Not quite as intense.

'It's just we haven't seen each other in a while,' Gabe added, 'almost as long as you and me, Rachel,' he said, with a smile and another slight wink.

'Almost,' she said. And she had to look away, pretend to check her mint tea.

'You are a good travelling companion, Gabe,' declared Khalid. 'Actually, I am driving to Agadir on Thursday, to see the wholesaler for my oils. Will you come with me?'

'I'd love to,' said Gabe. 'Nothing would delight me more.'

'*Bon. Alors.* We leave at dawn, though? Is that OK with you, my friend?'

'Sure. I like an early start.'

'*Fantastique,*' said Khalid conclusively. He stood up. 'I must return to work now.' Gabe rose too, as did Rachel, winding her scarf tighter around her neck. Khalid shook her enthusiastically by the hand. 'Tonight,' he said.

The way he said it thrilled her. Rachel imagined how the city might look after dark. How the gallery would appear, all lit up. She suddenly felt like she had been scooped up and placed inside a magic carpet, like the ones in those Arabian Nights cartoons she had watched on the *Banana Splits* show, with Teddy. The carpet was being rolled around her and she was inside ready to be transported into the night and all its mystery.

'*Tonight*,' she repeated, and Gabe looked at her with a smile so tender and reminiscent of the one she had known before, far from here and long ago, that she felt she was already being carried away, into the night, her destination unknown.

# Chapter Twenty-One

Rachel waited in the lobby on a vast amber sofa. Opposite her, a family with two teenage boys waited to be picked up for a sightseeing trip. In the corner, flicking the top of a ballpoint pen, was that businessman, whose gaze she avoided. Gabe was in the third taxi she saw pull up.

'You look lovely,' Gabe said, walking towards her, as Rachel was swished through automatic doors into the startlingly hot air and the swansong of the descending African sun.

'Thank you,' she replied. She was wearing a black 50s dress, with cap sleeves and a full skirt with a net petticoat underneath, plus sling-back sandals with a kitten heel. Over her shoulders was a black crochet shawl. She was tempted to say 'So do you', briefly wondering if Gabe would laugh and say 'This old thing?' as he tugged at the open collar of his white shirt.

He had walked her back to the Bab Agnaou gate after they had left Khalid's studio. She had got into a taxi, him waving her off; two people who had bumped into each other and spent a convivial morning in an artist's studio, drinking mint tea. She had pretended she'd felt safe then, in his company. That it was all a breezy nothing. Now, in a laden heat and with the sun lowering in the sky, she didn't feel safe at all. Rachel knew that much of her excitement about the evening was nothing to do with this magical city, or the anticipation of that lit-up gallery on the Rue Céline. It was that when the magic carpet was unrolled and she toppled out of it, Gabe would be standing there.

He was tall and incredibly handsome in white shirt and chinos. His hair was still slightly damp from the shower, his face warm and velvety-looking. His smile, directed only at her, a treat. Oh, she knew the setting was a manipulation. That heady holiday feeling of being dressed up for the evening, as the shadows cooled and the evening light flattered, an artifice. She was aware that in the seduction of a night's promise, on sun-kissed skin, many might feel something that wasn't entirely real. Drifting-apart married couples felt that the romance was still there. Unsuited first daters who'd met on the beach at lunchtime thought that tonight was the start of something amazing. Rachel didn't want to be seduced into feeling something transitory and illusory and dangerous too, but she was already worried. She was already in fear of falling, at the very sight of him.

Gabe kissed her briefly on the cheek and she smelled the lemon musk of his aftershave. He walked her to the door of the taxi and helped her into the back seat, before scooting round to the other side.

'OK?' he asked. Their thighs were close on the tan plastic of the back seat.

'Yes,' she said.

The taxi mooched off the turning circle and out of the gateway of the hotel, the guard raising a slow arm to herald them past.

'So, how are you?' asked Gabe. 'What did you do this afternoon?'

'I swam,' she said. 'How about you?'

'I lowered myself nonchalantly into a plunge pool,' Gabe said, and Rachel laughed, despite feeling her cheeks colouring at this image. 'I'm staying in a riad,' he added.

'In the medina?' Rachel had seen photos of riads in the library's guidebooks. They were Romanesque guest houses built around a central tiled courtyard, often with a small, very pretty pool. She had wanted the protection and the predictability of a big hotel, with a large swimming pool. It had been busy when she'd gone looking for a sun lounger this afternoon: splashing kids, bobbing adults, elbows like broken wings slapped on the sides of the pool, faces raised to the sun.

'Yes, I've stayed there before, once or twice. It's great. Have you had dinner?'

'No,' she said. She had heard clanking from the Majorelle dining room while she was in the lobby, and inhaled the scent of spiced meat and fragrant rice. 'I hoped there might be . . . snacks . . . at the party?'

Gabe smiled at her. 'There should be snacks,' he said. 'I haven't eaten yet, either.'

She shifted slightly up the seat and looked out of the window. The sun was a low, bold orange; it kept up with them, as they drove into the city.

'How many nights are you here?' Gabe asked.

Rachel turned to him. He had a triangle of velvety skin in the open collar of his shirt, at his throat. His eyes were fringed with eyelashes she was jealous of. *I shouldn't be feeling like this*, she thought. *I shouldn't be here, sharing this back seat with him. I should be safe somewhere, anywhere else.*

'Three,' Rachel said.

'Then we leave the same day.'

She nodded, while the sun, riding with them in her window, mocked her mixed emotions. She twizzled her wedding ring around her finger and sternly reminded herself of Jonny's voice, his laugh. Her husband. Her safety. She should have phoned him tonight, but she hadn't. She felt treacherous.

177

Gabe asked her what she thought of the weather in Marrakesh; she replied. He asked her if she liked the food; she said she did. He enquired if she was planning to do any sightseeing while she was here; she said she was. She became a stilted doll in a big black netted skirt. Stiffly resisting the unwanted seduction of his face, his voice, his thigh on the seat.

The taxi dropped them at Bab Agnaou gate. It was almost dark now; lights were beginning to come on: bright yellows within tiny shops, little lamps on the front of the mopeds, coloured lanterns overhead and single bare bulbs glimpsed through intriguing doorways. Stallholders now nestled inside, at desks, and looked up as people passed. The evening crowd wandered, and Rachel and Gabe walked deep into the medina.

The door to the gallery was open. Two hurricane lamps flickered either side, on the uneven ground, and Rachel recalled the ones along her front path on the night of the dinner party. How Lee had knocked one over while ambling up to the gate with Teddy, his arm around her shoulder, at the end of the night, waving a goodbye for both of them with a lit cigarette.

'After you,' said Gabe.

Rachel stepped inside. 'Oh, it's pretty!' she exclaimed.

There were more hurricane lamps along the tiny ante-hall, lighting their way; the arch to the gallery was strewn with fairy lights, and the gallery itself a magical grotto, with small spotlights over the paintings. A few people were gathered there already, Khalid at their centre.

'Shall we get a drink?' suggested Gabe.

'Yes, please.'

They hadn't spoken much as they'd navigated the maze of alleys of the medina. Rachel had been concentrating on reminding herself she was married and to not do or *feel* anything stupid. Scolding herself for this attraction, which would be fleeting at best, destructive at worst. Jonny was her life, her balance and her stability. Jonny was the blaze of sun that had wiped away the fog of her life. Jonny was the driftwood she clung on to from a sea of past sadness and chaos. There was no room, no *reason* for another man. Her resolve tonight? To be bright and buoyant. Unruffled. This was just a moment in time that would slip into those that had gone before, she told herself. Into the past. And she never wanted the past to change the present.

There was a small table at the left of the gallery. The ubiquitous mint tea brass urn presiding over proceedings. Some glasses of fresh orange juice. A cluster of filled champagne flutes.

'Bubbly?' asked Gabe. 'Isn't that what you Brits call it?'

'Yes, please.' Yes, that was what she'd be tonight. She'd be fun and bubbly. She took the glass Gabe handed to her. 'It looks lovely tonight, the gallery,' she said.

'It's a great space,' agreed Gabe. He looks so relaxed, decided Rachel. She doubted *he*'d given himself a good talking-to as they weaved through the streets. And once again she thought he'd lost some of the edge he'd had, as a twenty-something. Some of his darkness.

'Gabe! Rachel.' Khalid's face was flushed, and his arms open wide. 'Welcome, welcome, *bien venue!*' He embraced them both, clutching them together. Gabe's glass of champagne was cold as it lightly pressed against Rachel's left arm.

'It's wonderful,' she said, once released. 'Thank you for inviting me.'

'Thank you for coming, both of you. Rachel . . .' Khalid added, studying her face, 'I have considered your offer,' he said, 'of exhibiting in your gallery. And I have an answer.'

'Oh, we don't have to do this now,' she said. 'We can talk about this later—'

'—*Tiens!* Later we party. My answer is "yes".' He grinned at her. 'But there are details to be *thrashed, non*? Can I telephone you, when you return to Oxford? Or you have a fax? I don't have email yet. Things are a little slower to get started in Morocco, you know?'

'Yes, yes, of course, we can work out all the details. Everything is in the brochure I gave you, the telephone number, the fax . . .'

'*Alors!* We will talk then, when you get home. And now we will raise a glass and have our party.'

'Thank you,' she said. 'Thank you, Khalid.'

'No, thank *you*. You are introducing me to Oxford and to England.'

'Kha*leeed*!' Khalid was swooped upon by a lady in red linen and scooped into another cluster of adulation. He waved an '*à bientôt*' to Rachel and Gabe from inside his joyful huddle.

'You've made quite an impression on him,' said Gabe.

'I guess I have!' Rachel was pleased as punch. She had secured Khalid. Her mission here in Marrakesh was done. She could walk out of here now and take a taxi back to the hotel. Take off her dress and hang it back up in the wardrobe. Call Jonny and tell him her news. But she was at a party in a gallery lit by hurricane lamps. She had a glass of champagne in her hand. And she wanted to talk to Gabe. Hadn't she just *wanted* to, every time she had met him? 'I'm so pleased,' she said. 'I didn't know how easy it would be.'

Gabe held out his champagne glass for hers to clink against.

'Some things are just very, very easy,' he said. 'Congratulations.'

'Thank you.'

They stood and drank their champagne and looked around them, at the paintings and the people and Khalid – the centre of everything – enjoying his night.

'Tell me more about *your* art,' Rachel said to Gabe. 'I know you've exhibited in Fargo, but I want to know everything that's happened since I last saw you.'

Gabe smiled. 'I just continued,' he said. 'Got better, I hope. I now exclusively do the biro drawings and a new gallery opened in town, and they liked my pieces. Then I slung my work over my shoulder and went a-hustling in Fargo. The gallery there took some of my work on and they have sibling galleries – in Vermont, in St Paul, Minnesota – and one in New York. A couple of drawings ended up in all three galleries.'

'Oh wow, so, your art is in New York?'

'Currently, yes.'

'Have you been to see it?'

'I have.'

'That's *fantastic*, Gabe!'

'Gee, you're going to make me blush, Rachel!' Gabe joked.

'More champagne?' A Moroccan youth, eyes sepia and unblinking, appeared in front of them.

She nodded and her glass was refilled. 'I'm so glad I'm here,' she said, after a while. 'That I've secured Khalid. I'm completely thrilled, actually.'

'You should be,' said Gabe, 'it's quite a coup. He's been courted by a few galleries in the last few days.'

'Really?'

'There have been some calls, some faxes. But you actually *flew* here.' He waited for the boy to refill his glass too. 'You know,' he said to her, 'I don't think you'd have had the courage to do that when I first met you.'

Another kind of woman might have said to another kind of man, 'What are you talking about? We only met four times. How could you have *known* me?' If they had both been different people she would have found his comment patronising. But Rachel knew he had sussed who she was right away, probably from his very first look at her. She was not mysterious; she was not opaque. She was just Rachel Trent; a woman so open a book that anyone could catch

181

her pages as they fell out. And he'd caught a couple of them, hadn't he, in 1986, and held them up to the light?

'No, I wouldn't have done,' she admitted. 'But I have a business to run now, and courage doesn't come into it. I'm investing in my gallery. I'm securing – hopefully – a brilliant and very commercial artist who will help its ongoing success.'

'You've changed,' he said, his eyes dancing at her.

'Well, of course I have. Who's the same in their twenties as they are in their thirties? Haven't you?'

'Yes,' he said. 'I've changed. I've grown up a bit, I hope. And one day I hope I'll really crack it, this life business.'

'Me too,' she admitted.

'And until then, there's art and there's work.'

'Absolutely.' She wouldn't tell him that as the years had passed and the children had not come, the art and the work, actually, were all she had. That Vivaldi's was her squidgy form in a white Babygro, her milky wide-awake nights, her summer days strolling under dappled leaves with a pram. She wouldn't tell him she had begged Jonny to agree to IVF, but he'd said it was too early, too stressful, too much pressure, that those clinics just wanted to make money, that if it was going to happen, it would happen, let nature do its thing . . . That she cried at night while Jonny continued to live each day as it came, as long as what came was success and book sales and dancing in the front garden. She had hope still, of course she did, but it was fading like the late summer sun.

A tall French woman wearing an unbuttoned man's tuxedo jacket and very red lipstick swayed into vision.

'We're going on to Cafe Arabe,' she purred to Rachel and Gabe, 'Khalid and I, and a few others. To the rooftop. Would the two of you like to come?'

Rachel looked around her. The party had already filtered out a little.

Gabe looked at Rachel. 'Would you like to?'

'Why not?' This Cafe Arabe place sounded intriguing. And she didn't want this magical night to end. Not yet. She wasn't ready to leave this man's side yet, either. It wouldn't harm, would it, going to this rooftop cafe? It wouldn't disrupt her life to spend one single night of it in Marrakesh, with these people and with *him*?

Khalid was trying to get their attention from the other side of the room. 'Yes?' he queried, his thumb up.

'Yes,' signalled Gabe.

Within a couple of minutes, they were back out on the alley among a shifting, heel-clacking crocodile of people bantering and joking; their hands on each other's shoulders or steering the smalls of backs; dropping behind or catching up to enter new conversations. Gabe and Rachel were somewhere in the middle of this infectious crowd – as stallholders stared and moped drivers beeped and slalomed – smiling at *bons mots* and laughing at the jokes of strangers, like people walking between one party and the next do.

Cafe Arabe had three floors. There was a ground-floor courtyard. A sumptuous first floor, saturated with rich reds and purples and golds. And a stone staircase to the roof, where a relaxed lounge-type restaurant area was bordered on all sides by a low cream wall and iron fretwork. The ramshackle skyline was misty and ugly-beautiful. A crane, like a nodding bird, on the far horizon was lit against the midnight-blue sky. It was only slightly cooler up here, where there were round mosaic-topped tables and cushioned curved benches and the late call from the mosque was an opera issued behind them. They gathered in the centre of the space.

'Oh!' Rachel exclaimed, as a swoosh of cool mist from the fretted roof softly sprayed her in the face.

'Every three minutes, I believe,' said Gabe, smiling at her surprise. 'To keep us cool.'

'I like it,' she said, noticing the tiny sprinklers above her. 'I like all of it.'

They gathered around tables set with bright bowls of nuts and mini tagines of lamb, fish and chicken.

'Snacks,' said Gabe, and Rachel smiled. She was happy here on this rooftop, with these people. She slipped off her shawl. She enjoyed the feel of the netting of her dress and the way it made her skirt rise and fall like a cloud as they all gradually took seats. She was a little drunk, she realised.

'Cocktails!' said Khalid, clapping his hands and calling over a waiter. 'For those who drink alcohol, of course. Mint tea for me and *mes amis* who abstain.'

Rachel and Gabe were seated with Khalid, the French woman and two other Moroccan artists – sculptors, they said – brothers called Amir and Amine, who appeared to finish each other's sentences. The table was wobbly. Gabe folded a linen napkin and pushed it under the wayward leg.

'OK?' he asked Rachel.

'Yes, I'm OK.'

'Would you like a cocktail?'

'Yes, please.'

She chose a Cosmopolitan. When it arrived, it was prohibitively strong, but she sipped on it gratefully as it was both cold and delicious. Khalid and Gabe and the French woman started talking about Berber art. The two Moroccan men engaged in earnest Arabic and turned away, gesticulating wildly and baring mirthful tombstone teeth. Rachel let the sound of all their voices wash over her.

'OK?' Gabe asked again. 'Sorry,' he added, 'Berber art not your bag?'

It seemed she had already drunk most of the cocktail. 'It probably is,' she said, 'it's just that I'm a bit drunk, suddenly. Is that allowed?

'It's allowed. Just be careful. You haven't eaten.'

He placed a bowl of nuts in front of her. She nibbled at them and drank a little more. Khalid got called to another table. The French woman drifted away. The two sculptors scraped their chairs to answer entreaties from guests at the next table, and Rachel and Gabe were alone. He was smiling at her – looking intrigued, curious. The stone of her engagement ring clonked on the mosaic tabletop when she set her glass down. She turned it so it nestled in place against her wedding ring.

'Did you meet Sarah in the art world?' she asked him. 'Your ex-girlfriend? Or is that nosy?'

'That is a bit nosy,' he said, looking amused.

'Oh, sorry. Ignore me. Please.'

He laughed. 'It's a perfectly legitimate question. I can answer you. Sarah's a biochemist.'

'Oh. Right.' Rachel did feel quite drunk. She took another nut from the bowl and popped it in her mouth.

'And all my other ex-girlfriends weren't artists, either – and there's been a few, since we met, if you're interested. God sure loves a trier . . .'

'No, I'm not, honestly. I just wondered . . .'

'Why I haven't settled down? Some people don't, you know. Some people just keep on messing things up.' He laughed again, but she detected a note of defensiveness.

'It's none of my business,' she said. 'I just wondered . . .' she repeated, 'about Sarah. That's all. Sorry.'

'I'm cold,' he said quickly.

'What?' At first, she thought he meant here, on this rooftop, although it was at least a hundred degrees.

'I'm cold. That's why things never work out in my relationships.' He smiled ruefully.

'Cold? I don't see you as cold.'

185

'Apparently they did. And they were right. They sussed me. Called me out. They could feel it. That I wasn't feeling it.' The darkness had come back. He drummed his fingers on the table. 'They could see I didn't love them,' he added. 'Or that I might never love them. And it was the trying that hurt them, and hurt me, too. I made things difficult when they should have been easy. It seems that's what I do, over and over.'

Gabe looked haunted. He looked like a lost boy. A tenderness came over Rachel for him that was almost sweetly painful.

'Do you think you're capable of love?' she asked delicately. Rachel wasn't sure how this conversation had become what it was, but they were in it now. The swell of it. The quiet. The rooftop reduced to a series of elements. The netting of her skirt. A shot of mist, from the ceiling. The muted clink of glasses at the neighbouring table. Khalid's laugh, somewhere far behind them.

'Yes,' he said softly. And she could see her face reflected in his eyes and they were sitting too close, way too close, and his knee was almost touching hers beneath the stiff, fronded netting, and her left foot had slipped out of its sandal and the ball of her foot was cool on the stone floor. 'I'm capable.'

Rachel nodded. She needed another jolting shot of mist, Khalid to come bowling over, the French woman with the lipstick to snake up and ask their views on existentialism, or something – to break this spell. At the same time, she wanted it to weave and spark forever. 'Sorry. I am being nosy.'

'You're all right.'

'I don't think I am.'

'You're really all right,' he said, in almost a whisper, and her heart strained against its tether, pulling dangerously from the carefully constructed life that housed it. 'You know something?' he added.

'What?' She was whispering too.

'You're more beautiful now than you were in Oxford, Rachel.'

She wanted to laugh, but she didn't want to laugh at all, as she had never forgotten the words he had spoken, that spring night in the village hall car park. And she was sharply aware of two things: the tragedy of recent disappointments and the capability this man had to make it all go away.

'My husband's a good man,' she said. 'I just need to say that, out loud.' She forced herself to select an image of Jonny from her mind: Jonny in his party shirt, red wine in hand, his palm resting on the piano in their dining room that neither of them could play. Jonny looking at her with all that love and laughter in his eyes.

'It's OK, what we're doing here,' said Gabe.

'It's not,' she said, shaking her head. 'I can't flirt with you, Gabe. And you shouldn't be flirting with me.'

'Then let's not flirt,' he said lightly. 'Let's just talk. We're not doing anything wrong.'

'But the fact we bumped into each other,' she said. '*Fate . . .*' She had resisted the notion of fate, until now – its clang, its cannon boom.

'It's not fate. I'm friends with an artist here in Morocco. You want to exhibit him. It's just . . . *life*,' he smiled. 'Life has brought us to the same place and here we are.'

He didn't see anything wrong, did he? He wasn't worried about anything. He simply said the things he wanted to say and put them out in the world with an unassailable confidence, free of the threat of consequence that weighed heavy on her these days. It was a strange kind of confidence, but not arrogance, and it carried with it no thought of the future, when her thoughts were always of the future. Rachel looked around the roof terrace again, looked for escape, looked anywhere but at him.

'Gabe?' A block of a man was standing at the table, the toe of his right shoe planted on the folded napkin under the table leg. 'I got to the exhibition late. I thought you might all be here.' He had an American accent. 'Where's Khalid?'

'Right over there,' said Gabe, pointing out a laughing Khalid gesticulating to the French woman. 'He'll be pleased to see you, Martin.'

'Can you introduce me?' said Martin. 'I don't want to go lumbering over there like a great heap.'

'You don't lumber, my friend.' Gabe hesitated, glancing at Rachel.

'Go ahead,' she said. 'I'm fine sitting here.'

Gabe got up, mouthing 'I'll be back' at her, and after a while, in which she drained the rest of her cocktail, she got up too – a little unsteadily – and found herself swallowed into a small enclave of people. A man grabbed her hand, kissed it, and started firing questions at her: was she from England, was it her first time in Marrakesh, where was she staying? *He* was from France. Toulouse. He was a tourist. But he knew Khalid through a friend of a friend.

'You have a new prime minister,' the man said. His tongue was too big for his mouth. 'Do you think he will be great?'

'Great, no. Good, maybe,' she said, trying to straighten her slurred words. 'They are never great, are they, apart from Winston Churchill, maybe?' She thought back to the costume Gabe was supposed to wear, more than ten years ago, at the village hall. Her wonderful Nanna's words, 'the grass isn't always greener, just because it looks it from a distance . . .' 'It's always the same,' she said. 'They arrive with a great fanfare and a few years later are ushered out in disgrace.'

He laughed, but she didn't know if he had understood her words or whether he was the kind of man to laugh at anything a woman said.

'I like the queen,' he said.

'Everyone likes the queen,' she smiled.

'And Diana. Even though she is now divorced, banished from the royal family.'

'A lot of people still like Diana,' she said, again thinking of Nanna, the Attagirl who had worshipped the royal family and once loved an American serviceman called Scott. 'I'm one of them.'

'Diana will be happy now,' he said, 'now she is free. She will be very happy.'

'I hope so,' Rachel said. She recalled a recent picture she had seen of Diana on the beach in Saint-Tropez, in the sun. She wasn't sure if she looked happy or not.

'Let me get you another drink.'

'No, I'm fine, thank you.'

'I insist.'

In moments she had another drink in her hand. She sipped at it to divert herself.

'You are with the American?' he asked.

'I came here with him tonight, but I am not *with* him,' she said, more crossly than she intended.

'Why not?'

'I'm married.'

'Oh, that's a shame. You would make a very handsome couple.'

'Of course we wouldn't. I'm married,' she repeated.

'You're not going home with him tonight, then?'

'No.'

He shrugged, made a pouty *moue* with his mouth. 'Would you come home with me instead?'

'Now you're beginning to offend me.'

He laughed. His teeth were black, at the gums. 'I'm joking,' he said. 'Just my little joke.'

Rachel wanted him to go away. *She* wanted to go. Her euphoria at being here tonight, on this roof terrace, among this interesting arty set, had dissolved in the air like another cool jet of perfumed vapour. She was on a work trip, far from home, almost making a fool of herself with another man. She was on a sunset rooftop in Marrakesh, drinking too much and pretending she was someone else. Someone who was prepared to risk everything.

'How you doing, Rachel?' Gabe asked. He was cutting in – again – she thought, like he had at that Blitz party. She was equally relieved, but there would be no swaying to Glenn Miller tonight, no epilogue in an empty car park.

'It's probably time for me to go back to the hotel now,' she said.

'You sure?' Gabe's face was concerned, lovely. Dangerous.

'Yes.'

'OK. Let me walk you to the gate to find a taxi.'

Rachel wanted to say no, she could manage, but she knew she would never find her way out of the labyrinth of alleys and back to the gate on her own.

'Yes, please,' she said. 'Let me just go and fetch my shawl.'

They made it down the stone steps of Cafe Arabe. They were absorbed back into the maze of alleys, quiet now, their store fronts shuttered. The mopeds gone. Only a few lights remained, in tiny high square windows, or via unwieldy Victorian-looking street lamps. As they walked, she stumbled on the cobbles and Gabe steadied her.

'Are you OK, kiddo?'

'Yes, I'm fine,' she said ruefully. 'Well, I'm drunk, but I'll be all right in the morning.'

'Do you have plans for tomorrow?' he asked gently, as they approached the Bab Agnaou gate. 'Would you like to go to the Majorelle Garden?'

'I don't know,' Rachel said truthfully. She had read about the Majorelle Garden in the library and had a leaflet for it in her room. It looked beautiful.

'You don't know?'

'No.'

'OK, I'll ask you again in the morning. I'll call you at the hotel. See how you feel?'

'Why?' she asked him. She stopped, on the cobbles; he stopped too. 'Why do you want to call me? Why do you want to go to the garden with me?'

'I like spending time with you,' he said simply. 'Is it a crime?'

'I'll let you know in the morning,' she said carefully.

A taxi was outside the gate. Gabe saw her into it and gave the name of her hotel to the driver. He helped tuck the net of her skirt into the car. She looked at him through the window as the taxi pulled away and he waved. When she got back to the hotel and walked quickly up the front steps, Rachel saw the businessman, leaning against an outside pillar, smoking. He stared at her, his eyes narrowed and searching, and she put her head down, picked up her skirts and almost ran into the lobby's muted light.

# Chapter Twenty-Two

The phone was ringing. Rachel rolled on to her side and grabbed her watch from the bedside table. It was 8 a.m. She picked up the receiver.

'Sorry, but you have to go early to truly appreciate the Majorelle Garden – the brochure I have in my hand describes it as an "oasis of tranquillity in the early morning light" and it truly is. I really hope you'd like to come. *Morning*, by the way,' Gabe added, and Rachel could feel the smile in his voice.

'Morning.' She sat up, assessed how she felt, and she felt OK. No hideous headache, no hangover. She had survived the night. Physically, anyway.

'I can be at your hotel in half an hour,' he said, 'if you'll be ready. Will you be ready?'

She thought about it. She should really stay in bed. She should really thank Gabe, decline nicely, and never see him again. 'Yes, I'll be ready,' she said.

'Great.'

'What do I need to bring? Will there be water? Shall I bring a snack?'

'You and your snacks!' laughed Gabe. 'We can buy water and snacks outside. Don't worry about a thing.'

'OK,' she said. 'See you in thirty minutes.'

Rachel showered and dressed quickly, not allowing time for further thought, putting on a white cotton sun dress, flat sandals and a lightweight kimono robe. Outside the lobby, Gabe was waiting. He was lounging against a taxi in a long-sleeved blue top and khaki chinos and holding a large bottle of water and a knotted napkin.

'I nabbed a couple of rolls from the breakfast buffet,' he said. 'Nobody apprehended me. So, I guess we're all set.'

'I didn't have you down for a rebel,' she commented chirpily, telling herself his voice, a delicious surprise to her again this morning, was nothing special. That his face was just a face, with not a single part of it to feel disproportionately thrilled by. 'Or a thief.'

'I have my moments,' he replied, 'and when snacks are required . . .'

They grinned at each other. Gabe opened the back door of the taxi for her, and she hopped in. She was doing well, she thought. Spectacularly well. They were friends going on an early morning sightseeing trip. She was bright and chirpy. Unencumbered by temptation. If she could resist him at a rooftop party after champagne, two prohibitively strong cocktails and a conversation that had become as weighty and seductive as the Moroccan night, she could easily resist him while trailing round some bamboo bushes on an early Wednesday morning . . .

'How late did you stay last night?' Rachel asked, doing the exact opposite and marvelling at the cobalt of his eyes against the pale blue of his shirt. Chirpy, she pleaded with herself. *Chirpy*.

'About another hour. We moved on to coffee and impassioned arguments on Monet versus Manet.'

'Whose side did you come down on?'

'Monet, of course,' he smiled.

'Of course,' she smiled back. They were motoring through the city. The traffic was light, street vendors were setting up, cafes were opening – the motion and trundle of a weekday morning. They talked simply about the climate and the people and the architecture. The beauty of the morning. They did not talk about last night, of fate and flirting, or their capability for love.

Eventually, the taxi pulled into a street that got increasingly pretty as they drove down it and came to a stop in front of an immaculate, high terracotta wall. At a small kiosk – at the entrance to the garden – they paid for two tickets and stepped inside Le Jardin Majorelle.

'Goodness,' said Rachel. 'It's so beautiful. It's like walking into a dream.'

It was delightful, an almost magical oasis of curated groves and chaste water gardens, weaved through by polished russet-red paths, with bright blue borders. Bamboos leaned haphazardly to the sky. Banana trees with enormous leaves looked on as jaunty grey-green succulents squatted among coconut palms.

'The garden was taken over by French fashion designer Yves St Laurent and his partner, Pierre Bergé, in 1980,' read Gabe from his brochure, as they walked in dappled shade and fragrant calm, and she wondered why she felt perfectly happy, here, in this moment, with him. 'Saving it from demolition.'

They stopped to appreciate the interlude of a blue-and-white miniature courtyard, its long mirror pond static under the cool lace of lily pads. A fountain, and blue and yellow earthenware pots, pretty punctuations.

'The garden was in quite a state of neglect,' he continued, by a tall palm that cast dimpled shadows on his face, and she suddenly felt perfectly unhappy, at being here, with him, in this perfect early light – as it was transitory, disloyal and hazardous, 'as it hadn't been touched since originally designed in the 1920s by the French painter Jacques Majorelle.'

'It does seem composed and coloured like a painting,' she commented, letting shades of happiness and desolation sweep through her body like curious ripples. 'It's wonderful.'

The garden was quiet; there was just the sound of the birds and the low murmur of other tourists. Rachel couldn't help but think how it would be if Jonny was here with her instead. Would she feel happy or unhappy? she wondered. Or would she just feel safe?

They passed a pristine villa, of Moorish design, also in bright blue, nestled among the fronds and spikes and drama of the garden; Gabe told her Yves St Laurent and Pierre Bergé lived there when they were in Marrakesh and she imagined them on its terrace, drinking coffee in the morning before pottering off into the garden. Beyond the villa, a young Japanese tourist with a parasol was having her photograph taken in front of a prickly gourd of a cactus. Her companion asked Gabe if he would take a photo of them both and Rachel watched as he directed them and made them laugh, despite the language barrier.

'Would you like to sit for a while?' he asked Rachel, after the Japanese girls had signalled their thanks with shy smiles and little bows.

'Yes, that would be lovely.'

There was a sage-green bench, in the shade of a bamboo grove. They sat and watched as a French family trailed through the arched trellis of a nearby walkway, the father patting the children affectionately on their golden heads as they gambolled through it.

'You have no children?' Gabe asked simply.

'Not of my own,' she said, looking straight ahead, 'not yet.'

'I'm sorry,' he said. 'You told me you wanted them.'

'Thank you,' she replied.

Rachel didn't turn to look at him. They sat for a few moments in silence. A bird chattered in the bamboo, then took flight. The sun glinted off the sprinkling water cascading from an immaculate fountain.

Then she looked at Gabe and she spoke.

'Children haven't happened for Jonny and me,' she said. 'Apart from Teddy, of course, who I love with all my heart, and

I've enjoyed and appreciated every day I've spent with her, but it's not . . . well, our own baby . . . and, oh, it's quite a long story, with no apparent end.' She knew her laugh was as hollow as one of the bamboo switches, yearning to the sky behind them. 'But we have *had* other children,' she added.

'Go on,' said Gabe. His face was kind, empathetic, listening. Rachel felt she could tell him anything in the world.

'Well, we've had children to stay with us. From Belarus.' She felt a little embarrassed telling him that. Like she had stolen an idea from him because he had been there, once. 'They've been to stay with us for recuperative holidays.'

'Oh?' said Gabe, leaning forward. 'That's interesting.'

It was Dana and Anthony Reed, the retired couple who lived in the Old Rectory, who had first hosted children from Belarus, when two boys had come for a fortnight in the summer of 1992. It added two years to the lives of children affected by Chernobyl – a stay with the uncontaminated food and clean, radiation-free air of the UK – Dana told her, when Rachel had asked. She'd been with the two boys in the park one morning, when Rachel was on her way to the gallery. Dana told her she'd got involved with an organisation called Trees of Light: a group of volunteers who travelled every spring to the Odinski orphanage in Minsk, to visit the children there and bring them aid boxes and love.

'Dana said they were called Trees of Light because the children in the orphanage measured the passing of time by the turning of the seasons,' Rachel told Gabe, 'and every spring – when the trees started to grow new leaves – they knew the volunteers would come again.'

Gabe nodded. 'It's a very poignant name,' he said.

'I thought you'd like it,' Rachel smiled. 'Well, Jonny and I – well me, mostly – hosted two children from Belarus the following summer, while Teddy was away with her mum on a forest camping trip. Two girls came that first year – Katya and Snezhana. Katya was tiny and very quiet, Snezhana was a robust little thing, surprisingly cheeky, and always asking for chips or ice cream for breakfast.' She grinned at the memory of them. 'For two weeks . . .' she paused, '. . . I became their surrogate mother. I brushed hair and did up bracelets, I tied shoelaces and dispensed Polo mints. We went on outings, organised by Trees of Light, to play parks and zoos and roller discos. I mean, I had done nearly all those things with Teddy, but her mum was always in reach, even if not always physically available. These girls were my sole responsibility.'

'It sounds wonderful,' Gabe said, looking at her carefully.

'It really was. I tucked them up in bed at night, I hugged them when they were homesick. I was the first face they saw in the morning when they woke up.'

Rachel sighed, happy at the memory. She didn't know if it was her fear of never becoming a biological mother – despite having tried for four years – that had compelled her to become a temporary one for two Belarusian children, but she had loved every minute of it. As she had waved them off at the airport, that first trip, she'd cried, as she knew she would never see them again, but the next summer two more children would come, and Rachel would be a kind of mother – and not just a stepmother – again.

'But we haven't had children for the past couple of summers,' she said. 'Jonny said it was too much noise when he was trying to work. Too much of a distraction. But I still write to all of them. Two girls and two boys. One of the girls is trying to come to England on a work visa.' She shrugged. 'You never know.'

'You're wonderful for doing it,' said Gabe.

'Thank you, but it was easy,' she replied. 'Some things just are.'

He smiled. Rachel looked down and noticed a tiny beetle making its way up his arm. He let it traverse his thumb and travel into his palm. She remembered shaking hands with him, in that spring of 1986, that soft pulp of his skin between his thumb and palm. *Funny the things you remember*, she thought.

'I have become a father,' he said.

'What?' Her heart started thumping, which was crazy, and she was instantly jealous, which was even crazier, and unfair. 'When?'

He nodded. 'I haven't long found out,' he said. 'I haven't even told Khalid yet. An ex-girlfriend, a very brief one, actually – all rather surprising – recently told me I have a three-year-old son.'

Rachel was stunned. 'You do?'

'Yes.' He opened his wallet and showed Rachel a photo of a boy on a swing: round face, huge cheeks, big toothy smile, eyes like Gabe's. At the sight of him, Gabe's own face lit up, and Rachel's heart swelled for him. He had a boy.

'He lives in Fargo,' he said. 'I've only met him a couple of times so far. Anne-Marie didn't want to tell me at all, for a long time. Because I hurt her . . . when I realised it couldn't be forever with her. When I moved on.' He looked tortured. 'Anyway, she found out she was pregnant not long after we split, and she – eventually – decided I had a right to know, after all this time. So now I know. He's called Jacob.'

Jacob, thought Rachel. Gabe has a Jacob. 'Weren't you angry?' she asked.

'Angry?'

'That you didn't know about him until now? That you missed so much time?'

'No,' he said. 'I can understand it. When I walked away from Anne-Marie, it was pretty final. Brutal, even, I guess. She hated me.' He shrugged. 'I can understand it.'

'He's gorgeous.'

'Yes.' He looked sheepish. 'You must think me a heel,' he added. 'All these ex-girlfriends. A son his mother didn't want me to know about. A messed-up past . . .'

'We've all got a messed-up past,' she said. 'But you are a bit of a conundrum.'

'Does it make you not like me?' he asked, the tease of a sad smile on his lips.

'No,' she said. 'It makes me wonder why you are still lost and wandering.' She wasn't teasing him this time. She wanted to hug him. She wanted to reach her arms out and gather his body to her and hold him.

'We both know why that is,' he said, that sad smile loosening. 'Hope over experience. The destructive need to keep looking until I've found what I'm looking for.' Gabe gazed at her, unblinking, his eyes soft in the morning light. 'But I have Jacob now . . .' he added, putting his wallet back in his pocket, 'which is really something. And . . . you? You and Jonny. Will you keep trying for a baby?'

She nodded. 'Yes. We have been for a long time. Too long.' She sighed and looked down at her hands. 'I want to do IVF, but Jonny won't hear of it. Says he doesn't want us both "fiddled" about with. Doesn't want to spend all that money, maybe for nothing. He says I'm only in my thirties. That if it's meant to happen, it will happen. But we've been trying for four years! Sorry.' She shook her head. 'You don't want to hear all this!'

'Yes, I do, Rachel.' His eyes were full of empathy.

'You know,' she continued, 'I don't know if I believe in fate or not, but I believe if you can help make things happen, then you should try. But Jonny doesn't want to. I've had to drop it. I won't constantly nag him. I can't. I can't be that woman . . . But it's such a flawed plan, isn't it?' she cried. 'And not really a plan at all. To let nature take its course, when nature might have already turned her back on us. Sorry,' she said, shaking her head. 'Sorry.'

'I'm sorry, too,' said Gabe. He took her hand and she felt exactly how she had when he'd taken it on the back step of the village hall. Like there was a promise in it, one that could never be honoured. 'I hope it happens for you. Or you can convince Jonny to try IVF. I hope things change.'

'Thank you.' The beetle was back. She watched as it crawled over the width of Gabe's forearm.

'Shall we walk again?' he said.

'Yes, please.'

Gabe gently flicked the beetle on to the bench. They set off, following the line of bamboos to a courtyard pond, its languid lilies still and silent.

'It's really beginning to warm up now,' said Gabe.

'Yes.' She could still feel the touch of his hand.

'Would you like to go to the Jemaa El-Fnaa?'

Rachel realised they were almost back at the entrance to the garden. 'The market square. Now?'

'If you think it's not too hot?'

'No, I'd like that.' She didn't want to go back to the hotel. She wanted more time with him. More of this golden time.

They picked up a taxi outside and travelled in bright sunshine, now, to the enormous market square, where it was astonishingly hot and dry and dusty and busy. Makeshift tents with sheets laid down for sellers to display their wares on were scattered as far as the eye could see. There were grinning toothless men brandishing snakes like multiple necklaces; chained-up monkeys baring their teeth and hissing; peddlers staring and shouting. It was crowded, noisy and exhilarating, but grottier than Rachel had envisaged and a lot less mystical. She didn't want a filthy-looking snake placed around her neck by a man with tarnished gold teeth. She didn't like being anywhere near the sinister chattering monkeys. It was as far as she could imagine from the tranquillity of Le Jardin Majorelle.

They wandered round for a while, but Rachel didn't feel at ease. She felt heckled, assaulted by the cacophony of sights and sounds and less than fragrant smells. She was too hot after all.

'Your riad's somewhere near here, isn't it?' she said.

'Yes. A few alleys away.' They had been lured to a fruit stall and Gabe was haggling over a punnet of figs, while Rachel waited in scorching heat. He pointed somewhere beyond the misshapen roofs of the cafes bordering the square.

'I've never been to one before. Can you show me?'

'You want to get out of here, don't you?'

She grinned. 'I wouldn't mind.'

Gabe settled on a price for the figs, and they walked wordlessly from the market square and into the familiar claustrophobia of alleys. After several endless turns, they came to a dead end and a studded brown door. Above them, pelmets of dyed yarn – astonishing coral pinks and tangerine oranges – hung drying in the sun from overhead cables, row upon fronded row. 'Rue de la Marchand' said a plaque over the door.

'Is this it?' Rachel asked.

'This is it.'

The door swung open to reveal a small hallway tiled in mint-green hexagons. As Gabe closed the heavy door behind them, the sounds of the medina were immediately muffled, and the hot air of the city banished. Rachel exhaled.

'This way,' said Gabe. The hallway opened out on to a tiny but breathtakingly pretty tiled courtyard – white and emerald and turquoise – with a round skylight in its ornate ceiling and a fountain trickling lazily into its small, chequered pool surrounded by drooping palms, and orange and lemon trees in cobalt stone pots.

'It's beautiful,' she said. 'So peaceful.'

'I always stay here,' he said. 'I get looked after really well.' She wondered if he'd always come here alone or whether he had ever brought someone to lie on the side of the pool with, on the cool and calm tiles. To move on from, eventually. 'Madame Ricard is an excellent hostess.'

'How many rooms does it have?'

'I'll show you.'

There was a kitchen, a *salle à manger*, two *salons* and a bar, all off the courtyard and all beautiful.

'What's up here?' she asked, as a short passage from the second *salon* revealed the bottom of a narrow winding staircase, dimly lit.

'The bedrooms,' said Gabe. 'Would you like to see?'

She nodded. They climbed the wooden staircase, muskily fragranced in its gloom, and reached a hexagonal landing hugging a tiled central plinth of navy and topaz, where wall-mounted lamps softly lit six dark wood doors interspersed with small keyhole windows. Rachel trailed her fingers along the doors as they walked.

'This is my room,' Gabe said, stopping at one of them. 'I don't suppose—'

'OK,' she said.

'There are no exterior windows,' he volunteered, as they stepped inside, 'to keep everything as cool as possible.'

It was semi-dark in his room – a blind not quite all the way down on its keyhole window to the hall – and Rachel quickly absorbed its details. A pair of sneakers neat at the edge of an ornate ruby rug. A jacket flung over a rosewood chair. Petals floating in a decorative bowl. Gabe's bed, half made, the covers crumpled and flung back at one corner; the pillows dented marshmallows. Rachel felt herself blushing as she looked at it, where Gabe slept alone, warm skin against cool sheets.

'It's lovely,' she said. The room smelled of his cologne. 'Perfect after a hard day's sightseeing, I should imagine.'

He wandered over to the bed and idly picked up a ballpoint pen lying there. She wondered if he would sit, pat the coverlet next to him and gesture for her to come over, but he put the pen in his pocket and went to the door.

'Want to go back to the courtyard and get a soda or something?'

'Yes, please.'

There was a small fridge in the beautiful bijou kitchen. Gabe poured two iced sparkling waters and they took them to the courtyard, where they sat on the tiled surround of the pool and Rachel trailed her hand in the water.

'Will you come out with me again tonight?' he asked. The sun was in her eyes, suddenly, from the circular skylight. She couldn't see his face. 'There's a restaurant I'd like to take you to,' said Gabe, 'if you'll let me.'

'Have you not got anything better to do,' she asked lightly, 'than to spend your evening with me? Nothing with Khalid?'

'Khalid is busy with the exhibition and the paintings. I'm seeing him tomorrow when we go to Agadir.'

'Yes, I remember.' She fiddled with the hem of her dress, where a drop of water had spilled, darkening a spot of it.

'I'd like to spend time with you, while we're here. I don't know when I'll ever see you again. I feel I need to keep arranging things, or you'll slip away.'

She looked up at him. There was no answer to this, as she would indeed slip away soon enough. Two more nights and she'd be flying back home to her life.

Gabe continued. She still couldn't see his face. 'I've been thinking a lot about seizing the moment,' he said. '*Living* for the moment. As it's only the moments in my life that really seem to matter. Nothing longer term can be relied on.' He must have moved his head, as she could see his face again. 'When moments come along, I want to take them. Planning for the future can be severely overrated, don't you think?'

'No,' she said. 'It's all long term for me. Planning for the future is what I do. In my rosy bubble,' she joked, knowing some things in it were far from rosy.

'Ah, yes, your bubble.' Gabe looked at her curiously. 'Well, I just want to take some moments, with you, if that's OK.' She looked down at her dress again. The spot of water had gone. 'We'll eat, we'll drink, we'll talk, and then you can get back to your future.'

She looked up at him. 'Where is it, this restaurant?'

'In the medina. It's called Dar Essalam. Hitchcock shot a scene from *The Man Who Knew Too Much* there.'

'Doris Day and James Stewart?'

'The very one. It's a little touristy, but quite spectacular. Would you like to go?'

She sat. She thought. The trickling water was still peaceful but no longer lulled her. She had Jonny. She was doing something she could never tell him about. Yes, she could say she went to the Cafe Arabe, the Majorelle Garden, this Doris Day restaurant, but she couldn't say she'd been there with him, this American man, Julia March's nephew. A man she had once danced with. A man who had told her she was beautiful.

'You're not doing anything wrong,' Gabe said, as if reading her thoughts, but she remembered the rest of his words, outside the village hall that spring night. If she weren't engaged, if she were free . . . She was acting like she was free, but she wasn't. Rachel wasn't free to go to parties and rooftops and restaurants with this man. She had a direction she was supposed to be travelling in.

But Rachel looked at Gabe, his blue eyes, steady on hers. His smile. And she felt herself plunging. Wouldn't she still be travelling in that direction, whatever restaurant she ate in and whomever she ate with? Would a tiny diversion matter before she continued on the conveyor belt of her life, uninterrupted?

The water trickled from the fountain, like minutes through the day, or a life through their hands, and her words slipped from her like fire.

'Thank you, I'd like to go.'

# Chapter Twenty-Three

The phone rang in her hotel room at 6 p.m. Gabe was picking her up at seven.

'Hello?'

'Hi, it's Gabe. Look, I don't think it's such a good idea. Tonight.'

'What do you mean?' Rachel's heart plummeted to the basement of the hotel.

'I don't think it's a good idea. Us going out together tonight. I think it's . . . dangerous.'

'Dangerous? Why?'

'It's dangerous for both of us,' he said, and she was surprised he was feeling danger, the man for whom there was no consequence, the man who lived in the moment. She waited for him to say something else, her heart protesting.

'We're not doing anything wrong, remember?' she said finally. 'That's what you said.'

'I think it might be a mistake, that's all. What do you think?'

She didn't want to think at all. That was the point. Hadn't she almost conjured herself into an alternate existence, while she was getting ready? Putting on her make-up, doing her hair, turning herself into someone else?

'Well, I've already got my dress on and I've spent half an hour trying to get my fringe to lie flat, so I think we should go,' she said.

'You do?'

'Yes. We're just going out to eat – people need to eat, right? – and talk and have a couple of drinks.' She was echoing his words from earlier. 'As two people who bumped into each other in a foreign city and are spending time together. That's all.' She just wanted to go; she just wanted this night. 'See you in the lobby at seven,' she said quickly, and she put down the receiver, her hand shaking, and her heart clambered up the lift shaft and clicked back into her body.

◆  ◆  ◆

The Dar Essalam had a grand mosaicked portico of an entrance, set into a russet-y pink wall. A queue of elaborately covered-up female tourists – long skirts swishing against gold flat sandals – was snaking its way through the mouth of the doorway, murmuring 'wow' at every turn.

'Wow,' said Rachel herself, turning to Gabe, as they stepped inside. 'You weren't wrong about this place!'

'Amazing, isn't it?'

It was mosaicked, every last inch of it – floor, walls, ceiling – in tiny geometric tiles of the most amazing colours: grey-y dusty blues, muted creams, crimson reds and soft browns, kaleidoscope-d in the most intricately geometric and lacy motifs. There were alcoves and steps and archways. Ornate wooden doors and gold fretwork screens and suspended lamps, casting low light. It was a window-less, beautiful tomb of a place, with a feast for the eyes at every turn. A cavern of a building you wanted to peer into every corner of – every detailed arch and border and scroll.

Behind them, more tourists entered: Europeans in over-long chinos and cotton blazers, whose lapels were overslung with cameras on leather straps. Encased in a bottleneck, Rachel and Gabe moved to the end of the lobby and stepped down into the main restaurant area where it was all blues and greys, with red and stone tasselled cushions on low banquettes and a black-and-white chequered floor. On the wall was a still of Doris Day and James Stewart having dinner here.

'There they are,' said Gabe.

'There they are,' said Rachel. She imagined Doris and James walking into this restaurant for the first time, like she was, and looking around them with wonder.

She and Gabe hadn't said much on the way here. The taxi driver had the radio turned up loud and Rachel was relieved Celine Dion lustily drowned out all attempts at conversation. In lieu of small talk, they had exchanged small smiles and looked out of their windows. Rachel knew Gabe was right, that tonight was dangerous. She knew it as soon as Gabe had stepped out of the taxi outside the hotel wearing a silky charcoal shirt, with the sleeves rolled up. Black trousers. Black suede boots. His nose and across his cheekbones a little burnished from catching the day's sun.

It would not have been too late to pretend she was ill, or say she couldn't do it, or run for her life, but Rachel had been powerless. She hadn't cared about anything but him. Not Jonny. Not Teddy. Not the gallery. Not Fincham St George. She hadn't known how not to sit in the back of a taxi with Gabe, speeding towards the medina on this hot Moroccan night, and she didn't know how not to be in this amazing restaurant with him, being shown to a low table by the maître d'.

'Please take a seat.'

Their table was in the far corner. There were two other couples already seated: a French couple, in their sixties – 'Our first time in Marrakesh, isn't it hot here?' – and a mother and daughter who volunteered, via the mother, that they were from Brixton, in London. The daughter seemed terribly shy and barely raised her eyes from the table.

The table was elaborately laid with stacked charger plate, dinner plate and bowl – in crimson and cream – on a white tablecloth. There were rolled gold napkins lolling in wine glasses. Rachel thought again of the dinner party in Oxford, just a few nights ago. How wine was sloshed on her carefully decorated table halfway through the evening, and the candelabra knocked over – both by Jonny, laughingly telling a very funny anecdote from his last book tour. How Lee, who the candelabra fell in front of, just left it lying there, one hand down the back of Teddy's dress. Rachel let the memory drift away. A waiter was bringing bowls of soup and a platter of large rolls.

'OK?' asked Gabe.

'Yes,' she replied. Their earlier telephone call sat between them. Her last dinner party sat between them. Her real life sat between them, as much as she didn't want it to. And there wasn't much space in here: two inches between her right knee and his left. There were a *lot* of tourists crammed into this restaurant and it was prohibitively hot. The mother from Brixton was fanning her face with a napkin. The French husband was perspiring freely. Rachel hitched the skirt of her slip dress up a little and tucked the fabric between her knees, allowing air to cool her ankles and calves. She had never felt further from home.

Gabe smiled at her and she suddenly thought she didn't want to eat a single thing. She wanted to lean towards him and kiss him, kiss his slightly sunburnt cheeks, the tip of his nose, his lips . . .

'Look out!' he cried, amused.

Two men in traditional Moroccan dress appeared from an ornate doorway and, carrying sitars and small stools, settled themselves in a small keyhole archway at the back of the restaurant. They nodded at each other and then, with wry smiles, began to play, wriggling their heads as they strummed, so the long tassels from the top of their fezzes swirled like helicopter blades above them, causing grins at the table.

Rachel attempted the soup. It was delicious but she was too hot and too distracted. After a while, the waiter took it away and brought a tagine in a huge bell-shaped dish. There were layers of couscous and meat and sauce and egg; there was over-forced politeness in the sharing of the dish between strangers, that erupted into giggles. The shy London girl smiled at Rachel before dropping her eyes back to her plate.

'You're not still a vegetarian?' she asked Gabe, as he spooned lamb and couscous on to his plate.

'No, I gave it up.'

The tagine was cleared away. It was a fast meal, moved along quickly, as though ticked off on a clipboard by an unseen tour operator, lurking behind one of the elaborately carved doors. Rachel got up to go to the loo, closeted halfway along another blue-grey, beautifully mosaicked corridor, and when she came back, the dining space was empty of half its tourists and the two couples they'd eaten with had transplanted themselves to separate tables on the other side of the room.

'A group of Germans left,' explained Gabe. 'An appointment with a hammam just off the Jemaa, apparently. We've spread out.'

The French couple waved genially at her from their new table. There was a smile from the Brixton mother, another shy flicker of eyes from her daughter. Rachel sat back down at their table *à deux*, knowing this to be a disaster. She half expected Gabe to say 'Alone at last', with a hint of gentle self-awareness, but instead he said, 'I forgot to tell you how much of a knockout you look tonight.'

'Thank you,' she whispered, as she returned her napkin to her lap and smoothed its corners. Suddenly, it was all a matter of containment – her heart inside her body, and the wrong words from flying from her mouth. Her will, what there was of it, was already leaving her.

'And can I mention you're wearing the same sandals as that night in the village hall? *Blitz over Fincham St George?*'

'You remember that?' She was astounded.

'I remember everything.' He had to lean back, as a waiter arrived at their table and solicitously refilled their drinks. 'I remember those sandals were a bit precarious for dancing,' he continued, once the waiter had glided off, and his eyes were locked on hers and Rachel couldn't look away. 'I remember you're squeamish about blood. I remember you cry sometimes, but you're very good at pretending you don't.'

'That's a lot to remember,' she said.

'Is it? I don't think it is if you're interested in a person.' She looked away, towards the musicians in the fezzes who were now gathering their sitars and shuffling through an exit archway, bowing and smiling. 'You don't think I should be interested in you?'

She turned back. 'No.'

'Why not?'

'It's not your role.'

'It's not my role?' There was that easy laugh, the one she liked so much. *What about the danger?* she wanted to cry. The 'mistake'? Where had that gone? But Rachel realised he had slipped back into the easy Gabe of this trip, the one who lived in the moment, while she was somewhere else. She wasn't in the moment; she was on the precipice of her entire life, like others had been before her. 'OK . . . Want me to change the subject?'

'Yes, please.'

He thought for a second. 'My grandfather worked with James Stewart once,' he said. 'Not on *The Man Who Knew Too Much*, but on *Mr. Smith Goes to Washington*. You seen that movie?'

'Yes, I think so. Once, maybe, with Nanna.'

'My grandfather was a camera assistant, he rode the dolly – you know, that track the camera goes back and forth on? It was his first and last movie, actually, as not long afterwards, he permanently damaged his hand in a boating accident, down at the beach.' He paused. 'We call our lakes "beaches" in North Dakota,' he added. 'Nearest we got. After that, he worked at the famous Kegs in Grand Forks, North Dakota – a roadside diner. He worked there for forty years, one-handedly flipping burgers and taking home spare buns to my grandma every night. *That* was a love story,' he said. 'Forty-two years of laughter and burger buns.'

'My great aunt and uncle were married for thirty-eight years,' she said. 'Although my nanna almost went off with someone else in the war, an American,' she added, hardly daring to look at Gabe, 'but she stuck with my grandpop, and they were amazing.'

'I'll ignore the parallels,' said Gabe, shaking his head, 'as long as you know you don't have to follow in your nanna and grandpop's footsteps.'

But she was, wasn't she? She had been living by Flo's grass isn't greener motto, keeping her view from the kitchen window the same. Sticking to the plan of sticking together, of protection, like her great aunt had protected her, but, tonight, Jonny had never seemed further from reach. He was a vague recollection of a faraway place she'd once known. A shadow on a wall, hard to make out. But Rachel knew she must return to that wall, and to him; to the props that both reset the foundations of her past and held her up. She was *sticking* with that. She had to return to what she had constructed to keep her safe.

'What was your parents' marriage like?'

Rachel was taken aback. 'I don't really want to talk about that.' He had remembered, then, about them. No one in Fincham St George mentioned Frances and Gary now, not even Linda at the bank, not now she had said too much. Jonny still said things like 'Past is past' and 'It's the future that's important'. 'What's the point?' was what he said the most. 'If it upsets you, what's the point in talking about it?' Jonny. She must focus on him. She must not let him get lost in the softly cast light of this very different man.

'OK,' said Gabe. 'How about, tell me three things about your parents and I'll tell you three things about mine.'

'You start,' she said. She didn't know if she was actually going to play or not, not when she knew the bitter truth about how her parents died.

'OK,' said Gabe, his eyes blue and considering. 'Number one. My dad was a devil at card games. Like, ridiculously, turn-the-table-over-if-he-didn't-win competitive. Mom would have to let him win. I'd sit behind her and watch her throw good cards away. He was *always* so goddam competitive . . .' Gabe shook his head. 'Number two was that they got married on a ranch. My mother was seventeen and pregnant with me. She wore a yellow sundress and was barefoot; Dad was wearing jeans and his trucker's hat. We have one photograph of the day. When they were happy. A third thing was that every Sunday in the summer, when I was growing up, they'd put me in the car and we'd drive fifty miles to Beaver Lake State Park, up in Napoleon, and we'd stop at the White Maid drive-in on the way home and we'd buy sloppy joes and eat them in the car park, on the back of the trailer. I like those memories,' he said. 'The last two, anyway.'

'Good memories,' Rachel agreed. She could see it all, in her mind: the ranch and the state park and the drive-in and his mum's yellow sundress. 'You said "was",' she added, 'about your dad. Past tense.'

Gabe smiled sadly. 'He died last year. Brain haemorrhage. Happened one day, out back, while he was sitting in a lounge chair. I found him. He just looked like he was asleep, you know? Just asleep.' He sighed. 'Mom's still alive, still in and out of facilities,

212

but out more than she's in now, which is good. She's got her own little place, just up the street from me.'

'That's good. I'm so sorry about your dad.'

'Thank you. Hopefully he's at some sort of peace, as he sure as hell wasn't in this life.' He shrugged. 'What can you do?'

'OK, here's three things about mine,' Rachel said quickly, before she could change her mind. 'Number one: my dad liked to keep fish. We had an aquarium in the downstairs loo and Dad had named them – even though most of them looked exactly the same – after the 1966 England football squad. "Geoff Hurst" was this yellow thing with a black stripe.' Gabe smiled. 'Number two . . .' She took a deep breath. It was a gamble, saying this, for her own heart. But something about the quiet look on Gabe's face made her do it. '. . . He had an affair, which was why they were killed in a car crash. Number three: every Tuesday and Thursday night I'd come downstairs in my nightie and watch *Coronation Street* with my mum, while she was knitting, and eat cheese and crackers. I liked the music on the opening credits and the way the clicking of the needles went in time with it. We both liked Deidre Barlow.' Rachel laughed. 'This will mean nothing to you!'

'That's a nice memory,' said Gabe thoughtfully. 'Aunt Julia likes *Coronation Street*. But you kinda skipped quickly over number two, Rachel,' he added softly. 'Your dad's affair? The car crash?'

She almost couldn't bear the concerned curiosity in his eyes. 'You know, I wasn't allowed to go to the funeral,' she said quickly. 'Kids just didn't. I had to stay at home watching *World's Strongest Man* and doing a paint-by-numbers of a panda. It was hot, that summer. I drew the curtains to keep the sun out. When everyone got back, Nanna gave me a packet of ready-salted crisps from the pub, and told me everything was going to be all right . . .' She tucked her hair behind her ears, placed her hands at the edge of the table. Gabe went to reach his hand across to hers, but she could see it coming. She moved them quickly to her lap, on the smooth napkin. 'And now I know what really happened. That night.' Rachel fell silent.

'Do you want to tell me—?'

There was a sudden movement from behind them. A rippling, tinkling sound; a perfumed frisson, and a raven-haired siren in a bubble-gum pink bikini top, one long glove and a jewelled skirt with tiny bells on it sashayed into the space, a rather alarming tray full of lit candles on her head. The diners clapped in surprise; the siren smiled enigmatically and, to a burst of music, she began to wriggle her hips, swinging her long dark hair from side to side and shimmying and turning, before travelling around the tables.

At Rachel and Gabe's, she held out her hand to Gabe, and gestured for him to join her, but he shook his head.

'I'm happy where I am,' he said, looking at Rachel. 'Thank you.' And the woman nodded and moved on.

After enticing someone else to dance with her and to wear the tray of candles, the lady finally disappeared, with one more wriggle of her hips, through a grey-blue arch, and another took her place – a belly dancer, who immediately dragged up a mortified teenage boy to dance with her, squirming with embarrassment and refusing to look in the direction of her cleavage. The music got louder and faster. She gestured, with a sweep of a graceful arm, for diners to come and join her. A group of beaming Swedes rose up straight away. The French couple followed. The London mother stood up and beckoned her daughter, who shook her head in horror. The rest of the tourists in the restaurant moved to the impromptu dance floor and some made a game stab at attempting the belly-dancing moves, to much general mirth, while others gyrated haphazardly to the music.

'I'm feeling a little pressure to join in,' said Gabe. 'What do you think?'

'I think we should dance,' replied Rachel. She wanted to. She wanted to get closer to him. She wanted to stall the rest of their conversation. The rest of the night. She wanted to suspend time.

Gabe stood and held out his hand to Rachel and, as soon as she took it, she was back in the village hall with him again. She was land girl, and he was US Navy officer. They walked to the dance floor, where they tucked themselves between a grinning double-denim Swede and a woman in the coral swish of a high-necked maxi dress, and started doing a silly ineffectual jive, just like they had all those years before. Rachel couldn't help but giggle; Gabe grinned at her. The dancers around them shifted and they had to move closer, abandoning the jive and dancing very close now. Gabe put his hands on her waist. Rachel moved into him. Let his hands graze her back. His hand moved up from her back and trailed into her hair. She placed her right hand at the back of his neck.

There was a sudden crescendo of Moroccan drums from the sound system and then the music stopped. They stood there, in the centre of the room, not removing their hands from each other's bodies.

'Do you believe in love?' he asked her. His face was very close. There was an urgency to his voice. 'Real love?'

'I'm married,' Rachel said, breathless from the dancing and the question. Her hand was still at the back of his neck.

'The two don't necessarily tally,' he said.

'Yes, I believe in love.'

'And do you have it?'

'Yes, I think so.'

'Then what is this?'

'I don't know,' Rachel said. 'I don't know.'

The tourists had slid back to their seats. Gabe lowered his hand from Rachel's hair, and she took hers from his neck and they melted from the dance floor and slipped back to their table. Gabe pulled his seat closer to hers, so their knees touched. He took her hands again.

'Are you happy?' he asked her, searching her face.

'Mostly,' she said, her heart thumping in her chest. 'Are you?'

'I find moments of happiness. This is a moment of happiness. And I lied.'

'What about?'

'Only wanting moments with you. I don't just want moments, I want everything. I want a lifetime.'

The rest of the room didn't exist any more. The people, the majesty, the history. All that existed was Gabe and the touch of his hands.

'I'm married to Jonny,' she said. It suddenly sounded like a death sentence. Something trotted out. A line. A truth that didn't matter. Not right now.

'And I'm worried that I've never felt this way before, and that I might not ever feel this way again.'

Rachel knew. That in another lifetime their souls were looped together, laughing at silly things in the newspapers or smiling over baked lobster in a Saturday night restaurant or sitting quietly, in a garden somewhere, not talking but just being *still* with each other. She could see it, this other life, with this man, when she was already at least a third of the way through her own. Her life was being married to Jonny. Teddy. All her reasons. Her scaffolding. Her proofing of the future. These things could not be dismantled. She could not break them apart piece by piece and make something new. Because of her mum and dad. Because of her nanna. Their blueprints. Their templates for life, good and bad.

'I can't explain it,' he said. 'I feel in another life . . .'

'I'd be your next girlfriend?' It was a miserable attempt at a joke. She was miserable.

'No. I feel in another life you might shake up everything I've ever known. I know I could love you,' he said. 'Really love you.'

'Don't,' she said. 'Don't.' Rachel had made her choice long ago. She didn't have an alternate lifetime in which to live with another man. To love another man.

'You feel it too, don't you?' Gabe asked fervently.

She couldn't look at him. She wouldn't answer. Yet, she only wanted to be here, right now, at this low table, in this restaurant where movie stars had once sat. She wanted to feel the warmth of him next to her. Look at his face, the way his mouth softly curled up at the edges when he smiled, listen to his voice, his laugh. Hear him say that he could love her. Rachel wanted to transcend time and have it suspended here, forever, like a hammock slung between trees on a summer's day.

'Tell me you feel it too?'

'We don't have another life,' she said. 'We only have this one.'

'We can change our lives,' Gabe said, but she shook her head.

'I can't just exchange the one I have for another.'

'You could do,' he said. 'You could . . .'

'I couldn't!' she cried. 'I made a *choice*, for a lifetime. I made a commitment.' She froze for a second, then she continued. 'I need things calm and predictable. Safe. Quiet. No change, no drama . . . I've had all the drama I ever want in my life.'

'Because of your parents? Tell me!' he pleaded. 'Tell me what happened the night they died.'

She braced herself, anchored her feet to the floor. 'I'll tell you what happened!' she cried. 'My father had an affair, a terrible grubby little affair that lasted on and off for *two years*. That shattered every hero-worshipping, foolish-little-girl notion I had of him. He didn't love her, he didn't even like her very much, from what I heard. But he wouldn't stop seeing her. He would just keep going *back* – back and forth – despite all the screaming and the

217

shouting, despite the periods of time when my parents pretended to try and keep things together—' The words were rushing from her, toppling over and over. '—until one night, when they were getting ready to go out for another make-up dinner . . .'

There was a new and terrible part to the story of that night, a part that was still shockingly fresh and sharp and searingly painful to Rachel. A detail that had been kept from her, after the accident, and for many years since, aided and abetted by a loving and worried and well-meaning Florence and Jim, who had shielded her from the truth. Who had kept up the tragic tale of an almost happy trip to an Indian restaurant that went catastrophically wrong . . .

Rachel had discovered what really happened eight months ago. She'd gone into the bank one morning with another cheque, another dividend from her father's solicitors, and Linda, a little distracted on that occasion, having to reluctantly divert from stamping a huge pile of paying-in slips, had looked at the cheque, muttered 'shame' and then, shaking her head, had added, almost incomprehensibly, 'Going to that bloody woman again . . .' Rachel, just catching her words, had asked what she meant and Linda, puce-cheeked and caught out, had spluttered, 'You *really* still don't know?' and had abandoned her glass cube – walked straight out – and taken Rachel to the cafe (where an aproned-Wren had looked on with concern) and shamefacedly told her everything.

'. . . They had another blazing row.' Rachel continued to press down on the tablecloth. 'But this time when my dad left the house, Mum ran out after him, in her dressing gown – hysterical – and she flung herself in the passenger seat and my dad drove off like a maniac, to frighten her, and the car crashed three streets away and they died. My mum and dad. They died.'

Only the police knew, and Florence and Jim, and the neighbour who had heard them arguing. And Linda, of course, for the neighbour had told her. Linda was so sorry, she really thought Rachel had known by then (wrongly assuming that Nanna Florence's tongue had been as loose as her own) and she'd tried to hug her across the cafe table, but Rachel had been cold, stone cold. She'd left the cafe and Linda and Wren, and had walked home, to Jonny, as a ghost.

'I'm sorry,' said Gabe.

'One of my mum's slippers had got half shut in the door and fell into a flower bed,' said Rachel absently. 'I saw it there the following morning. Do you know, that was there for three days, that slipper, until someone picked it up . . . ?' She had always wondered what it was doing there.

'I'm sorry, Rachel,' Gabe repeated. 'I'm so, so sorry.'

'Thank you.' She was still processing it, the truth of that night. The terrible domino effect of her father's actions and her mother's. How the flutter and the beating of wings could smash through any glassy veneer of home or comfort. She didn't blame Nanna for not telling her, as the truth was horrible. She loved her and Grandpop for wanting to protect her from it. And Jonny had said not to dwell on this new part of the story, to keep her eyes on the future, like he always did. 'I . . . I need peace in my life, I need contentment,' she challenged, raising her voice a little. 'I need things stable, steadfast. That's what I've chosen and it's more important to me than ever. Being with you is not contentment. Being with you is turning my life – everything calm and peaceful and safe about it – upside down! But yes, I feel it too,' she said sadly, as she knew her words, her convictions, meant nothing in this moment. Her resolutions had already turned to dust. 'Of course I fucking well feel it too.'

'Let's get out of here,' he said.

He grabbed her hand and they fled through the mosaicked tomb of the dining space, through the labyrinth of the ancient building and back out on to the darkened alley. They hurried through the maze of the medina and within minutes found themselves in the heaving expanse of the market square at night, where she feared if Gabe let go of her hand she would be swallowed up into the crowd.

The Jemaa was a streak of people and lights, like Khalid's painting. Gone were the snake charmers and the dusty monkeys and in their place were rows of coloured lanterns, laid out on rugs. Kids' light-up spinning toys cascaded through the air in neon reds and greens and blues. Restaurant hustlers called out random Western pop star names to clusters of tourists ('Hey, Mariah Carey!' 'Hey, Liam Gallagher!') to get laughs, custom, punters.

'Where are we going?' she asked. Behind her, a Moroccan tour guide patiently admonished two sheepish teenage girls for wandering off from the group.

'I don't know,' Gabe said. 'I just want to walk with you. Go anywhere. Be with you.'

They walked through the maze of streets without speaking. They didn't let go of each other's hands, although it was forbidden. Everything was forbidden, for Rachel and Gabe. They found themselves in a dead end of an alley where yarns hung above them like judges' robes and there was a studded doorway. Rue de la Marchand.

'You have an early start in the morning,' Rachel said, her words just above a whisper as she thought of his room, his bed. 'Agadir.'

'Yes. Five a.m.'

A man brushed past them.

'Evening,' he said, English accent. 'Are you coming in?' He unlocked the door and propped it open for them.

Gabe and Rachel looked at each other. The man waited. Behind them, the final call to prayer echoed across the city.

'No,' said Gabe, and the man shrugged in a suit-yourself fashion, stepped inside and the door closed. 'I'll find you a taxi,' he said to Rachel. 'See you back to the hotel.'

The taxi driver smoked out of his open window and played loud Moroccan dance music. The hotel was reached too soon. The driver tapped at the meter, lit up another cigarette. Gabe came round to open Rachel's door for her. She got out, her legs shaking.

'Rachel,' he said and his mouth was on hers and it was like everything they had ever needed or wanted was in this moment, *this moment*, and she wasn't sure where his hands were, on her waist, her hips, round the back of her, she didn't know, but hers were round his neck, pulling him to her, bringing him closer, closer, and she was sure she had never felt like this before, because how could she, when nothing had ever felt like this?

'Oh God,' he said finally.

'Gabe,' she said, the taste of him on her lips, her tongue; his fingerprints on her soul. And his mouth refound hers and she didn't want it to stop because once it stopped, it was the end. Yet Rachel knew she had to be the one to choose the ending. And the ending had to be now.

She pulled away, although it was like wrenching her soul out of her body – a flamed soul he had touched with burning fingers – and throwing it in the gutter.

'Goodbye, Gabe,' she muttered, and she fled from him into the lobby, where the lights were dimmed and there was a solitary concierge on reception, staring at her with disinterested eyes.

'You sad he's gone?'

'What?'

That awful businessman was by the lifts. She walked to the furthest one and faced the steel doors.

'Your man, he no come in. You sad he's gone?'

Rachel ignored him. She just wanted to get to her room, to the cool turned-down sheets.

'You want me to come up? To fuck?'

He stank of coffee, strong cigarettes and assumption.

'No, no, I don't want that,' she said, willing the doors to open. 'Go away, please. Please just go away.'

'You OK, madame?'

She turned and it was the concierge. 'Is this man bothering you?'

'Yes, he is.'

'*Monsieur, allez, allez!*' the concierge said to the businessman, as though shooing away a fly. And something in Arabic.

'Thank you, *merci*,' she gabbled as the lift doors opened, and she was swallowed mercifully inside.

Rachel got into bed with her clothes on and lay there, eyes wide open, staring at the ceiling in the pitch dark for over an hour. Until the phone rang.

'Hello?'

'Will you come to my riad tomorrow night? Come to my place. Will you?' Gabe sounded breathless, out of himself.

The phone felt big and grey and plastic in her hand. The air between her mouth and the receiver was heavy.

'Yes,' Rachel said. 'Yes, I will.'

# Chapter Twenty-Four

Rachel woke at 5 a.m. with a jolt, catapulted into the reality of morning. She stared at the narrow straw of light in the almost-closed curtains. Listened to the crickety whir of the air con and the trundle of a suitcase being wheeled up a distant corridor.

Marrakesh was awakening. She imagined Khalid turning up in a dusty car to an alley behind Gabe's riad, Gabe throwing a bag into the boot. The pair of them winding down the windows and turning up the radio before setting off on their road trip to Agadir. She imagined herself tonight, going to Gabe's riad and into his bed.

Rachel knew there wouldn't be a moment today when she might think she wouldn't go, when she wouldn't envisage being with him, in that dark, closeted room, inside that jewel of a riad and nestled among the streets and the mystery of the medina. She would live these hours at the hotel, and wait for evening. She would wait, and then she would go to him.

At 6 a.m. she flicked idly through a magazine, focusing on nothing. At 7 a.m. she sat on the balcony and watched tiny bubbles of cloud teeter on the horizon then give up in deference to another clear-skied day. At 8 a.m. she called down to reception to pre-book a taxi for 6.30 p.m. At 11 a.m. she went downstairs and bought a coffee and a paper in the lobby, which she didn't drink and didn't read. At midday, she headed to the pool to lay supine on a sun lounger. At four o' clock, she came back up to the room, had a shower, laid out a strapless green dress on the bed and stared at the contents of her make-up box. At 5.30 p.m. she was ready. At 6.20 p.m. she grabbed her bag and opened the door.

'Surprise!'

'*Surprise!*'

Jonny was standing in the doorway, Teddy was on tiptoes behind him, holding up a banner that said 'Birthday Girl!' in pink bubble writing.

'Happy birthday!' cried Jonny.

'Happy *birthday!*' echoed Teddy and she blew into a loud party popper, like a lizard's tongue, which poked Jonny in the ear.

'Oh my God! What are you doing here?' exclaimed Rachel, an ashen-faced ghoul of terrified laughter and crashing relief and huge, huge, bitter, bitter disappointment, and she wanted to scream and cry but she also wanted to throw herself on them – her family – and never let them go, but Gabe, Gabe, Gabe . . . oh God, *Gabe*.

'My fabulous editor gave me an extension,' beamed Jonny, walking into the room and looking around him, pulling back the curtains and peering out of the window, then flinging his bag on to the bed, 'and you can extend your trip by a couple of days, can't you? So here we are! A bit spur of the moment but Teddy was up for it, weren't you, darling? Although I literally had to prise her away from Lee.'

'Let him miss me,' shrugged Teddy. 'And, you know, free holiday.' She came to hug Rachel, briefly letting her breathe in the solace of the faint teenage perfume on her neck, before mooching out to the balcony.

'And it's your birthday!' Jonny exclaimed. 'We couldn't let your birthday pass with you so far away! Come here!' And he put his arms around Rachel and held her tight. She clung to Jonny like he was a bobbing buoy in the sea, and she an out-of-her-depth fool, surprised by an unexpected undercurrent. *I've been saved*, she thought. Saved, again. How close she had been to the edge. How close to losing everything.

'Cool pool,' remarked Teddy, from out on the balcony.

'So, what are we going to do,' said Jonny, loosening Rachel from his neck, 'to celebrate your birthday evening?'

'I don't know,' mumbled Rachel. She looked at Jonny's face. At his hair. At his arms. At his T-shirt. His neck. Everything that was so safe and familiar about him. *How different he is*, she thought. *How different to Gabe.* And she nearly threw herself down on the bed and sobbed for everything she had and hadn't lost.

'Well, I've already planned something,' said Jonny proudly. 'And you look ready to go.'

'I was going down to dinner. On my own,' Rachel added unnecessarily.

'Well, *we* need to get changed,' he said, heading for the bathroom, joyously shedding clothes as he went. 'We probably smell like a butcher's armpit. Quick shower, Teddy,' he called to his daughter, 'and then it's off to the Dar Essalam, birthday girl!' he said to Rachel.

She froze. 'Dar Essalam?'

'Most famous restaurant in Marrakesh,' Jonny declared from the bathroom doorway. 'It's going to be great!' He disappeared, closing the door behind him.

Rachel sank down on the bed. She couldn't go back there. Not after last night. And she and Gabe had been seen. They had looked like lovers, she knew they had. She spread her fingers on the cool top sheet and tried to think clearly. Could she say she had already been there, on an organised trip or something, with the hotel? Could she say she'd heard it was overrated, and suggest going somewhere else? How could she tell Jonny she had been there for dinner last night, with another man?

She sat on the bed and vaguely registered the late-evening shrieks of people still in the pool, overlaid with the early percussion of cutlery and crockery. She felt she was being rushed through a tunnel. Jonny emerged from the bathroom in a cloud of steam and good humour, the white hotel towel shackled round his middle.

'Bathroom's free!' he called, and sat next to Rachel on the bed, placing a warm hand on her shoulder. It already felt like he'd been in this hotel room for days. 'We're going to have a fantastic night,' he promised.

They were whisked by taxi to the eternal dusky pink of the medina – back to the alleyways and the womblike, mosaicked entrance of the Dar Essalam – Jonny and Teddy exclaiming with delight at every turn. It was the same man on the door but if he recognised Rachel he didn't show it. The maître d' seeing them to their table – the *same* table; she knew it would be – didn't show it either. Neither did the strumming men with the spinning tassels or the raven-haired woman with the tray of candles on her head, or the belly dancer who pulled Jonny up from his table to dance with her like an eager clown. The only face she feared letting on that she had been here before was her own. Every bite she ate, every sip of drink, every false laugh or smile was painful, and she marvelled that no one else noticed that.

'Would you like another drink, darling?'

'What?' Rachel had been staring into space. It was nearly the end of the evening and knowing Gabe had been waiting for her was pulling at her guts like fishing wire. The Birthday Girl. Not lit up by love and family, like she was pretending to be, but plunged into darkness by near infidelity and treachery and utter misery. This was a betrayal to Jonny and Teddy, a betrayal to Gabe, a betrayal to herself.

'Isn't it marvellous, darling?' Jonny threw his arm around her shoulders and gathered her nearer to him. 'Don't you just love it here? Aren't you glad we came?'

'Yes, I'm glad,' she lied. 'Very glad.' Rachel wanted to flee this table, like she and Gabe had last night, and run through the maze of streets to him. She wanted to pound on the door of the riad until he let her in. She wanted his lips on hers again. She wanted the delicious, forbidden wrongness of him.

When the evening was over and they stepped out into heat of the medina, Jonny suggested a horse and carriage ride, which turned out to be endless. They trotted through streets narrow and wide, under arches, while people gaped from open windows. They hurtled past green hedges and dusty, broken fences. They waited in traffic and careered freely around roundabouts, mopeds beeping joyously at them.

She searched for Gabe, in the streets, knowing he wasn't within them. Had he turned the light out now, in his room? Was he lying in his cool, dark bed and hating her? Jonny squeezed her hand and the hooves clip-clopped and the whipped-up breeze flicked at her hair, and she thought, *I must turn the light out now, too. I must accept it. That I am married. That I have been saved from myself tonight.*

'I love you,' whispered Jonny, leaning in to her. 'Happy birthday. Are you OK?'

'Yeah, you don't really seem with it tonight,' offered Teddy, from the other end of the green leather seat.

'I think it's a touch of sunstroke,' lied Rachel, her heart full and treacherous as she smiled weakly at her stepdaughter. 'I got a bit burned today. But, yes, I'm OK.'

'I can't wait to get sunstroke tomorrow,' Teddy replied. 'I'm going to burn myself silly.'

Clip-clop, clip-clop. Time swept on. Rachel took a long, silent breath, in and out, to the rhythm of the horse's hooves, and with each breath she tried to come back to herself.

◆ ◆ ◆

Rachel awoke to Jonny taking a long phone call with his new editor, Bunty, punctuated by hoots of laughter and some earnest debating about character motivation. Teddy was out smoking on the balcony, in one of the hotel towelling gowns; she had slept on the camp bed in the dressing room area. As soon as Jonny put the phone down, it rang again. He snatched it up.

'Hello . . . hello? Nobody there,' said Jonny, placing the receiver down. 'I thought it might be Bunty phoning me back to say she's increasing my next advance.' He grinned one of his infectious grins and headed to the bathroom.

'Was that Lee?' called Teddy from the balcony. She had a pager, some new-fangled thing, and was waiting for Lee to contact her on it.

'No. It wasn't anybody, love,' said Rachel. She sat up heavily in the bed. Oh God, it was Gabe, wasn't it? Gabe calling her.

Rachel had not slept well. She had dreamed she was on an eternal horse and carriage ride she couldn't get off of, carrying her to the sea where it entered the water and kept on clopping, against the tide, until she woke up with a start, spluttering for breath.

'Are you OK?' Jonny had asked again, in the dark, his head heavy on the pillow next to her.

'Yes,' she had lied, again.

'I'm just popping out to get a paper,' Rachel called out to Teddy, moments later. 'See you both down at the pool.'

She slid down the corridor like a stoat and then down in the lift. She felt sick as she slid on to the back seat of a taxi and terrified as it glided out of the hotel gates, but she knew she had to see him.

'Rue de la Marchand, please.'

The taxi pulled up in the narrow street behind Gabe's riad. A woman opened the door as Rachel was about to knock.

'Hello, can I help you?'

'I was looking for one of your guests,' said Rachel, nervous. 'Gabe McAllister?'

'Mr McAllister? Oh, he's gone, I'm afraid.' The woman spoke with a French accent. 'He left early this morning – I think he brought his flight forward.'

'Oh. He's gone?'

'Yess . . .' The woman spoke like Rachel was slow to understand. 'He's not here. He's gone back to the States. I'm sorry. You're a friend of his . . . ?'

'Yes. Did you see him, before he left?'

Rachel didn't know what she was hoping the woman would say. That he looked sorrowful, a hollow version of himself, like she was, her insides so sheer and fragile a stranger could run their fingers through them?

'No, I didn't, sorry. As I said, it was very early. He was gone when I opened up at six.'

Rachel nodded and walked away.

◆ ◆ ◆

'You were gone ages!' Jonny noted, poolside, when she arrived with the newspaper.

'They'd run out. I had to walk to the kiosk down the road.'

She lay on a sun lounger without taking her sundress off. She looked up at the indigo sky, the sun sizzling like a fizzing aspirin in a glass of water. She heard the mid-morning lapping of the pool, the slapping of water against the filter. The buzz of the drinks machine. A lawnmower in the side gardens. A drill, somewhere within the hotel. She didn't want to close her eyes. To enter the dark miserable cavern of her brain. Rachel wanted sunlight and heat to saturate her, to burn Gabe away so she would be free of him and what had happened between them in this hot and majestic city of fire and of dust.

'You'll boil like that,' said Teddy from her own lounger. She was all teeny bikini, carrot oil and toes painted in Chanel Rouge Noir.

'I *want* to boil,' said Rachel.

The trail of a plane lazily streaked the sky like Gabe's had earlier this morning. He was halfway home now. He would continue with his life, continue searching for what he was looking for, but it wouldn't be her. She was home already, entrenched in it, buried in it, right up to her soul – the home that was meant to erase her past, all parts of it, and all its pain – but she would not forget the path she hadn't taken, that other life she had imagined, if only for a moment. It was love and it was loss, and it was hope and it was fear. It was a silvery thread pulled through her very being, like that plane trail across the sky, and it had gone.

# AUTUMN

20 OCTOBER 2008

# Chapter Twenty-Five

'Morning, Rachel!'

Robin Stipple, current manager of Fincham St George's Village Veg, and brilliant wielder of the charcoal pencil, gusted into the gallery on an autumn breeze, a russet-y leaf settled in his sandy hair like a bobby pin.

'Morning, Rachel!'

In his slipstream bustled Felicity – yellow rain mac, tiny lace-up boots – an absolute killer with watercolours. 'Great to get out of that drizzle,' she said, setting her tote bag at the end of the semi-circle of chairs and beginning to take out paintbrushes and palettes. 'My barnet looks like I've spent a week in the Bahamas.'

'You wish!' chimed a laughing voice. Kaye Bruce, local florist and lover of pastel crayons, swooped in with her artist's portfolio tucked under one flapping sleeve of a voluminous cape. 'Morning, Rachel. Who do we have today?' she asked, as she plonked her case on the floor.

'Tim,' said Rachel. She was at the back of the gallery, watching happily as her artists filed in. 'Morning, everyone.'

'Oh, I like him!' cried Sheetal. She was sloping in backwards, dragging her retro bag on wheels Rachel knew was filled with every medium: watercolours, oils, pastels, coloured pencils, charcoals and acrylics. 'He sits so nice and still.'

'Let me help you,' said Felicity, holding the door open for her. 'Oh, yes,' she agreed. 'We love a non-fidgeter.'

The rest of the class arrived and settled themselves behind easels, as weak sunlight streaked in through the gallery window and lit up their expectant faces. There was always a palpable anticipation at the beginning of a class: two hours' suspension from work, home, children and responsibilities; a quiet time with nothing required but silently dipping paintbrushes into water, or softly smudging a line of charcoal with a smutted finger.

'Sorry I'm a bit late.' Wren squeezed through the door carrying a giant sketch pad and a fluffy pencil case. Rachel smiled affection-ately at her friend's curly hair tied up in a wobbling bun, her roots needing doing (at forty-eight, didn't they always, for the pair of them?), and at her DM boots, still going strong.

'You made it,' Rachel said.

'The assembly didn't go on as long as I thought,' grinned Wren. 'Cute singing.' She had five children now: her youngest, twin girls aged seven; her eldest, teenagers. She came to embrace Rachel in a huge hug. 'Good to see you.'

'And you, Wren.' Rachel held her friend tight. They were close again. It had taken a while, but they knew the secrets of each other's hearts once more, and Rachel had needed her friend more than ever.

'Hi, everyone,' said Rachel, once Wren was settled. 'So, we have Tim again today,' she announced formally. Tim emerged somewhat sheepishly from the back room, in blue jeans and a stripy jumper. He would be keeping his clothes on; it was not a life drawing class, it was portraiture. Faces, whole bodies, clothes. No sniggering. No goosebumps. Rachel pulled a chair forward for him. 'Arrange your-self how you like,' she said.

'OK,' said Tim good-naturedly. He sat down and crossed his long legs, folded his long arms across his lap and pushed his glasses further up his nose. A few of their class shifted their position to get a better angle. Wren put her reading glasses on and leaned forward in her chair.

'Glass of water before we get going?' Rachel asked Tim.

'No, I'm good, thank you.'

Tim was new to the village and had wandered past the gallery a couple of weeks ago, coming in to offer his services, as he used to do life modelling years ago when he was a student. Rachel always needed people and Tim was an excellent find. He had a very interesting face – a great beard – and could sit for ages without moving a muscle.

The class set to work, looking and sketching. Wren had taken her jumper off and was wearing a T-shirt that said 'The Naughty Noughties', although she and Rachel had decided the Noughties didn't really have an identity at all, not like the 70s, 80s or 90s, but they supposed there was still time.

Rachel walked round the class making encouraging noises and suggestions. She loved these sessions and was glad she had decided to do them. She thought at first no one would come, when she introduced art classes at Vivaldi's in the spring of 2003, but they had, and people in the village seemed to really enjoy them.

Tim coughed. He shifted marginally in his seat but returned to exactly the same position. The pencils shuffled. The paintbrushes swished. Rachel tried to empty her mind of the rest of the day and what it might hold. She stood behind Wren and gently pointed out a perspective issue with her drawing, at which Wren declared 'Bugger!' and started frantically scouring at one of Tim's shoulders with the rubber at the end of her pencil. Rachel was crossing the gallery to fetch her a more forgiving one when there was a sudden rap on the window.

All heads turned. It was Teddy, wearing a bright orange jumper dress, a red scarf, and a sheepish grin.

'Sorry,' she mouthed. 'Sorry to disturb you,' she repeated, once Rachel had stepped outside. 'How's it all going?'

'Great,' said Rachel, gently shutting the gallery door behind her. 'You OK?'

'Yeah, I'm good. I'm free today until four o'clock so I thought I'd pop by.' Teddy was thirty-one. She had recently dyed her hair brown and it was the colour of bark, with a stripe of mossy blonde at the roots. She *was* good at the moment. She was great, in fact. 'How's Dad? I just knocked at the door to say hello but he wasn't there.'

'He's in Belgium,' said Rachel. 'Did I not tell you?'

'I can't keep up with him,' laughed Teddy. 'There's that many book tours. It's nice to see you, though.'

'And you. It's always wonderful when you drop by. How's university life been this week?'

'It's been fab,' smiled Teddy. 'Another week as the oldest student in town.'

Teddy was a mature student, in the third year of a degree in marketing at Oxford Brookes university, where she insisted they called her Tatiana. It had been a long and winding road to get her there, punctuated by the debilitating potholes of addiction that had surfaced in her life, deadly and dark and waiting, by the end of the 1990s, when her occasional pot habit turned into a reliance on alcohol and a downward tailspin. Teddy lost the dead-end jobs she'd been surviving in. She holed herself up at Lee's, drinking vodka, smoking weed and eating toast and Marmite all day. She ignored Jonny and Rachel knocking at the door, or calling her, or begging her to get help, even when Rachel started going every day, after she had finished at the gallery, and rapping on the sitting room window until Teddy eventually relented and let her in.

Rachel researched all the treatment programmes she could find, and Teddy was in and out of them for six years, getting better, starting her life again, leaving Lee (sometimes), guiltily resuming her dead-end jobs and her dissatisfaction, falling out with her mother – who had spent much of the decade in a toxic relationship with a man who worked in corporate finance – falling back into alcohol addiction, then getting help before starting the whole cycle again. It had been awful, unrelenting, endless. Then, in 2005, Rachel found a place in the Oxford suburbs called The Gables, a red-brick converted schoolhouse with ivy growing over the front and hopes growing within, it seemed, as Teddy emerged from it after two months like a newborn foal, unsteady on her feet but ready to live a new life, ditch Lee for good – Rachel hoped – and go back into education.

'But you're enjoying it still?' asked Rachel. 'The course? The life there?'

'Yeah, it's good,' shrugged Teddy. 'I'm still enjoying it. There's a book club night in halls tonight. They threatened to do one of Dad's but I managed to steer them on to *The Hunger Games* . . .'

'I'm so glad,' said Rachel, 'about all of it,' and she was. Her bond with Teddy was stronger than it had ever been. Their ability to confide in each other. Their friendship. She valued it immensely, when other ties in her life had come undone, to trail and to trip and to cause injury . . .

'And you and Dad?' Teddy said, a frown suddenly clouding her face. 'You'd tell me . . . if there was anything to worry about, wouldn't you?'

'Anything to worry about?' Rachel laughed. 'There's nothing to worry about! Dad and I are absolutely great.'

'Great,' echoed Teddy faintly. 'Well, you're busy. I'm going to go back to Brookes.' She stepped forward and allowed Rachel to give her an enormous hug – all their hugs were, these days – then she trotted away up the path, waggling her fingers in farewell over her shoulder.

'Bye, Teddy,' said Rachel. She stepped back into the gallery, to the quiet of the flick of pencils and the crumble of pastels. The time ticked on and, before she knew it, Tim was standing up and stretching out his limbs and the artists were putting away their materials, shrugging on their coats, saying 'See you next week', as they let cool October air in through the open door of the gallery.

'Do you want to come over tonight?' asked Wren on her way out, pulling her jumper over her head and making her bun wobble. 'Or are you . . . ?'

'Still haven't decided,' smiled Rachel, swilling rainbow cups of water down the sink.

'OK, keep me posted,' replied Wren, eyes wide, and picking up her sketch book. 'And when's Jonny back from Belgium?'

'Three days. Two nights. Back on Wednesday. I'll text you. Whatever happens.'

'You better,' Wren said, with a mock pout, and she flurried out of the door. 'Let me know.'

After everyone had gone, Rachel sat down at her console table and ticked off who had attended the class. She then tidied the gallery, stacked the chairs and closed a forgotten window she'd optimistically left slightly open at the beginning of the session. There had definitely been a change in the air in the last couple of days, when a prolonged Indian summer had finally sloped off, to be replaced by cool breezes and the need for jackets and boots – the anticipation of early frosts, Bonfire Night, hot chocolate and soup-making. She knew it gave people a feeling of sadness, that summer was over, and the long, cold winter was waiting ahead, but for Rachel the feeling was one of things being swept away – like freshly fallen leaves – and replaced with something new. She liked the seasons. Hadn't she told someone that once?

'Out you go.' The little black cat who sometimes wandered in was visiting again. She softly shooed him out before slipping through the door herself and walking home. She was closing early today. The drizzle was gone now and under a pale sun a gathering wind was gently whipping at the piles of leaves crouching at kerbs. Wood smoke was coming from somebody's chimney. The dogwood hedge on the lane was beginning to turn a buttery yellow. And there was an early pumpkin keeping watch on a swept doorstep.

At home, Rachel eased off knee-length boots and shook off her coat, before grabbing a cardigan. She boiled the kettle and rooted in the cupboard for a handful of roasted almonds. Everyone was getting so healthy these days. Eating virtuously and listening to Coldplay. Even Jonny sometimes liked to break up the week with sushi and a bento box, ordered from the new Japanese restaurant in Oxford, while after Lee's last play – still painfully written, still sparsely attended – he had asked her to lay on quinoa and goat's cheese quiches followed by caramelised pineapple, back at the house, for the small party to toast Lee and all the wishful thinking that was involved in him attempting to be a playwright.

Rachel sat down to her laptop at the dining room table with her old Snoopy mug and her tea, and a silence nicked at by the ticking clock on the mantelpiece. She had some emails to answer. Some gallery business. Things were a little tough at the moment. There had been a massive financial crash this year, which started in America and had swept across the Atlantic; businesses were going under, houses were on the market at massively reduced prices and still not selling.

'What can you do?' was Jonny's habitual comment, before returning to checking his place in the *Sunday Times* bestseller list. His book sales hadn't suffered, but soared. As the year began to draw to a close, readers were escaping into Nikita's exploits more than ever.

Rachel closed the laptop, took her tea and walked into the sitting room. Her old brown leather Filofax, its one curled-up corner as familiar to her as the grain on the wooden coffee table it lay on, was where she'd left it this morning. She drew a figure-of-eight with one finger over its worn cover, wondering how many years she'd had this thing. Since the early nineties, wasn't it? Jonny had given it to her for a birthday. The address book inside was long out of date. She used to write Jonny's important dates in it as well as hers, but not any more. They had separate diaries, separate calendars. They had a lot of separate things these days. Activities, time . . . And things had gone missing, too, like they often did in long marriages. Things like wallets and screwdrivers and that shirt – 'You know, my favourite one! Have you lost it in the wash?' – and meandering affectionate conversations over endless bottles of red wine. And fidelity.

Inside the front flap of the Filofax were empty stamp books and old receipts. A couple of photos of Teddy when she was small. A Polaroid of Margaret and Malcolm, Jonny's parents, on lounge chairs in their back garden. The back flap usually contained her stack of newspaper and magazine clippings from the last decade, but the stack was still on the coffee table where she'd placed it, this morning, along with its green paperclip.

She picked up the leafy stack and brushed her forefinger over the top, bringing it to rest on the very last clipping, which had not been held by the green paperclip, like all the others. It was a sliver from the back pages of a newspaper she had clipped more recently. It was secret. It held within its black-and-white lines a decision she had not yet made.

Rachel lingered on it for a moment, wondering about fear and future and forgiveness, then she started at the beginning and leafed through the clippings again.

# Chapter Twenty-Six

Rachel's first mention as a gallery owner, in any kind of publication, had been in London's *Evening Standard*, no less. It had been no more than a small square, in the Arts & Entertainment listings, back in late 1997, but the mention was that her acquisition of Khalid Ziani for Vivaldi's was quite the thing.

She held the clipping in her fingers, rubbed her thumb over the words, thought how nervous she had been about this exhibition, how she'd imagined it might not happen, right up to the date of its opening. Even when she and Khalid had arranged its finer details – conversing by telephone and by fax and then, tentatively on his part, email – and even when he notified her he'd carefully shipped ten of his paintings to Oxford, she still worried he might change his mind. He'd told her, on one of their early phone calls, that a few days after her visit to Morocco there had been two more what he called 'sniffs' from contemporary galleries in London, one in the East End and one opposite Regent's Park.

'Swanky,' she'd said, fearful, and she'd fretted, right up to the wire, that he would skip her and her little gallery in Oxfordshire and go instead to them, but he didn't. He came to Vivaldi's and it was a huge success. Rachel sold every single one of his pieces and attracted a lot of attention, including that of the reporter from the

*Evening Standard* who came down from London to see Khalid's paintings.

'Simple killer instincts,' Jonny had said proudly. At the time he was still number one on the *Sunday Times* bestseller list, with *Nikita's Game*, so was hugely magnanimous with his praise, throwing it around as often as he threw himself celebratory parties, which was often, that October. 'You got it, babe. You are setting *trends*.'

'I don't know about that,' she had said, wriggling with shyness under his arm across her shoulder, standing in front of the mantelpiece before a rictus crowd of people in her sitting room, there to toast Jonny's success, not hers. He had added her to the end of his speech, had beamed and told his crowd about Vivaldi's and her Moroccan artist and the man from the *Evening Standard* who'd arrived in Fincham St George in a taxi and a grey raincoat. She had been bashful, but it did appear Vivaldi's was on the map and once the art world knew it was there, it was easier to lure other fantastic artists. There was the French painter from Dunkirk who did the most amazing spring sunrise landscapes. The young wunderkind from Shoreditch who did miniatures of London's spires, in the cold grey of winter. And the brilliantly evocative sketches of roses by a local artist, in her eighties, that she discovered by accident. And then she started taking chances.

Rachel sipped her tea and flicked to the next clipping. In 1999, she appeared in a local newspaper, the *Oxford Star*, in a feature about local female entrepreneurs on the cusp of the millennium. There was a photo of her standing outside the window of the gallery, leaning against the glass in a summer frock. She'd been asked about her plans for the year 2000 and she'd said her goal was what it had always been, to showcase art that people would love. She had just nervously signed an artist who was a little off piste, but as the new millennium rolled from winter to spring, then summer, David Todd turned out to be a massive hit. He painted very detailed, very close-up portraits of elderly people, in vivid colours, and luckily Vivaldi's customers had found his work as amazing as she did.

The next clipping made Rachel smile at first, then feel incredibly sad. In 2002, the gallery was doing great business and attracting a wide clientele – she had discovered another daring and brilliant artist: an abstract painter called Marie Selps, who applied seeping, weeping streaks of colour to huge abstract canvases – a risk that had paid off, despite a few sleepless nights over her decision. A local luxury lifestyle magazine, *Oxford Living*, interviewed Rachel for a frivolous feature about what was in her fridge. Rachel had been nonplussed at first but decided all publicity was good publicity and had moved Jonny's beers and the chocolate mousses and replaced them with lettuces, organic milk and posh cheeses. The magazine had taken a glossy photo of her, all poker-straightened hair and tawny lipstick, and put it next to a photo of her show-shelf of glamorous continental cheeses.

When the feature had come out, Jonny had read it aloud in an amused scoff. Rachel had laughed and said no one was going to read it anyway – who on earth would be interested in the contents of her fridge? But she noted Jonny seemed strangely jealous over it – competitive, almost.

'That's very *celebrity*, that is, talking about your fridge,' he'd said, rummaging in it later for Bavarian cheddar ('We should start buying this for real. I like it.'). The next day he phoned his publicist and asked them to get word out he'd got a rather engaging garden shed. Then, a few nights later, when they'd been to the pub and she'd been applauded in by a local wag with a shout of 'Hey, I liked your lettuces, Rachel!' and, to Jonny, 'Look out, she'll soon be more famous than you!', he'd forced her to drink whisky with him when they got home and he started talking in a low, strange voice Rachel had to strain from the other end of the sofa to hear. He started with a long monologue about his current work in progress, that he was struggling with it. It was difficult, he said, when he had so much on his mind.

'Writer's block?' she had asked, nursing the whisky she didn't really want. 'You never get that.'

'Not quite that,' he'd said. 'I'm thinking more of diversions, distractions, digressions.'

She didn't understand what that meant, but he'd crept his fingers towards hers along the sofa cushions and had held her hand fast. He'd smiled at her, a smile that could still light her up inside, when she let it. A smile that could still reignite that enduring feeling of the relief she'd known after that business in Morocco.

The smile had morphed into a sigh and Jonny had let go of her hand and gone on to talk about a reader of his, again in that low, strangled voice Rachel struggled to hear. This reader was called Kim and she had written to him twice a week for a month, he said. Her letters were personal and intimate; she seemed to want to bare her soul to him. She had scented each page generously with Coco Mademoiselle.

'Why are you telling me all this?' Rachel was leaning further towards Jonny, as his voice had gone right down into his throat and she could barely make out anything at all.

'Because there's more. She felt we were kindred spirits . . . she wanted to meet up with me, take me for a drink . . .'

'Next thing you'll be telling me you had an affair with her!' said Rachel, and Jonny turned crimson and leaped up from the sofa.

'Don't, *don't*!' he said wretchedly. He was suddenly alarmingly pale and as twitchy as a rattlesnake. He was pacing around the sitting room, wild of eye, and running his fingers through his cropped hair.

'Oh God,' groaned Rachel, frightened, 'you've had an affair.'

Jonny slumped theatrically at her feet, pawed at her shins like a wretched dog. He asked her, did she not remember the pale pink

244

envelopes that started to arrive for him? Did Rachel not wonder why they had disappeared from the stack on his desk?

'I'm ashamed to say that one day, in a very weak moment, I *called* her,' Jonny said. 'On the number she had added so brazenly to the bottom of her letters.'

'And were they beautifully written?' Rachel asked abstractedly. 'The letters?' She was swallowing down every terrible emotion that was bubbling up inside her. Fear, revulsion, grief, an awful feeling of déjà vu that he was the same, wasn't he, the same as her father? Her father who had escaped from home so many nights, who had called another woman, too, from those holiday payphones. Who had conducted a dreadful affair. How could Jonny turn out to be the same? How could he do this to her?

Jonny considered her question for a moment. 'A little eccentric and rather too flowery, but yes.'

Rachel felt utterly repulsed. 'Right,' she said. 'So that's why you called her. The perfume. The beautiful letters. The adulation. You simply couldn't resist, could you?'

'Forgive me? Please?'

A rising anger threatened to spill out of her like fire and engulf them both, and this room, and this house, and everything she had tried so hard to build around herself. To send the whole lot up in flames. 'Tell me the rest of it first,' she managed to say. She needed to hear it, his betrayal. She needed to hear every horrendous, heart-breaking word.

Rachel was shaking as Jonny related the rest like a short story from a cheap anthology. A story cloaked in coy euphemism and weak metaphors. He had called Kim and met her in a pub in King's Cross and she had been startlingly and absurdly funny, but quite nuts, really, and they had – well, they had gone to a hotel and . . .

'Dot dot dot,' said Rachel drily, but she had to press both hands firmly down on her knees to keep herself together. Her heart was already in pieces, piercing her skin, trying to break out of her, but she must contain it, contain her devastation. 'Just fill in the dots, Jonny.' Already, she knew she was going to forgive him. Already, she knew she wouldn't allow this to shatter them. That she must keep going, clutch everything tightly to her, the parts of her life . . . *Home, family, security*, the tripod she was shackled to, the shipwrecked raft she must cling to.

'It was different,' Jonny started rambling, 'as I'm sure you're going to ask. How it was.'

'I'm not going to ask anything,' she said, her thumbnails scouring against each other. She was not going to ask anything more. She was going to winch up all her terrible emotions and stuff them in a bag inside of her, stow them away. Her anxious, angry mother would have handled this quite differently, she thought. Frances would been screaming by now, hysterical, likely to run out of the front door in her dressing gown, losing a slipper in a flower bed . . .

Confrontation and drama and tragedy. That's how Frances would have played it. But Frances had not been going through IVF.

Her tea now cold, Rachel set down the clipping from *Oxford Living* and watched through the window as an ochre leaf slipped from an oak tree and drifted to the damp ground. Next on her lap was the piece from the *Arts Magazine*, a national magazine, very prestigious, who did a piece on the gallery in 2005 entitled 'The Four Seasons of Rachel Trent', which she loved, as it totally got what she was about. The article also featured a very flattering photo of Rachel standing outside Vivaldi's in a red jumpsuit and made mention of her great aunt Florence Toms' time as one of the Attagirl Second World War heroines, as Rachel had been asked about inspirational women in her life. It was also the first article to *not* mention she was the wife of bestselling author Jonny Trent. She had watched Jonny very carefully for a couple of weeks after that.

Jonny had behaved himself after Kim. He had asked for con-
firmation of Rachel's forgiveness every day and she had provided it,
for a time. She had allowed them to continue, on their set path. To
follow the compass that kept them stable and stopped the ground
beneath her feet from shifting.

On her lap were two more clippings. The top one was from
earlier this year – June. She was included in a two-page spread
called Gallery Owners to Watch, in none other than the *Sunday
Times*. In the photo, she was sitting behind the console table in the
gallery, resting her chin on her hands, reminiscent of one of Jonny's
author snaps, and looking, courtesy of clever lighting, pretty good,
when she had felt about as bad as you can get. The evening before
this photo had been taken, Jonny had told her about the Woman
in the Blue Dress.

This time there hadn't been a confession over whisky. Instead,
an embarrassingly clichéd discovery of lipstick on a collar had led to
a confrontation in their midsummer garden, with the sun making
a slow descent over the arbour. The admission, when it came, was
accompanied by the clinking of a gin and tonic and the lazy squeak-
ing of a cast iron filigree chair. This had been no crime, Jonny had
pleaded, not like Kim. It had been no more than a flirtation and
some kissing, in a wine bar.

'What shade of blue?' Rachel had asked coldly.

'Cobalt,' Jonny had replied. He said the Woman in the Cobalt
Dress had approached him in a London bar and said – disingenu-
ously – that she knew him from somewhere but couldn't think
where. She had pressed a drink on him and another, said Jonny
had beautiful eyes, the kind of face she'd like to see on her pillow
in the morning, all those awful, cheesy, predatory things that men
usually say. Jonny said he had begun to embody a character, at this
point, that of a man under siege.

'I felt weak,' he said, 'so *weak*,' as though there were something inherently interesting about that. He and the Woman in the Cobalt Dress had started kissing, right there up against the bar. A scenario he had simply been presented with and felt compelled to explore.

'It didn't go beyond that,' he said, and Rachel felt she had been wheeled out like a prop and placed centre stage of an awful drama; she could see the wings, unlit, grassy, and longed to rise towards them, from her chair.

'The bad novella is not even your genre,' she had commented with a bitter laugh, and she'd wondered if the grass Jonny had found himself on had been greener, or just different.

'I know,' he'd said, but he looked relieved she had made a little joke. He clearly thought – yet again – that being so honest about this encounter absolved him. That as he had offered it, freely, and given enough background and motivation, like those Post-it notes he made for his *Nikita* works in progress and stuck on his study wall, it would all be OK. She had forgiven him once before, hadn't she?

Rachel had left the garden, then, on the pretext of fetching more ice, her legs stiff as she walked across the lawn, her arms hanging uselessly by her sides. How *careless* he had been about the whole thing, she'd thought, as she stepped into the house. So careless to have left that stuff on his shirt. So careless about their marriage. But it also didn't escape Rachel that she had once done the same thing – kissed a man in Morocco, on the steps of a hotel. Did that make her careless, too? And if they were both careless, then what did anything really matter?

'I love you and it will never ever happen again,' Jonny had called after her as she'd crossed the lawn, and he'd said that to her again this morning when he'd left the house for Belgium. That he loved her, and she shouldn't be in fear of anything happening while he was away.

248

'I'll miss you,' he'd added, with a silly look on his face, and he'd given her a silly wave too, from the back of the executive taxi, as it took off from the kerb.

Rachel pushed her empty tea mug further away from her and looked out of the sitting-room window again. A blue tit skittered along the edge of the bird bath, then flew into the cooling air.

Letting Jonny's second indiscretion go had involved actively engaging muscle memory from the first. She'd carried around all the reasons she should forgive him – the many smooth bars and poles that made up the framework she'd erected to keep her life and Teddy's safe and secure – but one night, about two weeks after Jonny's garden confession, she'd let those poles and bars clatter to the ground. It had been a really hot night, and she'd lain awake in their bedroom, while Jonny snored beside her, and listened to the Roman blind slapping against the open window. That morning, a June morning when she'd eaten breakfast in the conservatory before leaving for the gallery, she'd taken a clipping from a newspaper. A sliver of newsprint she had slowly and meticulously cut from the *Daily Telegraph* and secreted in her Filofax. A clipping that, ever since, she'd wondered what she might do about.

Rachel looked at that clipping now, held it between finger and thumb. It could be a telegram or an invitation or a flyer about carpet cleaning. It could be blown out of a window and down the street on a gust of autumnal wind, to be caught in a tree. It didn't contain many words.

*Gabe McAllister, renowned US artist, is holding an exhibition of his work at the Yale Lights Gallery on The Strand, London, from 20 to 25 October. The artist will be in residence in the capital for the week of the exhibition.*

Today was the twentieth. She'd already made her decision, hadn't she? She'd made it the night the blind had slapped against the glass. She'd made it, in a secret part of herself, both times Jonny had betrayed her. And she'd known it by the hotel pool in Marrakesh as the sun had scorched her skin and she'd watched a plane trail cross the sky . . .

That if Rachel had the chance to see him again, she would take it.

# Chapter Twenty-Seven

'Hi, again.'

Oh, wasn't it awful when you bumped into someone you knew, but not that well? When you were going somewhere that you needed to be completely and utterly alone in your thoughts for.

Tim, the non-fidgeting life model, was standing on platform one at Fincham station. He had a satchel slung across his middle and was nibbling on a pasty he must have bought from the Millennial Smoothies kiosk. He was wearing different shoes to this morning – pinky suede ankle boots, with raspberry-coloured laces. *He should wear those in classes*, Rachel thought fleetingly, in the midst of her absolute frustration and annoyance at bumping into him, *it would be a nice detail for my artists . . . Oh bloody hell, why is he* here?

'Hi,' she said. She felt compelled to come to a stop next to Tim, when she really wanted to sail on to the safety of an empty spot further up the platform. She eyed it longingly as Tim turned to her.

He looked delighted to see her. 'Where are you off to?'

'Erm . . . London.' His easy, lanky form was blocking the sky, like a Lowry figure.

'Oh, anything nice?'

'I'm going to see an exhibition.' Her smile was rigid, her heart thudding.

'Oh, fantastic,' he said. 'Whose?' He shifted his satchel further up his shoulder.

'Oh, I can't remember the name,' she said vaguely. 'Grant somebody.'

'Great,' he said heartily, and she was truly glad he hadn't picked up on her desire to flee, but she couldn't focus on him. Her eyes scanned around her: a poster for a new internet bank, a waiting couple entwined in scarves, the station car park, where her little Golf was parked, and she was sure that was Nancy's Beetle, three cars up from hers . . . hadn't Teddy said something about her mother having a new man who lived in Bagshot – some reformed-hippy type who worked in advertising but played the pan pipes at the weekends, which Jonny found eye-rollingly hilarious . . . ? She allowed thoughts of Nancy to divert her. They'd seen her last week, at the pub. She'd been at the bar flogging replica aftershaves from a large canvas bag to anyone who dared show an interest. She'd peered at Rachel and Jonny as they came in, under her watchful and wary fringe, simultaneously spritzing a wincing punter on the wrist with 'Dior Savage'. 'Well, I hope you enjoy it.' Rachel was forced to look at Tim again.

'How about you? Where are you going?' Each word squeezed from her was a colossal effort.

'I'm going to my brother's for the weekend. He lives in Richmond.'

'Oh, nice.' She smiled sweetly. She was going to be stuck with Tim the whole way to Paddington, wasn't she . . .

'Here it comes,' announced Tim happily, and the train, sleek and mallard green, rolled into the station and came to a stop, pistons belching. Rachel didn't move; she was rooted, still hoping for a reprieve – that Tim would say 'Cheerio, then', and bound off to his own door, so she could head to another.

'After you,' said Tim.

'Thanks.'

Wanting to scream, Rachel stepped forward and alighted the train. She turned left into the carriage; Tim followed. She chose an empty seat by the window and Tim scooched himself next to her and stretched out his long, rangy legs, with a contented sigh.

'Be nice to have some company on the journey,' he observed, as the train revved and moved off. Rachel silenced a primeval growl of despair. 'My wife's already there,' he said. 'At my brother's. She gets on really well with my sister-in-law. They've had a couple of days doing stuff together. Shopping. Cream teas. I've never asked you,' he added, 'are you married?'

Rachel fluttered the fingers of her left hand like the traitor she was. Her rings glinted in the weak sun from the dirty window.

'I'm not that observant,' shrugged Tim. 'I'm the opposite of all those artists trying to do me justice.'

'Ha!' she said. She smiled. He was a nice man. She hated him.

'How long have you been married?'

'Seventeen years.' She wondered what he would say if she added *but despite that, I'm about to go and track down someone I nearly had an affair with eleven years ago, to say 'sorry' for not having an affair with him.*

'Congratulations,' said Tim. 'We've managed forty-two.'

'Well, congratulations to you, too,' she smiled. Their wedding anniversary had gone largely uncelebrated this year as Jonny had been away in New York at the time (he was now famous in the US, his books having been discovered and raved about in an interview by Tom Clancy, no less) and Rachel had felt disinclined to mark another milestone so recently tainted with cobalt blue . . . 'He's a writer,' she added. 'Jonny Trent?' Two words usually met with delighted surprise.

'Jonny Trent . . .' mused Tim, tilting back his head and flickering his eyeballs at her. 'No, sorry, I've not heard of him.'

253

*Oh, Jonny would be furious*, she thought. 'No reason you should have done,' she said. 'But yes, he's incredibly successful.'

'Which genre?'

'Russian spy thrillers.'

'Ah. I read Bill Bryson and P.D. James.'

'Nice.'

'Have you read *An Unsuitable Job for a Woman?*'

'Several times.'

There was a pause. Tim brought out a packet of Mentos from his satchel with somewhat of a flourish. 'Would you like one?'

'No, thank you.'

'I'm sorry I've not heard of Jonny Trent,' he said. 'I must look him up. How wonderful,' he said, 'the two of you. The gallery owner and the author.' And Tim talked on and on about his wife of forty-two years and all her little ways, and how she and his sister-in-law had hit it off straight away, bonding over adding a spoonful of sugar to a chicken casserole, of all things, and he *did* wonder what they were having for dinner tonight, and whether there would be a pudding too, but he was usually lucky. His wife had ever such a sweet tooth, had done as long as he'd known her, which was . . . ooh . . . forty-seven years now, fancy that . . .

Rachel sat and smiled at his face as he talked, but behind her smile she was roiling. Jonny was probably in the bar already, possibly deciding whether to ruin things again, or not, and she hoped he *was*, as wasn't that what she was doing right now? Ruining the wavering peace of their lives? She was going to see another man. A man who even the *thought* of was making her heart beat too fast and her insides barrel.

She'd thought about Gabe a lot since Morocco. Not every day, but enough. Enough so that he was still a beautiful shadow in her life. She thought about him when she drove in the rain or heard a The Cure song or when she saw an old Doris Day movie or there was a summer's day so hot the sun melted into the sky. She remembered how he made her feel.

Tim was still talking, recounting some anecdote about his wife. 'And finally, when she sat on them, her head dropped off!'

This is not what Tim said, but it was something like that. Rachel smiled indulgently at the unheard comedy of his conclusion, wondering if she should have laughed at other points she hadn't been concentrating on.

'So, what's it like being an author's wife? Is he terribly temperamental?' Tim grinned. As he'd been talking, the trace of one of his front teeth had remained imprinted on his bottom lip. 'Marriage is a funny old game at the best of times,' he observed. 'Easy to fall into, hard to stick to, wouldn't you say?'

'Oh, yes,' she said. *Very easy to fall into*. Especially when it's a giant safety net offering you lifelong refuge from a blown-apart world. When it's Jonny Trent rocking up with a ready laugh, a big hug and a promise to take care of you, always. 'And yes, he *is* temperamental. But he's very funny with it, so that's OK.'

'Humour smooths over the roughest of seas,' nodded Tim sagely. 'Pippa and I would certainly tell you that. Do you have children?'

'No.' She said it too quickly, too painfully.

'Oh, well, not everybody does. Sorry.' He turned away from her, heightened colour in his cheeks, to the far window, where pithy raindrops suddenly appeared – blasted sideways – and she turned back to her own window.

Jonny had finally agreed to IVF in 1999, suddenly hankering for another baby and, maybe, a son. They embarked, with hope, on the injections and the hormones and the tiny paper cups and the stress of it, just like Jonny had said. Yes, he had been wonderfully supportive, cracking jokes throughout the whole strenuous process, but it was challenging. And exhausting and frustrating and

255

disappointing. Especially alongside all the trouble and pain Teddy was in at the time. Rachel knew the stress of it had probably led her husband to King's Cross, and surprisingly funny Kim.

Tim chuckled to himself. Was he thinking about sugar in casseroles again, Rachel wondered, or the million different ways he and Pippa sweetened their marriage with a sprinkling of humour? Within a few minutes, he nodded off, and Rachel continued to stare at the sideways rain on the window. She had thought she would have children. She assumed she would have *more*, in exchange for this life she had chosen and stuck with. Yes, Rachel had the gallery, of which she was enormously proud, but she thought she might be allowed a payoff for her duty and her allegiance, for her love and her forgiveness. For living with the same view from the kitchen window, day after day. But no babies had come, the IVF hadn't worked, and now she was forty-eight and it was too late. After the fourth try, Jonny had hugged her fiercely and had said, with a huge sigh of relief, 'Oh, well, we gave it our best shot, didn't we? And we have Teddy.'

She had gone to Wren, then. Rachel had literally run from the car following their last journey home from the clinic and gone to Wren's door, sobbing, where her old friend had held her and sobbed with her. Now Wren knew everything: Gabe, Jonny's cheating, the entire shape of the pain Rachel had been going through. Rachel sent her a quick text.

*I'm going*, it said.

*Oh God*, came the instant reply. *I'm with you in spirit! Please let me know what happens.*

And here she was being carried towards London, as grey clouds blanketed the sky like washed sheets that had fallen to the ground and been rehung. To a man from her past. To Gabe.

'Sorry, I appear to have had forty winks.' Tim looked around him, as though in fear of chastisement, and drew back his long legs. 'Whereabouts are we?'

'We've just gone past Reading.'

'Ah. Not long, then. Journey's flying by!'

'Yes,' she muttered weakly. It was the longest journey she'd ever known.

Tim chatted at her all the way to Paddington, as fields gave way to the backs of terraced houses and strips of narrow suburban gardens, blustered by autumn, then to high-rise flats and London Borough parks, with primary coloured apparatus. And as they got nearer and nearer to London, Rachel was chickening out.

She didn't have to go to the Strand. She could go to Covent Garden instead, have a mooch around. Or she could go to one of the big art galleries, do some research, get some ideas. Either suddenly seemed preferable to turning up unannounced to a gallery and telling a virtual stranger she was sorry for something that nearly happened eleven years ago, which he probably no longer cared or thought about.

Inevitably, the train glided into Paddington without a care in the world, while her cares were stacked like tin soldiers. Tim hitched his trousers at the knees and stood up, brushing imaginary crumbs off his thighs. Rachel stood up too, relieved, as they got off the train and made their way to the concourse, that he was going to say goodbye to her here at the barrier.

'Well, it's been a pleasure,' said Tim. 'Enjoy your exhibition and I'll see you at the next class. You've booked me for next Thursday, haven't you?'

'Yes, please. Same time, if that's all right. And same to you. Your weekend, I mean. Have a lovely time, Tim.' And she felt horribly guilty because he was a nice man.

'Bye, Rachel.'

'Bye.'

She walked away from him – free at last – still thinking she could easily go to Covent Garden and wander around some boutique shops. She found the entrance to the Underground and waited for the Bakerloo line train to Embankment. Stared at her lap as she sat in the half-empty Tube carriage, her useless hands flopping against each other like birds. She came out on to the Embankment into chill October air and low, stately grey skies and, taking a deep breath, headed up it, to the Strand.

# Chapter Twenty-Eight

It was a few degrees warmer in London but the drizzle that started as soon as Rachel left the cocoon of Embankment station was unforgiving. Umbrellas went up above the heads of raincoated people, handbags balanced on elbows and briefcases shoved under arms to accommodate them.

The drizzle and the grey drove her forward; the beating of her own heart forged every step. A couple embraced cinematically in a side doorway, the woman's arms looped around the man's neck. 'Let's get a room,' Rachel thought she heard the man say, but she may have imagined it. Turning on to the Strand, the drizzle didn't let up, and when she arrived at no. 472, Yale Lights Gallery, she walked straight in, heart beating in double time – past a large sketch of a wintry tree, black ink on grey, in the window – before she could change her mind.

It was cool inside, no warmer than out on the street. There were white walls. A matt black floor. Gabe's trees everywhere. She stood and felt the dampness of her coat, her hair, her skin, and the settle of her disappointment. He wasn't there. Well, what *was* she expecting? Gabe to be standing there, admiring one of his own works, a Bic biro behind his ear? That he would just turn and say 'Hello'?

Her quietening heart felt foolish. Of course he wasn't there. Why would it be that easy? And wasn't it easier *this* way – that she could walk back through the door and go home to her life? Rachel stood in the middle of the gallery and tried to bring all parts of herself back into line, to reassemble the bricks and bolts and buckles of stability she had shunted out of place by coming here. To realign her heart, before she turned and left.

'So, yes, that will certainly attract the before-dinner crowd . . .'

A young man was coming through a doorway at the back of the gallery. He had one of those headsets jammed on to a mop of red hair, so it seemed he was talking to himself, but another man emerged from the doorway behind him, rubbing at the back of his head.

'And what do you think of the positioning of the . . .' The other man had stopped, in the middle of the doorway. His eyes were crinkling in surprise.

'Hello,' he said.

'Hello,' said Rachel.

The young man looked over at Rachel, then back at Gabe. A blush came to his freckled cheeks. 'Well, I have all that to be getting on with,' he said. 'So . . . shall we leave it there, for now? I'll text you later?'

'Yes, please,' said Gabe, still looking at Rachel. 'Thank you, Adam.'

Adam nodded and hurried from the room. 'Good afternoon,' he mumbled to Rachel on his way out.

'Good afternoon,' she said quietly.

'Is it really you?' said Gabe. He did not move from his position in the doorway.

'Yes, it's me,' she said simply, like a child.

'Well, damn.' He stepped forward, almost in a run, and flung his arms around her and hugged her tightly. His jumper was indigo wool; he smelled like she remembered, the same aftershave – lemon and musk. She was aware of his left hand at her right shoulder blade, her right hand somewhere in the middle of his back, her chin pressed against his collarbone. She knew she was right to have come. She knew she was wrong to have come. She felt the *same,* and she was sorry, and she was glad.

'Damn,' he repeated, after a few seconds. After forever. Gabe drew back from her; he held her at arm's length. He looked into her face, her eyes, while she searched his. He had grey temples and sideburns, his hairline had receded, just a little, like the tide had gone out on it; his eyes were fanned by starburst lines that now graduated down his cheeks. 'How are you?'

'I'm good, thanks,' she said, 'really good.' All the years she hadn't seen him concertinaed into this moment. All the moments she'd thought of him saturated her heart like ink into a ball of cotton, and now it was heavy and a deep, rich red.

'I'm good, too,' he nodded. 'It's been a long time.'

'It has.'

'How did you know I was here?'

'I saw it in the paper.' Rachel drank him in, her eyes swallowed every aspect of his face and his hair and his skin.

He nodded. 'I can't believe it's you,' he said, not taking his eyes from her. 'After all this time. It's such a surprise. Shall we walk? Do you want to walk?'

'We can walk,' she replied.

He was already grabbing his jacket. Rachel smoothed down her hair. Touched her finger to her lips to see if her lipstick was still there. They moved from the gallery into the drizzle, like a whole decade and more hadn't slipped silently past them, an ocean of absence. They set off together down the Strand, like they were just two people. Two work colleagues popping out for lunch, or a couple from the suburbs wandering this beautiful city as autumn tourists. Not two people who had only met each other twice and who had oscillated on the brink of something, then had lost each other. Two people who'd had no expectation of ever seeing one another again.

'You're not too cold?' asked Gabe.

'No, I'm OK.' She was in a roll-neck, and a trench coat and a little silky scarf.

'Shall I stop and buy an umbrella somewhere?'

'No, no need. Thank you.'

She remembered his side profile, every inch of it.

'So, you're well?' Gabe asked.

'Yes, quite well, thank you,' said Rachel, stilted and shy. She feared looking at him in case some awful maelstrom of emotion burst from her. Regret, mostly. 'And you?'

'Yes, really well, thanks. A bit wet,' he added, and they both braved a laugh, Rachel curious at how hers sounded, in the cool damp air she was sharing with Gabe. 'I haven't been to England for a long time,' he continued, 'and I've never been here in the autumn before. It's muted . . . compared to the fall in North Dakota. It's mild and well . . . atmospheric.'

'Dreary more like,' Rachel said. She risked a glance at him as he laughed again. She remembered that laugh and all the years of trying to catch it again, in her memory.

'I like it,' he said. 'I like all the greys. So many different shades of them.'

'Yes, all of them drab.'

His eyes were bright and amused under the grey skies. She was playing her part well, she thought. Calm, mildly amusing. It involved great effort. 'I thought you liked the change in seasons?'

'I do,' she replied, 'Just not grey and drizzle – when the sky sits on us and the rain is neither one thing nor another. I'd prefer a proper downpour.' She remembered the Fincham St George car park and the downpour that day. The stair rods. And wondered whether he did, too.

'We can still go and buy an umbrella somewhere.'

'No, it's OK,' she repeated. *Calm. Not amusing at all.*

'So,' he said, tugging Rachel gently on the sleeve of her raincoat as they stepped around a halted passer-by, 'you saw the ad for the exhibition?'

She brushed a ruler of hair out of her eye. The drizzle had already formed a spider-spun haze on Gabe's hairline. He had his hand up at the collar of his grey jacket, closing it against the misting rain. When he'd put it on, before they left the gallery, she'd clocked the wedding band.

'Yes,' she said. 'You're doing so well, aren't you? With this exhibition and everything? How about stateside?'

She was an utter idiot. *Stateside?* Who said *that?*

'I'm doing OK,' he said. 'They have me permanently in a gallery in Fargo and I show in New York, still, occasionally. And Paris, possibly, next year.'

'Paris? That's great, Gabe, really great.'

'Thank you.'

They were on the Embankment now; there was less drizzle, more breeze, off the water. They joined the walkers and the detoured shoppers and those heading off for fun on one of the boozy pub boats.

'I love the Embankment,' Gabe said, as they automatically slowed their pace. 'Even the lamp posts are glorious.' She looked along the herald of them, stretching into the distance. 'We don't get anything like this in Jud.'

'How is Jud?' she asked brightly, not that she really wanted to know, in too much detail, because that meant his life there, his daily trips to the diner, his evening walk. His wife. Oh God, he was married, what was she doing here?

'Jud is Jud,' he said, 'it's always the same.'

'Current population?'

'Seventy-two.'

'It's going down.'

'People come and people go, and Jud just is,' Gabe said, and there was a strange melancholy to his words, and she wondered about his wife, and about his mum, too, but she was not ready to ask. There was so much she was not ready to say. So much she wouldn't be saying, not now. Instead, she said, 'Any new murals?'

He smiled. 'There's a horse one. On a wall down on Domsey Street. It's kinda cute. Not exactly Banksy but, you know . . .'

She grinned back at him, but she felt sad. *There are so many gaps between us that can never be filled*, she thought. Over ten years of lives lived apart, in other towns, in other countries with other people. With husbands and wives.

'Jonny's books were all over duty free when I landed,' he said.

'Oh, he's all over everywhere,' replied Rachel. 'He's doing tremendously well. A huge success,' she added vaguely. 'Just like he always dreamed of.'

'Great,' said Gabe. 'And you? The gallery?'

'The gallery's doing well, thanks.' It was her turn to fold up the collar of her coat against the rain. 'Well, there's a bit of a downturn, actually, because of the recession, but I'm confident we'll get past it.'

'How's autumn?'

'Autumn's good. I have two new artists in my autumn window. One who does ghostly Northern cityscapes, another who uses smoked glass to depict suburban decay. Both seem to be generating interest.' She was really proud of them both.

'I'd love to see them.'

'You won't be visiting Aunt Julia on this trip?' As soon as she said it, Rachel wished she hadn't. She didn't want to sound like she hoped he would be.

'I don't have time. And she came to see me in the summer. Quite the gallivant, still, is Aunt Jules,' said Gabe with a smile. 'European tours, visits to America, she even went to Southeast Asia last fall.'

'Amazing,' Rachel said. 'Good old Aunt Julia.' It was a relief he wouldn't be coming to the village. She couldn't have him ambling the streets, turning up to things, heading left on to Sidmouth Street . . . There was a sweet pain to imagining him there she couldn't begin to quantify.

'How's your mum?' she asked.

'The same,' he said. 'At home sometimes, away others. It's all still a struggle for her. Life. But I'm in Jud, when she needs me. I'm not going anywhere as long as she's around.'

Rachel nodded. They walked in silence for a few more moments.

'Actually, I've looked you up,' confessed Gabe. 'I've seen photos of the gallery and read a couple of articles about you. I know Vivaldi's has been a great success.' He paused, brushed some rainwater from the top of his head. 'And what you keep in your fridge.'

She laughed. 'It wasn't a true representation. I may have gilded the lily.'

He laughed too. 'I'm glad it's all going so well for you,' he added. 'Recession permitting.'

'You too,' she said shyly. 'I've looked you up, too.'

They both glanced away from each other. Gabe to the murk of the river and a gull that was circling overhead. Rachel, to the buildings on their right – the white stuccos and the red bricks and the grandeur.

'Oh, someone's left a book,' Gabe said. He stepped over to a bench and picked up a paperback that was lying on it.

'Graham Greene – *The End of the Affair*,' he said, and she remembered how he'd been introduced as the Quiet American, by

265

Dray Briggs, in Christie Wetherington's sitting room. She blushed a little at the memory. 'Have you read it?'

'Yes,' she said. The word 'affair' hung in the cool air when it shouldn't. 'Better leave it there,' she said. 'Someone might like it when it's dried off, about next May.'

Gabe smiled. They walked a fraction further, then he stopped by one of the glorious lamp posts.

'Would you like to go and get a coffee?' he said. 'I know a little place not far from here. It's warm and dry and the coffee is good.'

'I'd like that,' she said. The walking had begun to feel aimless; her hair was wet and her suede ankle boots were beginning to seep. She'd like to go and get coffee with him. They could talk and find out just enough about each other's lives to satisfy their curiosities. He could ask her more about Jonny and the gallery; she could ask him about his wife and congratulate him on finding his perfect half at last. For no longer being a lost and wandering soul. She'd apologise for coming and say it had been lovely to see him.

'Great,' he replied, and they fell into step again, as a seagull above the Thames wailed a poignant cry.

They would go for coffee and talk some more and then they would say goodbye.

# Chapter Twenty-Nine

The coffee shop was called Sullivan's and it was a tiny nook at the ground-floor corner of a brand spanking new hotel called the Zee. The Zee was all glossy chrome and glass; Sullivan's had brown smoked glass windows and a door with engraved lettering on it, like a private detective's office in the movies.

'Adam introduced me to this place,' said Gabe, as they stepped inside. They shook off their wet coats and Gabe hung them both up on pegs just inside the door. 'It's been here since the 1970s, apparently. The owners refused to move . . .' He smoothed down a bunched-up sleeve of Rachel's trench coat, on its peg; a strangely intimate gesture that made her blush. '. . . when the hotel went up. So, the hotel just built itself around it.'

'It's charming,' she said, looking about her. The coffee shop had brown leather booths, low-slung drop-pendant lamps in danger of kissing cream melamine tabletops, pale mocha walls and a black herringbone oak floor. Heaps of coffee beans in hessian bowls were lined up on the dimly lit counter, behind which a woman with a static beehive and cat-eye spectacles sat on a high stool. The whole place was terribly Old School and Rachel loved it.

'Over there OK?' said Gabe, pointing to a booth in the far corner. Rachel nodded.

The melamine table was veined with scratches but utterly spotless. The brown leather of the booth's banquette was cracked, and creaked as they sat down, both of them uttering a comedy 'oof'.

'Getting old,' laughed Rachel.

'Wait till we try to get up again,' grinned Gabe. He sank back against the seat and she caught another waft of his aftershave. She wondered if his wife had bought it for him. If she said 'I like this on you' in the mornings, when he kissed her after breakfast, and she drove off to her crisp little office job while he slouched to his drawings . . . 'It's . . . well, it's amazing to see you again, Rachel,' he said, bringing her back from Jud, North Dakota, to London, in the rain. 'It's kind of miraculous. And, well, it's floored me, actually. I wasn't expecting to see your face again.'

'I wasn't expecting to either,' she said. 'But when I saw the ad . . . I had to come. I hope you don't mind.'

'I don't mind,' he said. 'I'm glad.'

'I thought you might hate me,' she said. 'Or be freaked out.' His gaze was steady, she could read nothing into it whatsoever, except he was polite and he was kind. 'One of the reasons I came is to say I'm sorry,' she said.

'What's your order?'

The woman with the beehive and the cat-eye specs had appeared at their booth. She spoke in a croaky cockney accent.

'Just a milky coffee,' said Rachel.

'I'll have the same,' said Gabe.

*How odd to be sitting opposite this man again*, she thought, ordering coffee, when he had flickered at the edges of her dreams for so long; a shadow she couldn't reach.

'What are you sorry for?' asked Gabe, after the woman shuffled off.

268

'For Marrakesh,' she said. 'For not turning up, for not explaining. I felt awful.' The words rushed from her, like she hadn't rehearsed them a million times in her head.

'I didn't feel that hot either,' he said, and his smile was still gentle, but his eyes held a trace of pain. 'I waited for you for a long time. Why didn't you come?'

'Jonny showed up. At the hotel. With Teddy. As a surprise for my birthday.' She sounded robotic now. Lame.

'It was your *birthday*? You never told me.'

'I'm not big on them,' she shrugged. She felt fragile. She felt like broken eggshell.

'That's why you never came.' Gabe picked up the little copper spoon from the sugar bowl and balanced a sugar cube on its tip, like it was a diver at the edge of a board.

'I came to your riad the next morning, to explain to you, but you'd already left. The owner told me you'd taken an earlier flight.'

'Yes,' he said. Rachel wanted to look away from his steady blue eyes, but she couldn't. Everything she'd felt that final night in Marrakesh was still with her, bright and tart under its painful cloak, for the moment not seized and the years that had passed since. 'I tried to call you that morning, from the airport. Stupid, really. I wondered if they'd put me through to the wrong room, but when I heard his voice . . . I'd called the night before. About nine o'clock.'

'I was out,' she said sadly. 'You're not going to believe this, but I was back at the Dar Essalam.'

'You're kidding.' His eyes widened, the sunbursts flared, but his voice was flat.

'Nope. Second night running. I had to do it all again. The tagine, the entertainment, the dancing . . .' Her voice faltered now; her mind took her back to *their night*, to being in his arms on that makeshift dance floor.

'We had a good time there,' said Gabe. His eyes did not leave her.

'Yes, we did.' That hot, sweet Moroccan night – and all the things they'd said and all the things she'd felt.

'I'm sorry.'

'No reason for you to be sorry. I'm the one who stood you up. It was one of those twists of fate.'

'And how did you see it?' he asked carefully, allowing the sugar lump diver to launch off the copper spoon. 'As a good or a bad twist of fate?'

'Both,' she said honestly. 'Both. I was absolutely gutted but I was also totally relieved. I could return to my life unharmed,' she smiled, with a hint of sarcasm. 'Well, almost. I'm not sure I've been quite the same since. But, hey,' she laughed, trying to make it sound like she meant it, 'it was a long time ago. It's water under the bridge, isn't it? Unimportant.' She attempted a shrug. 'But I did want to say I'm sorry.' Oh God, it meant nothing really, did it, that word? *Sorry*. It was the tiniest tip of a devastating iceberg that had unearthed itself and was drifting off to sea. Nothing about her and this man felt unimportant.

'Apology accepted,' said Gabe, his gaze steady. 'The . . . disappointment was pretty rough. Even for a hard-ass like myself.'

'For me, too,' she said. 'And I've never been a hard-ass.' She grinned, despite the splintering of emotion inside her. The rendering of her heart into shards. 'What must you have thought of me?'

'I thought the same of you I always have.' He picked up another sugar cube between his thumb and finger and rolled it between them.

*And what is that?* she thought. *Can't you tell me? But does it even matter now?*

'So,' he said slowly, 'all in all things have been pretty good for you, since we last met?'

270

'Yes, it's been good,' she said. 'It's been successful, for both Jonny and me.' She thought again of the Filofax clippings, of all of Jonny's framed book covers decorating the walls of his study. 'It's had its ups and downs too,' she said, dulling her words with a rather tedious euphemism. 'Aren't they inherent in any life? You're married,' she added simply.

'No,' he said.

'You're wearing a ring . . .'

'Yes,' he said, looking down at his hand. 'But I'm not married any more. She died.' And his face crashed in on itself a little and Rachel couldn't help but lean across the table and place her hand on his.

'Oh God, I'm so sorry.'

'Thank you. It was cancer. Fucking ovarian cancer. My poor dear Anne-Marie . . .'

'Jacob's mum?' asked Rachel quickly. 'You got back with her?'

'Oh, you remember . . . Yes, we got together again. It was a good thing, particularly for Jacob. For a while at least . . .'

'I'm so sorry. I'm really sorry she died,' repeated Rachel. 'It must have been awful for you.' *He found his true love, after all*, she thought, *his real love.* He had found her and then she had died.

'The grief,' he muttered. 'The grief has been persistent and utterly terrible. No, don't feel sorry for me,' he said, looking up at her with eyes full of pain. Hers had filled with tears, her heart swelling with empathy for him. 'I don't deserve it.'

'I don't understand.'

'The guilt,' he said. 'The *guilt* has been worse.'

'That you couldn't save her?' Rachel's eyes filled again.

'No. That I didn't love her.'

She curled her fingers around the static flat of his hand. 'Tell me,' she said. 'You can tell me.'

There was a croaky cough from behind them and it was Cat-eye Specs, with their coffee in enormous beige speckled mugs, which she set down on the table before croaking back to the counter. They sat in silence for a few seconds, then Gabe spoke.

'I saw Anne-Marie in Fargo whenever I visited Jacob. She and her husband would drop him at the park, in the early days. We'd say "hello" and "goodbye", nothing more.' Rachel nodded. She thought of all the stilted Nancy drop-offs, the resentful looks, the awkwardness. 'Then, as he got older, it would be at the skateboard alley, or the shopping mall, or I'd rent a room and he'd stay with me for a coupla days. They'd always both be there, dropping him off – I think the guy didn't trust me, or something. Then one day, about two years ago, it was just her. The next time, he wasn't there, either. Turns out she wasn't married any more, that the guy had taken his time to show his cards – to her, at least – but he'd turned out to be seven shades of asshole. Then, a coupla days later, I walked into a bookshop down from the gallery I was showing at, in Fargo, to buy something for my mom's birthday, and there she was, behind the counter. New job . . .' Rachel could feel his wedding ring under her fingers. She was trying not to be gripped by a horrible and irrational jealousy at the 'meet cute' at the bookshop . . . 'Anyway, I guess we started something up again. We got on well. Way better than back in the day and, well, she was Jacob's mother, you know?' Rachel felt a shot of pain go through her. 'And she didn't seem to hate me any more,' he grinned, 'so there was that. We dated, and after a while, she and Jacob moved in with me, in Jud. We decided to get married. We got married on a Friday lunchtime, and on the Monday she started getting pains she dismissed at first . . . and, well, it turned out she had cancer.'

'How awful,' whispered Rachel. She hated herself for her jealousy, when this was how the story had ended. She hated being jealous that Gabe and Anne-Marie and Jacob had been a family, when it was so short-lived and so sad.

'And here's the punchline: I didn't love her,' said Gabe bitterly. 'Everyone said she was perfect for me . . . and she *was* perfect. She was sunny and optimistic, right to the very end. She was a good person, kind and funny, and an excellent mother. I cried for six days straight after she died, and I cried so hard because I never did her justice. I never fully loved her, not in the way I should have done, even though I pretended to. Boy, did I pretend to!' He thumped his hand on the table. Cat-eye, from across the room, raised one thin eyebrow, then returned to her magazine. 'She loved me, I know she did. Completely and fully and properly. The way real love should be. And I tried so very hard – because hadn't I screwed it up so many times before? Hadn't I continued to screw it up – and believe me, Rachel, I *had* done, since Morocco. And I so wanted to get it right. To feel right – but I never felt the same way. Isn't that terrible?'

'No,' said Rachel, squeezing his hand. 'I think you did love her. She was the mother of your son. She made you happy, it sounds, and it sounds like you made her happy, too. She must have felt loved. Wasn't that enough? I'm sure it was enough, Gabe.'

Gabe sighed. 'I don't know,' he said. 'I don't know.'

'I think you're being too hard on yourself. Maybe what you had was as good as it gets. Maybe that grand, passionate, all-consuming, once-in-a-lifetime love is a myth, anyway.'

'Is it?'

His eyes met hers and held them fast. Everything in her body stilled – her heart, her blood, her breath, her soul. The years fell away. The future, all her best-laid and formulated plans, became suspended – out of reach. She knew it wasn't a myth. She knew it was real. Wasn't that really why she had come?

The lady behind the counter dropped something with a clatter, causing them both to break their gaze and look round.

'Butterfingers!' she called out grumpily.

Rachel turned back to Gabe. 'You had something good with Anne-Marie,' she said. 'I'm sure of it. I think you need to hold on to the good stuff. The lovely things.'

'The lovely things have gone,' he said. 'And now I'm just sad, and who wants a man who has sadness running through him like letters in a stick of Brighton rock?' He flashed a caustic smile at the Graham Greene reference.

*I do*, she thought. 'But you have Jacob,' she said.

'Yes, I have Jacob. But he's fourteen now and he hates Jud, and he hates me more because his mother's not here. He'll be off as soon as he can, I know that, but I have to stay, because of Mom . . . Anyway,' he said, and he exhaled, long and low, as if attempting to expel a brace of demons from him. 'Jesus! How goddam self-indulgent! Tell me about you, Rachel,' he said passionately, and he leaned forward and placed his thumbs under his chin. 'Tell me your ups, your good stuff . . . What you got?'

'I haven't got a lot,' she said. 'Well, I have stories . . . haven't we all got them, by our age?'

'Old as the damn hills.' They shared a wry smile. 'How's your stepdaughter?'

'Teddy is good, at the moment. She's thirty-one, she's at university as a mature student. She's had her ups and downs too. Big ones. Addictions, you know. Drugs. Alcohol.'

'Oh, I'm sorry.'

'And a really bad boyfriend, who still lives in the village. The scourge of our lives, actually, although unfortunately Jonny doesn't see it that way. But she seems to be over him now. She's finished protesting "But I *love* him!"' Rachel smiled wryly and sipped her coffee. 'Do you know what he once did? Reversed his car over her

274

foot, breaking her ankle in three places.' It was in the late 90s, when things were already pretty bad. 'She was standing at the edge of our drive. He jumped in the car and reversed, furious and too fast.' Rachel winced. Teddy had refused to go to the police about it.

'That must have brought back bad memories,' Gabe said gently. 'I'm sorry.'

'Thank you,' she said, and she truly appreciated the look on his face, his empathy, him remembering the story of her parents, after all this time. 'I told her then it's not the *I love you*s, it's the *life*, something my nanna always told me.' An image of Florence came into her head and she wondered, as she sometimes did, what others jewels of Nanna's life had been in that lost tin. 'And she's free of him now. It's the life you live that matters. Don't you think so?'

'I think, ideally, it should be the life *and* the love,' said Gabe sadly, and she knew he was thinking of Anne-Marie. 'You said Jonny sees things a different way, about this Lee?'

'Oh, Jonny *invests* in him – unbelievably. Lee writes these terrible plays – awful self-indulgent dirges, set in Oxford, like Steinbeck gone wrong.' Gabe grinned. 'And Jonny funds local productions of them, at the Oxford Playhouse, while Lee waits for his big break that never comes . . . Jonny doesn't have a problem with Lee. Besides, he's too preoccupied with his writing. He's too famous. He's too busy cheating on me . . .'

'He's *cheated* on you?'

'Yes, twice, that I know of, and he may be cheating on me again, this very minute. If he's in a bar, which he probably is – see, I told you I had stories.'

'Which bar is he in?' asked Gabe, as if he planned to storm off to it, right now, and haul Jonny out on to the street.

Her laugh had a bitter edge. 'One in Belgium. But any bar might do – anywhere there's the deadly combination of slavish female fans and booze.'

Gabe's eyes were cool and studied. 'You haven't left him.'

'No, well, I don't leave, do I?' She sipped again at her cooling coffee. 'Stable and steadfast, that's me,' she said, thinking of her words in Morocco. 'I'm sure you've guessed I haven't had children,' she said. 'We tried IVF, four times. It didn't work.'

'I didn't want to ask.' Gabe's eyes were now full of sympathy.

'I stayed for that. Initially. The process. The hope. Both went on for a long time. And, also, I just . . . stayed. I stay for Jonny and I stay for Teddy and I stay for me.'

'To keep things safe and peaceful,' said Gabe. 'Your design for life. So, how's that working out for you?'

'Really well, obviously.' Her smile was sarcastic.

'And why are you here?'

'I told you, I came to say "sorry".'

'You've left your safe, peaceful life to come and tell me that?'

'I haven't left it.'

'*So why are you here?*'

'Look, can we change the subject?' she said.

'Sure. OK . . . well, I got a dog.'

'Ah. Name?'

'Red.'

'Not *Ol'* Red?'

'Yup. I'm just a walking American cliché with an American clichéd dog. Actually, he's not old. He's a service dog who didn't quite make the grade. The Service Dogs for America centre has always been in Jud – they've seen me around.' She saw the pain behind his wry smile. 'Seems I'm the perfect match for one of their lovable dropouts.'

'And does he walk down to the diner with you?'

'Every day. Once for breakfast, and again at four in the afternoon, for coffee and pie.'

'And does Hal give him a bowl of water?'

'He sure does.'

'That's a nice image,' Rachel said. She could see them so clearly, Gabe and Ol' Red – trotting at his heels – walking up to Jud Bar & Grill in sun, wind, rain and snow, as the seasons turned.

'I'll give you another,' said Gabe. 'The soppy fella lying in a basket while I brush the endless burrs off his coat.'

They both laughed.

'It didn't go away, did it?' Gabe's face was suddenly serious.

'What didn't?' Her heart halted.

'This. Us. This feeling.' He paused. 'I wrote you an email in 2001,' he said.

'Did you?'

'Yes. I looked up your email address, at the gallery. I wrote you, oh, it was all sorts of nonsense, talk of fate, destiny, missed chances, all of that crock. That you were still the most beautiful woman I'd ever met. That I felt I could love you, if you were free. That I would *love you*,' he added simply. 'That true, once-in-a-lifetime love.' He looked tortured. 'I didn't send it. I knew you were never going to turn up at my riad, that night in Marrakesh. I knew you would never leave. I just wanted to say how I'd felt when I was with you, and that I've felt like that ever since I first clapped eyes on you.' Gabe drummed his fingers on the table. Rubbed at the back of his head. 'Well, there you are,' he said. 'Would you like to say something?'

'No?' She tried to breathe deeply, tried to centre herself, hold on to reality, maintain a grip on her life. Her life that mattered. Her life that was everything to her.

'Please can you say something?' pleaded Gabe.

'I can't.'

'Not even if it's the last time? Not even if we'll never see each other again? This is it, Rachel, we'll never get another chance.'

Rachel felt for her bag on the banquette. She was ready to stand, to flee. To rush out of here and never see his face again. All she had to do was rise from the table and walk away. But it killed her, that thought. She wasn't sure how she'd continue to breathe if she never saw his wonderful face again. Or heard his voice. Or sat with him, like this. Just sat with him. She took her hand off her bag and placed it on the table.

'No, it didn't go away. It never has.' The words welled from her, like an exhalation. 'I think that I would love you, too.' She had loved him from the first moment she saw him, in the wake of Mrs Bottomley's fragrant skirts, at the Wetheringtons' lunch party. From the moment he had spoken, and observed that her face was like sunshine, when his was like a beautiful bomb going off in her life. And she had loved him ever since. Hopelessly, irrevocably, disastrously. But what to do with it? What to do with this love? There was nowhere for it to go.

'Are we going to do anything about it?' asked Gabe gently. 'This could-have would-have love?'

Her knee-jerk response was to say 'no', to follow the blueprint, to not wander from her path to see if the grass was greener, to avoid catastrophe – but then he moved his hand across the table and laid it over hers and she needed him, she wanted him, she couldn't bear to let him go. Suddenly, this moment was a here and now she wanted to grab hold of, clasp within her, cleave to her searing soul like a feathered wing that threatened to take flight, and she felt a yearning so desperate, and a compulsion so physical, it overwhelmed her.

'Yes,' she whispered.

'Yes?'

'Yes, I'd like to do something about it. I think I'd like to go upstairs.' She would leave Jonny. She would leave him tomorrow.

'Upstairs?'

'To the hotel. If you'd like to, that is.'

She saw him gulp, just a little. 'I'd like to,' he echoed quietly. 'If you're sure?'

She nodded. 'I'm sure.'

'OK then,' Gabe said, and he stood up from the table and held out his hand to her and everything they were about to do was in the touch of that hand. How they stood up, just looking at each other. How Gabe left a crisp ten-pound note with the chit on the table and she reached for her bag. How, not saying a word, they walked over and took their coats from the coat stand – him the grey jacket; her the trench coat – and shrugged them on.

The door creaked as he opened it for them – not the one they had come in through, from the street, but another door; a door that led from the coffee shop to the soft cream and caramel plush of the lobby of the Zee Hotel. She stood back as Gabe walked up to the check-in desk; avoided her reflection in the mirrored glass of the gilt and chrome lift, as it carried them to the sixth floor; watched as Gabe tried three times to get the key card to work in the door of their room; and inhaled as the light finally went green and the handle turned, and the door swung open.

Gabe silently took off his jacket and laid it on the back of a chair. He turned to help Rachel with hers and she let it fall on top of Gabe's, with shaking hands. Then he stepped towards her and softly undid the scarf at her throat, letting it slip to the carpet, and she gasped as he kissed her in the soft well of her throat and traced his hand along her collarbone, and she yielded her body to his.

# Chapter Thirty

Sometime in the early hours, in the drowsy half-sleep of a quiet hotel room darkened by heavy drapes closed against London skies, Rachel recalled a moment. A moment from that stolen late afternoon in the tumble of hotel white sheets when her face and Gabe's were close, and their lips had just pulled apart, and Gabe's eyes were a blue made almost black by the dusk that was slowly invading the room.

'Not yet,' he'd whispered. And she'd closed her eyes and tried to hold very still and his breath on hers was fast, and in time with her own.

'I can't . . .' she'd breathed, and he slowly slid his hand up her palm and intertwined his fingers with hers with exquisite pressure.

'Not yet,' he'd whispered again, and this moment was forever hers, it was forever theirs and, as it lingered, those mere hours later, as darkness blanketed London with the ashy dawn yet to usher it away, she almost imagined it held enough love to sustain her for a lifetime.

◆ ◆ ◆

A ribbon of cool grey sliced between the gold drapes. A white sheet was tangled around a leg and a bicep. The duvet was upside down and its button fastenings clipped like shells against Rachel's hip bone. She had an arm across her stomach she liked looking at, an arm with the remains of a tan from a North Dakotan summer, dark hairs, all foresting in the same direction, and a freckle that was cause for delight. She had no idea what the time was, and she didn't care.

'Morning,' came the voice from the pillow beside her.

'Morning.'

Rachel shifted position and turned her head so she could see him.

'How long can you stay?'

They had made love yesterday afternoon like two people for whom love was a rare, precious, and transitory gift – painful and sweet. They had made love like it was a new and novel thing that existed only for them. She had clung to Gabe and the rest of the world, all of it outside this room, had stopped.

*Borrowed time*, Rachel thought, in the sheets made warm and supple by their bodies. They had snatched at time, and were rummaging through its contents like scavenging crows, sifting through every piece, holding fragments up to the light and burrowing others within them, to prolong it – to stretch time as far as it could be stretched.

'I can stay today and tonight,' she said, as though it was perfectly fine to be living on borrowed time, 'but I have to go home tomorrow afternoon.' And the time was borrowed because now, in the cool light of the morning, Rachel wondered if she really did have the courage to leave Jonny.

Gabe nodded and pulled her back into his arms. 'Then that's all I'll ask of you, for now,' he said, kissing the tip of her nose. 'Today and tonight and tomorrow morning.'

They rose, finally, at about eleven o'clock and Gabe phoned down to reception to extend their stay by another night. They showered – together – then Gabe went down in the lift and ran across the road to Marks and Spencer's, where he bought Rachel a three pack of boy short knickers and two plain black T-shirts, and a packet of boxer shorts and a chambray shirt for himself.

'Romantic,' she said, on his return, when he unceremoniously threw the packet of knickers on the bed.

'Love is a three pack of functional underwear,' Gabe replied. 'Would you like to go to the National Portrait Gallery today?'

'I'd love to,' she said, sitting on the edge of the crumpled bed in a hotel dressing gown, and they shared a smile – the two borrowers of time, the stealers of imagined futures – as both time and future were already turning their backs and running out on them, stealthily moving past the door of their room and down the quiet corridors and out on to the grey streets of London below.

# Chapter Thirty-One

Their visit began fun and light. They were lovers, sightseeing in London. They were a carefree middle-aged couple in coats and boots (although Gabe took his coat off, halfway round, and slung it over his arm, as he was hot), who spent a leisurely two hours in the National Portrait Gallery, starting on the second floor, in the Tudor Gallery, where they stared at the ruffled collars and the stately dress of England's Tudors and Stuarts.

They held hands, moving slowly through the space and taking in each portrait – a young Elizabeth I, vulnerable and exposed-looking; Henry VIII, full of himself, inevitably – gently commenting or pointing out details they liked or colours they found entrancing. They stopped at the painting of Shakespeare for a good five minutes, lingered over Jane Austen – a small sketch done by her sister ('I would have liked to have had a sister,' commented Rachel, 'to share it all with'); impersonated the stern faces of the military men, to make each other laugh, and savoured the seductive stoicism of the royal mistresses.

On the first floor they travelled from Victorian times to modern days of royalty and fame: portraits of princes and explorers and prime ministers and actors. Rachel loved the more abstract photographs with the wild splashes of colour; Gabe the huge kaleidoscopic ones with the microscopic detail. They stayed longer on this floor, soaking up the many faces of culture and history, and the stories that were etched on their skin and in their eyes.

'Are you hungry?' Gabe asked her, after they had debated Mick Jagger and exalted at David Attenborough.

'Starving,' replied Rachel.

They went to the cafe in the basement, supped tea from a pot for two, ate chicken salad sandwiches and shared a slice of carrot cake. They talked about art and artists, Rachel's plans for the gallery, Gabe's next tree project. They smiled as a family on the table next to theirs sat down in a flurry of coats and stripy scarves and laughed as the youngest child pulled chocolatey gap-toothed faces at them over an enormous slice of fudge cake. If Rachel had a sadness to her laughter, then Gabe surely noticed. If he placed a hand on her knee under the table – and pooled in his eyes was the empathy of a million silent 'sorry's and a thousand unsaid 'I understand's – then she was grateful to him.

She texted Wren, holding her phone inside her bag. *All fine, tell you everything when I get home!*

A text immediately came back. *Glad you're OK.*

Gabe took a biro from his jacket and did a little sketch of her, on a napkin. She liked the look of concentration on his face as he worked, the way each stroke of the pen was considered. It was a sweet likeness, if a little too flattering.

'I look too young,' she protested.

'You'll always be young to me,' he said.

After lunch, they paid to see the temporary exhibition on the ground floor, 'A Photographer's Life' – a mix of uber-celebrity portraits and very personal family photographs by the famous New York photographer Annie Leibovitz. They trailed around – first, hand in hand, then separate, as certain photographs drew them more than others. Rachel found the portraits both fascinating and poignant. The celebrity portraits were huge and ostentatious. The personal pictures were small – harrowing reportage shots from Sarajevo in 1993, a photo of Leibovitz's late partner, Susan Sontag, among an assault of hospital wires and monitors as she was loaded into an air ambulance. There were several photos of Sontag, as she lay ill and dying of cancer; they were so personal Rachel wasn't sure how she felt about them. She peered at a tiny photo of Annie Leibovitz's father, then stood back to take in an omnipresent Bill Clinton in the Oval Office.

Gabe was the other side of the space, standing in front of a small and painfully intimate captioned photo of Susan Sontag laid out in her favourite dress at a New York funeral home. He was staring and staring at it.

'Are you OK? Do you want to go?' asked Rachel, after moving silently over to him. She found the photo disturbing and invasive, although it was beautiful. She found the whole exhibition unnerving, actually, having thought it would be celebrity razzle-dazzle only – all 'Whoopi Goldberg in a bath of milk', and not images that cut deep to the cycle of life and pain.

'No, I'm OK,' said Gabe, not taking his eyes from the photo. 'They're all amazing, aren't they, these photos? How they tell their own stories.'

'They're highly evocative,' agreed Rachel. She didn't want to look at this photo any more; Leibovitz's intimate recordings of a life coming to an end were landing within her like fragments of mirrored glass. 'Are you sure you're OK?'

'Absolutely,' he said, but he looked devastated.

'Oh, Gabe,' said Rachel, laying her hand gently on his shoulder, 'you did your absolute best for her, I'm sure of it.'

He shook his head. 'No,' he said. '*No.*' Then he turned to her and clasped both her hands. 'I want to be with you, Rachel. More than just this. More than today and tonight. More than what you've given me.' He turned and pulled her into his arms. 'I want to be with you.' His cheek was hot on hers. His voice a whisper. Rachel could feel his heart beating through the soft wool of yesterday's jumper.

'Don't ask me,' she whispered to him. 'Don't ask me yet.' Her resolve to leave, to make a new life with another man, had continued to drain from her since she woke this morning. Rachel was afraid. She was scared of tipping over the boat she had been sailing in for so long, with her along with it. What if she landed too hard? What if she crashed?

Gabe held her tighter. Eventually he said, 'Right, but I will, as I have to. I *will* ask you.'

'OK,' she said, breathing him in, breathing in this moment, for it was all they had. She only wanted to exist in this day, this hour. Tomorrow was a place she was petrified to travel to. 'OK.'

They stood together like that for a while, with her loving him, until Rachel sensed there was a man in a tweed suit behind them, resisting the urge to cough so they'd move on.

'Let's go,' said Gabe, stepping back from her, and taking her hand instead. 'Let's go and get some fresh air.'

They stepped out of the gallery and walked to Trafalgar Square, letting the desolate mood of the exhibition lift from them and the fast-moving clouds in the low sky swipe it away. Trafalgar Square was busy. It had recently rained, and the lions were slick and black and shiny, the fountains jaunty. There were chatters of people taking photos and wandering about, chomping on huge slices of pizza and Big Macs straight out of the box.

'My first ever visit to Trafalgar Square,' said Gabe, a sudden cheeky look on his face. 'I'm going to act like a proper tourist.' He made Rachel laugh by leaping from her side, levering himself up on to one of the plinths, then clambering up and sitting astride one of the lions, jiggling his legs in glee and pulling silly faces. If he belonged to her and she to him, she would have taken a photograph of him.

'You're an idiot,' she called to him affectionately.

'An American in London!' shouted Gabe. 'What can you do?' He eventually climbed down from the lion, letting three teenage boys shin up to take his place. They walked together to one of the fountains and perched at its edge, looking around them.

'I was expecting pigeons,' said Gabe.

'The mayor cleared them all up. Last year.'

'I'm kinda disappointed.' He smiled, looking around him. 'I love London,' he said. 'In another life I feel I could live here.'

'Me too,' said Rachel, 'in another life. Actually, I've always had a secret dream to open a gallery here.'

'Perhaps it shouldn't be a secret,' said Gabe.

There was sudden loud laughter from beside them. A couple, both in their sixties, Rachel guessed, both wearing glasses with bright blue frames, were roaring with delight at something on the man's phone.

'Relationship aspirations,' whispered Gabe, with an impish wink.

'Yes,' said Rachel.

'You'd look nice in glasses like that.'

'Stop it!'

'I'd like to grow older with you. I'd like to laugh like that with you, every day.'

Rachel fell silent. She watched as the couple began falling about laughing at something afresh, the man reaching into his coat pocket for a handkerchief to dab his mirth-filled eyes.

'I don't think I can wait,' said Gabe, and Rachel turned to look at him. 'I want to ask you. Would you leave Jonny? Would you leave him, to be with me?'

Rachel refused to look at him; she let her eyes land on every other person in Trafalgar Square. This was too big for her. The weight of it, too enormous. She had given her body to him and her heart, but her future? That was something which had always been ring-fenced, guaranteed. She couldn't answer his question.

'You make it sound so simple,' she said. 'It's almost as though Jonny is barely a concept to you. Or an obstacle so slight he can be swatted away. I realise,' she said, 'that the thought of him has never stopped you. From how you've been with me. Why is that?'

'I don't know Jonny,' Gabe said. 'I've never met him. I just feel you should be with me. That we belong together. It's always kinda been that simple.'

'It's not simple,' she said quietly. 'I'm not certain I'm brave enough to dismantle what I've built, what we've built, Jonny and me. I was taught to stick at things, you know. To just try and stick at things.' She was nearly in tears. She felt wretched.

'But you don't have to stick at things, not these days,' said Gabe. 'These are the days when you can do what you want.'

She turned to face him. 'Do you really think it's that different for women these days?' she said. 'That they can just make choices and execute them? When they've been brought up, still are brought up, to make themselves second in everything. To keep things together? To keep families together? To not feel they can just leave?' *How can I leave Teddy?* Rachel thought. *How can I upend Teddy's fragile sense of balance?*

'You shouldn't be second in anything,' said Gabe simply. 'And he has cheated on you.'

'And now I've cheated on him . . .'

'So, you're not happy any more – it's been proven – so you can leave him.'

'Not without paying too high a price.'

'What *is* the price?' His eyes searched hers.

288

'My peace of mind!' she cried. 'My stability. My home. My family. Teddy. Protecting Teddy! I love her so much. We've been through so much, she and I. I lost a lot when I was a kid, I need to keep everything – everyone – safe around me. If I left, I'd be repeating history in some awful way. Causing damage. Colouring outside the lines . . . rocking the boat. Oh, I don't know, I don't know if I'm brave enough. What would I do? Where would I go?' She felt panicky at the thought. She couldn't dismantle it all, could she, all the parts of her life?

'You could come to North Dakota and live with me.'

'And replace one view from a kitchen window with another?'

'What does that mean? You could open a new gallery, in Fargo maybe, wherever you like. Or I could come to England. I like it here. It suits me. I hope Jacob would like London too. We could all get a little place here, maybe?' Extra light came into his eyes. The sunbursts at the edges of them concertinaed.

'All those grey skies . . .' She shook her head.

'There's grey skies everywhere. The view from your kitchen window would often be the same, wherever we are. No one can escape the grey of life all the time. But we'd be happy, Rachel. Really, really happy.'

She closed her eyes. She tried to see it. A little place in London, or living with Gabe in North Dakota . . . walking to Jud Bar & Grill on spring mornings with him and Ol' Red and Jacob. Relaxing on Gabe's front veranda on summer evenings. Strolling in the fall through red and amber leaves. Looking out of the kitchen window at Gabe's oak tree in the winter, with the clear stars above it. Living in the after-haze of his guilt and his grief over Anne-Marie? Sitting where his late wife had sat at the breakfast table and feeling her shadow? Making a home with Gabe and Jacob, and being a step-mother again in a real mother's absence?

Rachel couldn't see it. She had Jonny. She had their life. She had Teddy, who still really needed her, and needed her and Jonny to be together. How could she just pack a bag and walk away from all that? Leave one man for another? Walk with a Jacob and not a Teddy? And she was worried she wouldn't be happy. That after she had pulled a life apart piece by piece, put what was left of it in a suitcase and then unpacked it – familiar clothes in an unfamiliar house, a pair of slippers placed under another bed – she would realise she had made a mistake, that the grass was just different grass, like Florence had said. But Rachel desperately wanted to be with him.

'Do you resent me for asking?' Gabe said.

'No. If you didn't ask, I wouldn't know you wanted it.'

'I do want it. I want you. But part of that is wanting you to be happy, and if you don't think you could be happy doing this, leaving him, leaving your life, then I understand. I really understand . . .'

She collapsed against him now, crumpled her face against the collar of his jacket.

'It's not a decision I can make straight away,' she mumbled into it. 'Just like that. I can't give you an answer right now. I need to think about it.'

'Of course,' he said, 'of course.' And they just sat there for a while, her head buried in his chest, and the couple in their sixties wandered away with a 'Come on, David,' and a 'Yes, dear', and more ready laughter.

'We need to move, because there's a dog on my foot,' said Gabe eventually, and Rachel laughed now, too, lifting her chin from the warmth of his collar. 'What can I say?' he said to the approaching apologetic owner, a girl in a bobble hat. 'Dogs just really like me. You know something?' Gabe said to Rachel, as they stood up, taking both her hands in his.

'What?'

'This. This is love,' said Gabe, and his smile was so tender and his eyes so blue and full of emotion that she raised her face and she kissed him – his cheeks, his chin, the space between his eyebrows, each ear lobe in turn and the tip of his nose – so she could remember. Remember every inch of his skin. Because in a few hours, she might only have her memory to rely upon.

# Chapter Thirty-Two

The sky boasted feathery patches of blue as Rachel and Gabe walked back to the hotel. The coffee and cream of the Zee's lobby was a welcome warmth. They rose in the lift and hurried along the muted corridor to their room, where they fell into bed for two, maybe three hours – neither of them wanted to count them now – and however long it was, it felt like far less than that. Time was a brazen thief, robbing them of their moments together, rushing them towards either a beginning or an ending, and the unknown of their future magnified every touch.

They eventually emerged and went downstairs for a casual supper in the hotel's French bistro, having neither the clothes nor the energy for the elegant restaurant on the mezzanine floor. They ate French onion soup and croque-monsieurs; they drank red wine and pastis. The atmosphere was laden with unmade decisions – as unmade as that hotel bed upstairs. The conversation was both stilted and free-flowing, tumbling and hesitant. They talked of the things they had seen and the things yet to see. Of art and of cities and of the seasons. They talked of everything and nothing.

'What's your favourite painting?' Gabe asked, as he tapped the stem of his wine glass. 'Ever?'

Rachel didn't need to think about it. 'It's Monet's *The Magpie*,' she said. 'The sun shining on freshly fallen snow . . . The surprising bright blue of the magpie's shadow . . .' she mused. 'The quiet beauty.'

'I haven't seen that painting for a long time,' said Gabe, 'and now I really want to see it again. I love it too. Monet will *always* win the Monet-Manet argument, in my book.' He didn't take his eyes off her. 'Shall we get the bill?'

'Yes, please.'

They returned to that bed, with no more questions asked or answers given – not yet – and they fell on each other, desperate to be sated, to wring every second out of the love they were so sure of, yet so uncertain of the future for. They breathed in every inch of each other, kissed warm scented skin with abandon, moved together achingly slowly to prolong, prolong, prolong . . . and Rachel knew in every caress Gabe was waiting for an answer.

Afterwards, they didn't sleep, not really – only brief corridors of slumber they emerged from to hold each other again, in the darkness, and whisper over and over again, 'I love you.'

In the morning, they extended their check-out time to the ticking bomb of 2 p.m. They slipped reluctantly from the bed at 1.45, after more flying tangled hours, showered and dressed. Gabe smiled hopefully at her as they went down in the lift to reception. Her heart was pounding; she felt light-headed, incapable of decision.

They approached the reception desk together. The young woman in the navy uniform looked up from her computer, but Rachel could only look at Gabe's face, his side profile, the beginnings of a five o'clock shadow . . .

'We'd like to check out,' said Gabe. 'There's a few items from the mini bar to settle up, please. Three miniature vodkas, a can of Pringles. It'll probably come to a couple hundred pounds.'

He winked at Rachel and the woman behind the counter got the joke. 'Certainly, sir.' She tapped precise baby-pink nails at her computer. 'That'll be £21.55 for the additional items. I'll just take the total amount off your card . . . I trust you have you enjoyed your stay at the Zee, Mr McAllister . . .' She looked up from her screen with a polished smile and bright eyes flicked with mascara. '*Rachel?*'

Rachel took in the young woman's features. The shape of her face, the colour of her hair; the aspects of the woman held quite obvious traces of the mischievous little girl she had once been. '*Snezhana?*'

'Oh my God! It's really you!' cried the girl, her face lighting up. 'Yes, it's Snezhana! I came to England, like I said I wanted to. I work in this hotel. I got a visa.'

'Oh, my goodness!' exclaimed Rachel, almost in sudden tears. 'What a surprise! Just look at you! You really did it,' she said, clocking Snezhana's smart name badge on her crisp navy dress.

'I really did it,' said Snezhana, looking fit to burst with pride, her cheeks, that reddened so easily as a child, firing up bright pink under her carefully contoured blusher. 'It's so great to see you, Rachel. Really, it is. I'm sorry for all of the times I asked for chips for breakfast,' she added.

Rachel laughed. 'That's really OK,' she said. 'It's *so* great to see you.' Her memories of the young girl flooded her – Snezhana snaffling bowl after bowl of ice cream morning, noon and night, or hurtling with an ecstatic yell down an inflatable slide at the nearby soft play centre, the pigtails Rachel had braided for her flying.

'So, what are you doing here, Rachel? At this hotel, I mean? And how's Jonny?' Snezhana asked, looking at Gabe. 'I miss his stories.' Jonny, when he could be persuaded, had told their young Belarusian visitors stories about dragons and dinosaurs before they went to bed.

'Jonny is great,' said Rachel. 'He's a bestselling author these days.'

'Well, I know *that*,' said Snezhana, 'I have seen him. I see his books at the airport.'

'Well, yes, you will do,' agreed Rachel. 'And I've been here to meet a friend,' she continued, reluctantly signalling to Gabe with an imperceptible tilt of her head. 'For my gallery.'

'OK,' said Snezhana briskly. 'Well, OK. That's nice.' She smiled a smile that had a million questions in it, all of which Rachel studiously ignored. 'So, thank you very much, Mr McAllister, I'll just print off a copy of your room charges.'

'Thank you,' said Gabe. Rachel watched as Snezhana turned and printed off a document on to heavy parchment paper, folded it expertly and put it in an envelope.

'Thank you,' echoed Rachel feebly. A guilt as thick and as heavy as a scratchy winter coat was bearing down on her. Weighing on her shoulders. Fastening itself to her with thick round buttons and snaking her in a wide belt that knotted itself tightly at her waist, squeezing her internal organs. The kind of guilt she knew would be impossible to escape from. The kind of guilt Gabe had talked about so painfully.

Snezhana gave Gabe the sealed envelope. 'Once again, I hope you enjoyed your stay, Mr McAllister, and we hope to see you at the Zee Hotel again soon.'

'Thank you,' repeated Gabe, tucking the envelope in his jacket pocket.

'Bye, Rachel,' said Snezhana cheerily, 'it's been so great to see you. I meant to look you up, but I've been so busy since I got here. London is just so incredible. But I could write to you, maybe. I have your address still.'

'That would be lovely,' said Rachel, that guilt now tightening around her neck and beginning to strangle her. She had written to Snezhana a few times since the girl had come to England in 1993, but had never received a reply. There had been no simulated mother-and-child echo, throughout the years; Snezhana had her own mother, after all, and Rachel was never meant to be one,

295

ultimately. Only to Teddy. Teddy, with all her problems, who was currently doing OK, but needed safeguarding and stability, and who Rachel was seriously thinking about abandoning. What sort of a person was she? Really, what kind of a person?

'Perhaps I could come and visit you?' offered Snezhana, 'I'd love to see you and Jonny again, and Tatiana. The three of you. I've never forgotten all our happy times together.'

'That would be wonderful,' said Rachel, with a stiff smile. '. . . And Katya, do you know how she is?' They had been at different schools.

'No, I don't,' said Snezhana. 'I heard there was some trouble in the family. A divorce. And now I don't know, I'm sorry.'

'OK, well, thank you,' said Rachel. She remembered Katya, quiet and polite, a laugh that was rare, but joyous, when it did burst from her. 'Bye, then, Snezhana.'

'Goodbye, Rachel.'

Rachel was already turning, already hurrying to get out of there. She felt she had been slapped in the face with the life she had lived up to this point; the life she had *wanted* to live. The person she had wanted to be. Happily married, a mother. A nurturer. Someone with a stable home and a secure future and a loving family. The woman she *had* been, who had dished up ice cream to two eager-faced girls and tucked them up in bed at night, smoothing fringes away from warm foreheads. Who had fiercely loved a stepdaughter like she was her own. *Not* a woman who frequented hotel rooms with men who were not her husband. A woman who created drama and trouble. A woman who might leap into a fast car and send it tragically off course.

Gabe tried to take her hand as they emerged from the doors at the front of the hotel. She shrugged his away, angry at herself.

'I can't do this!' Rachel cried at him. 'I shouldn't have done this!'

'What's the matter? Whoa, hey, slow down!' She had set off at pace in front of him. Walking up the street.

'We're in this together, aren't we?' he said, trying to catch her up. 'We love each other, don't we? There's nothing to regret here.'

*Regret.* He had spoken of his own heart being full of regret. Regrets were so easily made. 'There *is* something to regret!' she exclaimed, stopping to face him. 'I've destroyed everything. Who I wanted to be! Who I used to be!'

They were at the door to Sullivan's, the smell of coffee diffusing on to the street.

'Who do you want to be?' he pressed.

'I want to be good. I want to be calm and happy, to not be like my parents. I want love and safety.'

'I can give you love and safety. I can give you everything, so you can be everything you need to be.'

'No!' she cried. 'It's not that simple! I'm in a life! I can't swap it for another!' She knew her words echoed the ones she had cried in Morocco.

'You would if you loved me!'

'I need to go, Gabe,' she said, turning from him again. 'I'm so sorry. I love you, I do. I've never loved like this. I've never felt this way before, about anyone, but I have to go back to my life. I have to go back.' She was sobbing now, into the chill coffee-dusted air. He tried to reach for her, to hold on to her, to her arm, to the tail of her coat, but it was too late. She had already slipped from him. She was already gone.

# Chapter Thirty-Three

Her seat was 14F, by the window. She had slumped in the first empty pair of seats she had come across, having no return ticket pre-booked and hastily having purchased one for any train to Oxford. At one point she had not imagined herself on the return journey at all: a downcast figure placing her folded coat on the seat next to her; a bereft woman crying her eyes out into tissue after tissue from a pocket pack hurriedly bought from a kiosk at Paddington station.

'Sorry. Can I?'

There was a woman standing by her seats, wearing a rustling cagoule and holding a McDonald's bag.

'Of course,' Rachel said, removing her coat from the seat, a silent 'bugger off' unvoiced.

The woman sat down, snapped into place her seat tray and plonked the McDonald's bag on it. 'Where are you travelling to today?' she asked.

Rachel struggled to not roll her wretched eyes. 'Oxford,' she muttered.

'Oh, me too.' The woman looked delighted. Was she hoping to make a new friend? Bond over a large fries? Rachel turned away and stared out of the window, at the platform, praying the woman wouldn't try to engage her in any more conversation. She wanted to wallow in her misery; she wanted to roll and roil in the stuff all the way home to Oxford.

The train doors beeped and shut. The tannoy chimed musically into life. 'This is the 11.47 Great Western Railway service to Oxford,' came a sing-song voice. 'Calling at Ealing, Hayes and Harlington, Slough, Maidenhead, Twyford, Reading, Tilehurst, Pangbourne, Goring and Streatley, Cholsey, Didcot Parkway, Appleford, Culham, Radley, Fincham and Oxford.'

Rachel groaned out loud. Damn, it was the slow train! She shouldn't have jumped on the first one she saw. Well, she would have *plenty* of time to think about her sojourn in London, she thought miserably – on this two-hour hell. *Forever* to mull over her utter desperation and torment at leaving Gabe behind. The train rumbled into life and trundled painfully out of the station, in a smug forewarning of the interminable journey to come.

*It's over*, she thought, as it sludged past graffitied walls and blackened sidings. Whatever she and Gabe had – that clutching, compulsive need for one another – it was over. There would be no more chances for them, no more miraculous, soul-inflaming, achingly melancholic meetings. This was it. They had come as far as they could go; there was no more track in front of them on which to travel. The only way from here was home.

'Yeah, so you know what I said to him? I said, "Do one, mate!" Yeah, yeah, I did. Well, what the fuck else could I do? He had it coming to him, mate.'

A man in a seat the other side of the aisle had decided to inflict his voice on the rest of the carriage. Rachel zoned him out and continued to stare out of the window. She allowed Gabe's face to take up her mind and her heart. His words, 'I love you'. His touch, in that hotel bed. She was frightened of forgetting how it had felt. She went over each stolen moment again and again so she would never forget. She would never stop loving him. But she had to go

299

home. The guilt was too much, the burden was too great. The seismic upheaval Rachel would have to execute to do anything but go home would destroy her.

'Would you like a fry?'

'Sorry?' Rachel turned and the woman next to her was brandishing chips at her. She had kindly eyes Rachel didn't need right now. 'No, thank you,' said Rachel. Behind the woman's offering, a good-looking young couple were walking noisily through the train, with drinks from the buffet car, in a paradox of unconscious attention-seeking. The girl, hanging off the back of the boy's jumper, giggling and silly; the boy, grinning at her like the sun had come out.

'Young love,' said the woman, stuffing a chip in her mouth. 'Warms the heart, doesn't it?'

'Yes,' said Rachel, turning away again. She closed her eyes. She had 'young love' once. She had giggles and promises and a sun that had come out every day, but it hadn't lasted forever. Once love was no longer young, and promises hadn't come true after all, it had ebbed away, and the sun had disappeared behind a cloud. Now, in middle age, she had experienced a seized and latent love so all-encompassing it was unbearable, but she wasn't fearless enough to take its chances. She wasn't strong enough to change her life for it. Rachel was running. She was running away from him. Further and further away . . .

She woke up at Slough. The doors clunked open and slid shut again. People came on to the train with darkened shoulders, shaking back their hoods, and the train noisily restarted. The woman sitting next to her was asleep, her chin down to her chest. Across the aisle, Rachel noticed a man was reading one of Jonny's books. *Nikita's Plan*, the one where Nikita tries to bring down the government of the lesser Russian state of Slovabornia. Rachel checked her phone. There was a text message from Teddy, sent earlier, at 12.21 p.m.

*Book club great success! Next week On Chesil Beach, no
Nikita!!*

She would normally have smiled at Teddy's words. There was
also a text from Jonny. It had come at 9.15 this morning, she
noticed, when she'd been in bed with Gabe.

*See you tonight! I fancy steak, if you can sort that. Thanks
darling. Things have been WILD here, those crazy
Belgians!! Xxx*

She realised that because of this horribly slow train, Jonny
would probably get home before her, hungover, no doubt, and in
need of cuddles. He might even come to the door to greet her, with
a huge, bemused smile and the boast he'd made dinner – once he'd
sussed there was no steak. That was assuming he believed the lie she
told by text yesterday, about going shopping in Oxford with Wren
today. Of course he believed it! Rachel would never cheat! Rachel
would never dare. And loving another man? Preposterous! Yet *he*
had been happy to ride roughshod over their marriage, casually
stabbing holes in it with his treachery and widening the punctures
from which love and respect had been escaping, with a slow hiss,
for years.

Jonny got what he wanted; everyone knew that. He was fearless. He took chances. If he were in her shoes, her miserable shoes,
and he was offered a love like she had found, he'd just think he
wanted it and he needed it, and he would grab it with both hands.
That was ambition for you. Self-service, which her husband was so
good at. *Sorry, Gabe*, she thought, *I'm so sorry . . .*

A teen in headphones in the seat in front noisily opened a
packet of crisps and started chomping on them. Rachel was starving now, but she remembered she had a packet of Biscoff biscuits

in her bag, stolen from the hotel room. She reached into the main compartment of her bag and rummaged, puzzled by a folded piece of paper she felt at the bottom, which she pulled free.

Unfolding it, she gave a small gasp. It was a piece of cream notepaper, torn from the hotel pad on the desk, and on it was a tiny sketch of a magpie, in black biro, and under the magpie were the words:

> *Fly where your heart takes you, Rachel. But wherever that is, you will always cast a bright shadow on my life.*
>
> *Gabe x*

*He must have done this while I was in the shower*, Rachel thought. She already had the little napkin sketch he'd done of her, slipped inside her coat pocket. And now this. These uncertain words. This wish and promise, and a little piece of his heart to keep. A tear landed on the creamy paper. It made the magpie's beak shiny, like the sleek gloss of the Trafalgar Square lion Gabe had climbed on to yesterday. More followed, unchecked. She cried and cried as raindrops streamed diagonally down the window. She felt like she would never stop. Tissue after tissue came out of the packet.

There was a rustling from her right. The woman in the seat next to her laid a gentle hand on her arm. 'It'll all be all right, you'll see,' she said kindly. 'You'll know what to do.'

'Thank you,' Rachel said. '*Thank you*.' But she didn't know what to do, did she? She had the sudden panicky feeling she had made a mistake. The train lurched, then came to an abrupt stop, causing the passengers to exclaim and tut, and the driver's announcements about temporary signal failure to be wearisome and light-hearted.

Rachel felt as paralysed as the train, as static, as stuck. Finally, it limped forward again and began to pick up a cumbersome speed. She leaned back in her seat and closed her eyes, letting all the images and words of the last two days swirl within her, to the turning of the wheels and the rumbling of the track. Round and round. Round and round. Further from him. Further from him. Six little words formed in her brain. *How can I live without him?* Six little words in her head as a refreshment trolley rumbled past. Six little words as the train undulated past electricity pylons and far-stretching fields and isolated cottages with autumn smoke billowing from their chimneys. *I can't live without him.* Five words. The train swayed and tracked through fields of muted green and ploughed earth. A lone scarecrow flapped ragged arms. Four words. *I could go back.* And then three, as the wheels continued to turn and the track was eaten up, yard by yard: *I need him.* As the three words became two: *Can I?*, the fields gave way to houses and gardens. Empty autumn afternoon gardens. And then, as the train coasted into Fincham station, like it hadn't just been the longest, most excruciating journey ever known on the British railway network, just one word: *Yes.* Yes, she would be with Gabe. Yes, she would leave Jonny. Yes, she could make it all work, somehow. She would go home, tell Jonny it was over, upend her life, turn it on its head and leave it in ruins, and then she would go back to London. To Gabe. To all-consuming, once-in-a-lifetime love. Jonny would be OK. Teddy was in a much better place these days. Their bond would survive. But Rachel would go back to love.

The passengers were gathering their belongings with relief. Rachel slipped her shoulders into her coat and zipped up her bag. The woman next to her stood up and was the first to make for the door, depositing her McDonald's bag in one of those under-seat bins.

'Thank you,' Rachel whispered to her departing form, and the woman was gone.

Rachel trailed behind the passengers queuing to get off the train. She stepped down on to the platform and hurried from it, clattered over the footbridge and made her way to the tiny car park. Her Golf was where she had left it two days ago, but it seemed another lifetime ago she was in this car, in this space of hers where everything was so familiar: the leather gloves stuffed in the side door pocket, the fir tree air freshener hanging from the rear-view mirror, and one of Jonny's books on the dash.

She didn't falter. She could do this. Rachel pulled out of the car park, determined not to shake, determined to be brave, and started driving home. The roads were quiet; it wasn't yet rush hour, but as she got to Metcalf Road, just off the short bypass, she slowed the car as she saw the flashing lights of an ambulance in the rear-view mirror. A minute later, she pulled over, along with three other cars, on to the side of the road, allowing the ambulance – its sirens now blaring – to sail past. She saw it turn swiftly into Piper Way. Checking her mirror, she pulled out again. When she got to Piper Way herself, it started to rain, and the swoosh of the wipers was a welcome distraction. Jonny would be waiting. She *was* going to do this. She let the sound of the wipers sweep her with determination. With resolve. She was almost home. Three miles and she'd be in the village. Silent trees wept either side of the road. Her headlights, on full beam, picked up cat's eyes like Hansel and Gretel's breadcrumbs.

The village was quiet, largely free of traffic. She slowed carefully on corners. Piloted to avoid a lone cyclist, his bike lights winking. She turned on to Hedge Hill Lane, crunched into the enormous puddle that always lurked there when it rained and, further up the lane, flashing lights were casting watery blue and white shadows, like out of season Christmas lights. Even before she reached Crofters, Rachel realised the ambulance, that ambulance she'd seen flying past, was parked outside her house.

# WINTER

2 December 2019

# Chapter Thirty-Four

Turkish delight had been one of Rachel's dad's favourites. A hexagonal box of them had sat on the windowsill in the sitting room, behind his chair, every year after Christmas, the plump cushions of dusted lilac treasures nestled in their papery compartments waiting to be selected. He savoured his Turkish delight. Gary liked to spread out his enjoyment of them. And when he bit into one, he always used to hold it up to the light, like a jewel, and examine the contrast between the floury exterior and the translucent lilac centre.

'Beautiful!' he used to say, popping the rest into his mouth, and Rachel's mum would find the empty box, sometime in March, on the windowsill behind his chair, and put it in the bin.

Funny the things you remember, thought Rachel. The dear memories of her parents so distant now, but yet so clear, and the realisation she had outlived Frances and Gary by twenty-five years. She was not only thinking about Turkish delight because Christmas was coming and she was idly compiling a list, leaning over the coffee table, of Jonny's stocking presents (chocolate Brazils, Mint Matchmakers and Lyle & Scott socks), but because this early December morning her view from the sitting-room window was a little Narnia. There was no snow for the White Witch, on her enormous sleigh, to come scudding into view on, but it was crisp and fearfully cold and there had been a haw frost overnight, which had tipped the front lawn and bushes in glittery platinum. A petrified child's glove, stuck cuff-first into the hedge, was rigidly waiting for its owner to recognise the raspberry red under its frozen saccharine topping and Rachel wondered who it belonged to, as she stirred her morning coffee. Teddy had owned a set like that once, in her early thirties: a beret, scarf and gloves ensemble Rachel had bought her from Accessorize in Oxford. Jonny used to sing 'Raspberry Beret' to her every time she wore it.

'Well, good morning, my dear!'

He surprised her, coming out of the conservatory like that. It was positively arctic out there at this time of the year. No one set foot in the conservatory between November and April, and it was so cold in the winter they stored wine in it, ready for Christmas.

'Goodness, you startled me!' Rachel said, from the sofa. 'What on earth were you up to in there?'

Jonny navigated the brass threshold between conservatory and sitting room – a well-known trip hazard – in tartan slippers.

'I went to get this,' he said, waving a copy of Len Deighton's *The Spy Who Came in from the Cold*. Jonny was thinner than he used to be, the skin on his hands a little papery. 'From the other bookcase. I couldn't find my usual copy.'

'Shut the door then,' she said, 'it's freezing out there.'

'All right,' he said dismissively, flapping the book at her.

Rachel watched as he shut the conservatory door then headed quite jauntily to the kitchen, in his roll-neck sweater and plum-coloured cords. He didn't need his stick any more, but it leaned against the wall just outside the kitchen door, its gnarled top a smooth-grooved walnut, just in case. If he had an author event, he always took it, for faux gravitas – an authorly prop to hook over the arm of his chair when he sat down. He laughed and said he'd always imagined himself with a cane one day, and perhaps a monocle. Why not go the whole hog now he had turned sixty and was properly *old*?

Jonny turned in the kitchen doorway, ballasting one shoulder against the frame.

'I've had a WhatsApp from Teddy?'

Occasionally framing statements as questions was an affectation Jonny had picked up from watching Australian soaps in the afternoons. *Neighbours, Home and Away* . . . He had lengthy breaks from writing now; the luxury of a hugely successful author not expected to put out books quite so often, after having been ill for so long following the accident. He liked the new routine, working in bursts of six months to a year, then having long periods off.

'Oh?' Rachel enquired.

'She can make the Winter Ball, after all? That thing she's going to is finishing earlier?'

'Oh, great.' Rachel was glad she was coming, it would be lovely to see her.

'She didn't say anything about Lee.'

'No?'

'But I expect that means he'll be coming, too?'

Rachel's heart sank. 'Yes, I expect so.'

Jonny nodded, then turned and walked into the kitchen. 'I've been thinking,' he called out, the inflection gone, 'for a while now, actually. I hope it's the right thing to do.' He reappeared in the doorway. 'I'm stopping the investment, in Lee's plays.'

'Are you?' Rachel had returned to her Christmas list, but now looked up again.

'Yes. Dear old Michael, God rest his soul, had been banging on at me for years to stop doing it. My new agent, too. And my accountant called me last week and said I was mad to be continuing. That fiscally it didn't add up. Really gave it to me straight, the fucker.' He laughed. It turned into a cough and he fumbled for a balled-up tissue from the pocket of his cords and spluttered meekly into it. 'Asked me exactly what Lee's prospects were, you know . . .

And, well, it might have been a bit rash—' A look of disquiet briefly flickered across his face. '—but the decision's been made now. No one could say I didn't do enough for the man.'

*I don't know why you always have.* 'Well, no, they couldn't.'

'I mean, he's not going to make it, is he? He's been saying so himself, recently. A lot, actually. This is a kind thing to do, isn't it?'

'Yes, I'm sure it is, darling.' She doubted Lee would see it that way, but this was Jonny all over. Act now, think later. At the same time, Jonny's confidence was not so robust any more, not quite so undentable. His sentences these days often had the codas of 'isn't it?' and 'shouldn't I?' and 'don't you think so?'

Lee was – dishearteningly – back in Teddy's life. Teddy had finished her degree, got a job in Oxford, for a telecommunications company, and a flat, and things had been going great, for a few years, until Teddy had walked into a book evening Jonny was hosting and Lee was standing by the fireplace, a roguishly charming look on his face. Teddy had succumbed to him again. She still had the job, but she was commuting to it from Lee's bungalow and things seemed as up and down with them as they always had been.

'Good, good. Well, as I say, that's the decision. I think he'll thank me, actually. Yes, I think he will.'

Jonny nodded emphatically to himself and stepped back into the kitchen. Rachel heard him switch the kettle on. 'There's a glove out there?' he called almost absent-mindedly.

'Yes, I know,' she called back (wasn't marriage mostly calling to the other person from different rooms?). 'I'm sure someone will come along to pick it up.'

'Teddy used to have a set that colour.'

'Yes, darling, she did.'

Teddy had been wearing the raspberry red scarf that early evening in October 2008 when Rachel had driven home from the station, preparing to leave Jonny, and seen the ambulance parked in their drive. Having just arrived to visit her father, the red scarf had been trailing from Teddy's neck when Rachel caught her streaking up the hallway in a dead panic as paramedics dealt with Jonny, who'd fallen from a step ladder in the kitchen reaching for the griddle pan on top of the cupboard, because he'd arrived home before Rachel and wanted to cook bacon – but had no idea where the regular frying pan was. He'd cracked his head on the quarry-tiled floor; he'd broken a rib on the way down as he'd glanced off the side of the oven. The damned fool idiot. That's what he'd called himself afterwards – many weeks afterwards, when he'd had the energy to be angry with himself.

The cut head and the broken rib were only the start of his troubles. Jonny contracted MRSA while he was in hospital, from an epidural needle, he maintained, and had to stay there for six months, in a yellow room on the top floor, overlooking the Maternity Wing car park, while doctors tried to make him better. At one point it wasn't certain if he would live – a halting, frozen week in November when time had stood still and each second of the day had to be dragged through like thick mud. And later, the following February, there was a week where they didn't know whether he would walk again or not.

'What's for lunch?' Jonny asked. He was now cheerily making his way from kitchen to study with a large mug of tea.

'I was thinking tomato soup and some of that thick crusty bread I got from Morrisons,' Rachel said, scribbling 'Fry's Chocolate Cream' on his stocking list. 'Are you making it?'

'Oh.' Jonny pulled a face. 'Well, I was going to write until one.'

'All right,' she said, 'I'll make it, you can clear up.'

He pulled another one and disappeared into the study. Jonny was starting a new project this week – his first book for two years. Nikita was now a grandmother and her grandson, Alexi, was heading up a splinter spy ring in St Petersburg. Jonny shut the study door. Rachel crossed off 'Fry's Chocolate Cream' and wrote 'Lindt Dark Cherry'.

'What's for lunch?' had been one of the rhythmic refrains of their days after Jonny had eventually come out of hospital. When Rachel no longer spent her days by his bedside, softly talking to him (when he was awake) or looking down on the car park as new dads carefully brought out new babies in car seats (while he was asleep) or waiting outside the yellow room staring at a poster about blood types while nurses did his personal care.

'What's for lunch?', 'What's for dinner?', 'What's for breakfast?' When Jonny was confined to their bedroom when he first came home, the quiet, endless days were punctuated by meals served to him on the tray with the picture of the ginger cat on it. They were punctuated by the click of the numbers changing on the old-fashioned digital clock on the bedside table, as Rachel carefully changed their bed linen twice a week, to keep Jonny comfortable. Or spritzed a linen room spray he liked and arranged fresh lilies. Or adjusted his easy listening radio station to the optimum volume. She sometimes sat at the dressing table and dealt with cards and presents from well-wishing readers – replying to them, filing them, sifting them for any Kims she would silently dispose of.

That quiet period was from spring to summer of 2009. In August, Jonny got out of bed and took up residence between a recliner in the sitting room and a wheelchair he called Betty, as he said it made him feel like an inmate in a Betty Ford clinic.

'That's a compliment!' he'd cry, wheeling himself round in it. 'It's all serene and calm here. Restorative. Film stars would think themselves lucky to get over the booze and the drugs *chez* Trent.'

He roamed around the house on Betty, in tennis shorts and a yellow jumper – the trundle of the wheels a daily percussion that soon became overlaid with non-stop talking; sometimes whispers. Jonny found sitting at the desk in the study uncomfortable, so he bought himself a Dictaphone and recorded ideas and snatches of dialogue for his books as he travelled the ground floor of the house. The trundling wheels and the whispers became a kind of daily lullaby – the rhythmic sound of a train going round and round an endless track. Rachel listened as eventually Jonny dictated whole books, and she washed the bed sheets, and she sprayed the linen room spray, and fiddled with the volume of the radio, and nursed her husband back to a full recovery – and it took six and a half years.

The study door opened again. It had a comforting creak neither of them could be bothered to sort. Jonny held out the tea mug. When she didn't get up and come over to take it, he set it on the floor.

'Something else I've been thinking,' he said. 'I'm going to try to come to the Winter Ball, myself, this year. Even if just for a while.'

'Good,' smiled Rachel. 'That will be nice.' He'd said a few years ago he found the neighbours tiring now and social dos – unless they were author events – utterly exhausting.

'If you don't mind dragging me around.'

'You're better now. I won't be dragging you around.'

At Jonny's author events he had an assistant, a lad called Sebastian, who helped him over doorsteps with his cane, when Jonny wanted to play that card. 'Better warn Sally,' Jonny laughed. 'Tell her to lay on the finest foie gras canapés.'

Rachel smiled. 'I'm sure she already has,' she said. Sally Henderson-Bright was on even more of a mission this year. She was apparently planning the Best Winter Ball Ever.

'I won't go to that funeral, though, on Thursday? I know just about everybody in the village is going, but nobody will mind, will they? If I don't show up? It's not like I've ever had anything to do with the woman?'

'No, I'm sure no one will mind.'

'They're bad enough when it's someone you knew well, isn't it?' He looked away, coughed theatrically into his hanky. 'You can talk to Sally at the funeral, about me going to the ball. She'll be there, won't she? Muscling her way to the front row with a black net over her face, like a low-rent Sophia Loren?'

Rachel laughed. 'I'll tell her on Wednesday. Sally and I are doing the flowers at the church the day before.'

'That's nice. OK, my dear.' He disappeared back into the study, calling over his shoulder, 'See you at one with the soup.'

The door creaked closed again and Rachel went into the kitchen. The funeral was written on the calendar, the date – Thursday 5 December – circled before the Winter Ball coming up on Saturday and after the flower arranging at the church on Wednesday she had agreed to, last weekend, when Sally had commandeered her in the greengrocer's and railroaded her into helping.

'You can come along and assist, can't you?' Sally had twittered by the satsumas, pressing on Rachel's anorak-clad arm with almond-shaped talons. 'I'll be there at ten, sharp. Abigail can take care of the gallery for you, can't she?'

'Of course,' Rachel had replied, while her shopping companion, Wren, rolled her eyes.

Rachel had employed an assistant, too, Abigail, when Jonny was in hospital and she needed help, and Abigail took the helm most of the time now at the gallery, doing all the admin and the day-to-day running of things while Rachel still curated and came in when she wanted to. It was a very good arrangement and she liked Abigail; indeed, there was a date on the calendar – the seventeenth – written in as Abigail's Party – which Jonny had scrawled a huge exclamation mark next to, in comic reference to the Alison Steadman classic. He'd also put a red ring around the Winter Ball on Saturday night. He often messed with the calendar – putting giant question marks next to things, querying 'Whisky delivery?'

314

or 'What's this?' He had not scribbled anything by the square of 5 December – the day of the funeral. It meant nothing to him, and he had no idea what it might mean for her.

'You liked Julia, and so did I,' Sally had smartly concluded, on her way out of the greengrocer's.

This was true. Everyone had seen a little more of Julia March in the last couple of years. The old lady had started sitting in the south-facing front garden of the Mill House, on a striped canvas-seated chair, in the afternoons, basking in sunshine in the summer or bundled up against the elements in the winter. She watched plane trails scope across the sky and chatted to the neighbours – soaking up the last rays of life and engaging in her community at last, it seemed to Rachel, and she often stopped to chat, Julia blithely entertaining and Rachel carefully making sure they never meandered on to the topic of Julia's nephew in America.

'See you on Wednesday.' Sally turned, by the cucumbers. 'Oh, by the way, has Jonny made a decision on coming to the ball yet?'

'Sorry, he's still not sure,' Rachel had replied, putting down the mango she'd been staring at distractedly, her mind temporarily elsewhere, 'but there's always a possibility.'

'Oh, absolutely he must see how he *feels*,' Sally trilled, all smiles, as Wren pulled faces behind her back. '*Entirely* up to him. It would be *gorgeous* to see him, though, our local celebrity! Cheerio!'

A famous author at the ball was always a draw; Rachel doubted Sally would be equally thrilled about Teddy pitching up – she and Lee had only been reluctantly invited to encourage Jonny's acceptance. Last December had seen a loud drunken row between the pair – both in their forties but sadly unable to know better – that ended with Teddy crying on Rachel's shoulder while Rachel stroked her hair, and Lee storming off to a casino in Reading.

*Jonny, Teddy, Lee*, Rachel thought, distracted momentarily by a pheasant outside the kitchen window, its feathers ruffling like a can-can dancer's skirts. The triangle of three were woven into the fabric of Rachel, a fixture in the middle of them all, as familiar and as worn as the floral sofa in the sitting room Jonny refused to get rid of.

*Home, family, security.* This was what she'd wanted, and this was where she belonged, at the age of fifty-nine, on castors that had formed permanent hollows in the carpet and with everyone's weight on her, as they relaxed against her worn cushions. She felt a stirring of resistance, often, but worried it was both futile and too late. Besides, she preferred to think about all this *weight*, that she was perhaps never meant to shake off, than to think about the event marked on the calendar for 5 December.

Julia March. She had been liked by everyone. And she had meant an awful lot to others. *Would he be coming?* Rachel had thought, rather selfishly, from the moment she heard that poor old Julia March had died – as Rachel walked home from the gallery and was accosted with the news by Julia's excitable next-door neighbour.

'Thanks for letting me know,' she'd said, before the excitable neighbour had fluttered off to spread the news elsewhere, but in her head Rachel's words had been *Will he be at the funeral?* and those words repeated and repeated there, as she'd continued home in the cold, until the thought of seeing him made her tremble and she'd had to cross her arms, in her big coat, and grip them at the elbows. She didn't know if Gabe was coming. Nobody seemed to. But the thought of him made the weight on those castors feel all the heavier.

Rachel traced her finger over the calendar, letting it rest on the 5 for a little too long, then she opened the bread bin, released a loaf of bread from its crackling cellophane wrapper, plonked it on the wooden chopping board she'd had since 1985, and set about slicing it, ready for lunch.

# Chapter Thirty-Five

'Here you are,' said Wren, handing Rachel a cup of tea. They had both been at St Edwin's since 10 a.m. this morning and had just finished tying the last bunch of white camellias to the end of the front pew. Rachel had roped Wren in for moral support in dealing with Sally, and her friend had been happy to help as she, too, had passed by Julia's front garden and chatted with her sometimes in the afternoons.

'Thank you.' Rachel had brought snacks of carrot cake bars and passed one to Wren. 'It almost looks like a wedding,' she commented. The church was looking pretty and smelled so fragrant, with the scent of fresh flowers supplied by Kaye the florist layered on musty notes of ancient wood and stone. Warm, too, as Wren had dragged out the church's ancient three-bar electric heater, providing a neon glow just off the altar.

'Doesn't it just?' agreed Wren. 'But if this is what Julia wanted, then I agree with her sentiment – give everyone something beautiful to look at and they won't be quite so sad. It's going to be a really lovely send-off, I reckon.'

Julia March had died in mid-November. When Rachel had got home from hearing the news that day, she'd stood in the kitchen for quite a long time, still in her coat – her thoughts reduced simply to '*Gabe*', over and over again. She'd eventually taken off her coat and chastised herself with some dreaded housework, scrubbing the front of the kitchen cupboards, but as she scrubbed she wondered, would he come? Would he come over for the funeral? And she'd thought of Florence, gone now, so long, and she wondered again, was the grass greener? Greener than what she had known?

'Is he coming?' asked Wren, among a mouthful of carrot cake.

'Who?' Rachel pretended.

'Gabe. Is he coming?'

'I don't know.'

'Do you hope he does?'

'I don't know, Wren!'

Wren understood why Rachel had stayed with Jonny for so long. Why she had cared for him after the accident. Why she had slipped into a role of protracted subservience, at home at least. At the gallery, Rachel continued to fly. She had recently discovered an unknown artist who had swiftly become a global sensation, and sales and interest had never been so high. She was also considering opening a second gallery somewhere. But Wren thought Rachel had done enough and should grab some true happiness for herself in her personal life.

Rachel didn't know. She still felt the weight of obligation and commitment and she loved her family. She loved her life, didn't she? The one she had built brick by brick. It included her success at the gallery *and* her family, who still needed her. She could resist in little ways, maybe, but there was no room for big change.

'Well, it's all looking *gorgeous* so far,' carried a clear, self-assured voice up the aisle, and here was Sally, clicking towards them in thigh-high boots that Rachel thought must have been very skiddy outside. 'Thanks for your help, girls.'

The 'girls' popped the last of their cake bars in their mouths and nodded. Wren winked at Rachel.

'My pleasure,' said Rachel, stifling a yawn that threatened to escape from her. She had not slept well last night. Often, she didn't. She assumed it was a post-menopausal thing – the 3 a.m. wake-up call, a nocturnal brain that liked to have fun with her, these days. Although it may have been something else entirely. 'What's next?'

'Lilies in vases on the sills,' said Wren mock-efficiently.

'Splendid,' said Sally, and she made a great show of taking off her leopard print coat and rolling up the sleeves of her cashmere sweater. 'Let's get on with it, then.'

The three women worked for another hour, placing delicate white lilies in vases on the smooth stone ledges in front of the church's stained-glass windows, and chatting lightly about nothing. At a natural break in proceedings, when Wren went to put the kettle on again, Rachel told Sally that Jonny might be coming to the Winter Ball now and that Teddy definitely planned to show up.

'Jonny is very welcome, as you know. Tatiana is less so,' Sally said. 'And she and that reprobate, Lee Hope, better behave themselves. I'm still considering barring him.'

'Hmm. How's Leonora's painting for the ball coming along?' asked Rachel, desperate to change the subject. She knew any sort of barring of Lee would be redundant, as he was a boneless rodent able to squeeze into the most unwelcoming of spaces.

'Yes, all good, she's finishing off the piece I commissioned, close to the wire though, of course – temperamental woman, but fabulous at snowy landscapes. Actually,' Sally said, looking at the dainty watch on her wrist, 'there's somewhere I need to be. I've got a man coming round about some cornicing. Got to have the place looking immaculate for the weekend, girls!'

'And I need to pop home and take the pooch for his afternoon constitutional,' said Wren, setting teas down at the end of a pew. 'I'll be back though, Rachel,' she added, giving her a quick squeeze. 'Won't be long.'

After they left the church together – Sally's heels echoing, Wren's Uggs shuffling – Rachel laid the last arrangement on the sill of one of the small stained-glass windows by the nave, then sat down in the front pew and took a breath. No, she had not slept at all well last night. In addition to her usual 3 a.m. wakefulness, she had been feverish with her own thoughts. *Would* Gabe come? And if he did, had he forgiven her? For running away in London all those years ago? For not taking a chance on them? And if he had, what did it matter? It was way too late now – too many years had passed, too many years etched on their faces and their souls with silvery fingers, and the memories of them being together mere punctuations to already written stories.

Rachel leaned down on the bench, supporting her head with her hand. No, that wasn't comfy enough. She stretched further and laid her head on her bent arm, on the cuffed sleeve of the jumper Jonny had bought her, with the scratchy wool. It tickled her nose as she lay there, feeling the heat from the electric heater. She brought her legs up on the pew. No one would know, would they, if she dropped off for a little while? Nobody would care. Least of all Wren, who would give a big hoot of laughter and offer her another cup of tea . . . ?

'Hello.'

There was a word at the edge of her dream about being on a Caribbean beach, the sand white and the peaks of the waves wistful. She was just about to have a sip from a pina colada and was considering a dip. There was that word again.

'Hello.'

She opened one eye. Then the other. There was a man standing at the end of the pew, holding an enormous flower arrangement exploding from the top of a massive white vase. His face was only just visible over the top of it. He had grey hair, receding at the temples. Eyebrows, also grey. Faded blue eyes that looked tender

320

and highly amused and were wrinkled in sunbursts of surprise. As he moved the vase slightly, she saw a mouth that was smiling at her in that old familiar way.

'Hello,' she said, from her prone position, as she was seemingly unable to move. 'Well, this is quite like old times. You come to Oxfordshire, you catch me doing something embarrassing.' Her tone was chipper, wartime Blitz-like. Inside, her heart was hammering her inside-out.

He was here. *He was here.*

'Is it embarrassing?' he responded, clearly struggling with the vase. 'My God, that's heavy,' he said, setting it down. She could now see dark blue jeans, navy suede boots and a buttoned-up overcoat. 'I think there's something rather charming about taking a nap in a church, don't you?'

'As long as I wasn't dribbling,' she said, sitting up now. She knew the heat from the three-bar fire and the scratchy jumper had made her face all red. Rachel attempted to smooth down hair that was probably the full bird's nest. Her heart, she could do nothing about. Her heart was as lost a cause as it had ever been in his presence.

'Nope.'

They looked at each other. Rachel took him all in: boots, jeans, coat, scarf, hair, eyes that were a mirror. He was heading towards old age and so was she, but she felt exactly how she knew she'd feel if she ever clapped eyes on him again: floored, overwhelmed, undone.

'Well, thank God,' she said. *What does Gabe think of me?* she thought. That she had unattractive wrinkles now, at fifty-nine, at the corners of her mouth. A wobbly chin. A lined forehead. That she'd lost it, whatever she'd had? 'I wondered if you'd come,' she added, in a voice she was now analysing for traces of self-sabotage.

Was it giving her away? 'Although if you were, I wasn't expecting to see you until tomorrow.'

'I've been sent to help out,' he said genially. 'I bumped into Sally Henderson-Something in the lane when I arrived at Aunt Julia's house – she looks exactly the same, by the way. She was roaming the village looking for a lost cornicing man, apparently – asked me if I wanted to make myself useful. Told me there should be a delivery outside the church and to bring it in.'

'I think it's going here,' Rachel said, pointing to a waiting stone plinth, and Gabe went to heave the vase up again. 'Wait, let me help you,' she said, leaping up from the pew. Together they moved the vase into position. 'I'm so sorry for your loss,' she added, as he swivelled it frontwards and readjusted one of the lilies. 'For Aunt Julia.'

'Thank you,' he said. 'It's very sad and I'll miss her like crazy but, how d'you Brits say it? That cricket thing? She had a good innings.'

They were standing too close to each other – Rachel could feel the warmth of his coat, of his skin, of his soul. She was relieved they seemed to have skipped the bit where they officially greeted each other – the handshake, the hug, the awkwardness. She went and sat back down on the pew.

'Yes, a *great* innings,' she said, taking him in again, noting how he still had hair that curled a little, round his ears. How the shadow of grief and guilt he had behind his eyes, the last time they met, had lifted now. 'We had a little chat a couple of weeks ago. She was really funny.' She *had* been very funny, from her garden chair, but Rachel hadn't been careful enough and Julia had somehow started talking affectionately about her nephew, Gabriel, her trips to North Dakota and how she had met him in New York once, he was an artist, did Rachel know . . . ? And Rachel had nodded and smiled and said how marvellous and other suitable things, while her heart had ached in its shell and her regrets swirled within her like clouds with no fixings.

'She was always funny.' Gabe came and sat next to her, on the front pew – at an almost safe distance. Rachel watched as he stretched his legs out. 'You know one of Aunt Julia's greatest sayings?'

'Tell me,' she said, almost not daring to look at his face now.

'"Time is a bugger."' He laughed, and his laughter echoed upwards to the gabled church ceiling. And Rachel looked at him, at the way his eyes radiated into merry crinkles, and she laughed too, despite her disquieted heart. '"Time is a bugger that always gets you in the end."'

'Indeed, it does,' she replied. '"Nobody leaves this place alive" – that was one of my dad's,' she added.

Gabe smiled. He tinkered with the cuff of his coat, adjusted the lining, then looked back up at her. 'You're looking well,' he said.

'Really? Well, you too,' she managed. All her emotions fluttered within her like the anguished feathers of a caged bird. 'Are you angry with me?' she added, in a quiet voice.

'No,' he said, 'I was never angry.'

She nodded. Silence crept into the church and sat there for a while.

'How's life?' he asked her eventually.

'Good, thanks. How about you?'

'It's good. Watcha been up to?' he asked with a smile. 'How's Vivaldi's? Well, I know, actually. Fantastic, Rachel.'

'Thank you.' She felt warm inside. Gabe had been following the gallery's success. Her current exhibitions were her best yet, she felt. 'And I know what *you've* been up to,' she added. 'Showing all over the world. It's brilliant.'

'I try,' grinned Gabe. 'How's Jonny?'

'He's fine, thank you.' She wondered if Gabe may have read something about Jonny having been ill, especially now he was famous in America. 'How's your son?'

'Twenty-five years old and a doctor in Fargo.'

'Twenty-five? Gosh! And a doctor? That's amazing!'

'Yeah, I know,' said Gabe, looking all proud. His face was such a surprise to her, but so familiar. 'And your stepdaughter?' he asked.

'Teddy still has a whole heap of worries at forty-two, sadly.'

'Oh, dear. Sorry to hear that. Did she get her degree?'

'Yes, she did. She's got a good job, actually. But she's with Lee again – the bad boyfriend – and that's the worry.' Teddy was one of the strongest roots tethering Rachel to her life, she knew. 'How's Jud?'

'A few more murals. A few less people. Population, currently sixty-five. My mom died,' he added sadly. 'Last year.'

'Oh, I'm so sorry.'

'Thank you. It was a blessing. She'd been unwell for such a long time. Thank you for the email,' he said.

Eight years ago, in 2011, Rachel had written to him. She had found the email address of a gallery in Minnesota Gabe was exhibiting at and dropped him a short note. It couldn't be expansive. There was no point telling him she had planned to leave Jonny, after London, that she'd changed her mind on the train home, then hadn't been able to do it, because of Jonny's accident and subsequent illness. There'd been no point explaining this was her destiny all along, to live in this Oxford village, in this life, and to think otherwise had been to entertain a fairy tale.

All she'd said, very simply, was that she was sorry she'd run away from him (*again*. Did she put 'again'? She couldn't remember. After she had sent the email, she'd deleted it). She'd said it had been wonderful knowing him. She'd wished him well. She had been aware that someone else would read her words before he did

– a bespectacled gallery owner or a young female intern, but she'd signed off with 'All my love, forever', which was possibly a touch melodramatic for the bespectacled owner, or a tad romantic for the hopeful young intern, who may have mistakenly wondered if there'd be another chance for the sender and receiver of this email. Who may have mistakenly believed goodbye was not forever.

'Thank you for yours,' she said.

It had been three months before there was a reply from Gabe, who explained the delay was because he no longer exhibited with the gallery and it had taken that long for the intern to track him down. He said he was sorry she felt she had no choice but to stay in her life, that he understood, but would never forget the time they'd spent together. He wished her well, too. He had signed off with:

*I wish you the very best life, Rachel. I wish everything for you.*

*Ever yours,*

*Gabe. X*

She had deleted that email, too, but not before printing it out, secreting it in her old Filofax – along with his napkin sketch of her, from the National Portrait Gallery, and his hotel note with the little drawing of the magpie – and spending the next few months (years? Yes, years) reading it over and over again, scouring between the lines for anger or indifference, fearing indifference the most.

She wanted to ask him if he had a woman in his life. Why there was no ring on his finger. She wanted to ask him everything he'd ever done in the last eleven years.

'You know the other thing about time,' Gabe said. 'The thing Aunt Julia didn't used to say?'

The church was silent except for the faint buzzing of the old electric heater and the sense of soft, sleety rain gently landing on the stained-glass windows.

'No?'

She hadn't replied to Gabe when she'd received his email. She was tending to Jonny – she was held fast to her life; there was nothing to be gained from further correspondence, no point in prolonging a pain so bittersweet it was like running her tongue along the edge of broken glass dipped in honey.

'Time takes things you care about further and further away from you,' he said, and she felt his gaze heavy on her, poignant and unbearable. 'Until you know you're never going to get them back.'

Rachel wasn't going to argue with him. Yes, that pain had faded, slightly, over the years, not to black, but to grey, the colour of the London sky above the Embankment, and Gabe's jacket, where she had once lain her head on his collar and breathed him in. She felt it on some days more than others, like when October drizzle coated her on her morning walk to the gallery and she saw a black umbrella, held high. Or on still summer nights that retained the heat of the day. Or during spring rainstorms in provincial village car parks. She always felt it.

There was a sudden click and a creak, behind them, of the great oak door of the church. A clattering of feet. The throwing of something, which landed with a soft plonk halfway up the aisle, like a beanbag on a sports day playground, but it was actually a rag doll with one leg, the other one having been unceremoniously torn off last week during a toys' tea party.

'Granny!'

A rambunctious little girl, red-cheeked under a bobble hat and a blonde, slightly-too-long fringe, came bounding up the aisle and to a skidding halt next to the doll – who was picked up and stuffed into a fleecy coat pocket – before leaping on to Rachel's lap and flinging her arms round her neck.

'Iris! What are you doing here?' cried Rachel in delight, both squeezing the little girl to death and peering past the woolly warmth of her bobble hat down the aisle. 'Is Mummy with you?'

'Mummy's having a fag outside,' said Iris matter-of-factly. 'Who's this man?'

'This man is called Gabriel,' said Rachel. 'He's come over from America.' She glanced quickly down the aisle again. 'I hope Mummy knows you're in here.' Teddy's only vice these days was smoking, and Lee, of course, the other addiction she had slipped back into as easily as a vole into a muddy stream.

'Yeah, we went to your house and Grandad said you were flower 'ranging. He was writing, but he let me sit on his chair.' She looked up at Gabe. 'Like the *Angel* Gabriel?' she enquired suspiciously, assessing him from beneath her fringe. 'Last Christmas I was the Angel Gabriel in the school show. I had to wear a sheet from Mummy's bed and shout at the shepherds that Jesus was going to be born in Beth'lem.'

'You did,' said Rachel, stealing a kiss on one of those delicious red cheeks. 'And what a delight it was, too. Six-year-olds,' she said, beaming at Gabriel. 'This is Teddy's daughter, Iris. My granddaughter.'

'Pleased to meet you, Iris,' said Gabe, holding out his hand.

'Pleased to meet *you*.' Iris held out hers then waggled it up to her nose, laughing, with her tongue out. She looked just like Teddy. She had from the moment she was born, a scrap of a thing arrived early at thirty-six weeks with a shock of dark blonde hair and a look of wide-eyed delight that she was here to wreak such love and such havoc. She was a little miracle, really, and Rachel absolutely adored her.

'She's what's known as a *caution*,' said Rachel, smiling indulgently at her granddaughter. Iris had come along to be a joyous stitch in the fabric of their lives; a piece of wonderfully colourful embroidery to brighten them all up. 'Granny sometimes has to get a little strict with her, don't I, Iris?'

'Strict and then sweets,' said Iris, and all three of them laughed. Rachel was a doting grandmother who practised a dual policy of guiding her granddaughter with kindly discipline and spoiling her absolutely rotten. She saw Iris as often as she could and had her over to stay frequently, which was always great fun for both her and Jonny, who adored her too. Rachel placed her cheek against Iris's and hugged her tight, noticing, from the corner of her eye, that Gabe was staring at her, a curious smile on his face.

'Grandad gave me a chocolate muffin,' Iris said, wriggling in Rachel's embrace. 'And he ate two himself.'

'Did he now? Grandad's supposed to be on a healthy eating plan.'

'He said healthy eating is for wimps.'

They all turned their heads at the sound of clattering at the door. 'Oh, here's Wren,' Rachel said.

'Goodness, it's cold out there!' Wren said, blustering through the door Iris had left wide open. The bottoms of her trousers were soaking wet. 'My faithful hound had me over down at Lay's Pond,' she said. 'Naughty mutt. Hello, Iris,' she said, striding up the aisle and darting a smile at the little girl. 'Oh, and who do we have here?' she exclaimed, pulling off her ancient Barbour jacket and flinging it over the back of a pew.

'This is the *Angel Gabriel*,' sing-songed Iris. 'From America.'

'Gabe!' Wren cried excitedly. 'Bloody hell. You're as good-looking as she always said you were!' Rachel blushed as Wren took him by the shoulders and gave him an almighty hug. 'I'm very sorry for your loss,' she added quickly, into his coat. 'Julia March was an amazing woman.'

'Thank you, I appreciate that,' said Gabe.

'Wow, Rachel,' Wren mouthed to Rachel over his right shoulder, her eyes wide.

'This is my best friend, Wren,' stammered Rachel. She wanted to unhook Gabe from Wren and get close to him herself, and the fact she couldn't made her feel desperately sad.

Wren unhandled him. '*Very* handsome,' she proclaimed, and Rachel wanted to reach out her foot and kick her best friend in the shin.

'I suppose so,' Rachel muttered.

'And here you are,' continued Wren, 'after all this time. When was the last time you were here?' Wren was playing with her, Rachel knew, as the story of Gabe had been recounted between them countless times.

'The spring of 1986,' said Gabe.

Gabe was looking at Rachel as he spoke and she blushed, remembering the Blitz, and dancing in the gallery, and the village hall. She glanced down towards Iris, who had pulled the rag doll out of her pocket and was winding its string hair around her fingers.

'Well, it's lovely to have you back. Do you fancy a cuppa, handsome American?'

'No, thank you, Wren,' said Gabe, 'although that's really kind of you. I've got to get back to Aunt Julia's.'

'That's a shame,' pouted Wren. 'But I guess I'll see you tomorrow. Bye, Gabe.' She gave Rachel's arm a quick pulse then headed for the small kitchen at the back of the church.

'You *suppose* so?' Gabe queried, after Wren had disappeared, buttoning up the neck of his coat.

Rachel laughed. Then shrugged. Then blushed again – although she was far too old for blushing – as she remembered them in that hotel bed in London, the storm of the sheets and the calm of their bodies. The heat of 'I love you' and the cool of 'How long can you stay?' – and it was the last thing she wanted to be thinking about right now.

'I need to get back,' he repeated, after a moment when she feared she might drown in his eyes. 'Nice to meet you, Iris.'

'Likewise,' said Iris precociously, flashing him a huge gappy grin.

'She's cute,' he whispered, leaning down towards Rachel. She caught the scent of lemon and musk, a little mint. She wanted to catch him, all of him, and never let him go.

'Thank you.'

'I'll see you tomorrow.'

'Yes. I really hope it all goes off all right,' she added, suddenly shy and formal, over Iris's head. 'As well as these things can.'

'Thank you,' he said, 'I'm sure it will.'

'Bye,' she said, and she was worried she wouldn't see him tomorrow, at the funeral. That she wouldn't have a chance to talk to him again. She felt the same and she didn't know what to do with this feeling. It was swamping her, taking her over, rendering her both powerless and strangely energised, with a redundant force she couldn't contend with.

'Bye, Rachel,' Gabe said, and he turned and walked down the flower-edged aisle of the church, tall in his black wool coat, as Rachel watched.

'Right,' she said, after the final flap of his coat had gone through the door and her heart had stopped listing. She patted one of Iris's soft woolly knees with a quiet sigh. 'Let's go and find your mum.'

# Chapter Thirty-Six

Rachel was right; she didn't see Gabe at the funeral, not to talk to, anyway. The church was full for Julia March, who had got to know all her neighbours at last, in the past few years, and Gabe was in the front row, eight or nine pews away. Sally Henderson-Bright's enormous black hat blocked her view of the back of his head and the only time she saw Gabe's face was when he stood behind the pulpit, grave and handsome, and read the poem of Dylan Thomas, 'Do not go gentle into that good night'. His voice was slow and steady, and his words elicited a low burr of appreciation among the admiring congregation. When Gabe sat back down, Rachel saw a gnarly hand reach forward from the row behind to pat him on the back.

Jonny, as promised, had not come. Rachel was sitting in between Mr Akim from the dry cleaners, who had a lovely singing voice for hymns, and old Donald Patience from the British Legion, who didn't, but made up for it in volume. Wren was with her staff from the cafe, behind. Nancy Littlen-Green was in the row in front, fidgeting and casting her eyes around. Rachel had seen her on the way in, peering from under a new ruby-red fringe and giving out curt little smiles. Nancy had started cleaning for Julia March six months or so ago; she had set up a business called Nancy's Spotless Cleaning Co., but it wasn't that spotless, by all accounts.

Sally's hat moved and Rachel could see Gabe in profile, leaning forward and handing a lady two people up from him a folded tissue. Since seeing him yesterday, her mind had been a sea storm of emotions, lurching between the man-made shore of 'it means nothing he is here' to the shipwreck of 'it means everything'. It settled on the shipwreck, with her buried underneath. Rachel had thought of nothing else but him. She had not wanted to ask herself the question 'Do you still love him?' as she was terrified of the answer. She *knew* the answer. She had accepted it, how things were meant to be – how the universe could keep tossing them in each other's paths but not let them share a life together. How it was all too late.

Of course she still loved him. She had loved him steadily and silently for over thirty years. While she had lived a whole other life. While the seasons slowly turned. And she was supposed to have everything she'd ever wanted, but maybe she had nothing at all?

'Oh, my favourite,' muttered Mr Akim happily, as the vicar announced hymn number 542, 'Amazing Grace'. And they all rose from the pews to sing and Rachel looked at Gabe again, a few rows ahead, and loved him with all of her miserable heart.

# Chapter Thirty-Seven

Gabe was one of the first to file out. Rachel watched him as he walked down the aisle, supporting an elderly person on each side.

'Didn't he speak well?' whispered a woman she didn't know, leaning over Mr Akim to tell her so. 'I often find the American accent quite grating, but I think it works on him.'

Rachel mumbled her assent. She couldn't take her eyes from him, walking down that flower-accented aisle, smart and sombre in his black coat and American shoes. She imagined him walking down the other flower-filled aisles of his past: walking hand-in-hand out of a tiny church in Jud, North Dakota, with Anne-Marie, full of hope after marrying her. Filing out of the same church after her funeral, his devastated son hanging on to his hand. Walking stoically past well-wishers' sympathetic smiles after the funeral of his father and, on a later day, his mother.

Oh, Rachel imagined it all. The poignant and pinnacle moments she had not witnessed. The parts of Gabe's life she'd had nothing to do with. They were strangers, who had met only four times across four decades – spring, summer, autumn and winter – and this was their final encounter.

She felt a nudge from behind and turned to find Wren smiling sympathetically at her.

'All right?' Wren asked.

'Yes,' Rachel replied. 'See you in the pub.'

Gabe passed her pew and he gave Rachel a short, heartbreaking smile, which she returned with one of her own, selected from a small catalogue entitled 'He's Not Mine and Can't Ever Be', and she let the deceit that she had tears in her eyes for Julia March distil in the air around her, as he passed out of sight, slowly down the aisle.

'Aw, it's all got to you, hasn't it, Rachel? Bless you.'

It was Sally – hat as wide as two bus lanes – halted at the edge of Rachel's pew, her gigantic Louis Vuitton tote coming in boastful contact with the posy of camellias at the end and knocking them to the floor.

'Hi, Sally. No, I'm fine.' Rachel bent and picked up the posy, painting a smile on her face bright enough to match Sally's, so much so that she felt like a silly bridesmaid in a winter coat.

'Lovely turnout though, wasn't it? Is Jonny not here? You must come to the pub with us,' Sally said, and before Rachel knew it, she found herself one side of David, with Sally the other, striding off to the pub down frosty streets where bare trees bent their heads and silhouetted the sky with twiggy branches. She looked desperately for Wren, but Wren was somewhere behind, with her young employees, one of them laughing, another enveloped in purplish vape plumes.

The pub was packed. Rachel was hit by the smell of buffet food and perfume and beer. It was hot. Coats were off, pints were in hand, a couple of men were already playing darts near the bar, and bored teenagers – clearly trying not to look so – were fetching plates of food for their elders. Rachel recognised nearly all of the faces – the villagers, her friends and acquaintances. Wren swept in with her crew and was immediately assailed by the local postmaster. Rachel couldn't see Gabe and was determined not to start looking for him.

'Drink?' offered David, stout and grey in a navy coat and a winter beard.

334

'A very dry, very cold Chardonnay,' trilled Sally.

'I'll have a gin and tonic, please,' said Rachel, depositing the flower posy on a small table behind her.

'How's the gallery?' asked Sally crisply, once David had disappeared into the throng.

'Good, thanks,' said Rachel, keeping her vision as tunnel-like as she could. 'Any more news on Leonora and her piece for the Winter Ball?'

Sally pulled a displeased face. 'All sorted, though,' she said, tapping her nose with her finger. 'I can't wait for you to see what we're exhibiting. It'll be a charming surprise for everyone.' She levered off her faux fur coat and handed it to a passing member of pub staff. 'So, when's Jonny's next book coming out?' she asked, turning back to Rachel. 'The last one was a hoot.'

'Next year.' Rachel focused on Sally's glossy lipstick, the well-powdered pores on her nose, her Hermès scarf – anything to keep her from looking round the room.

'Good, good. He's doing ever so well. Nancy Littlen-Green told us it's over thirty years since the Fordham Hotel accident, is that right? When he first arrived on everyone's radar, rather dramatically.'

'Yes, it is,' said Rachel. 'Thirty years. He doesn't really talk about it now, finds it all a bit painful. Nancy mentioned that?'

'Well, yes. She cleans for us, you know. Though the jury's still out on whether we're going to fire her or not.' Sally leaned forward in a powdery, conspiratorial whisper. 'Cigarette butts in the loos,' she whispered. 'All a bit slapdash. And she lets herself be visited. Twice now I've discovered your Teddy in the house, drinking a cup of my very expensive Columbian coffee, and, once, that objectionable Lee, sitting bold as brass on one of our chesterfields and scoffing a bloody coconut macaroon. I don't know how Nancy can stand him.'

'Apparently she likes him and thinks he's a great potential son-in-law,' said Rachel. She grimaced. 'I think Teddy knows my silence speaks otherwise.'

'Silence? You don't ever tell him he's a toxic prick?'

Rachel laughed. 'Jonny likes him, so no.'

'Oh, *I* would . . . and I'd tell him he puts on terrible plays. I mean, God, even a rat wouldn't want to tread *those* boards!' She narrowed her eyes. 'Unless he's got some sort of hold over you all?'

Rachel shrugged. 'He has over Teddy, and there's not much we can do about that.'

'I suppose not,' said Sally, tilting her head to one side. 'Anyway, we might sack Nancy when she gets back from her holiday. She's off tomorrow, for some winter sun, with some new man, apparently. All right for some, eh? "Said the woman who goes on four foreign holidays a year"!' she smirked, laughing throatily at herself. 'So, I do hope Jonny will grace us with his presence at the ball, and tell me, will he go back on the road again, with the new book? It was ever so funny, that story he told us about the guy who came up to him in Germany and asked Jonny to autograph his . . .'

Rachel had seen him. She'd let her eyes roam around the pub and Gabe was behind the bar, visible through the heads of a clamour of middle-aged women. He was pulling a pint. His jacket was off and his sleeves were rolled up. At the risk of sounding like a clamorous middle-aged woman, he looked devastating. He caught her eye and grinned at her across the room. This one said he was pleased to see her, and could she come and rescue him? And hers, in return, was a very different smile from the earlier catalogue.

'Here you are.'

It was David, back with the drinks.

'So,' he said, passing them round, 'when's Jonny's next book coming out?'

'Would you excuse me for a moment?' said Rachel. 'I need to check on the . . . Thank you so much for the drink . . .' She moved quickly through the crowd, 'hello'-ing to faces and avoiding being stopped and searched for information about Jonny's new book, or Teddy's troubles, or Lee's terrible plays, or even how her beloved Iris was getting on at school.

'Rachel!' Wren's hand reached out to her. The other held a large gin and tonic. 'You OK? You going to talk to Gabe?'

'Yes. I'm so nervous, though. I mean, *look* at him!' They both flicked their eyes over to the bar, where Gabe was concentrating on perfecting the white frothy head of a Guinness.

'Is he single?' Wren asked admiringly.

'I don't even know,' Rachel said miserably.

'Let's just go with him being single unless you find out otherwise. You deserve him,' said Wren. 'He's lovely and so are you. Report back!'

Wren never made a secret of her distaste for Jonny, these days. 'Too big for his boots' was how she summed him up, but Rachel, although inclined to agree, still felt the dragging pull of loyalty and longevity. The safety of the number of years already accomplished. The tranquillity of a settled life without rolling or pitching. So why was she now making a beeline for Gabe McAllister?

'Hello.'

Gabe had just finished serving a 'punter'.

'Hello,' he said. 'Thank goodness you're here. I've been roped in and I'm struggling to cope. There's been a run on salt and vinegar crisps, and some heinous-looking things called Scampi Fries have just sold out . . .'

Rachel laughed. She couldn't help it. She loved seeing him. She loved seeing his face, his smile. 'Didn't you go to the pub in 1986?' she asked. 'Scampi Fries are a very old stalwart.'

'I didn't have the pleasure,' he replied. 'I was too busy dressing up as naval officers and visiting local art galleries.' How could she forget either moment? 'I love the old juke box,' he added, glancing over to it. Rachel followed his gaze – the strains of Rod Stewart's 'I Don't Want to Talk About It' started up. 'Do you know, the one in Jud Bar & Grill has been there for over sixty years?'

'Almost as long as you and I have been around.' She liked this older version of him. It suited him. There was a calmness and an easy humour he inhabited well – a mantle he wore effortlessly that he hadn't when he was young.

'I guess so. *We're so bloody ancient*,' he said, in a comical stilted British accent. 'Hang on a minute . . . Can I be excused?' he asked the real barman, and he scooted round the bar to her.

'Thank you for coming today,' he said, lightly touching her on the arm. 'I think it went well.'

'It did,' she said, praying he wouldn't notice the heightened colour that must have risen to her cheeks at his touch. 'And you did well with your reading.'

'I did a lot of practising.'

'You never would have known.' Because of the packed pub, they were standing too close to one another; she was afraid he would know exactly how she was feeling.

'Public speaking's not really my thing,' he said, and Rachel thought there was still so much they didn't know about each other and would never get the chance to. 'Are you not with Jonny?' Gabe added.

'He didn't come. He doesn't go to funerals unless he absolutely has to.'

'Good move, I can't blame him for that. Do you want to get something to eat?'

'Yes, please.'

They squeezed their way to the buffet. In another lifetime, Gabe would have extended his hand behind him for her to take.

In another lifetime, they would have belonged to each other. They arrived at the buffet, a spread with a few Julia-requested surprises from her travels. There were Vietnamese spring rolls, Thai fishcakes and some New York pastrami on rye toasts, eliciting a few murmurs of 'What on earth is this?' and 'Oh, give it a go, Margery!' from the crowd.

With plates loaded, they pushed themselves into a quiet corner. Only a few heads turned. Rachel saw Sally's swivel on its black cashmere stalk, but she refused to catch her eye. Wren flashed her a quick encouraging smile.

'Very nice,' said Gabe, popping a pork dumpling in his mouth. His hair looked really silver in this light, she thought, but he looked absolutely lovely. 'Oh, let me help you.' She was trying to take her coat off one-handed, as she was stifling. Gabe laid it over his arm with a smile, reminding her poignantly of when they went to the National Portrait Gallery, and the love they had shared in those two nights and two days. The memory of that had kept her warm for a long time. Now it was a bittersweet remnant of a dream she had once had. 'Will you be at the Winter Ball on Saturday?' he asked.

'Well, yes, I'm always there.' She was acutely aware of the sartorial limitations of her Funeral Dress – which had never intended to be such. A black knee-length dress with a keyhole detail at the neck she had bought for parties, but instead had worn to six funerals this year: the last, a month ago, Jonny's mother, Margaret, leaving Malcolm to potter sadly around their maisonette without her. The dress made her look dull, and black was no longer flattering. Rachel would *hardly* be attractive to him now, like he was to her. Ageing was not an equal opportunities employer. 'Has someone been telling you about it? It's quite the event in Fincham St George.'

'I'm going.'

'You are?' She almost choked on her Vietnamese spring roll.

'Yes. I don't fly home until early Sunday morning – I've a lot of sorting to do at Aunt Julia's. Sally invited me. She's going to exhibit one of my paintings on her stairs.'

'The big show piece?' Rachel was flabbergasted. 'How come? Another artist was working on something for it!'

'Sally said she couldn't commit, was taking too long, didn't want to give Sally something she wasn't happy with. Precocious,' grinned Gabe. 'And by that, I mean Sally. After I bumped into her yesterday, she came to see me at Aunt Julia's. What can I say? I felt sorry for the woman. And all that pouting and pleading . . . I can't imagine many refuse Sally and live.'

'Well, no.' Rachel laughed, but her brain was whirring. Gabe was coming to the ball. She didn't know whether to be happy and excited or fearful and troubled. 'Do you have time to do a painting?'

'I already have one. One of my trees. I did it when I was here in '86.' He shrugged. 'Well, it's more of a sketch, really. The idea for a later piece. It's been in Aunt Julia's attic. Sally seems happy with it. So, you *are* going?'

'Yes. And Teddy and Lee, and Jonny, maybe.' She felt she had to construct an armour around her. Throw up her scaffolding, as she would need it, to survive the Winter Ball with Gabe there. 'If he's up to it.'

'Up to it?'

'Jonny hasn't been well.'

'Oh, I'm sorry to hear that.'

'I thought perhaps you might have read it somewhere, about him?' she said hesitantly. 'I think he did an interview in the *New Yorker* recently, where he talked about it.'

'No. I've studiously avoided all mention of Jonny Trent, to be honest.'

'Oh, well, he's OK now, but he was ill for a long time. I was his carer, basically. For about seven years.'

'Seven years?' Gabe's eyes were searching hers. Was she going to tell him that after she'd fled from London she'd changed her mind and was planning to come back to him, but Jonny had suffered an accident? Her heart raced at the thought.

'Yes. As I say, he's OK now.' What would be the good in telling him, when her mind had been changed for her and life had since settled into a stasis that had become, over time, a comfort blanket? When she and Gabe were both on the precipice of sixty and it was far too late to start changing lanes and lives now? 'He's got a new book coming out next month,' she said mechanically. There was all this *stuff* inside them, she thought, all this *life* – stuffing that could not be removed without spearing a slit into their fabric and dragging it from them.

'Well, great,' said Gabe. He looked distracted. Was he thinking about the seven years and where they had fitted into the last decade? 'I liked Iris,' he said eventually. 'Your love for her shines from you.'

'Does it?' Rachel smiled with pleasure.

'Absolutely. It's lovely to see. You make a beautiful grandmother.'

'Is that a compliment? You're making me feel ancient again.'

'Yes, it's a compliment.' Gabe looked tender, serious. She wanted to melt under his gaze. 'You have a good life here, Rachel, don't you? The one you always wanted.'

'Yes, just what I always wanted,' she said, like a mantra. And many parts of it were. Her house, an easy relationship with Jonny – settled, since the accident, into a quiet contentment of domestic routine and occasional light bickering. Teddy, and their bond. The gallery. And Iris, the light of her life. 'And you?'

'Just me and the mutt, over there in Jud.'

'Ol' Red?'

'No. He's gone, I'm afraid, but I have Brando now to keep me company. An old springer who's still very springy indeed! I got him in the summer.'

341

She smiled. Her heart filled with the image of Gabe strolling up to the diner with his new dog, while summer turned to autumn and the leaves turned amber. 'Not lonely, then?'

'No, not too lonely. It's really very lovely to see you again, though.'

'You too,' she said softly. *He's single*, she thought. Not that it mattered. She was devastated at his continual fleeting presence in her life, like an autumn leaf catching in her hair and then flying away.

'I'm glad I'll get to see you, one more time,' he said. 'At the ball.'

Someone pushed past them, a Staffordshire bull terrier of a man, forcing them together. Rachel could smell Gabe's aftershave. The warmth of his skin. She wanted to place her head on his chest and cry. She loved him. It was as simple and as heartbreaking as that. She loved him. A hand clamped on Gabe's arm and they drew apart. Dray Briggs was standing there in a black polo neck; in his mid-seventies now, he looked like an aged *Milk Tray* man.

'Hey, *you're* American,' Dray said loudly to Gabe. 'Settle an argument about Trump for us, will you?'

'I'm no expert on Trump,' said Gabe, with a curt smile. Rachel wondered if either of them remembered the other from the 'cutting in' episode at the 'Blitz over Fincham St George'.

'You'll have to do.' Dray increased the pressure on Gabe's arm and steered him off. Gabe raised both hands in apology.

'Sorry,' he mouthed. 'I'll be back,' he said out loud. Rachel was being tapped on the shoulder, now, by an elderly woman with soft skin like faded parchment. She spoke with a wavery voice, warm with age. 'Hello, dear. Lovely send-off, wasn't it?'

'Yes, really lovely, Mrs Peters . . .'

'When I go, I'm going to have the same sausage rolls.'

'Yes, very good.' Rachel watched as Gabe was dragged off.

'Do you have any pictures of frogs at the gallery?'

'Frogs? No, not at the moment.'

'My granddaughter likes frogs.'

'Does she?' Gabe was the other side of the pub now, disappearing from sight.

'When is Jonny next having a book out . . . ?'

Rachel didn't see Gabe again until about forty minutes later. She had been drawn into five or six different satellites of people. She'd made contributions to conversations about global warming and the new bypass on the A34. Wren had signalled that she had to go, back to the cafe, that she'd catch up with Rachel later. When Rachel finally broke free, from a discussion on the best bollards of the area, she spotted Gabe in the pub's doorway, seeing people off. He was shaking hands, laughing at old duffers' old jokes, helping elderly ladies over the threshold. *This old lady ought to go home, too*, Rachel thought, take off her Funeral Dress, put her black bag away and have a nice cup of tea, with Jonny. She ought to be content in the life she had chosen. But every time she looked at Gabe, she wasn't content at all. Every time she saw his face, she longed for him.

Rachel made her way to the door and Gabe, her coat still over his arm.

'Rachel,' he said simply, and he held his hand out to her. As their skin made contact, palm to palm, her heart flooded with emotion. His smile said everything that had ever been said between them, and hers was a mere trace, an echo, of what she felt for him. 'Here's your coat,' he added, and he slipped it from his arm.

'See you on Saturday?' she said, suddenly fearing some catastrophe had taken place in the past forty minutes that meant he would no longer be going.

'See you on Saturday.'

A sweep of relief. A stay of execution. A stay of her heart's dissolution. *Thank God this is not the end*, she thought, as he helped her into her coat. And she smiled at him one more time – for now – and stepped over the threshold of the pub and into the cold street, where a heedless sleety rain was falling on to the naked winter trees like confetti.

# Chapter Thirty-Eight

Lee was at Crofters. Well, he was just leaving, as Rachel got home from the gallery on Saturday afternoon, after one of her art classes. As she walked up the drive, he appeared at the front door in his builder's overalls.

'Rachel,' Lee grudgingly acknowledged.

'Hi, Lee.'

'Is Jonny all right?'

'Why, what's the matter with him?' Fearing something physical was wrong, Rachel was poised to dash past him into the house and straight through to the sitting room, but Lee flashed her a cracked smile.

'Nothing like that,' he milled. 'But he's not been quite himself. He's just told me something I really didn't want to hear.'

'Oh?' *The investment*, Rachel thought immediately, not wanting to get involved. She kept her face neutral.

'Yeah.' Lee's face briefly set and looked off into the distance. 'Slightly out of character. Never mind,' he added, attempting to look affable. 'It's probably for the best.' He set off down the front path. 'See you tonight, Rachel.'

*He took that rather well*, she thought, as she stepped into the house and went into the kitchen to make some tea. On her return from Saturday art class, she and Jonny always had tea and cake. Saturdays were always Saturdays – calm and familiar.

'Rachel?' Jonny was calling from the sitting room. '*Rachel!*'

'Coming!'

'Ah, there you are.' He sat up. 'I'm glad you're back. Could you please take my slippers off for me? My feet are really hot.' She knew he couldn't get down to them so she crouched and took them off for him, placing them on the carpet.

'You told Lee?' she asked.

He flapped her words away. 'Thank you. Thank you, Rachel. And never mind all that, I need you to do me a favour, darling,' he said, wriggling his toes in his thick socks. 'Please. After you've collected Iris from ballet later, can you go to Nancy's and pick up something for Teddy?'

'Nancy's? Can't Teddy go herself? What is it?' Iris was coming for a sleepover tonight as Teddy's babysitter had fallen through (rather, she hadn't organised one) and Jonny had happily agreed to sacrifice his place at the ball to look after her. He loved spending time with Iris and said he wasn't bothered about going now anyway, that he was tired – Rachel wondered if he also wanted to avoid Lee, after dropping his bombshell.

'It's a dress she's got stored at Nancy's,' said Jonny. 'You know how tiny their place is, and Teddy's hippy doodah with the free food in Swindon today is going on longer than she thought. She says she won't have time to pick it up from Nancy's after, so can you fetch it and drop it over to the bungalow? I've got Nancy's key, Lee's just given it to me.'

'Well, why can't he go?'

'Plastering job. He won't get home until long after Teddy. And I may be better but I can't walk all that way, even with my blessed stick. Could you, pretty please, *for Teddy?*'

Rachel shook her head at the woeful disorganisation of Lee and Teddy's life. 'I've never been into Nancy's house before.'

'She's on holiday with her new bloke. She won't know. Could you?' Jonny had that silly, pleading look on his face.

'Oh, all right.'

'Fantastic. Thank you. And a nice slice of coffee and walnut and a cup of tea, for now,' he said, patting the seat next to him.

'No,' she said, leaving the room without a backwards glance. 'You can go and get that yourself, Jonny. I've got some paperwork to do for the gallery.'

◆ ◆ ◆

Iris's feet, stamping in wellies over ballet tights, skittered on Nancy's front porch while she waited for Rachel to heft the stiff front door open with her shoulder.

'Why have we come to Nanny Nancy's again, Granny?'

'I told you, Iris. To pick a dress up for Mummy.'

The door swung open, whacking the hall wall with a thud.

'There,' Rachel said, wrenching the key back out of the lock and putting it in her coat pocket. 'Come on then, lovey.'

Iris stepped inside the hall, her red wool coat over her tutu, hair in a cute bun and cheeks coral from the cold. 'It always smells funny in here,' she said, wrinkling her nose. 'Nanny Nancy is a bag lady.'

'She's not a *bag lady*,' laughed Rachel. 'Wherever have you heard such a thing?'

'She has a lot of bags,' shrugged Iris.

It was cold in the hall, colder still at the mouth of the sitting room where the curtains were drawn against the blanketing dusk and seasonal burglars, possibly, and there was a smell of some potent 80s perfume Rachel couldn't place, mixed with the ashy remains of a coal fire from a 1960s brick fireplace.

'It's so dark, Granny, I can't really see.'

'Hang on,' said Rachel. The switch to the overhead light didn't work. 'I'll put a lamp on.' She could just about make out the end of a sideboard and a tall lamp. She felt for its switch, which was not on the stem but on the sticky cord that trailed down the back of the sideboard. She pressed it with a dull click.

The sickly white glow from the lamp illuminated a silver-grey carpet, a sagging sofa with a lilac throw chucked over it and a faux leather pouffe with an ashtray on the top. Hanging plants in raffia baskets were drawing-pinned precariously to the ceiling. A fleece with an embroidered wolf on the back was flung over the top corner of the door. And random items littered the sideboard the lamp was on: magazines, crusty-looking mugs, a Rubik's cube, an old set of dominoes and a copy of Jilly Cooper's *Riders*.

'I hope Nanny Nancy clears up before you come over,' she said.

Iris shrugged, bringing her shoulders up to her ears. 'Not really.'

Rachel remembered Florence's cottage, clean and cosy. The reclining chair, the little cocktail cabinet, the Charles and Di memorabilia. 'I don't think Nanny Nancy's cleared up since 1985,' she muttered. 'Do you want to wait here, and I'll go and get Mummy's dress?'

She went quickly up the stairs to what she suspected was Nancy's room – unmade bed, handbags everywhere, a half-closed curtain – then a spare bedroom, where there was a wardrobe with a dress covered in black cellophane hanging on the front. She grabbed it and came back downstairs.

'OK, good girl, we can get out of here now.'

Rachel went to turn the lamp off again. As she reached for the sticky cord, she noticed another miscellaneous item, at the edge of the sideboard. It was a tin. It was burgundy, flattish, hexagonal, with gold edging; it was being used as a coaster and had a stained mug sitting on it.

Rachel removed the mug, picked up the tin and turned it over in her hands. She ran her forefinger over the shallow lacquered sides and the small brass lock.

'Come on, Granny, let's *go*.' Iris was in the doorway, pouting impatiently.

'OK,' said Rachel. She slipped the tin into her coat pocket, turned off the lamp and took Iris's hand in hers. 'Let's go.'

# Chapter Thirty-Nine

There was lots to do when they got home. A snack of cookies and milk, and riding on Grandad's back around the sitting room, although Granny said it wasn't such a good idea, but Grandad insisted on going round three times and neighing like a lame horse. Top Trumps – *Frozen 2* edition. Teatime – Iris's favourite: fish fingers, chips and peas – then a bath, with lots of bubbles, and getting into pyjamas and watching Granny fill a hot-water bottle with the special fluffy sheep cover, before bed.

Rachel loved all these activities with Iris, every moment treasured. From the moment she'd been born, as Rachel would readily admit to herself, Iris had been a salve for all the babies of her own she hadn't had. Every hug, every kiss that she could plant on the little girl's cheeks helped to ease the pain and memory of those years, long ago now, of trying so desperately for a baby. Jonny's parents had always adored Iris, too. Malcolm escorted her to his tomato plants and Margaret would make her huge discs of chocolate shortbread; and now it was only Malcolm, her hand in his was even more precious.

'Night, night, Granny,' Iris said, after Rachel had kissed her on alternate cheeks six or seven times, making her laugh, and had tucked in all the teddies and the rag doll, pulled the Elsa duvet right up under her chin and smoothed hair away from a hot little forehead. 'See you in the morning.'

'See you in the morning,' said Rachel, and she stood in the doorway for a minute or two, just staring at her granddaughter as she squeezed her eyes shut ready for sleep, and then it was time to go and talk to Jonny.

Jonny was at the kitchen table doing the crossword. Rachel went into the utility room and fetched the tin she had found at Nancy's. She placed it on the kitchen table and pulled out a chair opposite.

'What's another name for a "despot"?' Jonny asked, without looking up.

'Do you know why this tin was in Nancy's sitting room?' she said.

'Eh?' Jonny looked up, a bemused laugh in his voice. 'What, this tin?' He tapped at it vaguely with his forefinger.

'Yes.'

'Never seen it before.'

'I have,' she said. She had the key to it, in the shallow drawer in the middle of her dressing table. She placed her stockinged heels on the rung of the chair. 'It was my nanna's tin. You went off with it one night, after I left it in a carrier bag in Lee's car.'

'You've lost me.' Jonny hadn't shaved, now he was no longer going to the ball. His eyes were amused.

'It was Sausage Night, I believe, at the pub.'

'Sausage Night?'

'Yes. I'd just come from Florence's house. Her tin was in a carrier bag with some nuts and other bits she'd given you. Lee dropped me off and I accidentally left the bag in his car. And you went to the pub.'

'You've got a very good memory.'

'Yes, I have. And the next morning, after you got home ridiculously late, the bag with this tin was missing. And today I find it in Nancy's sitting room.'

'*When* was this? It must have been a bloody long time ago if Florence was still alive.'

'Nineteen eighty-six.' Rachel knew the events of that week. She knew the year. It was the year Gabe had first come to the village. The year she had danced to The Cure in the gallery and cried in the rain in the car park. The year she'd first been offered another life.

'Christ, Rach, that was over thirty years ago!'

'I know. You didn't get home until two in the morning, Jonny. I remember, because you broke my mum's porcelain cat.' She pressed her toes against the rung of the chair. 'Were you having an affair with Nancy?'

'Good lord, that's a leap! What on earth has brought this on?' He raked fingers through his sparse hair. Picked up the tin and put it down again.

'Can you please just answer the question?'

It was not such a *leap*. Jonny coming home so late. The tin, being at Nancy's. Jonny always protesting too much about Nancy, about how pleased he was to have got away from her, his strange insistence on not even looking at her, back in those early days, at drop-offs and pick-ups. A tendency, after he'd been round to her cottage to fix something, for evasion, but at the same time a spewing of too much information. Plus, of course, dropping far too often that Nancy was 'unfocused' and 'untidy' and 'discouraging', in comparison to Rachel's virtues, but now all these things seemed like awful masks, or even clues, especially in the cold light still cast from Kim and the Woman in the Cobalt Blue Dress.

'Were you sleeping with Nancy before we were married? When we were engaged?'

351

'Well, of course not! Nancy? Blimey, I was lucky enough to get away from her the first time! Why on earth would I go back for more?'

'Well, I don't know. Because it was easy. Because she wanted you. Because she was beautiful. Because you could?'

She imagined him knocking on Nancy's door after *Sausage Night* and staggering into her sitting room. Pouring the contents of the carrier bag on to the sideboard. Drunkenly scoffing Flo's gifts, before he and his ex-wife shagged each other on the silver-grey carpet. And Flo's burgundy tin had got forgotten about, among all the miscellany on that sideboard, and lain next to a dodgy old lamp that illuminated their affair for months, possibly years.

'No! Of course, not, no!' Jonny started to cough, something he liked to do as a distraction measure – he'd be reaching for his stick next, struggling to get out of his chair. 'Why are you even accusing me of this?' he said, reaching round for his stick, but it was not there. He sat back in his chair. 'Has someone said something to you?'

'Who, Nancy? She's barely spoken three words to me in thirty years. No. I found the tin – shouldn't that be enough?' And all the other clues, she thought. All those other tiny things that were pointing directly to this, if only she could have seen them.

'You're being ridiculous. Maybe Teddy took it round there, or Nancy found the bag in the pub or wherever, I don't know. It's utter nonsense!' He glanced at the clock. 'Haven't you got a ball you need to be getting ready for?'

'Yes.' Rachel didn't have a lot of time. She changed the tone of her voice. To cajoling, understanding. Forgiving. 'Oh, Jonny. We weren't yet married,' she said. 'You weren't doing anything wrong. You were, in effect, still a single man. You may as well confess, darling. It doesn't really matter, all these years later, does it?'

He sank a little more into the chair, flicked his eyes down to the table. Rachel knew him. His urge to confess, his rash need to blurt things out, be forgiven and move on. She could see him weighing things up. He was wrestling with his urges like an old dog with a deflated football.

'Come on, Jonny, you can tell me. Won't it be better when it's out in the open? You don't want ghosts from your past catching up with you, do you?' She spoke to him like she did when she was taking his shoes off or bringing him a lovely cup of tea.

'Well . . .' he hesitated. 'Can we go back to our nice quiet life if I tell you?'

'Yes.'

He gave a big, world-weary, unburdening, do-we-really-have-to-go-there? sigh. He looked frail, defeated. 'We *may* have slept with each other a couple of times,' he said. 'But as you say, we weren't married then. I hadn't yet made vows to you. It was a last hurrah, really. A silly bit of nonsense, for old times' sake. It meant nothing at all.'

He looked an odd mixture of relieved, triumphant and defiant. He was waiting, now, for her to tell him it was all right. She watched as the expression on his face morphed into uncertainty. 'You slept with her when we were engaged!' she said, a quiet detonation. 'In that golden time. When it was all ahead of us. No, we hadn't yet made our vows to each other, but the promises were there, weren't they? Our promise we would be together forever, and yours that you would take care of me.'

Her hands were clutched at the edge of the table, her thumbs hooked underneath. She liked the rough feel of the wood. She liked that her thumbs were stopping her sliding to the floor. It *had* been a golden time, hadn't it? That golden time had kept her going so often – Jonny's promises of love and of care – and, in recent years, since his accident, she had come to believe in them again, his good and simple promises. That life could be calm and secure. That theirs might not be the grand and all-consuming love she'd supposed when they first got together, but it was a sustaining sort of love, it was a *lifetime* sort of love. It was a love she was content to have chosen.

'I stopped as soon as we were married,' protested Jonny. 'I thought that was OK.'

Rachel's voice remained quiet. 'You thought it was OK to be planning to spend your entire life with me, when all the time you thought *it was OK* to amble over to Nancy's gaff and give her a shag, for old times' sake?'

'I was young,' he said. 'A lot of the time I was drunk.'

She laughed bitterly. She felt sad and flattened. And she felt very, very old. He was entitled, that's what he was. Entitled into thinking he could promise one woman and shag another. Entitled to the thrill of Nancy wanting him and being able to dole himself out to her, to all that gratitude. Never give one man all your power, that's another thing Flo used to say to her. Never place too much of it in one person's pair of hands. But Rachel had done that, hadn't she, because Jonny had said his pair of hands was safe?

'I'm late. I have to get ready for the ball,' she said coolly. She picked up Florence's tin and went upstairs to shower and dress. She didn't wait to absorb Jonny's hangdog expression as he waited for forgiveness. Rachel wanted to park him, his grubby affair and Nancy Littlen-Green somewhere in the recesses of her mind and get ready to go out.

Hanging on the back of the bedroom door was a high-necked, long-sleeved, baby-pink silk dress, with a scarlet underskirt that kicked up when she walked. Jonny had declared it a 'showstopper' when she'd shown it to him; she felt it was a little daring, but sod it, she was damn well going to enjoy wearing it, despite her turmoil of emotions about the night ahead. The dress on and her hair up, she sat at her dressing table and pulled out the shallow velvet-lined middle drawer to search for the diamante hairclip she was probably far too old for, then reached her hand further, to the very back, and felt for the tiny key she had left there over thirty years ago. At first, she thought it had gone, but she spread her fingers to the right-hand corner of the drawer and there it was, cold and small. She fetched Florence's tin from the bed, turned the key in the lock and prised the lid open. Inside was a thin stack of photos and she carefully lifted each out, in turn, being careful to hold them at their edges.

The first was of Florence and Jim on a roller coaster, that moment when the cart comes rolling back to the start, before the riders get off, and faces are flushed and exhilarated and relieved. The second was of Flo and Rachel, and Rachel's mum, when Rachel was about three or four, all sitting almost comically solemnly on a park bench with 99 Flakes. The final photo, at the bottom, was of a group of laughing young women, Flo at their centre, in front of an ATA utility plane – all windswept hair, sensible shoes and smart uniforms. They all looked proud and joyful.

*These are snapshots of Nanna's happiness*, Rachel thought. Her life in the air, her happy marriage to Jim, an afternoon with her daughter and her granddaughter. She plucked the photo of Florence and the Attagirls from the base of the tin and was surprised to see, under it, a tarnished silver locket. Rachel held it in her hand and let the chain trail down to her dressing table. She tried to open it, but it wouldn't budge. After trying again – she really had to go – she undid the clasp and fastened the locket around her neck, then she grabbed her shoes and bag, and went downstairs.

Some terrible True Crime documentary was blaring from the sitting room. Rachel put her head round the door.

'I'm going, Jonny. Keep the landing light on, please, in case Iris needs to get up in the night, won't you? She sometimes wakes up for a glass of water.'

'Yes, I know.' He glanced up from the television, abashed-looking. 'I'll turn this down now, so I can hear her,' he said, reaching for the remote. 'I've got stories on standby, too,' he added with a small smile, 'in case she needs one.'

'You always have stories,' said Rachel, her hand on the door frame.

'Have a nice time.'

'Thank you.' She turned to go.

'I'm sorry,' he called after her, and she stopped in the doorway, absorbing his drawn and sheepish face, 'about all those years ago. I'm sorry if I've hurt you. Please say it doesn't change anything, our life together. Will you think about it, while you're out? Think about our life together and maybe forgive me when you get home? I know I've done a couple of terrible things . . . but they were mistakes, Rachel. Just silly mistakes that mean nothing, compared to you and me. Will you think about it?'

She nodded. His eyes were pleading. 'I don't know,' she said. 'Maybe I'll think about it.'

'Hey, we'll have our own party, shall we? In January, maybe, when my new book comes out? A lovely little party? With those caterers we like?' He gave that slow grin she knew so well and had loved so often. 'Wouldn't that be nice?'

'I guess so.'

'We could celebrate *us*, Rachel. All those years.'

'Yes,' she said. 'All those years.'

'Great.' He looked pleased. 'See you when you get home?'

Rachel nodded. Turned to go. She let the image of his smile fade before she had even left the room. 'See you when I get home.'

# Chapter Forty

Rachel was glad of the walk. The evening was crisp and very cold. The threat of frost was already in the air and preparing to settle on trees and bare prickly hedges, to crystallise in the early hours. Rachel liked the sound of her heels on the brittle tarmac of the pavements, her dragon's breath in the darkness. She'd just passed Vivaldi's, and her grandpop's bench. A couple of taxis travelled by slowly, like beetles. She pulled her coat more tightly around her.

'Hey,' called a voice, 'want a lift?'

The second of the taxis had slowed to a stop beside her and beyond a wound-down window were an elderly Christie and Martin Wetherington, in their shiny best on the back seat.

'No, thanks,' Rachel called back. 'I'm happy to walk, if that's OK.'

'Sure?' Christie was beautiful in cream and opal.

'Absolutely. See you in there.'

The taxi beetled away, its tail lights sharp red in the black of the street. Rachel quickened her pace. She could see TV squares of colour in front rooms where Saturday-night curtains were not drawn; *Strictly Come Dancing* watched from takeaway laps. She walked, relishing this chance to let her emotions seep from her and escape into the night air.

*Nancy*, she thought. Nancy with her bad mothering and her terrible fleeces. Nancy with all her men and her under-fringe eyes. Nancy hadn't fitted in with Jonny's plan – when he had wanted a successful career and a nice house on Hedge Hill Lane, and to become one of the respectable, party-loving corduroyed neighbours – but he'd still wanted her, and the whole of Rachel's early life and love with Jonny was a lie.

He had betrayed her at the start of it all. He had set up a repeatable pattern she'd not been aware of, in her hopeful youth. That he would betray, and she would forgive. That's what Rachel knew he hoped for. She would get home tonight and Jonny would be waiting for her, with that same contrite expression and maybe a hot chocolate and some sandwiches, plus the hope she would end up saying it didn't matter, that it was such a long time ago, that theirs was a life worth sticking to, as what else did they have but this life? There was a chance she and Jonny might end up laughing at something stupid, and plan that party in January, and decide to surround themselves once again with this past decade of quite content marriage they'd shared and not let what happened at the beginning unearth it. Jonny would hope that what she'd always wanted was still what she needed, and it was too late for anything else.

There was a crackle up ahead. The sound of a twig breaking underneath a dress shoe. He walked with steady footsteps, his head slightly down. He had a green scarf wrapped round his neck and a long, dark winter coat.

It was Gabe.

Rachel was too far away to call out, but not near enough to quicken her pace and catch him up, without breaking into a ridiculous run. She didn't want to be ridiculous, with him. He was a ghost, wasn't he? Time had taken him so far from her, she couldn't reach him now.

When he reached the gate of the Henderson-Brights, she watched as he walked up the path, was framed momentarily by the glow of the light of the porch and then was swallowed into the house.

◆ ◆ ◆

People talk of a party having a 'buzz', but this one was positively erupting as Rachel stepped inside. The chatter was at high velocity, there was some lively jazzy music being played by a swaying quartet, over to the back of the entrance hall, and the huge space was a shifting, drink-balancing, hooting and chuckling sea of black mostly, punctuated by the bright jewel colours of ball gowns. Sally was in a bright red dress; Wren, grinning madly at her, in green, and standing with her husband; Sheetal, from her art classes, in chartreuse, over by the bar. Rachel would be pale pink with a flash of scarlet.

People were in clustered circles. She could see Christie and Martin greeting people with hugs. Rachel started making her way over to Wren.

'Rachel!'

Teddy and Lee were in her path. Lee in a dinner suit, Teddy in a dramatic shroud of a dress: asymmetric taffeta and tulle, wrapped around her body.

'Thanks for dropping the dress over, that was a big help.' Teddy was smoking and hanging off Lee's arm with her free hand.

'No problem, love. How was the ashram day?'

Teddy pulled a face. 'It was OK. A bit rubbish. Is Iris in bed?'

'Yes, of course, all tucked up and fast asleep.'

'Thanks, Rachel.' Teddy flashed her a warm smile clouded in smoke. 'Oh, I know, shouldn't be smoking indoors. I'll go outside in a minute.'

Lee was standing straight-backed, hands in pockets. 'How are you, Lee?' Rachel asked.

'Yeah, all right, thanks,' he responded, his face still set and grim. 'I'm just going to the bar. Champagne, ladies? Sorry, Coke for you, Teddy.'

'Yes, please,' said Teddy, ignoring his little barb.

'Thank you, Lee.' Rachel watched Lee slope off into the crowd of glamorous, party-best people. She couldn't see Wren now but noticed Sheetal, out of the corner of her eye, coming away from the bar with a glass of champagne. She waved to her. Sheetal hadn't seen her, but another arm waved at her instead. It had the black sleeve and white cuff of a dinner jacket and it belonged to Gabe, emerging from the bar too, holding a pint of beer. Rachel hated that her heart lurched, that her pulse quickened, and her cheeks flushed at the sight of him. It was far too late to be feeling any kind of frisson, any semblance of danger. Even the knowledge of Jonny's latest and oldest revelation newly tucked inside her, like a grubby vintage railway ticket, didn't assuage her belief that the ebb and flow of time had stolen any right she may have to love him.

Still, she waved at him too, and returned his smile, before he was hedged off by another guest and into conversation.

'How was that funeral you and Dad went to?' asked Teddy.

Rachel turned back to her, trying to still her breathing. 'It was just me,' she said. 'Dad didn't go.' She wondered if Lee's swift exit to the bar and overly grim face was because he was angry about Jonny stopping the investment. *I won't bring it up*, she thought. It was always best to leave well alone with Lee.

'Oh right. Was it a good turnout?'

'Yes, there were lots of people there.'

'I heard some exciting nephew came over for it, a dishy silver fox from America? What was he like?' Teddy's kohled eyes were warm and intensely curious.

'I didn't really see him, so I couldn't tell you.' Rachel kept her own eyes on Teddy. She would not let them wander the room in the hope of seeing his face again. She would not betray her heart, thumping sadly in her chest. 'But he's the artist whose work is featured tonight so you'll probably get to meet him, if you want to.'

'Oh, is he? I didn't know he was an artist. And I thought Leonora Wotsit was supplying the art?'

'She bailed out.'

'Ah, that's a shame. Speaking of bailing out, because apparently she's staying out there and may not come back for Christmas, did you hear my lovely mother's in the Bahamas?'

'I did.' Rachel managed a smile she knew was tight and forced. She didn't want to talk about Nancy. She fingered the locket at her neck and thought she must try to get it open when she got home tonight. Rachel wanted to see the photos Flo had put inside, of her and Jim; she wondered if they were ones she'd never seen before. She would open it after the hot chocolate and the sandwiches and the begging for forgiveness. Oh, there was Gabe again, talking to Sally and David. He raised another hand in 'hello' to her; she did another feeble wave back.

'Who's that?' Teddy craned her head. 'That's not the silver fox, is it? Why is he waving at you?'

'I have no idea.' She put her arm around Teddy. 'How are you doing?' she asked her kindly. 'How are things at the moment with Lee?'

Teddy pulled a bit of a face. 'They're OK,' she shrugged.

'Are you happy?' Rachel hadn't seen Teddy on her own for a while. Lee was always there, or Iris, of course. She could never ask her how she really was.

'It doesn't matter if I'm happy or not,' said Teddy. 'We're a family.' For the first time Rachel was struck with something awful – what if Teddy was following *her* blueprint, of all these years, to stick with something, no matter what? To keep on driving even after the wheels had come off? 'Oh, look, Lee's back.'

Lee was carrying their drinks on a small tray. Teddy and Rachel both took theirs, Lee removed his pint glass and leaned to place the tray at the base of a nearby pillar. As he righted himself, a man in animated conversation in the next circle jogged Lee's arm and beer sloshed over the top of his glass and down the front of his tuxedo jacket.

'Hey, watch it!' Lee said, eyes immediately blazing to the man, who turned out to be Bill Tennant from the parish council.

'Sorry.' Bill was a timid fella, overly apologetic at the best of times. 'So very, very sorry.' He pulled a handkerchief from the breast pocket of his jacket and started dabbing at Lee's with it.

'Get off me, man!' Lee put an arresting hand on Bill's lapel and stepped back from him. 'No, sod off, it's all right.' Bill melted back into his circle, red-faced. Teddy was laughing sheepishly, her hand to her mouth.

'And you can fucking shut up as well, you stupid cow!' snapped Lee and, with one corner of his top lip snarled, he jolted his glass spitefully in her direction, causing foamy beer to slop over her dress. Teddy looked down at the dress and then up again, shocked. She clawed at Lee's sleeve.

'Sorry,' she said. 'Sorry for laughing. It doesn't show, honest,' she said, tapping at his lapel, and she was right, the beer didn't show on Lee's jacket, but it did on Teddy's dress, a dark splodge like a psychologist's ink blot.

'I need to talk to Carl Abara about a job,' said Lee, grabbing her free hand and pulling her into the throng. 'Come on.'

As Lee dragged her away, Rachel shot her stepdaughter a 'What are you doing?' look, her heart breaking. Teddy returned it with her own 'What *can* you do?' shrug. Teddy was going willingly, as she always did, and it devastated Rachel.

She stood for a while, desperately looking around for Wren and wondering which backup circle to join, despite Bill from the parish council chucking her sheepish smiles from the edge of his. There were any number of people to talk to here tonight: colleagues, regulars to the gallery, neighbours, villagers. As lovely as most of them were, she didn't particularly want to talk to any of them.

Sally glided up, a rustle of chiffon.

'Rachel, *hi*! How lovely to see you. You're looking *gorgeous*! Have you seen the exhibit yet?' She grabbed at Rachel's fingers.

'You look beautiful, Sally. No, not yet.'

'Oh, you must. Gabe's work is just wonderful. Come, come,' Sally said, sliding a cool palm around Rachel's and leading her through the black and jewelled crowd of dinner suits and dresses. 'Let's go see it now, if we can *get* to it. It's causing quite the stir.'

There was a crowd of people on the landing of the grand double staircase, and they were all looking up at the large framed piece hung on the wall there. The crowd this year was larger than normal, due to chatter about Gabe being a big name, Rachel suspected. The sketch, done in blue biro, was huge. She wondered which tree in the village it was. Among its branches were tiny hearts, cracked down the centre or weeping, like melted candles, or severed into two long and narrow parts. It was stunning. It was stark and bleak, its branches were like reaching signposts to the past and the future.

Rachel stood and looked at it for a very long time.

'It's really amazing.' She turned, but Sally had gone. Gabe was standing next to her instead, staring at her with a soft smile.

'Thank you.' He smiled; her heart keeled. There was frisson, there was danger, all going nowhere. All posthumous, for them. Time had failed them, finally, by running out.

'Oh, it's you,' she said, her voice a fabricated light froth, a party greeting. 'Are you creeping up on me?'

'Yes, I expect so,' he said, and in another life Rachel would have taken her hand and placed it gently on the side of his face, to feel its warmth. 'Do you really think it's amazing? It's kinda . . . sketchy.'

'It's wonderful,' she said. 'I can't believe it was here in the village, all this time. That you even *did* it when you were here, all those years ago.'

'I did it in a couple days,' he said. 'In between endless errands for Aunt Julia and going to parties and visiting the local gallery . . .'

'Quite the social whirl,' Rachel laughed, wondering just why it was his eyes had such an effect on her, always. Why they were the most beautiful shade of blue she'd ever seen.

'I met a bunch of nice people,' said Gabe. 'Some I won't ever forget,' he added seriously, and they both stood and looked at each other for a while, Rachel weeping inside for this man, this man she could never have had. 'You look stunning,' he said, after a while. 'I like the flash of scarlet.'

'Thanks. I try to scrub up, for an old 'un,' she said, looking down at her dress.

'Could you ever just take a compliment?'

'No?'

He smiled and so did she. A woman in a green dress stepped closer to them, her hair a spun-sugar helmet. They were in the way now, of guests trying to view the painting, so they moved to the top step of one of the grand flights of stairs.

'Careful,' said Gabe, steering her towards the railing. 'Don't want you falling.'

*I already have*, she wanted to say. *Over and over again.* Instead, she said, 'When are you leaving?'

'Always trying to get rid of me,' Gabe laughed. 'Tonight. Well, tomorrow morning, first flight, 6 a.m., but I'm driving straight to the airport when I leave here. Giving myself plenty of time.'

'A good plan,' Rachel agreed, although her heart was breaking at the thought of him going. Of him driving away from her forever.

'I always have good plans,' said Gabe, 'but you know what they say about the best-laid ones . . .'

'I do,' said Rachel. All her best-laid plans had and hadn't come true, she thought. Yes, she'd got what she wished for in her life – home, family and security – but there had been a price. Jonny's inconstancy, the trials of their beloved Teddy and . . . Gabe. The loss of Gabe. 'How did the sorting go? Of Aunt Julia's things?'

'The packing up of a whole life? It's gone OK. It's all done, at least. All the things she had to show for her life, her travel souvenirs, the trinkets and the tokens of her marriage, wrapped and boxed up. I found some wonderful photos. It was . . . well, her falling in love with Uncle Trevor that took her away from her country and her family, but it was worth it, you know?' Gabe sounded sad. 'It was really worth it, for her. She told me once it was a love that took her breath away.'

'Lucky Aunt Julia.'

'Yes, lucky Aunt Julia.' His gaze didn't falter. His eyes were clear and steady. She could see his irises, the light playing on them, the stretches and spirals of colours rippling from his pupils.

'Gabe . . .'

A very excited mini tour group flooded the platform, fronted by Sally, back again – a flock of bow ties and plunging necklines.

'Yes, this is the artist,' Sally said proudly to them. 'Gabe McAllister.' She opened her right arm out to him like a conductor. 'No Jonny?' she said accusingly to Rachel.

'No, sorry,' replied Rachel. 'He's babysitting.'

'Shame. So many people I wanted to show him off to. Never mind, we've got Gabe. Gabe is one of the top painters in New York,' she trilled to her audience.

'North Dakota,' corrected Gabe.

'North *America*,' summarised Sally.

'Ooh,' said one of the women, placing a hand on Gabe's back. 'You clever old thing. Tell me . . .' and she started grilling him about where he got his ideas, how long it took him to do his artworks, did he like to have music on while he worked, was he ever so temperamental, as she'd heard a lot of artists were . . . And Gabe was swept away from Rachel and down the stairs. A retreating hand waved an apology to her; she raised a hand to him in return. She didn't even know what she'd been about to say to him, and he'd be going soon. Going for good. She was gutted, panicked. There was a cold rock inside her chest, stopping her from breathing normally. Time was running out and soon he would be gone, and she just wanted to talk and talk and talk to him until that moment. She wanted him with her for each and every one of those precious seconds.

Rachel walked down the flight of stairs, not able to see him at all now. She was beckoned over by a neighbour, engulfed in a swirl of chat and champagne and loud laughter. Of merriment and early festive cheer. She ate canapés; she drank champagne. She took an occasional and reluctant turn on the dance floor; she was returned to more circles of conversation. Small talk, bigger talk, questions, questions. How's Jonny? When's his next book coming out? How's the gallery? Is Wren here? (Where *was* Wren?) Round and round; repetition on repetition. She stared at taffeta and lace and stiff white collars and bow ties relaxed and loosened and elaborately curled hair slowly flopping, flopping. Gabe was not in her orbit, or the fringes of her vision. In between sympathetic smiles to waffling-on neighbours, she looked for him. In gaps taken in uttered exclamations or laughs at feeble jokes, she scanned the crowd for his face, but there was no sign. Had he left already? Had he gone without saying goodbye?

She excused herself from the loud, braying circle she was currently being interrogated in, this time about the explosion and

Jonny's subsequent rise to fame, what had he been wearing when he'd been found wandering the streets of London, dazed and confused, yet so handsome . . . ? saying she was going to the Ladies. She went into the cloakroom, which was thankfully empty, and leaned her hot cheek against a tiled wall. *Had he gone? Had he gone?*

'Rachel!' Wren was sweeping in, her floor-length dress catching in the door handle. She disentangled it and pulled Rachel to her. 'There you are! I had to bloody well go home, didn't I? Jackson was sick and the useless teens couldn't cope, apparently. Rory's stayed with them all – good luck to him, quite frankly – and I got to come back,' she grinned. 'So, have you spoken to Gabe yet?' she asked.

'Yes,' said Rachel miserably. 'But now I don't know where he is. I don't know if I even should be speaking to him again.'

'Of course you should! And what will you say when you do? Are you going to go to him? Go with him?' Wren grabbed both Rachel's hands and gazed at her imploringly.

'I don't know,' said Rachel, shaking her head desolately. 'I don't know what to do. I found something else out about Jonny tonight,' she added defeatedly. 'That he cheated on me with Nancy before we got married.'

'Oh, for God's sake!' Wren exclaimed. 'Why am I not surprised? Go and grab Gabe before it's too late!'

'I don't know what he's feeling!' cried Rachel. 'He's given me no indication . . . And he flies home tomorrow.'

'I can guess how he's feeling,' said Wren. 'I saw how he looked at you in the church. Go and make a new life!' she entreated. 'We can all manage without you, I promise you.' Rachel didn't think so. *Just look at how Teddy and Lee have been tonight*, she thought. 'And the gallery? You can do that anywhere, you're so brilliant at it! London, New York, North Dakota . . . Go out there and talk to him and then come back immediately and tell me how you get on. I need to take my bra off and put it back on again. Damn those strapless bras!' Wren felt herself around the middle. 'I think it's slipped all the way down. Go!' she repeated, giving Rachel a quick hug. 'You're brave and you're awesome and you deserve this.'

'I'll have one more look for him,' said Rachel dejectedly, and not at all convinced by Wren's words. She felt it was too late for her and Gabe. She feared he had gone. But as she came out of the bathroom, there Gabe was, standing by a pillar, a gentle smile playing on his lips as he watched revellers on the dance floor. He saw her. He was walking over.

'Hello.'

'Hello.' Her heart expanded and contracted; she was both lost and found.

'I've been looking for you,' he said. 'I'm leaving now, and I'd like to say goodbye, if that's OK. Shall we?' He gestured to a glazed exterior door that led to the garden. She nodded.

'Here, take my jacket,' he said, as they stepped outside. 'It's freezing out.'

Gabe was right. The sky was midnight black with stars starkly visible. The air was almost deliciously cold and clean.

'Mild for North Dakota, though,' she commented nervously, pulling his jacket closer around her and feeling the residual heat from his body. If only she could wrap herself in him forever, but he wanted to say goodbye.

'Positively balmy,' said Gabe.

There was a pergola, at the far end of the garden, in the moonlight, on a raised platform. He led her towards it through damp grass that licked her calves and helped her up its narrow steps. Once they were standing, under a roof of slatted wood and twisted vines, he took both her hands and she shivered, but she was not cold. His eyes were a sapphire blue in the moonlight. His mouth was beautiful.

'Rachel,' he said.

She was drinking him in. She was committing his face, his hair, the way his bow tie sat at his throat to memory. For what was left of her future. She was already feeling what she knew she would feel when he walked away from her.

'Gabe.' Her voice wavered, she feared she might cry but she didn't want to, in this still, quiet garden. Her tears would be futile, and Rachel wanted to see him with clear eyes, this final time.

He took a deep breath. 'I met you a long time ago,' he said, and he didn't take his eyes from hers. 'I met you when I was a young man, impassioned, a little erratic,' he grinned, the merest trace of a wink at his left eye, 'a hopeful yet hopeless romantic with big dreams and big ideals. A bit of a prat, to coin an English phrase.'

She shook her head. 'You were lovely.'

'I met you again when I was an enthusiastic thirty-something,' he continued, 'living for the moment and for art and for travel.' She smiled at the memory of him, then. Of Morocco. She let her thumb trace along his. 'I met you again when I was grief-stricken and full of guilt, when I'd cared for someone who'd meant so much to me, but not enough.'

'I'm sorry,' she said, like she had done all those years before.

'Thank you,' he said softly. 'The guilt and the grief fade, in time, and you only remember the good stuff. I think it's important to.' He exhaled. 'And now I've met you again, as I come to say goodbye to my beloved aunt. As I return to the little village of Fincham St George and here you are.'

'Where else would I be?' she asked, with a sad smile. That was the question, wasn't it? *Where else would she be*? She had met him, one spring, when she was so certain her life was all plotted out, that nothing could have punctured the shield she'd thought was invincible around her. She had met him again, one summer, when, after so much disappointment, she had been intoxicated by his lust for life. And again, one autumn, when she had been betrayed in her marriage and needed him so very badly. But life's planned course always came first, for her. So desperate had she been for the things she thought she wanted, so determined had she been to make things work, to *stick with it*, Rachel could never change her life for him, to *be* with him, and now she had met him again, it was all too late.

'The years have passed,' Gabe said, shaking his head, 'the days, the weeks, the seasons. Yet here we stand together again, outside another English party.' She looked towards the house. The lights. She remembered the village hall, her silly headscarf. The figure in the car park emerging from the trees and walking over to her. 'It's been so good to see you again, Rachel.'

'You, too.' She couldn't bear it, this final goodbye. She pulled his jacket tighter.

'Do we think the universe is trying to tell us something?' he asked. 'The way it keeps bringing us together?'

'I've always found the universe to be incredibly silent,' she said sadly. 'I don't think it knows anything. And I thought you didn't believe in fate?'

'I'm not so sure now,' he said with a smile. 'I'm really not sure. But there are things I *do* know,' he said. 'And I want you to know them too.' His look was so tender, so warm. 'I still feel the same.'

Her breath, warm into the cold air, caught in her throat. 'It's been such a long time,' she whispered. 'I didn't know . . .'

'Rachel,' he continued. 'My feelings for you have never changed since I first set eyes on you. When I saw you in the gallery, when I danced with you. When I saw your tears and heard your laughter. I knew then. I still know now. I've tried to live other lives, with other women, to create other loves, but they haven't been *it*, for me. It always comes back to you. I guess I was young and stupid when I said to come find me if you were ever free. You've never been free. But what I said still stands. Everything I've ever said to you still stands.'

'I can't be free,' she said, shaking her head, knowing suddenly and tragically she could never go to him, because of Iris, because of Teddy, because of her life, but her heart swelled at his words.

'I know. You have your life, Rachel, your home, your grand-daughter, your stepdaughter, Jonny and the gallery. I know you treasure all those things. I know they're all the things you've been looking for.'

They were, she thought desperately. They were the anchor of love and dreams she was chained to. She couldn't leave them. 'And you? Have you found anything you've been looking for? There in Jud? I can't bear the thought of you being unhappy. Please tell me you've been happy?'

'I've been OK,' he said, with a wry smile. 'I have Jacob, he's a good kid, he makes me happy. Apart from that, I've just been liv-ing in Jud, population seventy-one and a half, for that half a man is me, without you, but that's the way it's got to be.' He smiled gently at her. 'I know I must leave you, here in your life. I've asked you to come find me. I've asked you to be with me. I know I can't ask you any more.'

'I was going to come back to you,' she said, her words com-ing out in a rush, her emotions spilling out of her. 'To London. I changed my mind on the train home, and I was going to tell Jonny and I was going to come back to you.'

'You were?'

'Yes. But Jonny had an accident. A fall. Just before I arrived home. Then he got ill. I had to stay. I had to look after him. That was the start of the seven years – of me being his carer.'

'Why didn't you tell me, back then, what happened?' Gabe's face was anguished, his eyes raking over hers.

'What was the point? There was no point. I couldn't leave Jonny then, he needed me. I had to look after him and I did so willingly, and with love, I hope. But before then I *was* coming back to you. I was coming to be with you.' Rachel was almost crying, but she would not let her voice break. She needed to tell him this.

'Your email.' He sighed deeply. 'It told me nothing. It contained nothing, Rachel. And I wrote you back and you never replied. You'd already broken my heart, when you ran from me in London, and then you broke it all over again.'

'I'm so sorry. I should have explained, I know that. I thought it was easier—'

'I get it, Rachel! I get the life you've chosen. It's what you've needed, but goddam it, I wish you hadn't. *I've* needed you! I've wanted you. I've wanted this great big love between us and that's never gone away!' He looked on the verge of anger. 'But why would you risk the life you know to go off with some American hick? Why would you take that leap? It would be such a big thing to do, the grandest of grand gestures. I know I was a damn fool to have hoped it of you.'

'I would have done, I would have done!' Now she *was* crying; tears like raindrops coming down her face.

'No.' Gabe shook his head. 'There always would have been something. Something to tether you to home. It's OK, Rachel.' He ran his hand through his hair. 'Your constancy and your commitment to what you think is right, to what you think of as your safety, is part of the reason I love you, but those things also keep you from me.' He sighed. 'I'm going to protect my heart now,' he said. 'You'll always have it. *Always*. But it's time to let you go. Time for us to let each other go.'

He gathered her into his arms, and she almost collapsed on him, softly weeping. She lay her head on the warm cotton of his shoulder.

'I just want to say, you're the most beautiful woman I've ever known,' Gabe whispered. The words came from inside of him. From inside his chest and up to her.

'Please don't say that,' Rachel whispered through her tears.

'When will I ever get another chance?'

She drew her head up to look at him. His face was the same as it had been on another English night, long ago. Full of the promise of a love she could never accept. And she hated herself then, for her *commitment*, for all the reasons that bound her to her life even when presented with the heartbreaking goodbye of this man.

Her marriage. Her duty to her family. Her fear of painful consequence. Jonny, who had fractured the shield he'd put around her, but had given her moments of joy: laughter and dancing in the garden; times of quiet contentment; times when they were mum and dad to Teddy, or granny and grandad to Iris, tucked up with her cuddly toys, safe and warm in their house. The blueprint of Nanna and Grandpop's wonderful marriage she had followed. The words of Nanna, who had chosen to stay and had had an amazing life. Who said the grass wasn't greener. But you'll never know unless you go and see it for yourself, thought Rachel, and Gabe was right, Rachel had never had the courage to take the risk.

'A part of me wants to leave it all and be with you,' she whispered. 'A part of me always has.'

'You won't, though, will you?' he answered, searching her face for the answer she couldn't give. 'You won't.'

Rachel shook her head.

'Then I'm asking no more of you except that I can silently and deeply love you for the rest of my life.' His irises were midnight blue, now, in the moonlight. Looking up at him, she had never seen a face she loved more, or hated more to lose from her life.

'You can do that,' she whispered, 'and I will love you. I have always and will always love you, Gabe. I'm as certain of that as I am of my inability to change my life and be with you. I'm so, so sorry.' The decades had slipped through her fingers, she thought, and he had too. Tonight, Gabe slipped away forever.

'Oh God, Rachel, I don't want to say goodbye, but it hurts to stay,' he said, and he wrapped his arms all the way around her and held her tight, so tight now, and she clung on to him, trying to save this moment in her heart, and she could feel his breath on her cheek, and the rise of his chest against hers, and the warmth of his skin, and she just wanted to hold him and hold him and hold him forever.

Gabe pulled away from her and she wanted to cry out. Then he bent down and cupped her face in his hands like it was a rosebud that needed to be protected from a late spring frost, and kissed her like it was the last time, because it *was* the last time. And in that kiss was all they had never had, and all they had lost, and all that would be empty and far from them in the years to come. It was the past they had never shared, and a future they would never see. This kiss had to last her for a lifetime.

'I love you,' he whispered.

'I love you, too.'

'See ya, kiddo,' he said. And with one last fleeting look, he turned from Rachel and walked back to the house, leaving only half of her behind.

# Chapter Forty-One

Rachel stood for a while, under the midnight sky, wanting every atom of this bone-cold night to seep into her and numb her body and soul. Gabe was gone. He was gone for good. She had never felt so cold. She had never felt so bereft. She wanted to feel *nothing*, but it was impossible. Rachel just stood, breathing in the loss, trembling under the dark wickety shapes of the winter trees and realising she was still wearing Gabe's jacket, which she gathered around her as she let the tears fall.

He was gone and she was hollow from the inside out. He was gone and she was alone.

There was a switching of bracken and a shiver of taffeta, to her right. She turned and Teddy was buffeting towards her, an angled cigarette in one hand.

Rachel quickly wiped the tears from her cheeks.

'Rachel? What's going on? Who was that man?' Teddy asked. Her heavily kohled eyes had smudged a little and she looked like an inquisitive doll.

'Just an old friend,' said Rachel softly. 'He's gone now.' She looked over to the door Gabe had disappeared through, from which he would never return.

'You were kissing!' said Teddy, wide-eyed. 'It looked like the dishy American. That artist, Julia March's nephew? It was, wasn't it?'

'Yes,' said Rachel, more aware than ever she was wearing his jacket and trying to draw its last warmth into her body. She tried to smile at Teddy. 'But we weren't kissing. We were just talking.'

'I saw you!' cried Teddy. 'Come on, I'm not shocked or anything! Why are you always trying to protect me?'

'Protect you? Because it's my job,' said Rachel. 'Or at least it's something I've been doing for a really long time. I love you. That's why.'

'I'm forty-two years old, I don't need protecting any more.'

'Don't you?' Rachel's voice was weary, her whole being so very tired.

Teddy shook her head. 'No. I saw you kissing. I saw the way he was holding you. The way he was looking at you. Good God, Rachel, is he in love with you?'

'He's gone,' whispered Rachel. 'That's all I know. He's gone now.'

'But how do you even know him? You're wearing his *jacket*, for God's sake!'

'I've met him a few times over the years,' said Rachel sorrowfully. 'That's all. It's nothing.'

'I don't think it is nothing! It looked like everything to me. It looked like love. It looked like . . .' Teddy flicked a centimetre of ash on to the grass. '. . . the kind of love every bloody person in the world's looking for!'

She gazed into Rachel's face. A cat streaked across the lawn in the distance, fur fluffed with cold.

'I'm never going to leave your father,' Rachel said quietly and sadly, after what had seemed an endless pause, with the night sky waiting. 'I need you to know that.'

'Why not?' Teddy's eyes were narrowed.

'Why not? Because we're married, because we're a unit, because we've been through so much together. My marriage is my life.' Rachel felt like her heart was shattering into a million pieces.

'A life based on a lie,' snorted Teddy.

'Why are you saying that?' Did Teddy know about Nancy? Rachel wondered. How could she know about that?

Teddy waved her cigarette in the air. 'The lie that it's true love, or that you're meant to be together. I know you two try so hard to be the perfect role models, always so desperate to show me how marriage could be, so I'll dump Lee and find myself what you've got. So perfect, so stable . . . It's a load of shit!'

'What on earth do you mean?' Rachel shivered in the cold – surprised and shocked.

'Oh, come on!' scoffed Teddy. 'All these years, you and Dad. "The perfect couple."' She did that terrible quotation mark thing with her fingers. 'I've never seen you truly happy. I've never seen *you*. It's always been all about him. His needs, his career, his daughter – yes, I know so much of what you've done is for me, and I see that, and I appreciate it and I love you and Lord knows you've been a much better mother to me than my own . . . And I know he's been ill. I know he's great fun, sometimes. But none of it has been love.'

Teddy's words sank into Rachel like blades. Teddy didn't know about Nancy, but it was true. Rachel had facilitated Jonny, indulged him and withstood the infertility and the self-centredness. She had kept the secret of his affairs in order to shield his daughter. She had cared for Jonny when he was ill. She had smoothed his ego, gone to bed with him night after night and loved him, to the best of her ability. She'd thought it was a stable kind of love, an enduring one, that was a good blueprint for a girl like Teddy, but she'd been wrong. It was why Teddy had accepted less-than-perfect in her own relationship for so long, because that was the standard.

'I won't leave the things that are precious to me,' Rachel whispered, and she felt colour rising to her cheeks. 'You, and Iris and my life as I know it, and yes, your father, for all he's done or not done, because . . . well, *I've* always done the right thing, haven't I? The

377

safest thing.' She fought to keep the anger from her voice. Anger that was rising within her like a long-dampened flame. 'Keeping quiet and laughing along and not being a nag and making sure there's no drama and not changing my view from the kitchen window.' Teddy looked mystified. 'That's what I've done, for years and years! As all the decades have passed and the seasons have turned. That's what I've done! Because the grass is not greener. It isn't!'

'Are you sure it's not?' asked Teddy. 'Dad doesn't need you. He just needs his career. Maybe you should seize what you've got going with that artist bloke. If that's real love. That real, only-happens-once-in-a-lifetime kind of love. It's so rare, isn't it, Rachel?' she said, and her mask slipped and she looked sober and raw and desperate. 'It's so, so rare.'

Rachel exhaled. The look on Teddy's face was destroying her. 'And you?' Rachel asked quietly, knowing she could only digest the truth of Teddy's words later. Away from this midnight garden. 'What kind of a love do you have with Lee?' She knew the answer.

'What Lee and I have is a below par, substandard, messy non-kind of love,' Teddy said sadly. 'It's not right, I know that. It's wrong in so many ways. But sometimes, when he looks at me, he makes me feel like the most special person in the world. They are rare, too, those moments. They have to be earned, with a lot of pain. But when they come . . . I guess I live for the moments when he looks at me like that.'

'Your last remaining addiction and the hardest one to give up,' whispered Rachel. 'I wish you could break the habit of him.' She reached for Teddy's hand, but it was batted away.

'It's the life and the love I know. It's easy, even though it's difficult. We have a child together. I haven't got the energy to start over, to find someone who's good for me. I've got too many issues.' Teddy laughed coldly and it echoed into the night.

'I think Lee's caused a lot of them,' said Rachel drily. But they had caused others – Jonny and Nancy and her. The blueprint they had designed.

'Who knows?' shrugged Teddy. 'We need each other, I guess. We can't do anything else now. I know I can't.'

'You're really not going to do anything about it?' Rachel asked. 'Never?' And she couldn't help but ask herself the same question.

'Nope. It's too late, isn't it? It appears we're both stuck exactly where we think we deserve to be. Let's go back inside.' Teddy had a pleading look on her face. 'Please. I can't talk about this any more. Come on.'

Rachel hugged her, feeling sorry and desperate and alone. Then Teddy took Rachel's arm and Rachel tried to steady her breath as they cut across the grass in their heels. She would go home now, as soon as she'd made her polite goodbyes, and she was already thinking about that crisp walk home, when ice would be forming on the pavements and she would take stock of everything that had been said tonight, and of her life. And when she got in, maybe she would forgo the sandwiches and the hot chocolate. Maybe Rachel would let herself in quietly and go straight upstairs.

As they reached the door, Lee was stepping out of it, hunched into his jacket and reaching into an inner pocket for fags and lighter.

'Ah, there you are,' he said, glaring at Teddy.

'I came out for some air,' Teddy said, and Lee held out his arm and Teddy hesitated for a second but then he hooked her under the armpit of his jacket, and she slotted in so easily with him and turned her face up to his with such misplaced love that Rachel knew it for certain. There was no hope. Teddy would never leave Lee, whatever anyone did, or said, or tried to be. And, as they all stepped back into the warmth of the hall, and Teddy peeled away from Lee, laughing and blowing him a kiss and saying she was just going to the loo, Rachel felt a surge of anger rise within her.

She tapped him on the shoulder.

'Can't you release her?' she said.

'What?' His eyes were steely.

'Can't you have the decency to let her go?'

'Who are you talking about?' he sneered.

Rachel's anger soared. 'You know who I'm talking about! *Teddy.*'

Lee laughed, long and easy and cutting, 'Why would I want to do that? I have the perfect life with Tatiana. She needs me,' he said in a cruel whisper, leaning into Rachel's face. 'And I find that very seductive. And it's a bit late to start saying this now, darling,' he added, like flinging a knife at her.

'I want to say it. It needs to be said out loud, Lee.' She was shaking. She was angry. It was time.

'Jonny's never had a problem with me.'

'No, and I really don't know why that is . . .' She froze. The blood cooled in her veins. What had Sally said? About Lee having a hold over them all? Seconds passed and her brain clicked through a number of markers. Why Jonny had invested in Lee for so long, why he had never pulled him up on his treatment of Teddy, or discouraged the relationship.

Suddenly, she understood. Lee knew about Nancy. He was there that night. Sausage Night – almost hilarious if it wasn't so awful – and other nights too, no doubt. He had dropped Rachel off and gone with Jonny to the pub, and he had probably deposited Jonny at Nancy's, too – maybe he'd even brought him home. But most certainly this toerag had known all about the affair. Perhaps he'd known about all of them.

'You've always had something over him, haven't you?'

'Have I?' Lee looked away rudely around the room.

'Yes, and he was relieved for me to find out what it was, actually.' She talked to the side of his face, but it didn't deter her. 'It doesn't matter, about you knowing any more. You don't have any hold over him, and Jonny doesn't have to worry about any consequences of stopping the handouts. Because I found out. About Nancy.'

Lee flicked his head back to her, his eyes narrowed. 'The handouts?'

'Yes, the handouts. Jonny's investment in your horrible plays.'

Lee's smirk dropped and so did the unconcerned mocking glint in his eyes, replaced by a fire of anger. 'He's stopping the investment?'

'Yes. You know that, don't you? He told you when you were round this morning. You said he'd told you something you didn't want to hear . . .'

'He told me he was postponing the opening night of *The Trampling of the Vines*, until April.'

'Oh.' She froze again. So, Jonny had chickened out, or postponed the inevitable. 'But well, yes, Lee, he's stopped the direct debits. It's over, your Bank of Jonny, the cash cow. You're on your own. You and Teddy. I wish to God she'd leave you!'

'Right,' he said. '*Right*.' He turned to her, eyes flashing. 'And you think that's all I have over him?'

She faltered. What was he talking about? 'Well, isn't it enough? That you knew all along he was sleeping with Nancy before we even got married . . .' The look on his face was starting to worry her.

'That's nothing,' Lee laughed. 'Nothing at all. Ask him about the other thing.'

'What do you mean? The affair he had with that Kim?'

'Who? Oh Lord, he really can't help himself, can he?' he laughed. 'No, the big thing you were never supposed to find out about.' His face was too close. 'Ask him about how he became *famous.*'

'What do you mean? Everyone knows how he became famous. The accident . . .'

Lee's face was now one of a man who had nothing to lose. 'Ask him for the part of the story he hasn't told you,' he whispered, then he shoved past her.

'Wait! Lee?' But he had gone, swallowed into the crowd. She made to go after him.

'Rachel, *hi . . .*'

*Oh, not now, Dray.* Dray Briggs, in a straining dinner suit, was blocking her way. His face was red and sweaty and tilted in the direction of her cleavage. 'How are we . . . ?'

'We're fine, thanks. I'm just on my way out, actually.' She tried to push past him, but he placed a meaty paw on her arm.

'Why are you leaving? We could have a dance, couldn't we? Take a turn. You look quite pretty tonight, for an old bird,' he said, placing a finger on her chin. 'And there's life in the old dog yet,' he added, giving a repulsive shimmy and a wobble of his belly. 'I have no idea why the young girls don't want to dance with me.'

'Because they're sensible,' she said, trying to squirm away from him. 'I've been avoiding dancing with you since 1986.'

Dray erupted in laughter and dragged one sweaty arm around her back, brushing the side of her chest and pulling her closer. 'That's a pretty locket,' he leered, fingering it with his other hand. 'Got a photo of me inside, darling?'

'No, of course not,' she said, trying to wriggle away. She felt a pull on her neck, then a release, and the necklace dropped from her and fell like water to the floor. 'Fuck off, Dray!' she said, pushing him off her with all her force. 'On behalf of all of us, fuck off.' And she bent to the floor to gather up the necklace, and the two tiny photographs that had fallen out of it, and she fled.

Rachel dashed to the front door, grabbed her coat from the rail and stepped out on to the front porch where the air she breathed in, in big gulps, was cold and fresh. She leaned against the door frame. She opened her hand. The locket and the two photos in her palm were lit by Sally's porch light and Rachel peered at them. One was a tiny version of the photo Florence always had on her mantelpiece – her in pilot gear, standing in front of the Spitfire, one hand raised in a salute. '14 October 1943' was inscribed in Florence's miniature handwriting at the bottom. The other was a photo of a stranger, a handsome man in a smart serviceman's uniform, with '6 April 1943' written across it, followed by two words.

'*Fly, Florence!*'

Someone was opening the front door behind her. Rachel quickly snapped the photos back into their resting places, dropped the locket in her bag and hurried up the lamplit pavement towards home.

# Chapter Forty-Two

'I wasn't expecting you yet,' Jonny said, and she knew he was both annoyed to be disturbed and a little drunk. There was a bottle of whisky on his desk. 'How was it?'

Rachel closed the study door. She didn't come in here very often. Copies of various *Nikita*s lined untidy shelves. Russian guidebooks littered the desk. A pair of shoes toppled on each other in the corner.

'Pretty much the same as usual,' she lied, leaning against the door and bringing her foot up against it so she could rub at her toes through her tights. 'You know how it goes. How's Iris been?'

'Great, wonderful, not a peep.'

'Good. Lee said to ask you about the accident.'

Jonny had not yet glanced up from his laptop. Now his rhythmic tapping stopped and he looked up. 'What accident?'

'*The* accident. The gas explosion.'

'I'm not with you,' he frowned. 'What about it? Why was Lee talking about that?'

'He said to ask you about it,' she repeated. 'He said to ask you for the truth.'

'I don't know what on earth you mean,' said Jonny flippantly, returning to the laptop. 'I've told the truth about it. I've been telling people for years,' he added, with a short laugh. 'Everybody's got thoroughly sick of it.'

'I told Lee your investments were stopping,' she said. 'He was really angry about it. Don't you think he'll eventually be angry enough to simply tell me himself? Whatever this is.'

Jonny blanched. He stopped typing again. 'You told him?'

'Yes.'

'Why did you do that?'

'Because I thought you had. When it turns out all you'd done was tell him you were postponing the opening of *Trampling*.'

'Right.' Jonny took a huge swig from his tumbler of whisky. A new crease branched on his forehead, short and deep. A vein pulsated. 'My damn accountant!' he exploded, half rising from the desk. 'I should never have been persuaded! I should have just kept the money going!'

'Please don't wake Iris up,' said Rachel calmly.

'Sorry, sorry.' Jonny dropped his voice, but not his anger. 'I could still go back on it, if it's so disagreeable to him . . . Maybe I could—'

'Did you also help Lee buy his building company, years ago?' she asked, and Rachel knew from Jonny's face that he had. 'There's no doubt he's going to tell me,' she continued, 'about what really happened. So, I think it's best if you do it first, Jonny.' Oh, she was cool, Rachel thought, really cool. But her heart was smashing through her chest.

'There's nothing to tell,' Jonny protested, but Rachel knew he was floundering; she knew he was becoming unable to resist the temptation to bare all. To make his second confession of the night. 'I thought it was all so long ago I was safe to stop the money,' he said weakly. The new crease in his forehead deepened. 'I've made the wrong decision . . .' His voice trailed off. 'Stupid. *Stupid.*'

'We can be truthful with each other, can't we?' she pressed, knowing that later she would have to be truthful with him too. 'Haven't you always been truthful, eventually?'

Jonny hesitated. Then he grabbed the tumbler of whisky, eyes blazing, and emptied the contents down his throat. 'Why do you think I let that slimeball be with my daughter?' he whispered, almost to himself, then he slammed the tumbler down on the desk. 'Why do you think I couldn't put a stop to it? . . . This fucking *hold* he's had over me all this time!' His face was all red and a vein was thumping in his temple. Rachel shushed him, thinking of her sleeping granddaughter upstairs, but a rage in her was already rising for Teddy.

'I made a mistake,' Jonny muttered, and she held her breath as she knew the confession would come now, like so many before. 'A long time ago, when I was a boastful and reckless man. I told Lee about Nancy.' Rachel nodded, encouraging him to go on. Jonny poured himself more whisky. 'Because, well, I was showing off, I suppose – because he looked up to me, thought everything I did was great, and I wanted to confide in someone who would do the opposite of condemning me for it. And, because he kept my counsel – kept it so well – I later trusted him with . . . something else.' He sighed deeply. He looked like he wanted to rise from his chair and escape, to anywhere but here. Then, wretched, he continued. 'Well, he guessed, actually, got it out of me. He was in awe of me. I enjoyed telling him stories that made his eyes widen with adoration and shock and surprise. And, well, I was drunk, that's God's honest truth, Rachel. Reckless and drunk. I really don't want you hearing it from him,' Jonny added quickly, his eyes suddenly childlike and beseeching. 'If I tell you, at least I can explain.'

'Explain, then,' said Rachel, trembling a little. '*Tell* me.'

Jonny took a deep breath. 'OK,' he said, looking utterly beaten, 'I'm going to tell you,' and when he started talking, she leaned back against the study door and let his words soak into her like poison.

'The afternoon of the accident, events started in the way I've always told,' he said. 'Six of us were in the ballroom of the Fordham, getting ready for two hours of authorly chat and literary pleasure.' He grimaced. 'There was me, Arabella the PR lady, the two women from the Fordham's Events team, Bertie's publisher – Giles Nicholson-Sage – and Bertie, of course.'

Rachel knew the five other characters very well, from Jonny's renditions. She knew Arabella had a shiny brown bob like a motor-cycle helmet, and huge cow eyes. Giles Nicholson-Sage had a smoker's laugh, and hair the colour of biscuits. The two women from Events both looked like varying versions of Tom Petty. And Bertie, well, he had been such a larger-than-life character, she could picture him by just closing her eyes.

'We were setting up for our book reading and Bertie's Q and A. Arabella was fussing round him, making sure his bow tie was straight, and briefing him on diplomatic answers should anyone ask him how much sodding money he earned.'

Jonny swished the liquid in his glass. Took a long shallow sip. *Already he's telling this story differently*, Rachel thought. Already his tone was different.

'Giles was on the phone to his assistant, booking dinner for him and Bertie at a Mayfair restaurant. The two women from Events were bickering about the best position for the huge card-board cut-out of Bertie. As if one of him wasn't fucking enough!'

Rachel braced herself against the study door. This was not the version of events Jonny had recounted countless times, over the years; he had always painted a jolly portrait of him and Bertie as amiable colleagues that afternoon, despite Jonny's fledgling status and the other man's huge renown – of it being the possible dawn of a great friendship.

'That Bertie was always so bloody full of himself!' said Jonny. 'I knew he didn't want me there – a small-fry author and his publisher was doing an old Etonian favour for mine. I was only going to have a few copies of my books on a side table; stand at the back of the room, while Bertie took centre stage in a yellow waistcoat and that ridiculous red bow tie. But he made a big show of being avuncular towards me. There was a lot of backslapping and "dear boy"s. A lot of condescending posturing. Oh, it was a happy little tableau, until that oven in the adjoining kitchen exploded.'

Jonny hesitated, looked at the words on the laptop screen he'd written tonight. This was the crossroads of the story; the cliff edge, thought Rachel. She could see Jonny was teetering on the edge of truth.

'I always said I was heading for the double doors at the end of the ballroom to open them for better disabled access when the explosion happened,' he continued, 'which is why I survived and no one else did, but that's not true. They'd asked me to, but I'd said something crabby about being an author not a "door marshal", and one of the Tom Pettys said she'd do it, after she'd sorted the chairs. In fact, when that oven exploded, I was scrabbling under a table to retrieve Bertie's lanyard, which the bugger had just dropped. Yes, I was creeping round him like Uriah Heep. Yes, I was hoping I'd get an invitation to that Mayfair dinner. I dived under that table like a bloody ninja, to court Bertie's favour, and when I came to, after the blast – the blackness and the dust of it – I realised that lanyard had saved me.'

Jonny's eyes had not been focused on Rachel; they'd been misted over, gazing somewhere over her shoulder, to that closed door, but now they returned to her face. 'I crawled out into the half-light and the rubble. And everyone was dead, except for Bertie.'

Rachel gripped the door handle below her right hand. 'Bertie? Wasn't Bertie already dead? Dead like all of them?'

Jonny had told the story so many times: he had headed for the double doors; Bertie and the others were already dead.

'He was still alive,' said Jonny, with a sardonic smile, 'the giant buffoon. He was lying on his back with his own cardboard cutout on top of him. I went over and dragged it off and there was a beam on him, across his chest – straight across that stupid yellow waistcoat. He was smiling at me and saying, "Get this thing off me, there's a chap." And I knelt down next to him and I looked at him smiling and I thought about everything that was going on in my life, and everything that wasn't. No book sales, no plaudits. No success. No one caring who I was. Certainly no one showing up for me that day – all the readers were for *him*, for *his* books. And I thought about how he was successful because he'd been a child star in that stupid programme about the bear, because of his stupid famous showbiz parents, and that because he was famous already, success as a writer came easily to him. He didn't have to work hard; he didn't have to prove himself. And you know what else I thought? That if I'd shifted that beam, I'd be at best a short-lived sidekick to his heroic survival; at worst, exactly what I was already – a complete nobody. Knowing him, he'd dine out on this accident for years. He'd play it down, laugh it off. Refuse me any glory. I'd be reduced to "that other guy who was there". He'd probably end up saying he'd saved me! It was a split-second decision, Rachel,' Jonny said. 'And not even an action, but an inaction. There was a chance he'd still be alive when the emergency services got in. Or a chance me removing the beam wouldn't save him at all. I left it to fate.'

'You left it to fate . . . ?' Rachel's voice was weak.

'Yes.'

'But you also knew this could be your lucky break,' she stammered. 'That if you were the lone survivor, emerging blackened and dusty from the wreckage of this horrible explosion and wandering the streets of London – *dazed and confused* – there was a chance for you to be someone.'

'Yes, there was that chance,' said Jonny. 'I left it to chance.'

'You left Bertie to *die*, and you walked out of those double doors, and through that fire exit, and on to the street.'

Jonny nodded.

'Wow. You played your part so well,' said Rachel, disgusted. 'Dishevelled and wandering on Wardour Street. Bewildered and despairing, at all the deaths. You wept at Bertie's funeral, if I recall.'

Jonny gazed off towards the blank and dark study window, the blind he had not bothered to pull down. 'It was so bloody hot that day,' he said. 'A scorcher. You expect rain, don't you? Grey skies, at a funeral, but it was a day for packing up the car and going to the beach.' He sighed. 'So many fucking people turned out. So many readers. At first it made me angry, how many of them there were. But that's when it started. I'd been in the papers, my face on the front pages, and the readers . . . they started to come up to me at the wake. They started talking to me. They were interested. Interested in my book. Interested in me. Because I was *famous* now. And then everything just took off. The book sales. Michael. I'd made it.'

'You'd *made it*? You make it sound like you'd worked for this! You hadn't worked! You could have saved Bertie Hinch-Wells, but you chose not to. It was a choice.'

'I *chose* this life. This fantastic life I've had, and I have worked, on all my books. I've worked really bloody hard. Bertie had had so many years of fame and success . . . since he was six years old.'

'So, you wanted what he had, and you took it?' Rachel was repulsed.

'I gave fate a helping hand, and everything since has been hard work. Blood, sweat and tears. Do I feel bad about it? Occasionally. Do I wish I'd never told Lee? Absolutely.'

He actually looked relieved, relieved he had told her, and his face told her he was waiting for her forgiveness. It wouldn't be coming.

'So, our whole life has been a lie,' she said.

'Yours hasn't,' he replied. 'Only mine, and only that small part. That tiny thing. The rest of it's been real, hasn't it, you and me?'

She shook her head. 'No,' she said. 'No, it hasn't. And this wasn't a *tiny thing*! It was a huge thing! It was a horrendous thing! And *Teddy*!' she cried, furious, devastated, wanting to fillet Jonny alive for the part of the betrayal that had shocked her the most. 'You allowed that absolute *snake* to dominate her life, to save your own skin! That is absolutely unforgivable, Jonny!'

'I'm sorry,' he said weakly. 'I'm so, so sorry.' But she knew he would do it again, should the same circumstances arise, every time. 'Are you going to go to the police?' he asked, a sudden wild look of fear in his eyes.

'And say what? You didn't commit a crime.' Her voice was cold.

'Are you going to go to Bertie's family?'

'He didn't have any family.' *Poor Bertie*, she thought. *Poor, poor Bertie.*

'What about Teddy – you won't tell Teddy, will you?' He looked desperate.

'No, I won't tell Teddy.' She couldn't inflict this new and terrible secret on Teddy. The protection of her stepdaughter must continue. She took a deep breath. 'But I am going to leave you.' His utterly shocked face nearly made Rachel falter. 'I'm going to leave you, Jonny, but not because of this. Or even because of Nancy, or the others you've betrayed me with. I'm leaving because – throughout it all – it's always, always been about *you*, Jonny. Because you have never encouraged me, or championed me, or supported me, not really. Because I thought, despite everything, it was all for Teddy – you and me, our marriage – but it turns out, it hasn't been. Everything was always for you.' She took another gulp of air and spoke on, despite his face, which was now crumbling before her. 'And I have lies of my own, I'm afraid. I've not been entirely honest with you either, Jonny. For thirty-three years I have loved another man. And tonight, I'm going to go to him.'

She had thought and thought, on the cold, crisp walk home; as ice began to settle on the pavements, like a frosted blanket. She had thought about love, life and her future and, as she reached Grandpop's bench, she'd decided she was going to leave Jonny. Sitting on that bench, she had made arrangements on her phone as her breath steamed into the cool night air. She was booked on the 12.10 p.m. flight to Chicago then the 4.05 p.m. (Chicago time) to Fargo, and a taxi would be waiting outside Crofters in the morning for an 8 a.m. pick-up.

'Who is it?' Jonny was desolate. She knew that for all his love of fame and success, home, family and security also meant a great deal to him, too. The comfort of it. The warmth. The blanket of the life that surrounded him. Rachel thought of Iris sleeping upstairs and she almost floundered. She nearly took her phone from her bag and cancelled all her arrangements.

'It's an American man,' she said, and her voice got stronger as she spoke. 'It's Julia March's nephew. I met him in 1986, and in 1997 and in 2008. And I've met him again now. I'm going to him. I'm flying to America and I'm *going* to be with him.'

Jonny's eyes flickered. Once upon a time he would have shouted, or he would have flung himself on her, begging her to stay. Now he did nothing, and she could see he was defeated, and accepting, and that was far more catastrophic.

When he finally spoke, all he said was, 'Could you . . . could you stay with me until morning?'

Rachel looked at the face she had woken up to every morning, at the body she had nursed and accommodated, at this man she had loved and given most of her life to. She looked at her husband and she whispered, 'Yes, I'll stay with you until morning.'

'Thank you,' he said, then he dropped his hurt and bewildered eyes to his laptop and began to tap again, his face becoming too blank and set for all he had told her, and all she had told him.

She hesitated in the doorway for a moment, then quietly left the study, closing the door behind her. In the hallway, she took her phone from her bag and called the second person in her contacts.

'Hi, Teddy? It's Rachel. Look, can you come over? Now? Right now?' She started to cry, as she spoke. 'Please come over. Come now? Thank you. Yes. OK, see you shortly.'

She fell to her knees, then, on the hallway floor and broke into sobs – choking sobs that consumed her whole body. She cried for Jonny. For the life they had spent together. For the love she had sustained for him. For all the laughs and all the good times. For all his lies. She cried for Teddy and for Iris. Her little family. And, after she was done crying, she lay her head on folded arms on the tiles and stayed like that until Teddy knocked on the door.

'Are you OK?' she asked Rachel, her eyes full of tears too. 'You've left him, haven't you?'

'Yes, I have,' Rachel sniffed, wavering at the sight of the step-daughter she had always been a mother to. 'I've told him so. But I don't know if I want to leave you and Iris. I'm not sure I can do it.'

Teddy nodded. She stepped into the hall and placed her bag on the bottom stair. 'You don't need to worry about me so much any more,' she said. 'I'm leaving Lee.'

Rachel wiped tears from her eyes with the back of her hand. 'You are?'

'Yes. Can I tell you about it? And then you can tell me what you're going to do?'

'Yes. Tell me, Teddy, please.'

Teddy sighed. She leaned on the banister. Rachel went and sat on the bottom stair, next to Teddy's little bag. The study door was shut. 'Well, after you left the party, I kept looking at Lee, really looking at him,' said Teddy, 'and how he was looking at me. I couldn't get the image of you with your American man out of my head. The way he was with you. Those moments I talked about, when Lee makes me feel special – *why am I living for those?* I thought. *Why can't I look at* myself *like that, in the mirror each morning? Why have I never seen myself as deserving of love?* Then I realised that look of love he treats me with, that I crave because it's so rare, is not real, it's a mask, because the million ways he looks at me, and the way he talks to me in between, are not right. I wondered if maybe one day *I* might deserve a man who looked at me like your American looked at you. Without me cowering for that look or begging for it or needing it like a drug. Do you think I could?'

She looked so plaintive and so childlike Rachel wanted to cry again. 'Yes, I do,' she said. 'I really do.'

'And I thought of Iris, sleeping peacefully and tucked up with all her cuddly toys, at your house, and I thought how much you'd loved me and always done the right things by me, how you'd tried so much to help me over the years, even if it meant staying with my dad for far too long, and now I need to do the right thing by her. To not bring her up in a toxic environment. So, I'm done,' said Teddy with a watery smile. 'I'm leaving Lee tomorrow. And I might even give up smoking, too, how about that?'

'Oh, Teddy!' Rachel exclaimed, and she stood up and Teddy fell into her arms, to be held long and tight. 'I'm so glad. You're going to be so much happier, you know that, don't you? You're going to be *free*.' And Lee would be left without Teddy and his career as a terrible playwright, she thought.

'I'm here for Iris and I'm here for Dad and I'm here for you,' Teddy whispered into Rachel's neck. 'I think leaving is the right thing to do, Rachel. Go to your American,' she entreated. 'Go to him and be loved the way you deserve for the rest of your life. We'll be fine. Me and Iris. We'll be absolutely fine.'

Rachel felt a relief as bright and as golden as the sun travel up her body. *I can leave*, she thought. *I can really leave*. 'I have flights booked for tomorrow,' she said, stroking Teddy's hair. 'I'm feeling now I can actually get on that plane.'

'You must,' said Teddy. She pulled back from Rachel. 'And Dad. How is he? Is he OK?'

'He's OK,' Rachel said. 'I think he'll be OK. And I'll see you soon, I promise. You and Iris.' Rachel's voice cracked. She struggled not to break. 'Whatever happens, I'll see you very soon.'

'We'll always be here for you, Rachel,' Teddy said. 'Me and Iris. *Always*.'

They hugged again, then Teddy went upstairs to check on her sleeping daughter, before creaking quietly up to her old room in the attic. Rachel then stepped into Iris's bedroom herself and kissed her granddaughter softly on the cheek.

'I love you,' she whispered, her heart swelling. 'I'll be back, I promise.'

Jonny was standing outside the study when she came back down.

'I'd like to go to bed now,' he said.

'Come on,' she said gently, and she helped him upstairs. She eased him out of his shirt and his trousers, and, as he lay back on the bed, she took off his shoes and gently placed them on the carpet, in a neat pair. He clambered under the bedclothes, like a small boy, and she pulled the duvet up to his neck, then she lay on top of the bed next to him and tugged the wool blanket up over her, before falling into a fitful sleep. At 7 a.m. she rose from the bed, showered and quickly packed a bag.

'You were loved,' she said, kissing a sleeping Jonny gently on the cheek and smoothing a piece of wayward hair back from his forehead. The sound of a diesel engine rumbled slowly up the lane and she walked noiselessly from the bedroom. 'You were loved, Jonny.'

# Chapter Forty-Three

When someone imagines a place, in their mind, for a very long time, or when they've seen it in their dreams, for years, often when they see it with their own eyes, it looks very different, but when Rachel looked out of the taxi window at Jud, North Dakota, it was exactly how she'd envisioned it. Jud was the inside of a lit-up snow globe. It was a snowy night scene from a Hallmark movie, or the front of a Christmas card. It was a patchwork grid of what seemed only a dozen or so tree-lined streets totally blanketed in pure white under dark skies, except for neat patches of cleared drives and the front of snow-topped street signs. Its charming weatherboard houses had picturesque front porches and swing chairs you might read about in books, illuminated by yellow-glowing lamps. It was a twinkling button of civilisation in a huge dark-white quilt of absolute nothingness.

Rachel had been driven through miles and miles of open prairies, settled under their dense cloak of snow, to get here. Past farm buildings and giant grain silos on the outskirts of the town. A lone house that became two, three, four. She wound down the window as the taxi turned into Central Avenue, Jud, and the shock of the cold air made her catch her breath, just like it had when she'd alighted the plane at Fargo airport, from the warmth and stuffiness of what her dad had always called a 'flying tin can'. Rachel had gazed in awe at the blank of the surrounding plains of the airport, as far as the eye could see, at a giant snow plough clearing a nearby runway and kicking up plumes of powdery snow into the black of the early evening sky. As Rachel had clonked down the metal steps with her carry-on case, her lungs had been full of crisp, cold air and her eyes full of snow.

'North Dakota,' she had whispered to herself. She couldn't believe she was actually here.

The flight from Heathrow had seemed never-ending, the change at Chicago lonely, as she'd wandered around duty free gift shops and eaten a sandwich from a wrapper on a hard bench. Her carry-on bag contained a few clothes and a washbag, as well as her hope and her heart, and it trailed behind her as she roamed Chicago airport, a little lost, but sure of the destination for that hope, and that heart. Rachel had messaged Abigail about the gallery, told her to hold the fort for now. She had caught sight of herself in a mirrored panel between shops, and was taken aback, as she sometimes was, at her ageing face, when inside she was still twenty-five years old and on the way to a party or a lunch do . . . But she was also a stepmother and a grandmother, and she bought Iris a teddy and she carefully zipped it into the front compartment of her bag. She carried her past with her, and it was not to be forgotten, but her future was her own now.

On the two-hour plane ride from Chicago to Fargo, she had tried and failed to sleep so instead had followed the journey map on her personal screen, transfixed by the little plane cursor that edged in increments from city to city, bringing her closer. She had watched with tired eyes as the 'time to destination' got shorter and shorter, until the plane landed at Fargo and she took that first exhilarating intake of breath at the open mouth of the plane.

Her cab driver, Patrick, drove up Central Avenue, cranking up the volume on the radio for the 8 p.m. news. The last leg of her journey, the two-and-a-half-hour cab ride from Fargo to Jud, had been quite entertaining. Patrick had talked non-stop about North Dakota and North Dakotan people – what they liked to eat and to drink, how they liked to spend their time. The average temperatures for each of the winter months. The hours of sunlight in the summer. When they first saw the tiny twinkling lights of Jud, in the distance, he'd asked Rachel why she had come so far, and she'd told him she was coming to visit an old friend.

'A romance?' Patrick had asked, and she'd wondered if her face, in his rear-view mirror, had given her away.

'Yes, a romance,' she had replied, with a small smile.

'I love it!' he'd declared, grinning from ear to ear under his fisherman's hat. 'I hope you get a happy ending, ma'am,' he'd added, 'don't we all deserve one?'

'I'd like to think so,' she'd said.

Her window still down, Rachel smiled as she spotted the mural that Gabe's mother had painted, of the pheasants, on the side of the saddlery store. Then she realised she had no idea where Gabe lived, not even the name of his street, so she asked Patrick to drop her at the Jud Bar & Grill.

'Sure,' said Patrick. 'You have a wonderful romance!' he called from beyond the closing passenger door. 'Do us all proud!'

Patrick slowly drove away on crunching snow tyres; Rachel wheeled her bag up a cleared pathway to the porch of a weatherboarded white-and-blue diner. Inside, there were neon bar signs and a dark wood floor and the smell of fried food and blueberry pie. There was a juke box in the corner, and three occupied tables with townsfolk bending over baskets of food, who all turned when she came in. And a grouchy-looking man behind the counter, wearing a white apron and a bald shiny head like polished glass.

'Good afternoon,' he grunted.

'Good afternoon,' she replied, and she was aware she probably sounded like Mary Poppins. 'Are you Hal, by any chance?'

'Yes, ma'am.' She wondered if he was only a half-second away from saying, 'What brings you to these parts?' The people staring at her from their tables refused to return to their food.

'Do you know where Gabe lives?' she asked. 'Gabe McAllister? The artist?'

'Gabe McAllister? Of course I do.'

There was a pause, while Hal checked her out. Her. Her bag. Her very English bobble hat with the pom-pom on the top. She waited and then she said, 'Can you tell me where, please?'

'Sure, course I can,' said Hal, the curiosity not having left his eyes. 'It's the house on the corner of Logie and Davis, with the giant oak in the front garden. Want me to walk you down there?'

'No, I'll find it. Thank you. Sorry, so which way do I go?'

'Straight up Logie, that we're on, ma'am,' he said, pointing towards the right with a robust arm cross-hatched with oven burns, 'then take a left.'

'Thank you.'

The occupants of all three tables continued to stare at Rachel as she left the diner and wheeled her bag back down its front path. She was glad of her fleece-lined boots and her jeans and her padded coat, as she walked up Logie Street, in the near-dark, and a few gently soft flakes of snow began to fall, but she wasn't cold. Rachel left the hood of her coat down and enjoyed the sensation of the new snow landing on her hair and face, and the earlier snow gusting down on her from trees that lined the street.

The roads were cleared but the pavements weren't, and her boots sunk into snow up to her shins. Feeling like a small child, she looked behind her at the footprints she was making, illuminated in the glow of an occasional street lamp. They showed where she was coming from and where she was going.

When she turned back to the path ahead, she saw him. A man in the distance. He was walking up the thick, blue-white pavement towards her, in the gentle illumination of the winking windows of the neat houses flanking the street. His hood was up over a knitted hat. He was wearing snow boots and thick mittens, and trotting at his side, making an exuberant trench through the snow, was a very shaggy dog.

Her face broke into a grin and a snowflake landed on her top lip and melted there, delicious and cool. Had he seen her yet? Would he grin at the sight of her, like she was grinning at the sight of him? Rachel's heart, bundled under all its unaccustomed layers, skipped a merry dance. Her whole being felt warm and lit-up inside. She continued on her path, making tracks in the snow. She knew where she was going.

On the flight to Fargo, as the tiny plane symbol had slowly edged along the destination map, Rachel had thought about a lot of things – the same things that had filled her head as she'd made her way home from the Winter Ball. The things that had caused her to stop and sit on the bench and take her phone from her bag. To make the biggest decision of her life. Over Milwaukee, she had thought about Jonny's lies and confessions. His ambition and his betrayals. Over Wisconsin, she had thought about Teddy's words, that Rachel and Jonny had actually provided the shabbiest model of marriage. That their blueprint *hadn't* been of love, despite all Rachel's heartfelt efforts, yet the briefest moment Teddy had witnessed, of Rachel and Gabe under the pergola, had been. And somewhere over Minnesota, as a stewardess had gently tapped her on the shoulder and handed her a welcome glass of water, Rachel had thought about the photos in her nanna's locket.

Gabe was raising an arm to her in the gently falling snow. His face was suddenly clear, in the lamplight, and he was smiling at her, his eyes shining in surprise, and the smile on her face was the widest it had ever been.

Her great aunt had not chosen Scott, the American serviceman, all those years ago. She didn't choose the love she had found over four days, but instead chose the love of a lifetime, but Rachel believed all the amazing things Florence had done in her life, with faithful and loving Jim at her side, she had embarked on because of Scott. She had met him in the spring of 1943 and was flying by the autumn. It was Scott who had seen something in her, wasn't it? Scott who had encouraged her to change direction, to *fly*. Maybe Scott had told Florence all about his life in the air, the day they drove in his jeep to Broughton Castle, and the night they danced at the servicemen's club. Maybe Florence had talked about her most secret hopes and dreams. By the end of that year, her nanna had flown Spitfires and Hurricanes. She had become the person she wanted to be. An amazing woman whose feet were on the ground, but whose head was in the skies, soaring high.

Or maybe she would have done it anyway. Maybe Florence was brave and fearless and awesome and knew what she wanted from life all along.

Gabe was getting closer. Rachel could see the flakes of snow landing on his cheeks. She laughed as he wiped a snowflake off the end of his nose and flicked it comically into the air. Rachel thought of what he'd done for her, and what she'd done for herself.

They had nearly reached each other. The snow was crunchy and satisfying at her feet. Gabe's dog was coursing good-humouredly through the soft white of it, at his master's heels. As the moonlight picked out the face she had always loved, she knew that in each season they had met, she had taken another step on the path back to him.

'Hello,' she said. They both stopped, both a little out of breath.

'Hello,' said Gabe. His cheeks were pinkish from the cold. His mittens had zigzags that reminded her of Charlie Brown's jumper.

'You're late for your afternoon stroll.'

'You're right,' he said, his eyes puzzled, curious and amazed, under his fur-lined hood. 'But I've been travelling. My body clock's all over the place.'

Gabe's dog gave a low snuffling sound and butted at his master's boots. She patted his cold furry head.

'I take it this is Brando?'

'Sure is.'

'Hello, boy.' Brando pushed his nose up into the palm of her hand.

'You're like a mirage,' said Gabe. 'A mirage in the snow. Where did you come from?'

'Heathrow. The 12.10.'

'I see. And you're here . . . because?' He didn't take his eyes from hers.

'Because of you,' she said. 'I thought the grandest of grand gestures was called for. I thought I'd come find you.'

'And here I am,' he said. 'Me and my ol' dog.' He looked at her quizzically. 'So, has something changed?'

Rachel nodded. 'Everything's changed.'

'OK.' He looked hesitant. 'And is that change for good?'

'Yes, it's for good.' Gabe had a little snow, she noticed, hedged along one of his eyebrows. It made her smile.

'And everyone's OK, back home?'

'They will be,' she said. 'I think it's all going to be OK.'

A gust of wind buffeted up the street, causing Brando's fur to ripple, and some snow, dislodged from an overhead branch, to cascade over all three of them. Rachel laughed and swiped snow off her fringe.

'Can I make a speech?' Rachel asked. 'I feel this is the perfect moment for one.'

'Sure,' said Gabe, his blue eyes dancing. 'You can make a speech.'

She loved his eyes. She loved his hair and his eyebrows and his cheeks and his chin. She loved his coat and his hat and his dog and every ridiculous thing about him. She loved that she was here. 'I thought about a lot of things on my long journey here,' she began. 'I thought that you'd sparked something in me, when I first met you, and that you'd changed me in some way every time since.' She spoke fast, the words tumbling out. 'That you'd challenged me, made me more ambitious, to strive higher and wider. You'd taught me that we don't have another life, we only have this one and we have to make it the best we can, for ourselves. That falling in love and being in love should be as easy as saying "hello". That love can sustain and nurture, but sometimes we need to fly!'

Rachel took a breath. She had thought all these things when she'd seen the photos that had fallen from Nanna's locket last night. She had thought Gabe had changed her life. It was a turning point, a huge part of the reason she'd decided to finally leave Jonny and come to him. 'But then, as my journey reached an end, and my plane came in to land, in that cold night air, I realised that wasn't true. It was *me*, Gabe. I made all those changes myself. Brick by brick. Day by day. Season by season. Through all those years with Jonny, I was building a business. The gallery – I did that, all by myself. I made it from nothing to the huge success I'm so, so proud of. I was building a family, with strong enough foundations to eventually stand on its own. I was building my own escape from my past and a route into my future. I was building *me* to be ready for *you*.'

Rachel grinned at him, relieved, released, exhilarated and ready. Wren was right, she deserved this. She had always been a bright shadow in her own life.

'Yes, it was you,' Gabe said, soft and still in the falling snow. 'It's always been you.'

There was a moment of silence. A rustling of wind in the trees, another scattering of snow.

'So, do you think you can still love me?' Rachel asked, in a quiet voice. She needed to hear it. In Jud. His home. So she knew she had come to him and this was *real*.

He stepped towards her. 'I only told you so last night,' Gabe said softly.

'There's a whole ocean between us and last night,' she whispered. 'You said you wanted to let me go.'

'I never *wanted* to let you go. I *had* to. Are you telling me I now don't have to?'

Rachel nodded.

'Then I guess sometimes time brings precious things back to you, after all,' he said. He clasped her to him. She could feel his heart through the wadding of his coat. 'I'm so glad you came to find me,' he whispered. 'You're the most beautiful woman I've ever seen.'

'I'm wearing a bobble hat,' she protested.

'Still can't take a compliment,' he smiled. 'But, to me, your face is like sunshine,' he said. 'Always has been. Always will be.' And Rachel felt very old, but very young. She felt like anything was possible. 'And yes, I can love you. Yes, I still love you. *I love you*,' he whispered in her ear, and she blushed.

'I love you, too.'

'I think we're both finally ready for each other at last.' He pulled back from her and searched her face. 'Where do we go from here?' Gabe asked. 'Home can be wherever *we* are, you know?'

'We can work out where we want to be,' Rachel said. 'In time. We don't have forever, but we have enough time, don't we?'

'Yes,' he said. 'I reckon we have just about enough. Hey,' he added, with a big smile, 'I'm no longer lost and wandering.'

'No,' she smiled, loving him forever, 'and neither am I.'

Brando, impatient, in the cold and the dark, gave a short indignant bark and began chasing his tail.

'Do you want to go to the diner with us, grab a coffee?' Gabe asked. 'Maybe some pie? Get into the warm?'

She nodded. 'I'd like that.'

'Shall we?' he asked, holding out a Charlie Brown mittened hand.

'If I take that, I might not ever let it go,' Rachel warned, with a huge grin on her face.

'Fine by me. Come on, boy.'

Gabe clicked his tongue, and Brando gave a small, shaggy bounce, and, while the lights of Jud winked and a solitary night bird, from the shadow of a wintry tree, took flight into the evening sky, the three of them set off in the snow towards the diner and Rachel knew, with Gabe, she was finally home.

# ACKNOWLEDGEMENTS

*Spring, Summer, Autumn, Us* was my 'lockdown baby'. I spent endless, uncertain days immersed in Rachel and Gabe's story and, although writing is always a joy for me, escaping into their lives every day was a wonderful distraction. I'm going to miss them, but shall tuck them away inside my heart along with all my characters.

Of course, Rachel and Gabe did not make it to the page by my hand alone. I have a cast of wonderful people to thank.

Firstly, huge thanks must go to my glorious editors at Lake Union. To Victoria Pepe, for believing in this story and loving Rachel and Gabe as much as I do, and to Caroline Hogg, for her exceptional care and attention to this book. I am grateful to the whole team at Lake Union for bringing *Spring, Summer, Autumn, Us* to readers so lovingly and expertly.

Thank you to my dazzling agent, Diana Beaumont, who really gets me and always has my back – you are an absolute star!

Thank you, as always, to my writing bestie, Mary Torjussen. I've said it before and I'll say it again and again, I couldn't do any of this without you!

Thank you to my husband, Matthew, for his sympathetic, patient and bemused ear to all my writerly waffles, and for putting up with my 'Go away!' face when he dares enter my little study . . .

And, finally, to the readers. Anyone who has ever read any of my books, I thank you from the bottom of my heart. Every word is for you.

# ABOUT THE AUTHOR

Fiona Collins grew up in an Essex village and after stints in Hong Kong and London returned to the Essex countryside where she lives with her husband and three children. She has a degree in Film and Literature and has had many former careers including TV presenting in Hong Kong, traffic and weather presenter for BBC local radio and as a film and TV extra.